IRONA
700

IRONA
700

WITHDRAWN

DAVE DUNCAN

OPEN ROAD
INTEGRATED MEDIA
NEW YORK

Cover design by Andy Ross

978-1-5040-0218-9

Published in 2015 by Open Road Integrated Media, Inc.
345 Hudson Street
New York, NY 10014
www.openroadmedia.com

IRONA
700

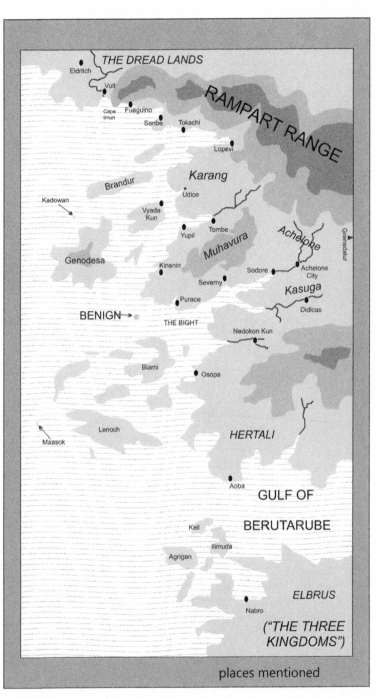

THE DREAD LANDS

Eldritch

Vult

Cape Imun
Fueguino
Sanbe
Tokachi

RAMPART RANGE

Lopevi

Karang

Brandur

Kadowan

Udice

Vyada Kun

Yupil

Tombe

Muhavura

Achelone

Grensdalur

Genodesa

Kinenin

Severny

Sodore

Achelone City

Kasuga

Didicas

Purace

BENIGN →

THE BIGHT

Nedokon Kun

Biarni

Osopa

Lenoch

HERTALI

Maasok

Aoba

GULF OF

Kell

BERUTARUBE

Ilimuda

Agrigan

ELBRUS

Nabro

("THE THREE KINGDOMS")

places mentioned

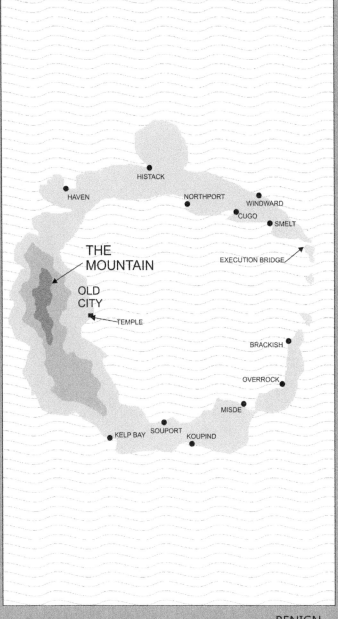

THE YEAR 700

I'm not going," she said. "It's a waste of time."

Crammed in, shoulder to shoulder around the tiny table, her brothers fed like starving sharks and did not meet her eye. Her father continued to chew, staring at the gap in the wall above her where a rotten plank had fallen out. He kept promising to mend it.

"We'd just walk until our feet hurt and then have to walk all the way back again!" This time Irona glanced over to the bed, where her mother sat, nursing the latest baby and surrounded by Irona's sisters, all waiting their turn at the food. Her mother was glaring warnings at her, and the three girls old enough to understand defiance looked terrified. Her father took another crunchy bite out of the onion he was holding.

He hadn't exploded yet. He never normally tolerated back talk, and she was only risking it now because tomorrow mattered to her and she thought he was sober for once. If he knew he didn't have to get up early tomorrow to take her into Benign, he would be free to get drunk as usual. It was worth a try. Almost worth a backhander or two. And he wouldn't want the goddess to see his daughter with two black eyes.

Irona tried again. "Sklom says Caprice almost never chooses a woman and certainly never anyone from Brackish. Only rich boys or priests' sons." Still no answer. "Besides, who would want to be Chosen anyway? The Seventy are a gang of thieves and tyrants. Making honest working people pay taxes so that they can own slaves and live in great palaces." Everyone in Brackish knew that.

The Matrinko home was certainly no great palace, just one room and a small loft. The girls slept in the loft and the boys on the floor. Not that Akanagure Matrinko was a pauper; he was a respected sea hunter, master and part owner of *South Wind*. The flesh, hides, and tusks he brought back fetched good money in the markets of Benign, but he had to pay a crew of twenty and his share of the profits was one-fifteenth and a twelfth, a lean catch to feed a two-digit family.

Still he did not heed what Irona was saying.

"Sklom's going to take me to watch the regatta." She had promised him he could kiss her after. She was looking forward to that even more.

At last her father turned to her. He was a huge man with an ugly, scarred face and broken teeth. "Stupid!" he roared. "You want to see your mother and me stripped naked and flogged at the whipping post in the market? You're stupid."

Irona recoiled. Her brothers smirked. One of the toddlers on the bed began to cry.

"How would they ever know?" Irona protested. "There are hundreds of people my age in the city, thousands! How can even the Seventy keep count of them all?"

He leaned closer, breathing onion. His voice was slurred by the gaps in his teeth. "They don't, Stupid. Their spies do. Women like . . . Won't name names. Know a dozen snitches right here in Brackish, and wouldn't they just love to tattle that Irona Matrinko didn't go to the choosing? Now shut up or I'll take a switch to your backside. Stupid, Stupid, Stupid!"

Irona subsided into silence, and the regatta floated away on a tide of might-have-been.

Tomorrow would be Midsummer Day, the first full moon after

the solstice. This would mark the festival of the blind goddess, the start of the year 700, and everybody's birthday. That day all children born in 684 were deemed to turn sixteen. They must go on pilgrimage to Caprice's temple, where they would swear to obey the laws and thus become citizens. Then they could marry, and the men might be called upon to fight for the Empire. That day, too, the goddess would choose one of them to serve her as a civic magistrate. But only rarely did she choose a woman, and never from an obscure hardscrabble outport like Brackish.

The day dawned clear and hot. From all around the city, crowds streamed inward to the center. None had farther to come than Akanagure Matrinko and his eldest, for Brackish lay far to the east, at the mouth of the bay. Although he expected to return almost every year for the next sixteen or more, this would be the first choosing Akanagure had ever attended. Back when he was a fingerling himself, Brackish had been just a fishing port. Since then, the city of Benign, bloated by the wealth of its empire, had grown and grown, spreading over much of the island of Benign, and a few years ago, the Seventy had recognized Brackish as part of the city. Taxes had gone up and thenceforth its children had been required to attend the choosing.

Before dawn, the candidates set out, girls mostly in groups with mothers, nervous, excited, whispering of possible betrothals. Irona's mother was still nursing a baby, and Akanagure wouldn't have trusted her to find the temple anyway. Boys fared mainly in gangs, loud, laughing, bragging what they would do tonight when they were men. The human tide surged and flowed, whispering and clattering like waves in shingle.

Regrettably, Akanagure had listened to Sklom Uroveg, his chief harpooner, who had advised him not to go by boat because the fares would be extortionate that day. Even if he got some of the lads to row him over in *South Wind*'s dory, they would have to pay in blood for a berth. Also, Sklom had said not to start too early. Things dragged until the choosing. The goddess always made her choice by mid-morning, and after that the current would run much faster, so they could save themselves a lot of standing around by delaying an hour or two. It did not take Akanagure long to realize that the young fool had been spouting like a whale, all froth and no sense.

Sklom had Irona following him around like a duckling, but Akanagure was of two minds about him as a son-in-law. Irona was tall and strong, already quite a beauty, likely to bear well and often. Akanagure could probably find a better match for her in Brackish—a deputy customs officer had a likely son needing a wife. There were also matchmakers in Benign who might do very much better, for a fee. On the other hand, no man on the island cast a harpoon harder or truer than young Sklom, and other sea-hunter captains were making him offers. Seals, whales, dolphins, dugongs, sea lions, otters, or walruses—Sklom was equally good with all of them. Marriage to Irona would tie him to the family.

Excited, frazzled, and dazzled, Irona had never been so far from home on land, although she had twice sailed on *South Wind* to help with the skinning. All her life the city had been the distant smear on the Mountain across the great circular harbor. As she and her father progressed around the shore, passing quays, jetties, beaches, and shipyards on their right, the buildings to their left grew steadily larger and grander. The smells of fish and weed waxed stronger, gulls grew noisier, and the wind died in the lee of the Mountain. But the buildings! The one with the gold dome was the Source of Chiala, Sklom had said, and the one with the white spires was the Source of Koupind. Dome, yes, but Irona couldn't see white spires anywhere.

She could see the temple, though, on the shore at the base of the Mountain. The temple was visible even from Brackish. There were many gods and goddesses, but only one temple. Caprice was patron of the city, goddess of the sea, of chance, and the only divinity ever shown in human form. Caprice was worshipped. Most of the others were feared: Maleficence, god of evil; Craver, god of lust, greed, and desire, who drove people mad; and Bane, the dreaded spirit of the death curse.

The day grew hotter. Irona's feet hurt already.

A wave sweeping in on the outside coast near Brackish would build higher and higher until it toppled down in mighty foam, but this human tide just filled the streets from wall to wall and then stopped. Her father began pushing his way through, dragging her by the wrist.

Standard dress in Benign was a smock. For the poor it was basically a sack with three holes cut in it, and Irona's was not much more than that. On the rich it morphed into a shapely, pleated tunic in bright colors and soft material. For the elderly and the priesthood it dropped its hem to the ground to become a robe. Hats were straw or cloth, brimmed or turbans or anything else; feet went bare or in sandals. One thing that never changed was that the Benesh left their arms uncovered. Possibly some ancient law had made sleeves illegal because felons were branded on their shoulders. Arms were admired or mocked. Poets rhapsodized about beautiful arms, male or female, hard or soft.

Sklom's harpooner arms were mythical, amazing. The way the muscle swelled when he lifted anything made Irona melt. He knew it too. He would bulge those muscles and watch her under those long eyelashes of his, devil that he was. Yes, marriage! Soon!

Being twenty, Sklom had attended the choosing four years ago and knew all about it. He had assured Irona that she had absolutely nothing to worry about. The goddess would take some rich trader's son from the Mountain; that was certain. And Sklom Uroveg would take her. Soon. Married or not. She had tried to slap him then and very nearly been kissed in the scuffle.

~

There were noises ahead, now, audible over the surflike rumbling of the crowd. Trumpets, drums. Ten at a time, Sklom had said. The new citizens were presented to the goddess ten at a time, and the bugle blew for each ten; the drum was for every ten tens. How many hundreds, Irona had asked, and he had laughed. At least two thousand, maybe twice that. If the blind goddess waited and took the last one, it would take all day, wouldn't it? This was the seven-hundredth choosing, and even in Brackish, people were excited about that, with much talk of great Chosen of the past whose numbers had been even hundreds, men like Eboga 500 and Eldborg 300, heroes who had helped build the Empire.

People, solid people, a chowder of angry fathers, frightened mothers, and the kids themselves, who—despite their common age—varied from bony girls and puny boys to bosomy young women and fuzzy faced young men, respectively. People grumbling, jostling, sweating, swatting at flies, complaining, scratching, pushing, swearing, sweating, spitting, shoving, muttering, breaking wind, sweating, scratching; all elbows and feet.

Irona was terrified she would lose a sandal and have to limp home in one. Her water bag was empty. Why hadn't they brought more water? Once in a while someone would faint and there would be cries to make room.

Then, at last, *at last*, there was an arch, a gate, and surely this was the entrance to Caprice's temple. Three streets converged there, and the crowd had set like cement, easing forward an eyelash at a time.

For another hour she watched that gate approach, while the bugles blew and the drums rumbled. Most of that time she was staring at the back of the same young man, watching his sweat-drenched blue-and-white tunic dry out because the sun was merciless and he was too parched to sweat any more. So was she. Her father was somewhere ahead of the man, still attached to her wrist, but they were too far apart to speak to each other.

Nothing lasts forever; one day the world itself would ebb. Noon came and went. As the shadows began to lengthen—but not lengthen enough to give her any shade—Irona reached the gate and found it constricted by bronze barricades to prevent people entering more than two at a time: adults on one side, adults-to-be on the other. Priests in dusty gray robes directed traffic. Their heads and faces were all shaven and sunburned; they looked weary and testy.

"Hat!" one of them shouted at her. "Take it off!"

Sklom had not warned her that heads must be uncovered in the holy place. Other candidates were passing their hats to their escorts, so Irona snatched off her turban, letting her hair fall loose over her shoulders. Her father took the turban, but let go of her wrist, and in the press they were pushed apart. And separated. Panic! They had not planned on that, had not agreed where they would meet later, and she had no idea how to make her own way back to Brackish. A storm surge of adolescents swept her forward into the temple and Father was gone.

Oh, Goddess, preserve me!

At least, for a moment, she was in blessed shade, a very narrow, high tunnel: dark, cool, and smelly. And then out into sunlight again. But now the pilgrims were walking in single file up a long, shallow ramp. On her right a sheer wall of white marble, scorching hot from the sun, on her left an open courtyard packed with people. Already she was looking down on them, frantically searching for her father.

Then, hearing exclamations behind her, she looked ahead and saw Caprice, sitting in a sort of alcove or niche. Naked and many times larger than man-size, the blind goddess was carved from white marble and wore nothing except a jade bandage over her eyes. She was very beautiful, very imposing. On her lap she held a shallow jade bowl, tipped forward, so that a frozen golden cataract spilled out between her knees to symbolize the wealth she poured into her city.

Platforms on either side of her, like the arms of a giant chair, were the flat roofs of other parts of the temple complex, and it was on one of those that the pilgrims were lined up in their sets of ten by supervising priests. But the way there was still long. The line stretched the full length of the courtyard, steadily rising. Then it doubled back. And reversed again, higher yet, so Irona still had to walk the length of the courtyard three times before she would reach the platform. But at least she now could watch the ceremony. A spindly bridge, probably temporary, connected the two sides. One by one, the pilgrims had to cross in front of the goddess, pausing halfway to bow to her. On reaching the far side they were adult citizens and free to go. Relieved that the long ordeal was over at last, they dropped any pretense of dignity, running to a stairway on the far side, then down into the crowd of waiting, waving, shouting parents. There was a scrimmage as families matched up, but eventually they would leave in pairs or threes by another gate.

So that was all right. That was where Irona would meet Father.

She could not possibly recognize him down there in that mob, but he must have picked her out by now and could follow her progress in the line. He might mark her by the boy in front of her, who was very tall and wore a stunning calf-length tunic of red and gold. He had two water bottles slung on his shoulder. Irona watched greedily as he drained another. She wondered if she might dare beg for a sip, just one. She had been brought up to despise beggars. But . . .

Her dilemma was solved by the girl in front of him, who had heard or seen what he was doing and turned to watch.

"Please? Just one mouthful?"

"Certainly not," he said. "I brought six bags and had to carry two of them myself. You should have thought to bring more. But, here, take the empty one. You can have it as a keepsake. I don't need it."

The canteen he offered her was made of fine goatskin with brass fittings, worth a lot of money. The girl's reply was a vulgarity that Irona had heard a few times around the harbor in Brackish.

"Bitch," he said. "Slut. You really think the goddess would ever choose trash like you?" He dropped the canteen and left it.

That ended their conversation. The weary journey dragged on. Trumpets and drums. Irona had been forced to come all this way just to walk across a bridge? What good did it do? The Seventy were tyrants, Sklom said, forcing people to do things like this just to show that they were the bosses. They could just as easily pick some rich kid in private and do away with all the pretense of the goddess choosing. Sklom was very brave to say that, because blasphemy could cost a man a flogging or worse.

Irona turned, feeling her hair tugged by the girl behind her.

"What do you do with all this hair?"

The speaker's tunic was grimy now, and sweat stained, but had been fine once and would be again, after a good wash. She spoke with a curious lilt, much like the tall boy in red and gold. Her own hair was curly, cut short.

"I keep it," Irona said. "What do you do with yours?"

The girl pouted and did not answer the question. "I'm Milosa Fotaz."

"I'm Irona Matrinko."

"That's not a Benesh name. And you talk funny."

"I'm from Brackish."

"You're not supposed to be here unless you were born in Benign."

"Brackish is part of Benign."

"Even if it is, which I don't believe," said the tall lad in front, who could not have helped overhearing, so closely were they packed, "how many Chosen have ever come from Brackish?"

While Irona was not enjoying the conversation, it did make a change from silent moping. "The Seventy added Brackish to the city about ten years ago. Who are you, and where are you from?"

"I'm Nis Puol Dvure. I live in the Dvure Palace. My great-grandfather was a Chosen, and so was his great-grandfather."

"I don't suppose the goddess will make the same mistake three times."

"That's blasphemy. If the priests hear you, you'll get whipped, probably branded."

"Would make a pleasant change," Irona said wearily. Nis Puol Dvure might be as rich as the Seventy, as tall and handsome as a god, with shiny black curly hair, and teeth bright as sunlight, but compared to Sklom's, his arms were *twigs*. They were also badly burned, like his neck, suggesting that Nis Puol Dvure was not accustomed to spending all day in the summer sun.

Pilgrims were fainting now, even some of those already up on the stage, waiting to parade past the goddess. There the priests could remove them, but they had no way to bring aid to those who collapsed on the long ramp, so their neighbors either sat them in the shade of the wall with their heads on their knees, or just stepped over them and kept on going.

As the third trek along the courtyard brought Irona level with the platform and close to the action, she was able to make out details of the ritual. First, the pilgrims were lined in a groups of ten by the priests. When their bugle sounded, they would file over to a huge marble box, elaborately carved and big enough to be a sea lion's coffin; each pilgrim in turn would reach in through a hole in the top to obtain a token that flashed gold in the sunlight. When they had reached the middle of the spindly bridge and bowed, they tossed the token into the goddess's jade bowl. Because of the tilt of the bowl, the token slid to the front edge and shot down the golden cataract between her knees, which acted as a chute. At the bottom it vanished into a hole, no doubt into some temple crypt for storage until next year. The newly recognized citizen was then free to run the rest of the way across the bridge and head for the stairs.

Every ten groups of ten the drummers at the back of the platform would drum. That was all. Irona Matrinko was being baked alive just so the priests could watch her play this silly game?

"How many?" she muttered. Her mouth was so dry she could barely speak. The sun was almost setting. It would be long after dark before she found Father and they got home to Brackish.

"Five hundred forty since I entered the temple," said Nis Puol Dvure. "This choosing is lasting longer than any in centuries. Maybe ever."

"I wish she . . ." Irona wished Caprice would make her holy mind up, but decided not to finish the sentence.

"We must be patient. Obviously the goddess knows exactly who she wants and is waiting for him to arrive."

Nis Puol Dvure had no doubts who that man was.

Eventually the ordeal ended. Irona was at the end of the ramp, at a gate manned by more gray-robed, shaven-scalped priests.

"Name?"

She could hardly find enough spit to make the words. "Irona Matrinko."

He blinked. "That is not a Benesh name. Where were you born?"

"In Brackish." If he tried to send her away after she had come all this way and stood all these hours in this heat, she was going to hammer his shiny skull up and down on the marble a few times. Just watch her!

"Brackish?" He looked to another priest and received a shrug. Perhaps neither of them had ever heard of Brackish. "Oh, very well. You were born in 684? Do you swear to obey the laws? Stand there. Next."

She advanced onto the wide platform to stand behind the long bony back of Nis Puol Dvure. He was too skinny to make a good shade tree. The trial was nearly over. Her head throbbed with the worst headache she had ever known. She could not swallow. She was fourth in her group. There were two more groups lined up ahead of hers. The group going through was almost done.

The trumpet sounded. The next line surged forward.

Why groups of ten? Why drums, why trumpets? Just so that the priests could know how many sixteen-year-olds there were in Benign? Who cared?

The boy in the lead arrived at the coffer and reached in through the hole in the top, having to insert his entire arm to the shoulder. If there were so few tokens left now, Irona wondered, would she be able to reach them at all? He brought out what she now saw was a shiny brass disk about the size of a man's palm. He hurried onto the bridge, bowed, dropped the token, and kept going, not even watching where it went. It clattered into the bowl and slid away. By the time it disappeared into the hole at the bottom, the boy had reached the far end of the bridge, practically skipping in his joy at being released. His friends must have a party planned for him, thought Irona. The girl behind him was already throwing her token into the goddess's bowl.

One more line followed, and then it was Irona's group's turn to head to the big coffer. As their leader reached in, the girl behind him, the one who had begged Nis Puol Dvure for a mouthful of water, slid to the pavement in a faint, almost cracking her head on the corner of the box. The crowd made no sound.

Without waiting for the priests to come and remove her, Nis Puol Dvure stepped over her. In spite of his height, he, too, had to insert his arm all the way to his shoulder. Then he straightened up, clutching his brass disk. Smiling, he walked onward to the bridge.

Irona reached into the big stone box as far as her arm would go. Her fingers fumbled around in vain for something to grip. A hand grabbed her wrist. Something cold and metallic was thrust into her hand. She squeaked in fear and let go. The grip on her wrist tightened. The token was offered again.

She took it, and her wrist was released. She brought up her hand, clutching the brass disk, and ran onto the bridge, eager to get this over with and unwilling to look down, because the railings seemed flimsy and the ground was a long way below. She saw Nis Puol Dvure toss his token into the bowl and watch confidently as it fell.

And fell. Just like the others, it slid down the golden chute and vanished. He stood there as if stunned, gaping in disbelief. Irona shoved him impatiently until he moved away. She threw her disk in turn and hurried after him. She had not taken two steps before the temple erupted in a thunder of drums and trumpets, cheers from thousands of voices. Bewildered, she turned to look back.

Her token had not fallen. It had remained in the goddess's bowl, miraculously stuck to the jade. Holy Caprice had granted a miracle to indicate that this was her choice. Irona looked at the priests on the far side and thought that they seemed as surprised as she felt. She did not know why the token had not fallen, but she was much more inclined to believe in priestly trickery than divine providence. Why would the goddess ever choose an ignorant, illiterate, impoverished girl from a remote outpost, barely even part of the city? No, Nis Puol Dvure had been the intended Chosen and something had gone wrong. That girl in front of him had not been supposed to faint.

A youth in a pleated sea-green tunic strode out from behind the goddess and came to the end of the bridge, waiting there for Irona, grinning widely and beckoning. She couldn't spend the rest of her life where she was, so she walked forward, and now the bridge seemed to sway far more than it had before.

He wore a collar of jade plates around his neck and held another like it in his hands. He also had a gold bracelet on his right wrist, a silver anklet on his left ankle, a ruby in one ear, and a sapphire in the other. He had bulgy eyes that made him look like an owl trying not to laugh.

"I'm Zard 699."

That number was written in silver characters on his collar.

"Irona Matrinko."

"Then welcome, Irona 700." He put the collar he held around her neck and closed with a click. "Too loose, of course," he said. "They always make them big, just in case, but tomorrow they'll adjust it to fit you properly."

The edges of the plates were smooth, not sharp, but the collar itself was cold, heavy, and alien.

The crowd was still roaring and cheering.

"Let them take a look at you, 700. Wave. And smile! All your worries are over. You're rich. You're made for life."

No, her life was finished. Father, Mother, brothers, sisters . . . and, worst of all, Sklom! All taken from her. Would she ever see any of them again? Even if she found a chance to run away, how could she get the awful collar off her neck?

"Come," Zard said. "Water and shade. You are allowed some time to compose yourself."

The offer was irresistible. Irona nodded and let him take her by the hand and lead her around the great statue, into the cool darkness of the temple.

"That's enough for now," Zard said, still smiling.

He had brought her to a small room, whose windows were masked by slatted shutters, making the interior cool and dim. Walls and floor were decorated with gaudy tiles, in complex patterns she could not make out and did not care about. She had slumped down in a huge padded chair, almost a bed, and Zard had handed her a beaker of water, which she downed like a scupper.

Holding out the beaker for a refill, she noticed that it was faceted like the broken ice she had chipped off *South Wind*'s cables in the northern seas. She had never seen colorless glass before. Zard poured water from a large jug, also glass. This time the drink was flavored with lime juice.

When she tried for a third, he refused. "Not wise to drink too much too soon. I know from experience."

"I liked the plain water better," she said hopefully.

"You should. That was from the Koupind Source. It'll have you turning standing backflips in no time."

Source Water was sold in Brackish by the mouthful for enormous prices, and even then it was usually fake or well diluted. Irona could not believe that she had just drunk a whole beaker of it, or imagine what that might cost. She leaned back in the heavenly chair and felt the healing magic seep through her like a rising tide.

"Your tutor will be here shortly," Zard said, with his perpetual grin. "She'll take you home and let you bathe in Source Water. No, I mean it! Or at least wash your face and arms to heal the sunburn."

After a moment, Irona held out the beaker again, and this time he refilled it.

"You were surprised to be chosen." He had a friendly face, the sort of face that was hard to imagine looking serious. The number on his collar marked him forever as one year older than she, but he seemed younger, still more child than man.

She nodded.

"The goddess does choose women sometimes, though. We have six in the Seventy at the moment, so you make seven. And fifty-five men."

"That wasn't what surprised me," she whispered. "They cheated."

The smile instantly became a look of horror. "Never say that! The goddess stopped the disk from falling. That was a miracle, so Caprice chose you." He frowned at her silence, or perhaps her expression.

"The man ahead of me was Nis Puol Dvure. He was certain he was going to be chosen. He seemed to be very rich." The priests had been bribed.

Zard's eyes widened even more, pale in the shadow. "They don't come any richer! The Dvures own half the Source of Chiala and about a third of everything else. Perhaps he did expect to be chosen, but goddesses don't make mistakes. Caprice wanted *you*, Irona Whatever-Your-Name-Was."

"There was a man in the box," she insisted. "A man who gave me that particular token. The priests asked our names as they lined us up, and somehow they passed a signal to the man in the box. He was told to give the special token to the third hand in our group. But the girl ahead of Dvure fainted and there was no time to change the instructions."

The carvings on the sides of the box were images of fish and shells, easily deep enough to conceal airholes or spyholes, or both.

Now the boy looked seriously alarmed. "You're wrong, 700! Only the goddess could make one token refuse to fall like that."

She suspected otherwise. "How about you, last year? Did you just pick a disk out of a pile, or did somebody give it to you?"

Zard squirmed, seeming younger than ever. "I took the first one I found."

"Had you been told you were to be chosen?"

"Of course not!"

That was a lie, too.

"You swear that nobody gave you a particular token?"

He tried to seem indignant. "If you think my family bribed somebody to have me chosen, you're crazy. They're well off, but not like that. The goddess chose me because the Seventy need me. I spoke five languages even then. I'm up to eight now." When Irona didn't comment, he added smugly, "I'm already making myself useful to the Seven, translating at meetings with allied envoys. Several Sevens have told me so."

Again, Irona did not comment.

He tried to seem cheerful. "But you know that this is the happiest day of your life, don't you? From now on you can have everything you've ever dreamed of!"

"Like the man I was going to marry?"

Zard 699 lost his grin yet again. "Chosen can't marry. But you could send for him! If your tutor doesn't mind. Ask her."

A tiny flicker of hope in the ashes of her dream. . . . "Send for him? To do what, to be what?"

"Your escort."

"He means gigolo," announced a new voice, a stern, haughty voice. Its owner was a tall, angular woman in a shimmering sea-green tunic. She went to a window and adjusted the slats, flooding the room with light.

Zard sprang to his feet. Irona followed his lead more slowly—not because of weakness, but because the padded chair was hard to get out of. Already the Source Water was bringing her back to life.

"Irona 700, ma'am," Zard said. "Trodelat 680."

Majestic as an iceberg, Trodelat advanced. She held out both hands. "Congratulations on being chosen, Irona. The goddess never makes mistakes. I'm sure she has very good reasons for wanting you among the Seventy. Yesterday, they elected two potential tutors for today's newcomer, one male, one female. I won, obviously."

She turned to regard Zard with high disdain, aided by the fact that she was taller than he. "And you, '99, should return to your own tutor and ask him to explain to you the difficulties of moving and storing thousands of brass disks. You have completed your obligations to 700 and are free to go." Evidently Trodelat 680 had been eavesdropping for some minutes.

Zard flushed angrily and stalked out of the room.

Still holding Irona's hands, Trodelat looked down at them and frowned. "Poor child! Tell me about yourself."

"My father is a sea hunter, part owner of *South Wind*. We live in Brackish. I have five brothers and five sisters." And one almost-betrothed harpooner.

"Can you read and write?"

"I know my numbers. I help my mother with the shopping."

"We'll teach you all the rest. How are your teeth?"

Teeth? Irona automatically bared them, starting to feel like a slave on the auction block.

"Remember to rinse your mouth every day with Source Water. And your hands, too. That will soon get them in shape." Trodelat released her and went to uncover another window. "Source Water doesn't let people live forever, but it does keep us healthy. The tide ebbs for all of us eventually, but those who drink Source Water every day stay healthy until they drop dead."

Trodelat herself, more visible now, was revealed as feminine perfection. Her skin was smooth as ivory, her eyes clear as gems, and not one hair was out of place or curled the wrong way. It seemed that curly hair worn short was the mode among the rich; Zard had it, and so had the Dvure boy. Trodelat 680's collar and sea-green tunic were obviously the uniform of a Chosen, but she expressed her individuality by wearing even more jewelry than Zard: rings, bracelets, a jeweled belt. Although her collar proclaimed her as being twenty years older than Irona, which would make her older than Mother, she certainly did not look it.

She was trying to seem motherly. "I know just how you feel; we all do. We all went through it, even the First himself. Being a Chosen is a very great honor, a very great responsibility, and very well rewarded. You will live like a queen all the rest of your days. The city gives you anything you want freely, so you are never tempted to accept bribes or play favorites.

"And don't worry that you don't know what's expected of you. Of course you don't! You receive a two-year education. I will be your tutor. That means I'll see you are housed and fed and dressed and taught all the things you will need to know to help run our great empire. Or almost all the things. We keep on learning all our lives. We work hard, but we are well paid. Now, we have years ahead of us, but have you any immediate questions?"

"What did you mean about thousands of brass disks?"

Trodelat made a scoffing noise. "That silly boy! You think that box could hold enough disks for every sixteen-year-old in Benign? After an hour or two, they would need arms like anchor chains to reach to the bottom! I imagine the temple has four or five hundred disks. It will certainly have teams of slaves to carry them back up. Of course there must be a way into the box from underneath, and when the basket under the hole is almost empty, it has to be refilled. You got your disk as they were making the change, that's all."

What she said did make sense. But Nis Puol Dvure had looked very surprised. However full of his own importance he might be, surely he could not have been so sure of being chosen unless he had been promised?

Trodelat was frowning. "Your token did not fall like the others, my dear. You were granted the miracle. I don't deny that priests some-times take bribes, but they can't work miracles. Only the goddess can. . . . Mm? You think you know how it could have been done?"

Irona nodded timorously. Who was she to argue with one of the Seventy or blaspheme against the city's patron goddess?

"Interesting," her tutor murmured, considering Irona with nar-rowed eyes. "Ignorance is not stupidity, and the goddess does not choose idiots. But I strongly suggest you do not voice your suspi-cions to anyone else. No one at all! Meanwhile, are you recovered enough to travel? Any more really urgent questions?"

They were going to make Irona Matrinko into Irona 700, who would be a different person altogether, and she did not want to be another person. "Who pays for all this teaching and feeding?"

Her tutor chuckled. "Very smart question! You do."

"I don't have any money."

"But you have something else of value. Tomorrow I will take you to a meeting of the Seventy. The First himself will be there, and most of the Seven, and the rest of us. I will present you, and you will take your seat among us. And thereafter, starting immediately, whenever we vote—to appoint a magistrate, pass a law, raise a tax, even to declare war—your vote will count as much as anyone's."

"And I vote the way you do?"

Trodelat laughed. For the first time her mood seemed sincere. "Well done! Very well done! Yes, that is my reward. During our tute-lage we follow the lead of our tutors. Your vote gives me a very slight advantage in the bargaining that precedes important votes. It's a sort of game, really. After our two years' tuition we choose seniors to follow, but then we call them patrons. Mine is a very fine lady, Obnosa 658. I almost always follow her lead in voting, although we all support our friends, too, and she understands when I ask for leave to differ on a vote. You will meet her tomorrow. Come, let us go home, to my home."

"Wait! What about my family?"

"I can write them a letter if you wish. If your father can't read, he can take it to someone who can. The law forbids you to see your family during your two-year tutelage. I know that is hard, and I wept when it happened to me, but it is for the best, believe me." Again she studied Irona's reaction. "They would have to kneel to you now, child."

Irona imagined them all kneeling to her, even Sklom. *And Father?* She shuddered.

Again Trodelat made an effort to seem motherly. "But think how proud they will be when they hear the wonderful news! How the neighbors will rush to congratulate them!"

Irona nodded, but it was much more likely that Brackish would throw rocks and insults, and perhaps even drive her family out of the village. They would consider that Irona had gone over to the enemy, the Benign bloodsuckers.

"A lover?" Trodelat was puzzled by her reaction.

"Oh, no! Betrothed." Not even that, really.

"Tell me about him."

"His name is Sklom Uroveg. He's a harpooner."

The Chosen grimaced. "And would you like me to invite him to come and live with you and be your servant?"

The thought was so impossible that Irona could only stare.

Trodelat nodded, satisfied. "I'll show you what I mean. Guard!"

The man she had summoned must have been waiting right outside the door, probably listening to every word, because he entered at once. He was a very large man, clad in a bronze cuirass and a skirt of bronze plates. He was armed with spear, sword, and dagger. His bronze helmet was elaborate, with a crest in the shape of a swan, and a gap at the back through which his hair hung in a thick braid. If the helmet was strong enough to be useful and not just decoration, it must be very heavy to wear. His arms were impressive, although not up to Sklom's standards.

He halted and thumped the butt of his spear on the marble floor. "Ma'am?"

"Jamarko, this is Chosen Irona 700, who will be living with me now."

He pivoted toward her, thumped his spear again, and went down on his knees. "Your servant, ma'am," he told her sandals.

Irona recoiled so that she almost fell back into the chair. Trodelat gestured encouragingly. Irona shook her head, not understanding.

"The correct response is, 'Rise, guardsman.'"

"Rise, guardsman." Irona could feel her cheeks burning, mostly because she knew that her ignorance had been deliberately thrown in her face.

She could almost swear that the soldier bore a faint smirk as he straightened up and glanced at his mistress for orders. He had an old white slave brand on his right shoulder, and a freedman brand, more recent, on his left. There were slaves in Brackish, of course, although her mother could not afford one. Father would not use them on the ship because he found them lazy and untrustworthy.

"Irona 700 and I will be returning to my residence," Trodelat said. "Two litters, and I want the best bearers."

"Always, ma'am!"

"No. This morning's were pathetic."

A dangerous glint showed in the big man's eyes. "I am rebuked. I will choose them myself, ma'am."

The shocks were coming too fast. Irona had never even seen a litter before that day, let alone ridden in one.

"We shall be mostly going uphill, my dear," her tutor explained as they headed through the temple to a gate on the inland side, "so you recline with your head at the front. It's more comfortable that way. Keep the gauze curtains drawn always, then you can see and not be seen. Order the outer ones closed if you wish. Today your bearers will follow mine. I'll explain how to signal your orders another day."

Irona had not realized how steep the city was. She felt sorry for the slaves who had to carry her litter. They were required to maintain a fast jog, while Captain Jamarko and his five armed assistants ran alongside or ahead. The stairs and alleyways were still crowded because of the festival—although Sklom had told her that the city was always crowded. One of Jamarko's men beat a drum to warn pedestrians to clear a passage. Anyone slow to move was roughly thrust aside.

The temple was located near the docks, in the Old City, built on the limited flat land near the shore, where it rubbed shoulders with warehouses, businesses, and markets. The Mountain rose steeply above it: not in a continuous grade, Irona now realized, but in innumerable shelves and terraces, separated by cliffs and chopped up by ravines. Traffic moved on human feet. There were few roads of any length, and many staircases, even bridges. At the summit, she knew, stood the First's Palace, where the business of government was done.

Feeling sorry for slaves and other pedestrians was a pointless exercise when she should have been admiring all the splendid buildings and spectacular views, but she arrived at her destination with almost no memories of those. The size of Trodelat's house amazed her. It had at least thirty rooms, and the one she was told was to be hers—all to herself!—was twice the size of her father's house.

There she was taken in hand by a couple of body slaves, whose names she had to learn again the next day. They washed her all over with Source Water, trimmed off nine-tenths of her hair, shampooed the remainder, and then rubbed it up with a sea marten fur. This, they explained, had the power to make hair curly and shiny and it certainly worked for her. She had not known why sea martens were so prized, although she knew how pleased her father was when his men managed to catch even a single one. They were smaller than otters, and yet so valuable that *South Wind* would put about at once and race straight home with this one tiny cargo, so that the pelt would be delivered fresh to the tanners. Sea martens were found only in the far north, so they were probably tainted by the evil of the Dread Lands.

The girls dressed her in a tunic of sea-green silk, which she felt much too short, and delivered her to a twilit terrace, where her hostess-tutor was waiting. As soon as Irona took the other chair, slaves began bringing out tables laden with food. Food! It was only then that Irona realized that she had not eaten all day. Slaves offered dishes and she said "Yes!" every time, until her plate was heaped like the Mountain.

Trodelat watched with amusement, taking little for herself. After dismissing the servants, she chuckled. "I am sorry, my dear! I was very thoughtless not to guess that you must be starving. Eat until you burst. I won't even talk. We'll have some music instead."

She turned to a set of chimes beside her and jingled three notes. That was a signal, for in a moment a group of slaves appeared with musical instruments and began to play. Irona did not recognize the music, or even like it much, but she was fully occupied with the food, and that she enjoyed very much. She had never tasted things so varied and delicious. She began to understand what Zard and Trodelat had meant about rewards, but she kept thinking that her mother would be mourning a lost child. And missing her principal helper.

The Midsummer moon hung huge over the bay by the time Irona had finished, when two male slaves carried away the tables and the musicians departed.

"That was wonderful, ma'am! I do believe that it was the best meal I ever ate."

"I could believe it was the biggest. And you don't call me 'ma'am.' Normally you do offer that respect to Chosen at least ten years older than yourself. And others who are not Chosen will call you 'ma'am.' However, because I'm your tutor, you will call me Trodelat, or 680. Just 'Eighty' would be too informal. Members of the Seven you may address as 'Your Honor' and of course the First is 'Your Reverence.'"

Irona nodded. But then her eyes wandered to the view, and it seemed that all the world was spread out before her. The island was shaped like the rim of a jar being used to ladle up water. Its eastern rim was submerged, although a few rocks and arid islets supported beacons to mark the best channels.

"Oh! I had no idea it was so big, ma'am-I-mean-Trodelat."

"Big? Big? Benign is tiny, child! Wait until you start your lessons and they show you maps. This is one of the tiniest islands, and yet it rules all the others, and much of the mainland as well, from the borders of the Three Kingdoms in the south to the Dread Lands of the far north. Not that you will have to worry about them until you have gained much seniority in the Seventy."

Why? How? Those questions would have to wait. Irona had never wondered about such things before, but perhaps in the future she would have to. Now her eyelids weighed more than two dead whales. She must not yawn. Yawning, she was sure, would be bad manners in Benign, because it was frowned upon even in Brackish.

"I should let you retire," her hostess said. "You have had a killing day." Her manner had softened since they met in the temple. Did she feel more in command now, here in her own palace, with dozens of slaves to wait on her? Or had she decided that her pupil was not going to cause her any trouble? "But let me explain two more things, if you can stay awake a little longer. But no! First, I must ask what else you want to ask me."

"Oh, nothing. . . . Well, I did wonder what happens after this tutelage thing?"

"Tutelage is a time of learning and a probation. After that, we'll find you things to do, ways to serve, and you will receive an income. A generous income! The harder and better you work for the city and the goddess, the better your reward. The Seventy pay me very handsomely to act as your tutor, and they cover your expenses. You get food and board, and I can supply any spending money you are likely to require, for clothes and lessons.

"But some decisions in the Assembly can be very close, and every vote may be valuable. Cooperation and exchange of favors are to be expected, but avoid outright bribery. You will never offer or be offered anything as vulgar as gold or silver. A Chosen rarely even thinks of personal money. But promises, favors, positions . . . For the next two years you will vote as I do, but we think of the long term, so there will be hints, at the very least."

Irona nodded. "I report them to you?"

"That would be wisest. Be polite, of course. The primary rule, always, is: *Never make enemies!* You have a lifetime job now, a vitally important job, and you will need help and colleagues if you are to achieve anything. There are persons whose policies I despise utterly, and yet sometimes I find myself voting with them, even soliciting their votes for projects of my own. Everything is done by cooperation and compromise."

Just like the hunters in Brackish dividing up the season and the hunting grounds! Irona had Trodelat figured out now. She was very much like Beigas, the wife of the Brackish harbormaster, who was spiteful and devious, a woman addicted to spinning webs of power. Probably all the Seventy were like that, sucking up the labor of the poor.

Again Irona fought to keep her eyes open. Her hostess must see that she was exhausted and battered by a day like no other, and yet she was deliberately dragging it out.

"The other thing we must discuss," Trodelat said briskly, "is sex. You do know about sex? I'm not asking about experience, just whether you have been told how male and female bodies fit together."

Irona had known for years how the squeaking of her parents' bed produced more brothers and sisters. "I've watched the dogs in the streets."

Trodelat chuckled. "That is a rough approximation. The law forbids the Chosen to marry."

Alas, Sklom Uroveg—what other girl would he clasp in his beautiful arms?

"The reasoning is obvious, I hope," Trodelat said in her usual imperious way. "And we are forbidden to own anything at all. I am granted this house and everything in it for my personal use, but when I die, it will all revert to the Seventy. That tall boy just ahead of you today—wasn't he a Dvure? He looked like one."

"Yes, he was." Why had Trodelat noticed him especially, out of the thousands of youths parading through the temple?

"Well, the Dvure family would happily make you the richest woman in the city if you were to marry him, or any of his brothers or cousins. You would then help them become the richest family in the world. That is why you are not allowed to marry anyone at all. Lovers are permitted, naturally. Children are expected, because that is what ensues. But when we die, all our wealth reverts to the Republic. Our lovers and children have no claim on it. It is a hard law, but necessary. Caprice has set us to rule all her people, and we must not play favorites."

Except themselves. They could live like emperors and empresses, while the poor went hungry. *Like lice, leeches, and lampreys,* Sklom always said.

"This is why Benign has prospered more than all other cities, whose rulers are corrupt and favor their families," Trodelat said, still lecturing. "There is one complication that I might as well mention now. We never have romantic affairs with one another. Mixing politics and pleasure can become very complicated and very heartbreaking. One partner or the other will be labeled a whore, selling sex for advancement."

She thought Irona was that sort of gutter slut, did she?

"I felt no mad impulse to throw myself into the arms of Zard 699."

Her hostess smiled thinly. "I should hope not! But you will eventually wield great power in the Empire, and power lends enchantment. You will have no difficulty in finding enjoyable companions. A strong young man in attendance is a great fillip to one's self-esteem. Copulation is very healthy exercise. Let me explain my own solution to this problem." She tinkled more notes on her chimes.

In marched Jamarko, without his weapons but still clad in a ton of bronze.

"Tell the Chosen how you came to be in my service." Trodelat leaned back with a smile that seemed curiously feline in the moonlight.

The big man stepped closer to Irona, sank down on both knees, and spoke to her sandals, as before.

"I was born one of the Havrani, ma'am. And when Benign—"

"She doesn't know what the Havrani were," Trodelat said.

"Beg pardon, ma'am. The Havrani were a barbarous tribe in the Muhavura Hills. We were too stupid to appreciate the benefits of civilization. Being only twelve, I was not old enough to fight in the Third Havrani Rebellion, so I escaped the fate of my father and brothers when our war band was crushed by the imperial army under the noble Byakal 633 and the survivors were put to death in the customary fashion. Instead, I was shipped to the markets with my mother and sisters. Where they went, I do not know, but I was bought by a slave trainer who brought me to this great city, cured me of my savage ways, and trained me as a house guard. I had the great good fortune to be purchased by Chosen Trodelat. After some years she freed me and appointed me her chief guardsman."

Freeing had requiring branding his other shoulder.

"And what else?" Trodelat prompted.

"She also made me her majordomo, in charge of all her household and estates. I am extremely grateful for her trust in me."

"And?"

After a moment's pause, Jamarko said quietly, "And she sometimes lets me sleep in her bed."

Trodelat, Irona was horrified to see, was watching this humiliation with undisguised pleasure, eyes and lips shining.

"And very good he is, too, although so far he has failed to quicken my womb. Go now, Captain. You may dismiss the staff. Get out of all that hardware and go to bed. I will be there shortly."

The women watched him as he marched away.

"You see what I mean?" Trodelat murmured.

On the surface, she meant that love could be bought and paid for as required. Somewhat deeper, that she was ruthless and expected her every word to be obeyed. Irona had already heard that message and did not believe the first.

"Oh yes. Thank you for being so frank."

Yet she was remembering a friend of her father's who had tamed a sea otter pup and kept it in his home. It had been a gorgeously silky, playful pet, until the night it ate the baby.

At long last Irona was permitted to drag herself upstairs to her own private palace. It glittered with fancy treasures—and she hated it. The Seventy were trying to turn Irona Matrinko into Irona 700, twisting her out of shape just as Jamarko, that once-proud young warrior, had been twisted into a lapdog to amuse his owner.

She must escape soon, but how? The jade collar had been given her, so it was hers. Father could get it taken off her and then sell the jade for a lot of money. The Seventy would never find her, and no one in Brackish would betray her to them. She would have to wrap something around her neck to hide the collar until she found her way home, that was all. And probably find a smock that wasn't the goddess's color, although the six or seven now in her closets were all that same sea green. Not tonight, though. Irona was almost asleep on her feet as she dragged them across the soft rugs to the great bed.

Tomorrow. She would escape tomorrow. Get up early . . .

Tomorrow brought a nonstop parade of people on their knees, calling her "ma'am" and eager to serve her. It began with a silversmith who adjusted the collar to fit her slender neck. Then came the teachers. The city had dozens of instructors dedicated to training the youths the goddess chose to rule it, supervised by a special committee of the Seventy, the Education Board. Now they had a new pupil to meet and appraise. Could she sing? Dance? Read? Write? Speak any better than that Brackish gabble? How much history had she been taught? *None at all?* Geography? Finance? Law? Irona's head spun. They thought they could turn an ignorant Brackish baby maker into a great lady in two years? Even granted that they all insisted her education would continue long after that, even if more slowly, the job was impossible.

By evening, Irona was again too weary to think of running away, even if she would dare try to walk all that way home in the dark. And evening was when the Seventy met.

Slaves carried her up to the very crest of the Mountain, to the sprawling marble complex of the First's Palace, where all the government business was done. After a quick tour of the public areas, Irona was led into a private little garden to meet the rest of the Chosen. Almost all of them were there, about fifty in sea-green robes and the Seven in purple. The women all swarmed on her with cries of welcome that she was almost prepared to believe were genuine. There were young men there, too, whose appreciation was quieter and more subtle, but certainly flattering. And even the older men eyed her approvingly. There were many references to great Firsts of the past who had helped build the Empire: Eboga 500 and Eldborg 300. No one mentioned 100, 200, 400, or 600, though, and Irona didn't give a sprat for the Empire.

For bloodsucking monsters, they seemed remarkably well behaved. The one who impressed her most was the slightly stooped, silver-haired Knipry 640. He actually kissed her hand, with a gleam of mockery in faded old eyes under tufted eyebrows as white as breakers. His age was confirmed by his collar, an incredible seventy-six! Old enough to be her great-grandfather.

"Brackish?" he murmured. "Somebody told me you're from Brackish?"

"I can't help the way I talk."

"Of course not, and I like it. Sailors everywhere have rough, hard speech like that, so they can be heard in the storms. Our slithery singsong would be drowned out by the winds and waves. But it seems to me that the Navy Board has an old, old petition moldering away in its in-basket. About Brackish . . . Something to do with a breakwater?"

Irona remembered much angry talk. "It's too short! It doesn't shelter the boats when we get nor'easters. Winds from the northeast, that is." *South Wind* had been damaged once.

Knipry nodded. She guessed that he had known all that and been testing her. "Then we'd better do something about it! We must thank the good folk of Brackish for sending us such a beautiful Chosen to show up the rest of us old relics."

Just minutes later, after Irona had been led indoors, welcomed by the First himself on his throne, and applauded by everyone else, that same Knipry stood up and asked for unanimous consent to amend the agenda, whatever that meant, by adding a vote to provide funds for a much-needed extension to the breakwater at Brackish.

It was then that Irona began to feel doubts. Might this disaster include some good fortune after all?

THE YEAR 702

*S*omehow Irona's escape plans kept retreating as she approached, like rainbows. They faded into visions of rescue. No, she wouldn't escape back to the hovel in Brackish; she would rescue her family and bring them here to the Mountain. When her two years were up and she was no longer a pupil, but a fully fledged Chosen, then she would have a palace of her own and unthinkable amounts of money, and she would have herself carried back to Brackish in a gilded sedan chair and invite them to join her and enjoy a better life. Her mother and her sisters, and some of her brothers. Maybe not her father. Certainly not her father! And meanwhile she must work hard and study hard and show them that she might talk funny and not know how to dance yet, but she could learn. She was not stupid. She could learn to be every bit as good a Chosen as that foppish Nis Puol Dvure would ever have been. She would have to learn to think like a man, though.

Sometime in those two years, her attitude changed yet again. Even if the priests or the Seven had been trying to force the selection of Nis Puol Dvure or some other candidate of their own choosing by means of a fake miracle, their own choice had certainly not been Irona Matrinko. Therefore, the goddess had thwarted them, so Irona truly had been divinely selected, and fealty to the gods required her to do her

*best to serve her city as a Chosen. She could fight the tyranny from the
inside instead of grumbling about it in whispers outside.*

*She discovered that stupidity could not be cured, but ignorance
could; while she was uneducated, she was smarter than she had ever
suspected. She was, in fact, a lot brighter than some of the other Chosen. She watched, listened, read, learned necessary skills, and cultivated the right people.*

*Although the Chosen were paid enormous stipends and the state
provided their mansions almost gratis, they had very large running
costs to meet and an imperial lifestyle to support. The salary for each
office was set by the First, who served for life and was therefore no
longer in competition. The offices that paid the most were much in
demand, but so were those that brought great prestige or power. It was
not quite true that the Chosen could not be bribed.*

"Busy days ahead," Trodelat remarked at breakfast. "Many positions
to be filled before Midsummer, including the elections for two of the
Seven. We must start thinking about some appointments for you."

She popped another grape in her mouth. She had a silver bowl
full of grapes, peeled and seeded by her kitchen slaves.

As was their custom, the two Chosen were beginning their
day with a light repast on Trodelat's terrace, enjoying its spectacular view of the city and the harbor. The sky was cloudless, as was
expected in Benign in summer, and by noon the sun would be hot
enough to melt bronze, a reminder that Irona had almost completed her tutelage. She had never made a fool of herself or her
tutor. She had not attempted to make any speeches in the Chamber—three or four years from now would be time enough for that.
Had she tried, the chairman might not have recognized her, and
at first her Brackish accent would have had the honorable Seventy
sniggering behind their hands. Now she had been taught to speak
proper Benesh, plus rudiments of rhetoric, history, reading and
writing, decorum, protocol, history, geography, finance, dancing,

music, poetry, and about a thousand other topics. After seven centuries, Benign knew how to train its rulers, even one who had been fished out of the cesspool by mistake.

"What do you suggest?" Irona asked, sipping Source Water. She had some plans of her own, which she had not yet mentioned to her tutor.

"Well, the choosing is coming up soon. You might go after the female tuition. There's almost no chance that the goddess will choose another girl so soon after you, so you win some free cash for wasting half a holiday."

A year ago, Irona had placed a jade collar around the neck of 701's Chosen, a gangling redhead, Komev, who looked as if he ought to be Komev 697 and might have been romantically interesting had he not been permanently labeled as being a year younger than she, and out of bounds anyway.

"But supposing Caprice lives up to her name and does choose another girl? I have no establishment of my own." Irona assumed that this was what she was supposed to say.

"Oh, you are welcome to stay on here. I have plenty of room. This place is far too big for me."

That would effectively establish Trodelat 680 as Irona's patron and give her three votes in the Chamber, instead of the two she had at the moment. Trodelat was angling for a seat on the Treaty Commission, which supervised the behavior of the tribute states. The graft involved in settling even one boundary dispute would make her many times richer than she was already, but probably she was more interested in the prestige. Although she never admitted it, Trodelat had her heart set on eventually becoming the first-ever female First. Irona could not imagine a worse fate.

"Surely I need something more permanent?"

"Oh, I meant as well. The choosing was just a thought." Trodelat mused, although she had probably been planning her next words for days or weeks. "With your background, perhaps the Harbor Board?

Or Supervisor of Fish Markets? Both good training grounds. Not romantic, but the romantic ones don't pay well.

"And," she continued, before Irona needed to think up any polite refusals, "it really is time you started wearing some jewelry. You are still as skinny as a fishing pole, too. People must think I don't feed you or trust you near my jewel box."

"I eat like a hog, '80, and you know it! If I stay slim, it's not from want of trying and certainly no fault of your excellent cooks." As for jewels, right from the first Irona had declined offers of loans of any of her tutor's adornments on the grounds that she would wait until she had earned such finery for herself. She had drawn that line purely on instinct, but two years' experience had promoted it into a personal statement. Although the Chosen never discussed their own backgrounds, they were always ready to gossip about one another's, and it had not taken Irona long to identify a few of the Seventy whose origins had been humble, although none as humble as her own. And she had noticed that the poorer their families had been, the more they were now inclined to flaunt their present grandeur, men and women both. So let them glitter and shine! She wore her sandals, her smock, and her jade collar, and that was absolutely that.

"Oh, look at those shadows!" Irona sprang to her feet. "I must rush! My dancing coach is eager to give me extra lessons."

"Not too eager, I hope?"

"That, too. That's why I insist on early morning classes. He's not as ambitious then!" Laughing at her own lie, Irona scurried away. Deception was not part of the official curriculum, but she was getting good at that, too.

Irona sent a slave to fetch a litter for the journey up to the First's Palace. Half an hour later, she slipped in through the public door of the Juvenile Court and took a seat in the front row. This was the fourth time she had sat in on the proceedings over the last couple of months. Members of the public who attended, mostly witnesses or relatives of the accused, generally shunned that conspicuous location, and the three justices must certainly have noticed her blue-green robe and jade collar. She was quietly—if not subtly—demonstrating interest.

Juvenile Court paid much better than the Fish Marketing Board, and she suspected that a seat on the bench could be hers almost for the asking. Minor offenses and first offenders were tried by district courts. Only crimes that might call for the death penalty came to the attention of the Chosen, and even the hardened cynics of the Seventy must dislike ordering children flogged or killed. Irona was repelled by such thoughts, but it was a job she was sure she could handle more sympathetically than people who had been rocked in golden cradles.

Capital punishment took several forms in the Empire, but one thing the executions all had in common was that the criminal was gagged first. A name spoken with a dying breath was a prayer to Bane. Nothing was more dangerous than a death curse.

The big hall was filling up, although she was still alone on the front bench. The four clerks filed in and spread their tablets and slates on their table. Then one of them went out again. He returned after a few moments, but that had been a break in routine. Irona warned herself not to read too much into what might have been just a hasty visit to the bucket closet.

The bailiff bade all to rise, so all rose. In filed the judges, but only two of them: Dilivost 678 in Chosen blue green and Mofe 632 in the purple of a Seven. All sat and the courtroom fell silent.

"The court regrets to announce," old Mofe mumbled, "that our learned Justice Podnelbi 681 has suddenly become indisposed and cannot attend."

A mutter of surprise from the spectators was too soft to produce calls for order, yet they all knew that the Chosen were all wealthy enough to afford the perfect health granted by a daily draft of Source Water.

"Fortunately, I see a possible substitute present. Chosen Irona 700, would you consent to fill in for our ailing brother justice?"

Irona was not merely willing but ecstatic. She was to be tested, and she prided herself on having never failed a fair test in her life. She nodded gravely. Rising and moving with dignity, as she had been taught, she went up to the judges' bench.

Eyes twinkling, Mofe swore her in as a judge. His hair was starting to gray and he had wrinkles around his eyes, but among commoners he would have passed as a fifty-year-old. Juvenile Court was a very lowly office for a Seven, so he must have arranged his election for his own devious reasons—to do a favor for someone, or to avoid election to something even worse a few days later.

Dilivost just nodded gravely to her. He must have agreed to this procedure, but he was reserving judgment.

Irona took her seat on Mofe's left. The judges' desk was sloped and bore no tablets or books, only a single slate and three black disks, which would be invisible to everyone else. She looked at them blankly. Old Mofe turned his over, to show her that the other side was white. "To show whether you agree or disagree with the suggested verdict," he murmured.

She nodded.

"First case?" he inquired.

The first case was a hulking bear of a youth who looked at least twenty. Two witnesses had sworn that he was only fifteen and had never attended a choosing. He was charged with brawling, which was not in itself an offense, and causing bodily injury, namely putting out a boy's eye with his thumb during the fight, which was. His family could not or would not pay compensation.

He pled guilty.

"What is the standard sentence?" Mofe inquired, likely for Irona's benefit, because he must know the entire legal code by heart.

"Branding and a hundred lashes, Your Honor," said the chief clerk.

"Has the accused any alternative to offer?"

The accused mumbled something inaudible and peered around anxiously. A man in military bronze arose in the body of the court.

"Navy will accept the accused, Your Honors."

Mofe turned his disk over to show white. Dilivost followed suit. So did Irona.

"The judgment of the court is that the accused shall serve in the military of the Republic until 717, and this sentence be tattooed on his right shoulder. Next case."

That had not been difficult.

The next one was a little tougher. He looked about ten but had been caught breaking into a house at night. With childish folly, he had picked the home of a stevedore who had three grown sons. The resulting damage still showed on his face and the sling supporting his right arm. He had two thief marks already, so he ought to have been taken to the adult court, whatever his age, but perhaps the bailiffs had thought he had already been punished enough.

"Your turn, Judge Dilivost," Mofe said softly.

Dilivost turned his disk black side up. In this case that meant death.

The other two concurred. Had Irona disagreed, she would have been outvoted. If she showed any mercy at all today, she would fail the test. At least until she was elected, she must be the toughest of the tough. The Seventy would not want a milksop chit of a girl in the judiciary, Juvenile Court or not.

The third case was tougher yet. The accused looked no more than twelve and had admitted to being a prostitute, but not to drugging and robbing a client.

"This is her second appearance on this charge?" Mofe inquired, although again he must know the answer.

"It is, Your Honor."

Mofe glanced inquiringly at Irona. She frowned and raised an eyebrow, wanting to be sure she understood.

He whispered, "So she hasn't eaten in four days. Not many of them hold out that long."

Perhaps not in his world, but down in the gutters, food came less reliably, so people grew up with hunger. Starvation was a standard technique to force a guilty plea and save the court's time.

Dilivost leaned closer. "Remand for two more days?" he whispered.

"Can we hear the evidence?" Irona asked, having missed the accused's first appearance before the court.

"We heard the plaintiff and told him he need not come back," Mofe said. "They had agreed to a fee of two copper fish. The idiot accepted a cup of wine first and woke up in an alley bare, um . . . totally naked."

"A fix?"

"We considered that, but decided not to press the matter."

A fix was any magical device, and its use or possession was punishable by the sea death, the harshest sentence the court could impose. At least this waif was not threatened with that.

"Your turn, 700," Mofe persisted.

Irona had spent long hours studying the penal code and she knew the standard penalty would be a branding and at least twenty lashes. A girl so scarred would be trapped in the gutter forevermore, unable to obtain a husband or even honest work.

"Slavery," she said. White side up.

The two men exchanged a very brief glance and concurred. The scarecrow tyke was led away to be sold. Her owner might still use her as a prostitute, although that was illegal, but she might be put to work in a sweatshop or food market. At least she would not be tied naked to the whipping post and half flayed; from now on someone would see that she had food and shelter. While Irona felt sick to her stomach at what she had done, she was sure that she had seen a flash of relief on the child's face when the sentence was announced.

"Next case. . . ."

When the court adjourned at noon, Irona had been accessory to eight executions, nine floggings, and three enslavements. So far as she could tell, she had not made anything worse and might have reduced a couple of sentences. Moreover, her fellow judges were not dismissing her as a bleeding heart.

"I approve of your advancement of slavery," Dilivost proclaimed as he congratulated her. "We tend to overlook that option."

"It brings in revenue," Irona announced with a straight face. To the rich, slaves were tools, ranking so far below their owners' status that normally only servants would even give them orders, but she had known quite a few slaves in Brackish and most of them had not been conspicuously less happy than the free.

Music, history, and rhetoric classes took care of the afternoon.

That night, the evening meal at Trodelat's house went better than Irona had expected. Her morning adventure had not come to her tutor's ears, so Irona was able to break the news herself. By not mentioning her previous attendances at the court, she could make today's participation sound like a pure accident.

Even so, Trodelat was suspicious. Her pupil was starting to slip out of her control. "You enjoy slaughtering children?"

"By no means, but I gather that every Chosen gets appointed to the Juvenile Court at least once, and the extra money would mean more to me now than it might twenty years from now."

Her tutor could only approve of this cold-blooded political calculation. "Very well argued! The election is tonight, is it not? I shall mention your interest to Obnosa. So far as I know, she has not promised to support any other candidate. As you say, the position is not coveted." A prestigious appointment for her pupil would reflect well on her own tutelage.

"Very kind of you, Trodelat." Obnosa 658, Trodelat's patron, had her eye on an upcoming seat among the Seven and was scrounging every vote and calling in all the favors she could.

~

At this time of year, the Seventy met almost every day, and always at sunset. Before each meeting, they would gather in a small, shady garden in the Palace, a nook known as the Scandal Market, there to scheme and trade among the greenery. Since few people, even Chosen, lived to be eighty-six, there were never as many as seventy Seventies, and some were always absent on imperial business. Most days less than fifty of the Chosen turned up in blue-green robes, plus the Seven in purple. The First did not attend in the garden.

Irona was expected to stay close to Trodelat, and Trodelat swam in Obnosa's shoal of toadies. Obnosa's patron had been one of the Seven and had died quite recently. She had failed to win the by-election for his seat, but in a few days, two more would become vacant and she was thought to have a good chance. As the most junior member of the group, Irona found herself on the outskirts, but that often happened and she welcomed the chance to natter with other juniors.

This evening she found herself openly stalked by a tall, cadaverous young man. She knew him, of course, because she knew them all. Ledacos 692 was eight years her senior and generally believed to have promise. Eight years was a difficult gap: should she address him by name or as "sir"? To see him without companions in the Scandal Market was surprising, but she let herself be cornered beside a marble statue of a priapic faun skulking behind an oleander bush.

"I hear you are a candidate for the Juvenile Court, 700," he said with no preamble.

"You have sharp ears, '92."

He grinned, so she did, too.

"Why?" he asked. "You enjoy killing children?"

"No. Because I know I can do the work, and it pays better than any other job that I have a reasonable chance of winning."

He nodded. "Good reasons. I'll see what I can do to help."

"Thank you."

"But my help won't be needed. Mofe himself is going to nominate you."

"You know this?" she demanded, astonished. All offices came with limited terms, and incumbents could not succeed themselves right away, but they had an unofficial right to nominate their successors. While that would rarely prevent other names being put forward, it was said to be worth fifteen votes as a gratuity for a job well done, and it was a courtesy to be returned in due course. In the case of an unpopular office like a Juvenile Court judge, nomination by a Seven would almost guarantee election.

"He told me."

"You asked him to?"

Ledacos's eyes twinkled. "No. We were discussing my future, not yours, and he wouldn't have suggested it had you not impressed him this morning."

"Well! Thank you again. And what are you hoping for?" Tit for tat, of course, except that he probably had a phalanx of supporters to follow his lead and she would bring nobody with her.

"Let's finish planning your career first. What else are you after?"

"I haven't decided." The court would not fill up her days. Something else might be tossed her way, and if not, there were always more classes.

Ledacos stepped closer and glanced around conspiratorially. "How about the Navy Board?"

"A woman?" she exclaimed, almost laughing aloud. Benign owed its empire and its wealth to its maritime trade and its navy. The idea of the Seventy letting a chit of a girl meddle with either was ludicrous.

But Ledacos wasn't laughing. "You come from a nautical family. Many of the Seventy know a little about shipping, but only because their families own ships or traded overseas. Have you ever been to sea?"

Irona did not doubt that he already knew the answer.

"Yes. I have sailed south to Lenoch and as far north as Brandur."

"Gods save us! You're better qualified than almost anyone. I know from experience that much of the Navy work can be arranged to suit your convenience, so your court attendance won't interfere. Best of all, you are clever."

So was he. Meeting his bright, metallic gaze she wondered why she had not remarked that before. His neck was a cubit long and sinewy, his face was all bone, hacked out of flint, his arms and legs were hairy, but the most notable thing about him was the presence of an intimidating mind. That explained why people spoke of him as someone to watch.

"I am very flattered, but—"

"I will nominate you."

That was a thunderbolt. Ledacos was completing a two-year term on the Navy Board.

"I am speechless," she said.

Again the sudden grin, making the angular face for a moment almost boyish. "Don't believe you."

"And you? I can't deliver more than one vote, but it is certainly yours."

"Treaty Commission," he said, with another quick glance around. "I have twenty-three promised, so you may well put me over the top."

Irona felt her hopes crash around her. "Ah, that's tricky. My tutor . . . I promised."

"Oh, of course," he said quickly. "I should have remembered that she is a candidate. You cannot go back on your word. But if she is eliminated in an early ballot?

"Then I shall be happy to switch my vote to you." Irona did not believe for an instant that Ledacos had forgotten that her tutor was one of his opponents for the Treaty Commission.

He smiled. "Thank you. We should separate before people start thinking we're plotting."

"We're not?" she said, laughing, but he was already stalking away.

Seen from the rear, he had good shoulders, tapering down to the hips of a snake. She wondered why he did not have his tunics tailored to make him look more fashionably plump.

Irona was almost free of Trodelat's iron hand. She would need employment, which now looked more promising than she had dared hope. She would need somewhere to live, which would bring complications of its own and might have to wait. And she would need companionship.

Not Ledacos 692!

Chosen were off-limits, otherwise sex was allowed, marriage not, but at social functions, a Chosen needed an escort. Trodelat's choice of a hired gigolo certainly did not appeal—in fact, Irona did not trust Captain Jamarko as far as she could see through a stone wall. But Trodelat had warned her many times that romance between two Chosen was guaranteed disaster. Although Irona had heard scandalous stories of past affairs, she knew of no gossip about anyone breaking that rule at present.

She headed off in search of Trodelat. As she approached the group around Obnosa 658, the great gong sounded, seven beats jarring teeth and toe bones throughout the Scandal Market. People began moving toward the door of the Assembly Hall.

Irona caught Trodelat's arm to pull her aside.

"I am told that Seven Mofe is going to nominate me for the Juvenile Court."

Her tutor's automatic smile melted into shock. It returned with an effort and open suspicion. "That is wonderful news, my dear! Have you found yourself a patron, then?"

"I am certainly being offered patronage. I did not seek it."

"Let's go and sit down and you can tell me all about it. I can advise you."

The Assembly Hall was much larger than it need be to hold seventy people, but it passed sound beautifully, so that even whispers could carry. The walls were thick and the windows kept shuttered by day. Now they were open, and the cooler evening breeze was starting to disperse the stuffiness.

But by the time Irona and Trodelat had entered the dim hall and found two chairs together and not too far from Obnosa, the time for chat had ended. A bugle call announced the entrance of the First, and everyone rose.

First Dostily 631 was showing his age, walking with a shuffling stoop as if the weight of his splendid scarlet robes was almost too much to bear. He crossed in front of the assembled Seventy, with the purple-clad Seven following in single file, although only five were present that evening. The First took his seat on the red throne, the Seven on their line of lesser, purple thrones, all facing the assembly. A table of secretaries off to the side waited to record the proceedings. The great bronze doors closed with thunder and the meeting was in session.

In theory, the First had very little power. He chaired meetings of the Seven. He set salaries and the terms of employment, but his changes did not take effect until after the next election, so he could not reward friends in their present offices. In meetings of the Seven or the Seventy, he could change the order of items on the agenda, so an item he disliked might never come to a vote. He could indicate his disapproval of a decision by calling for a second vote, which would often result in the first result being overturned to please him. In practice, those rights had always been sufficient to let most Firsts run the Empire to their own satisfaction.

It was the Seven who set the agenda for all meetings of the Seventy. As Chosen themselves, they participated in the discussion and voting. They also took turns at chairing the meetings, the chairman always sitting farthest from the First. That evening it was old Mofe 632, who had presided over the Juvenile Court that morning. He accepted a slate from a secretary and read out the excuses of those not present. All were absent from the city on state business, except for one who had been granted a day's leave to bury his mother, and Podnelbi 681, who was indisposed. That announcement raised murmurs of surprise and alarm. An indisposed Chosen was almost certainly on his deathbed, and only the poor died as young as thirty-seven.

Irona was probably more shocked than anyone. If Podnelbi had not faked his absence from the court that morning, then her chance to show her mettle on the bench had not been a political favor; it had been a direct intervention by the goddess, just like the girl who had fainted to block Nis Puol Dvure's choosing.

Mofe read out the first item, election of the next Inspector of Fish Markets.

Dreadful silence.

Mofe called on the retiring inspector to recommend a successor. The lady in question rose reluctantly and spoke a name, which was a sure way to earn a lifelong enemy. Red with fury, the nominee came forward to be recognized. There being no other nominations, he was declared elected. The First might decide to increase the stipend in the future, to make the office more attractive.

Director of Street Cleaning drew a surprising three candidates.

Then came nominations for tutor for the next male Chosen. This brought more interest, because of the second vote it brought, and the possibility of a lifetime client after the two-year tutelage ended. Three men were nominated and went to the front. Hands were raised, and the winner was declared to be Ledacos 692, with a clear majority over both opponents combined. Almost certainly he had won because he had been nominated by a Seven, Knipry 640.

"Making his move," Trodelat whispered as the candidates returned to their seats.

"What?"

"Ten years since he was Chosen. Future Firsts all start by building support in their twenties, then serving terms on all the major committees in their thirties. Then they can hope to make the Seven after they've turned forty."

Trodelat herself was thirty-eight, and not conspicuously a power broker yet, so far as her pupil had noticed. The rules might be slightly different for a woman, though, because they were so few. Irona had no chance to think about it, because now Obnosa was rising to nominate Irona 700 to be tutor for the next Chosen—should the blind goddess be so wayward as to choose another woman so soon, although no one would say that in mixed company.

Heart thumping, Irona went forward to bow to the First and stand at the front. She felt like a slave at an auction, a sudden insight that startled her. A Chosen who refused an appointment might face drastic penalties, so the highest and lowest in the land were similarly bound to serve. She tried not to remember the children she had condemned to slavery that morning.

She was surprised to see smiles of approval everywhere. There were no other nominations. Approved by acclamation, she bowed to the applause and returned to her chair, still shaking. She did not expect Caprice to send her a protégée, but the cash reward for just standing by all day was considerable. And once the goddess made her choice, Irona's own tutelage would end and she would be free of her dependence on Trodelat.

The climax of the session, and the most important position to be decided that evening, was the seat on the Treaty Commission. Most of the other cities and islands in the Empire were officially independent states, bound by treaties of alliance. In practice they had to do as Mother Benign told them, submitting their annual monetary and manpower levies, and the Treaty Commission oversaw their compliance. It wielded enormous power. Of course, no Chosen ever accepted bribes, but friendly gifts were always available, and senior officials like the Treaty Commissioners might be offered bars of gold or teams of slaves.

Five candidates were nominated, so several ballots would be

needed. The first one eliminated Trodelat. Irona was not at all surprised when Ledacos won by an overall majority in the second. He
was the big winner of the evening; he had made his move. He was
one to watch.

He was also, in another sense, easy on the eyes—skinny or not.

The following evening two of the three candidates Ledacos nominated won election. The evening after that, he nominated Irona 700
to be his successor on the Navy Board. As she rose to go forward, she
heard some angry muttering. She was supposed to hear it: A woman?
A child? Even if her sponsor had gathered enough votes to elect her,
the First could call for reconsideration, which would surely overturn
her election. Having been elected for life, the First need never worry
about making enemies.

But Ledacos had not finished. "Irona 700," he informed the
assembly, "comes from a seafaring family and is very familiar with
ships. She has already sailed as far south as Lenoch and as far north
as Brandur."

In its sheer brevity, that announcement greatly overstated her
experience and knowledge. She had served as a narwhal skinner, not
a sailor. But it was enough. Two other men had already risen to nominate. Both promptly sat down. At last everyone understood why the
goddess had chosen Irona, and she was elected by acclamation.

Now she certainly had a patron, and Ledacos had put his client
on the Navy Board as his own replacement. He was indisputably the
new man to watch in Benesh politics. And Irona 700 had her feet on
the rungs of the ladder.

On Midsummer Day, Irona was collected before dawn by a troop of
soldiers and rushed off in a litter to the choosing. Already the streets
were crammed with people, but her guards charged through like a
pod of orcas and took her safely to the temple of Caprice.

The blind goddess's priests did not kneel to her. After two years, she had come to expect everyone to kneel to her. But they did escort her to Ledacos, who was eating an interesting-looking breakfast in a small room to the right of the goddess's elbow. Its windows provided a clear view of the platform and the coffer below, and of the first pilgrims filing up the long ramp as the first rays of the sun lit the temple spires.

He rose and pulled up a chair for her. The move unsettled her, for that was a courtesy that juniors extended to elders. The Chosen were very fussy about seniority.

"Source Water?" He poured her a beaker. "Koupind, I think. It has that peppery touch on the tongue." He was impressive, radiating confidence and interest, the man on the way up. His tunic was a decorous knee length and the regulation sea green in color, ornamented with a small sunburst in seed pearls over his heart; personal adornment was limited to one heavy silver bracelet and a ruby ring. In Irona's opinion, those merely emphasized the hairiness of his wrists and fingers.

She had a little speech prepared. Before she could recite it, Ledacos beat her to it.

"I was impressed by your performance on the Juvenile Court that day, 700. You seem to share my philosophy of government."

Irona had never given a thought to philosophy of government. "Um . . . What do you mean, exactly?"

He smiled. "Well, please don't tattle this to any of the senior antiques among the Seventy, but I'm a cynic! I think most rulers try to do too much. Too much good, I mean. Do great good and you will inevitably do great evil also. I think our guiding light should be to do as little evil as possible. The secret is to choose the course of action that does the least amount of harm."

She nodded uncertainly. Taxing people who couldn't keep bread on the table, wasn't that evil? Conscripting boys to be marines and get killed, wasn't that evil? How about burning half an allied city because it was late with its tribute? She would have to think about this, perhaps ask her teachers for some lectures on philosophy of government. Her education had not ended yet.

"Of course," he continued, "sometimes that principle would lead us to do nothing, but sometimes nothing is the thing to do, don't you agree?"

Was he just playing with her? Leading her out of her depth to watch her flounder? She countered with her prepared speech.

"I congratulate you on your recent successes, '92. You have marked yourself as the man to watch among the Seventy. I am honored to regard myself as one of your clients."

"Thank you. I have also made enemies." Then came one of his rare smiles. "But also some friends, I hope?"

Again she was thrown off balance. Fortunately, she did not have to comment, because in walked lanky, red-haired Komev 701, clutching a jade collar. He flashed a smile at Irona and attempted to kneel to Ledacos.

"Up! You don't need to kneel to me, '01!"

The boy flushed. "Sir, my tutor has taught me to—"

"Your tutor, if you will forgive my saying so, is a stuffed walrus. Mine taught me that Chosen never kneel to other Chosen. Now help yourself to as much as you can carry." He waved at the loaded table. "And don't call me 'sir.'"

Komev hesitated. "Is it possible to change tutors, '92?"

Ledacos regarded him in silence while nibbling a fig. "I suppose it might be permitted, but you would make lifelong enemies of your present tutor and all his clients. As would whoever took you on."

"Oh."

"Tough it out for another year," Ledacos said with more sympathy. "684's not a bad man, just a little too rigid on protocol, and you'll do better getting too much of that than too little. He's had a lot of administrative experience, so listen to what he tells you. Next year at this time, if you want me as your patron, I will be honored to accept you as a client. I've been keeping my eye on you, and so far you look most promising."

Komev's flush turned as red as his hair. He began loading food into a silver bowl with both hands. His idea of what he would need was astounding.

"They're starting," Irona said from the window as the first brass disk went slithering away down the chute. "Does the goddess ever choose one of the early birds?"

"She is reputed to have chosen the very first in line a century or so ago," Ledacos said.

Whether that was true or not, Komev believed him. Grabbing up his bowl and the 702 collar, he tore out of the room to wait downstairs for the next Chosen.

"Come and eat," Ledacos said. "Our young friend overlooked a few scraps. We may be here for hours. You kept us waiting long enough."

"Me?" She returned to the table.

"Two years ago. I was here with Trodelat all day."

He did not quite roll his eyes, but she pretended that he had.

"My tutor, or former tutor, is not a stuffed walrus! I am quite certain of that, because I have helped skin walruses."

He laughed. "Goddess preserve us, what a horrible thought! No, but she does pall after a few hours. By the way, I have never seen anyone look more surprised than you did when you were Chosen."

"Likely not," she said carefully.

He studied her for a moment, that clever-clever mind analyzing. "You thought that the Dvure boy was supposed to be the one and the girl fainting spoiled the plot. But what plot, Irona? How could they rig the choosing?"

"I have no idea." To put her suspicions into words would accuse her own father of using a fix.

Ledacos shrugged. "One day I hope you will trust me enough to tell me."

"One day I may understand why the goddess wanted an ignorant girl for her Seventy."

"To sit on her Navy Board. I was elected to Navy two years ago because my father was a sailor who earned distinction in the Battle of Byakal-Krida. But he had been a rower in a galley, and when I knew him, he was a mere carpenter. Still is, by the way. Have you been home yet?"

"No."

"Send someone to make inquiries first. Otherwise you may be shocked by the changes. Or more shocked by what hasn't changed. And don't make the mistake some Chosen make, of snatching their families up from poverty and installing them in mansions. Better just to send them regular money so they can live where they've always lived and lord it over their neighbors."

Irona thought her family would much rather not remind any of their neighbors that they had a daughter among the Seventy. The Seventy collected taxes.

"Talking of mansions," Ledacos remarked, "you need a home of your own now."

"I know I do." As long as she lived with Trodelat, Trodelat would try to manage her. Now her new patron was starting to do so.

"And a staff to run it. Even the most junior member of the Navy Board is expected to do some entertaining."

Horror upon horror! Already she worried about the workload she had taken on and all the preparatory learning it would need. She was appalled to think of the labor involved in choosing a home, hiring servants, training them. She would need a majordomo to run the place, and the thought of someone like Captain Jamarko in her bed made her feel physically sick. She rose from the table and went over to the windows to stare down unseeing at the boys and girls filing by, and the new-fledged citizens running to the exit stairs.

Ledacos had followed her, for his voice came from close behind.

"Podnelbi 681 is dying. Source Water does nothing for him now. His tide will ebb before tomorrow's dawn."

"That's very sad," she muttered, not looking around. What was her patron hinting at?

"His home and all its contents revert to the Property Commission. The Sebrat House—do you know it? The commission currently has six or seven abodes it can offer you at purely nominal fees, but Podnelbi's place is quite modest. Some of us live like emperors, as you know, in mansions of a hundred halls. Other go the opposite extreme and are too frugal to uphold the dignity of their office. But Sebrat would suit you very well."

She knew the house, and it was certainly humble compared to most.

"I would feel like a ghoul, storming in there to loot before his corpse was cold."

"He has two children." Ledacos always seemed to know everything. It was a very annoying habit. "His daughter is already safely married off. His son is a trainee lawyer, I believe, and betrothed to marry the daughter of a very rich silk merchant, but of course both of those arrangements will go by the board now. Their mother is a freedwoman, Velny Lavice. The moment 681 stops breathing, she will be given two days to get out, and there will be guards on the door to make sure nothing is removed except the smock on her back. The same goes for his entire staff, about ten of them, I think. A very modest establishment."

Trodelat had twenty.

"What are you suggesting, patron?"

"Please never call me that, 700. They will all be out in the street. I am suggesting that tomorrow morning you inform the Property Commission that you are interested in taking over Sebrat House as is. Or I can tell them for you, if you wish. I have some influence there." He must have clients everywhere. "Then, as soon as it is practicable, you interview Velny. She would make an excellent housekeeper for you."

The drums and trumpets continued, the disks slid away down the chute, but Irona was not seeing the choosing ceremony now. A ready-made establishment was a dazzling prospect, almost too good to be true. But she had already learned to analyze every word the clever Ledacos 692 uttered.

"How old is the son?"

"About your age, maybe." Ledacos shrugged, implying a lack of interest in young men.

Irona swallowed. There were more hints and clues floating around this conversation than gulls around a fishing port. She had met Podnelbi's son at social functions. He was a year or two older than she was and fabulously handsome. "Are you suggesting that I take over the son as well?"

After a pause, Ledacos said softly, "Gods forbid that I should even dream of it."

Her heart jumped. She was not sure when sex had appeared on the agenda, but probably when he came to stand so close that she could almost feel his breath on the back of her head. It was certainly there now.

She spun around. "I was not aware that romance was part of our arrangement."

The inquiring smile vanished. His face hardened. "Nor was I."

"Good," she said. "Almost the first thing my tutor told me was that sex and politics do not mix."

"Mine told me the same thing, ten years ago."

Nice try, though.

She nodded, hoping he would not grab her and kiss her, because she did not trust herself to resist. She would certainly not scream for rescue. Once she had been fascinated by Sklom Uroveg's harpooner muscles, not understanding that Sklom was stupider than the seals he slew. Ledacos's arms were adequate, if a little on the hairy side. As were his legs.

Feeling her face flush scarlet, she turned back to the window.

"I would be very grateful if you would drop a word to the Property Commission about Sebrat House, Ledacos."

The crowd roared, trumpets and drums . . .

"Already?" He joined her at the window. A boy—a barefoot child in a dirty rag—was standing on the bridge, petrified with horror. Komev 701 was striding out to greet him, seeming to grow taller with every step.

"That?" Ledacos whispered. "He has rickets! Truly the goddess is blind."

"Was she blind two years ago?"

"She was insanely cruel to make you a Chosen as well as me. That mite is never sixteen!"

Irona ignored the first remark as if it had been a slip of the tongue, which it might have been, except that Ledacos's tongue wore cleats.

"He may have been starved all his life," she said.

Komev had actually gone down on his knees to set the collar around the boy's neck, and he was still almost as tall. The new Chosen was weeping.

"I think you'd better go down right away and provide some assistance," Irona said. "701 is out of his depth."

"So am I. He needs a woman. Come with me." Taking her wrist so she could not refuse, Ledacos led her out of the door.

By the time they had run down the stairs, Komev had brought the boy into the cool peace of the recovery room, away from the thousands of eyes. The priests had not yet brought refreshments for the new Chosen, but he was sitting on a chair, feet swinging, and stuffing himself from the remains of Komev's breakfast in the silver bowl, which Komev was holding for him. The collar seemed ready to slide down over 702's shoulders and pin his arms.

Komev 701 looked up with relief at the arriving reinforcements. "Meet Dychat 702."

Irona knelt beside him and looked into the red-rimmed, terrified eyes.

"Welcome, Dychat. Don't eat so fast."

He dropped a half-eaten prawn back in the bowl and cringed as if expecting to be struck.

Irona tried again. "I just meant that you'll make yourself sick. There's no hurry. You will never be hungry again."

His hand reached for the prawn as if it had a life of its own. He might be thirteen, but eleven seemed more likely. He needed a bath, several baths, and a thorough delousing.

"Anything else you want?" she asked.

His chin trembled. "My mother?"

But did his mother want him? If she had wanted to be rid of him, she could have told him he was sixteen and sent him off to the coming-of-age ritual. Then he would be legally an adult and on his own. Truly, Caprice was well named.

The priests arrived, alarming the child even more, until he saw the spread they were laying out and was told he could help himself. Then he rushed to the table and tried to stuff his mouth with both hands while the adult watchers didn't know whether to laugh or weep.

Outside, the seemingly endless parade of adolescents trooped across the bridge. The counting had changed, though. Now there were no groups of ten; postulant priests simply counted heads going by and signaled for a drumbeat or trumpet call as needed. Why be so careful before the choosing, and less so afterward?

Eventually Ledacos told Dychat that he had better stop or he would burst, and would he like a ride in a sedan chair? Instantly worried again, the boy asked what a sedan chair was, but then agreed that it might be fun.

"We'll go to my house then. Irona lives nearby, so you'll be able to see her again quite often. Won't he, Irona?"

Of course, she agreed, wondering if she ought to acquire some building blocks or a skipping rope for the new Chosen to play with.

~

Azalka 660 was a tall, stiff woman whose mouth looked as if she disapproved of most things, but she greeted Irona warmly enough when she arrived at Sebrat House. Azalka was the senior commissioner of Property and had the house in her gift, so far as assigning it to a Chosen was concerned.

"Too small for most, but a fine starter home," she declared. "The view from the terrace is especially fine. Shall we begin there?"

A fast tour of house and grounds took about half an hour and left Irona overwhelmed by splendor. She had visited many mansions in the last two years, but not with an eye to owning any of them. Sebrat House was small by Chosen standards but a hundred times larger than her parents' home. It was lavishly decorated and furnished, and even Azalka gave grudging approval of the designers' taste. Irona had expected to find servants present, but wherever she went, from the grandiose master bedroom to the cavernous kitchens, she saw no one. Yet a fire smoldered in the kitchen range, and no speck of dust lingered anywhere.

The tour ended in the ballroom, which was the only part of the building that Irona had visited before that day, and which commanded a breathtaking view of the city and its great circular bay.

"A very fine neighborhood," Azalka said thoughtfully. "Were I not chair of the Property Commission, I might crave it for my own."

"Neighbors?" Irona had already registered that the mansions flanking Sebrat were several times grander.

"Seven Knipry this side, Chosen Ledacos that side."

He had not mentioned that cozy little arrangement. Irona had not been pursued by a man since Sklom bulged his biceps at her; now none dared express interest in her. Possibly Ledacos's hints had been no more than some sort of ruling-class compliment, but the potential for future flirtation would add some spice to life. The fact that only a high stone wall would now separate her from her patron was the deciding factor. She was going to accept Sebrat House.

"Can I possibly afford this?"

Azalka chuckled. "If you can afford to feed eight or nine servants, you won't notice the rent. Say two dolphins a month?"

"If you were to rent it to a citizen?"

"Two or three hundred." Azalka smiled with the joy of power and took her companion's assent for granted. "You can move in at any time. I mentioned to the servants and other residents that you might wish some of them to stay on. Would you like to interview them now?"

"Er . . . yes." The prospect would only get worse if she delayed.

"Ring a bell when you are ready, then. I must run. I have a meeting of the Ad Hoc Sumptuary Laws Committee at noon, such a bore. Please excuse . . ."

Her voice tailed away as she hastened to the door. Irona went over to the nearest bell rope and tugged. She considered sitting on a chair of intricately carved narwhal ivory and was deterred by visions of it collapsing under her. She wandered back to the windows to enjoy the vista. Sebrat stood higher on the Mountain than Trodelat's house.

Within seconds, a woman entered and approached. She was swathed in black, so that only her arms were visible. Irona rose and held out hands to greet her, but the newcomer dropped to her knees, then lifted back her veil, keeping her eyes lowered. She looked far too young to have a son of about Irona's age, but that just meant that Chosen Podnelbi had provided his paramour with Source Water. Her shoulders bore the brands of a freedwoman. Even in grief, she was beautiful.

"I am Velny Lavice, ma'am."

"Please rise."

Velny shot her a surprised glance and almost imperceptibly

shook her head. A freedwoman ranked above a slave but below a citizen and infinitely far below one of the goddess's Chosen.

Irona might make mistakes, but she must not admit to them. The last time they had met, Velny had been mistress of the house.

"I insist! We are not yet mistress and servant and may never be. At the moment I am merely a friend come to offer sympathy."

Velny rose, Irona embraced her, then led the way to a couch.

"I am told that the law evicts you with disgusting haste. Have you family to go to? Other plans?"

"None, ma'am."

Not even the married daughter? "It was suggested that you might be willing to stay on here and run the establishment as my housekeeper."

"I should be deeply grateful for such mercy, ma'am, and would serve you to the very best of my ability."

"Then we are agreed. What would you pay a housekeeper?"

"Between three and five dolphins, ma'am, depending on her performance."

"I heard seven, so seven it shall be. Now what other staff do we have?"

Two cooks, four guards—of whom the two juniors doubled as porters—three gardeners, two cleaning maids, a valet, and a ladies' maid. Extra help was brought in for banquets. The total was more than Ledacos had said, but probably the minimum needed to run a place this size. Six were slaves, who required no wages but would expect to be freed after twenty years or so.

"I have no need for a valet."

"I believe he has already received at least one offer, ma'am."

"Good. Please keep on the others, except any you feel do not merit employment. Now, you also have a son. I met him once, here in this room, but I confess I forget his name."

"Vlyplatin Lavice, but he has no training or experience as a servant, ma'am."

"Of course not. Tell me about him."

Again the surprised glance, gone in a moment. "He is nineteen and was articled to an attorney."

Was? "And betrothed, I was told."

Velny nodded, her expression bitter. "That also." A living Chosen could advance the fortunes of a family or a legal firm, a dead one could not. What future did Vlyplatin have now?

"The blind one can be cruel. Is he here now? I wish to speak with him."

"Ma'am, he is in deep mourning."

"I understand."

Looking worried, Velny curtsied and departed. She had probably been in deep mourning herself until an hour or two ago.

Irona went back to the window. After a few minutes, she realized that a slim young man had entered in silence and was kneeling at her feet, staring in silence at the floor. He wore only a rag around his loins and had clearly been rolling in dirt: hair, face, limbs, and all his visible torso were filthy. He would proudly walk the streets like that for a month, displaying his grief, but he was close to naked, and so embarrassed to be interviewed in private by a young woman that his blush showed through the grime and stubble. Deep mourning for men also included a limited diet and sleeping on bare floors. And in spite of it all, Irona was very conscious of his incredible good looks and warned herself that she must not let them warp her judgment.

"Oh. Um, Vly . . ."

"Vlyplatin Lavice, ma'am. At your service."

His voice was a deep growl that ought to belong to a much older, larger man. She remembered the voice.

"Stand up, please."

He rose but did not look at her.

"My sorrow on your loss, Vlyplatin. I watched your father in Juvenile Court a few times and was impressed by the care and dedication he brought to every case. The Seventy will miss him. His death has probably struck you harder than anyone, even your mother. Have you made any plans yet?"

He shook his head and swallowed hard, as if he was still close to tears. He was young to lose a father, young to be thrown out with nothing into an uncaring world.

"I seem to recall standing in this very spot a few months ago with a couple of other Chosen and a visiting Lenochian, while you pointed out some of the sights to him. Would you do so again, please? As if I was a stranger to Benign."

He blinked in surprise and almost pouted, as if any distraction from his mourning was an imposition, but then he turned to the window and did as she had asked. His growl had a true Benesh lilt, much more acceptable than her own voice, which still carried dregs of Brackish.

When he pointed out the Source of Chiala, she interrupted. "Explain to me about the Sources. Why does Benign have three?"

"You would have to ask the goddess that, ma'am. No other city has more than one, and of course that explains much of our prosperity, or did so early in the city's history. It is indeed strange that such a tiny island should have come to rule so great an empire."

"Go on. Keep talking." He was as easy to listen to as to look at.

"Well, Benign has the world's finest harbor, sheltered by the Mountain from the westerly winter storms, and I expect it had fine forests back then, for timber to build ships, and we grew rich exporting Source Water. Our republic flourished because we had three Sources, so no one family was able to control all the income and impose its . . ."

He was articulate, poised, and quick-witted. She threw irrelevant questions at him, but he had guessed that she was testing him and performed as required, answering them all if he could, fielding the rest. She wondered if he would rebel if she asked him to sing for her.

"Thank you," she said. "Impressive! I have engaged your mother as my housekeeper and will keep on all, or almost all, the servants. But you have been raised as a gentleman."

"I would be extremely grateful for any employment, ma'am, no matter how menial."

"I will not demean you. What I need is an escort." Not someone like Captain Jamarko, whom Trodelat dragged to every social engagement, jangling like a smithy in his armor.

Vlyplatin's head whipped around, and he looked right at her for the first time, staring in amazement.

"Whose duties, I stress, will end at the outside of my bedroom door."

He blushed scarlet and dropped his gaze again. "Escort a *Chosen*?"

"You would," Irona said, anxious to dowse emotional fires, "have to dress better than that, though."

He grinned at the floor. Even his ears were red. "Of course, ma'am."

"Gentlemen carry daggers, sometimes even swords. Have you had any weapons training?"

"Just a little, ma'am."

"I would see you got more, as much as you can benefit from. If you have the agility, I would have you become an expert swordsman. You would be free to complete your deep mourning ritual. I have been entrusted with two important offices, so I will be receiving many social invitations. I need someone to escort me to them and be my host when I entertain here. I repeat that I do not expect you to be my lover. I will pay you five dolphins to start with, probably more later, and you will have to dress like a gentleman. Would you be willing to perform an escort's duties?"

Apparently too overcome to speak, Vlyplatin prostrated himself and kissed her sandal.

Irona moved in three days later, requiring only one bearer to carry her meager possessions. Trodelat seemed genuinely sorry to see her leave, and Irona knew the old nag was going to be lonely with only her bronze-plated gigolo for company. And she . . . She must not think about her next-door neighbor.

Except that she did, of course. They met often, both socially and in the Scandal Market, but never alone. Ledacos was already powerful enough to have acquired a permanent train of clients, and young Dychat 702 stuck to him like a barnacle. Many times, by the end of a long evening, whether of work or play, he went to sleep and Ledacos carried him out in his arms.

Housekeeper Velny was reserved, respectful, and extremely good at her job. She almost never showed her feelings, yet Irona could still detect the bitterness she was hiding. The blind goddess had been kind to Irona, but most unkind to Velny. That was not Irona's fault, and she could only hope that Velny did not grudge her her better fortune.

Vlyplatin Lavice proved to be a shy young man, pleasant enough but strangely docile compared to the adolescent male hellions she remembered from Brackish. In the last two years, she had rarely even spoken to people of her own age. She could not tell whether he was just unsettled by his father's death or was naturally timid. A few days after her arrival, she thought of a way he could make himself useful while still living on crusts and roots and dressed like a hermit fresh out of the wilderness.

"My father is Akanagure Matrinko, a sea hunter and master of *South Wind*. My family live, or did live, in Brackish, four doors seaward of the chandler's store on the road to the lighthouse. I have not spoken to them since I was chosen, and I want to know how they fare. If possible, I would prefer that you do not let them know why you are inquiring, but that may be difficult, for Brackish folk are a tight-mouthed lot." Sklom? What was he doing these days? But Sklom could wait.

"And," she added, "I insist that you wear sandals, for it is too far to go in bare feet; you will lame yourself." She wanted to order him to eat a good meal, too, but she was certain he would disobey.

~

Vlyplatin returned very late and showed great distress as he broke the news. *South Wind* had gone down with all hands in a storm during the winter before last. Irona's mother had remarried—as she would have had to do to feed her brood—and had moved, probably into Benign itself, but possibly to the mainland. Her husband's name was unknown, or at least had not been revealed to a nosy young stranger.

The young man was weeping by the time he had finished his report; he seemed to feel more hurt than she did. Two years had blunted her pain, but his bereavement was still an open sore.

She said, "Thank you. Now we have something in common."

THE YEAR 703

*T*he Benesh navy had built and sustained its empire. Its ships carried its trade and applied its military strength. Naval vessels were galleys, mostly single decked, although the larger biremes were gradually being adopted, for sailing ships, being limited to square sails, were awkward and unreliable, incapable of doing much more than running before the wind. Galleys were manned by freemen, not slaves, and Benesh troops were marines, rowers at sea, soldiers ashore.

Empire building relied on a deceptively simple technique. Each new territory conquered, or just bullied into submission, was required to pay tribute in the form of fighting men, who swore allegiance to Benign and ultimately went home with Benesh citizenship. A large kingdom might supply and maintain a dozen galleys, fully manned, while small cities would contribute men only. Each time the Empire extended its borders, it grew richer and stronger, and so its own citizens had to share less of the risk in the next expansion.

But a navy largely manned by provincials was like a rich man's armed bodyguard, a potential threat in itself. The Seventy were well aware that any so-called ally or group of allies might rebel at any moment and then their naval contingents would surely turn coats also. The government's Geographical Section kept a watchful eye on every

other navy, and its Treaty Board would rapidly move to confiscate any
ships it viewed as superfluous to their owners' needs.

Being a Chosen was a great honor and very well rewarded, but it was
a full-time job. Juvenile Court and Navy Board filled Irona's life. The
Navy Board, especially, was so important that it ranked five Chosen,
at least one of whom must be a Seven. The members sat at a crescent-
shaped table facing their staff of a dozen or more clerks, shipwrights,
and senior sailors, who were seated at two long, straight tables,
which joined the head table to form the shape of a U. The room was
frequently stuffy and overcrowded; its ancient frescoes of sea battles
were fogged by centuries of smoky oil lamps. The Navy Board had
several duties, but the most important was delivering fighting men
where they were needed; the Army Board's responsibilities began as
soon as they stepped ashore.

As Ledacos had told her, much of Navy's work required personal
study of reports, and that could be done at her own convenience, but
the meetings could never be avoided, and many problems were spun
off to subcommittees, usually consisting of two Chosen and a couple
of clerks. The subcommittees commonly met in private homes, often
sitting well into the night.

As the most junior member, for the first half year of her two-year
term, Irona rarely opened her mouth in meetings of the full board. The
first time she did so she blundered badly. The senior member of the
board was Seven Knipry, who had "rewarded" Brackish with a better
breakwater for "donating" Irona to the goddess. He had been Ledacos's
patron and now could best be described as his ally, for he promoted the
younger man's cause, having few ambitions of his own and being convinced that his chance ever to be elected First had long passed. Yet he
was still both sly and spry, and he kept meetings running at full gallop.

"Letter from the Treaty Commission," Knipry announced,
"requesting transportation for Commissioner Ledacos to visit Osopa
and Biarni. Commodore?"

"Good tryout for *Green Gull*," proclaimed a white-haired sailor at the head of one of the side tables.

"Can she be ready by full moon?"

"Aye, if I threaten to keelhaul her skipper."

"And who shall we send along to witness her maiden voyage, eh? Her trials, I mean. Chosen Irona?"

Irona should have jumped at the chance of a trip on the navy's latest and largest galley, but not when Ledacos was going along. That was altogether too neat an arrangement, and she was certain that he had set it up with Knipry. The snide crack about maiden voyage was confirmation.

"Full moon would be a bad time for me, sir."

The sudden silence seemed to clang like a bell. Then Knipry offered the perk to Rasny 650, who accepted with enthusiasm. Obviously such treats should not be refused, and a girl who wanted to be counted one of the boys should not hint at women's problems. She was offered no more goodies after that.

She was young. She would learn. But her blunder rankled, and it was small consolation that the trial of the innovative new bireme turned into a near disaster. *Green Gull* almost rolled in a minor squall and came limping home to Benign in disgrace. The designers were soundly flogged and then fired.

It was just after midwinter when Caprice smiled on Irona again. The city was cowering under a winter storm, and the board met by lamplight at the bitter end of a very wet, dark, and blustery afternoon. The air was rank with the smoke of whale oil. Everyone was anxious to leave and prepare for the annual Navy Ball at the First's Palace.

The board was discussing pirates.

Specifically, it was discussing a man who went by the name of Captain Shark. Shark had been running a flotilla of anywhere up to a dozen ships for several years, at great cost to the Empire and its commerce. The Geographical Section's spies had learned that he was holed up for the winter in Udice, a tiny port in Karang. Army had been alerted but had retorted that Karang was a desert, without water, roads, or inhabitants. Some fisherfolk lived in hamlets like Udice, but even they had no access to the interior. At this time of year, Shark might as well be on the moon.

"Tar and burn him!" Knipry roared. "By the time we can go after him, he'll be long gone out of there. We'll have to mount a major naval campaign in the spring, sweep the whole coast."

Not wishing to display ignorance, Irona rarely asked questions, but she had grown skilled at picking up information from hints. Why, she wondered, not just turn the job over to Vyada Kun? It was a smallish city ruling a biggish island of the same name—she knew that because she had been there. It was close to Udice and it had war galleys. It was a vassal state, so why not just hire a sea hunter to deliver a letter ordering Vyada Kun to clear up the nest of pirates on its doorstep? After a few moments, she realized that the board did not trust Vyada Kun not to be in league with the enemy.

Knipry cut off discussion with a slap on the table. "Nothing we can—"

"Sir?" Irona had her hand up, for the first time ever.

Knipry stared at her as if he had forgotten her name. "Yes?"

"I ask for a recess."

Four men exchanged angry glances. A recess was called only to discuss very secret matters, or when the members were seriously divided and needed to shout at one another. The Navy Ball . . . But Irona 700 had never spoken up before and obviously must be granted the courtesy of a hearing for that reason alone.

"Recess." The chairman pushed back his chair. The Chosen retired to their withdrawing room just behind their table. It held a circle of five chairs, nothing more. Some of the lamps had burned out, so it was even smokier and dimmer than the meeting room. Knipry slammed the door without suggesting that anyone sit down. It had been a very long afternoon.

"Yes, 700?"

"I have been to Udice."

His eyes widened. "How? When?"

"The spring of 700. I sailed on my father's boat and we put into Udice to trade for their winter's catch of seal pelts."

He scowled suspiciously at that, so the other men did the same.

"And they let you go?"

They were thinking of a pirates' fortress. She shrugged and smiled.

"Why not? It's just a very small fishing village at the end of a fiord. It's sheltered by cliffs and has good water. Maybe four hundred people, eighty able-bodied men at most. But I think we can snuff Captain Shark there." She could sense the favor of the goddess. "In fact, I am sure of it."

The old man frowned. "Everybody sit!" Even before all buttocks were in place, he barked, "*How?*"

"How many men does Shark have? Three or four hundred?" She saw her audience fidget. They wanted no analyses from her, only facts; so she switched to facts. "When sou'westers blow—as they usually do at this time of year—it is very easy to get into Udice and almost impossible to get out. By the time they know we're coming, they're trapped."

Four men seemed to deflate like bubbles.

Knipry sighed. "And how do we get there? Galleys can't put out in this weather, my dear. They lack enough freeboard. About a third of the allied craft have gone home for the winter, anyway, and most of our own are in dry dock, being refitted." He started to rise—stupid child, wasting time.

"Why galleys?"

He sat down again. "The Empire has little else."

She was nodding to show that she had read the reports. "But fishing boats go out in winter. Sea hunters do. Let's requisition a hundred of their boats. Pack twenty marines in each, a dozen would do. If the goddess wills, a sou'wester will have us at Udice in eight or ten days. If they try to break out, we swarm them like bees. The beach there is too long to defend, so Shark's men can't stop us landing. If they try to escape inland, we take their ships and let them die in the desert while we wait for a northerly to blow us home again."

Objections exploded like the beat of raindrops on the shutters: rations, seasickness, water casks, the fleet scattered by storms, lost in fog, compensation . . . Irona just sat, watching old Knipry, who was listening to the clamor and saying nothing.

Finally he leered. "I can't wait to see those fat-cat officer slobs with their fancy brass helmets being ordered aboard stinking little fishing boats. It's an insane idea, but it's worth looking into. I can laugh myself to sleep at nights just thinking about it. You can have a committee. Who do you want?"

Irona glanced around the group and shot an inquiring glance at the youngest one there, after herself. Fialovi 694 was another Ledacos client, and so her natural choice. He nodded vigorously.

Knipry rose. "The kiddies have it, then. Report as soon as possible. Absolute secrecy." He turned to the door and then paused. "Is there anything else we can't postpone until another day? In that case, let's go, get ourselves fancied up, and prepare to face the music."

He led the way back into the Council Chamber and adjourned the meeting. On the way out, he whispered to Irona, "Well done, my dear!"

"You're welcome, darling," she retorted, but not until he was safely out of earshot.

Wherever she went, Chosen Trodelat required her escort, Captain Jamarko, to trot alongside her litter. Perhaps he smelled no worse while streaming sweat than his leather-based armor did at any other time. Irona was kinder to Vlyplatin, insisting that he travel in a litter also. One evening, about a month after becoming her escort, he had sent for a double sedan chair instead, so they traveled together, facing each other.

She approved and that became their practice. That was how they went to the Navy Ball on that stormy night, with eight bearers, four guards behind, and two link boys running ahead to light the way.

The Navy Ball was the highlight of the social year, crammed with ship captains, office staff, senior navy contractors, and their respective wives or, in very rare cases, husbands. All the Seventy were there with their consorts. Even the First's Palace could barely hold such a number, and senior Chosen had to wait in line to disembark from their litters or carrying chairs.

There was music, but the floors were too packed for dancing, which Irona regretted. Dancing was one of the few things she could do better than almost all the rest of the Seventy. Instead of dancing there was drinking, circulating, and gossip. There was ogling, too, but there she was mostly the oglee, rarely the ogler. As the evening wore on and the wine continued to flow, Vlyplatin also received his share of appraising glances due to his flawless profile, and that night he was looking even more godlike than usual in a tunic of gold samite. Youth helped, of course.

Once Irona found herself close to Fialovi 694. "I can't make it tomorrow until late," he said.

That suited her well; she had plans for the day. "Come to dinner." It was her committee; it would meet at Sebrat House.

He shook his head. "Love to, but it will have to be after dinner."

"I'll wait up," she promised.

They drifted apart in the crowd. Vlyplatin did not ask; she did not tell. She never discussed business with him.

But later she ran into Ledacos and his latest consort, who looked younger than Irona and was voluptuous in the style of gravid sea lions. He was fickle, changing mistresses frequently.

Polite chitchat was exchanged. Then: "Did you ask her?" he demanded of Vlyplatin, without preamble.

Vlyplatin's answer flashed back. "She won't tell me, sir. You'll have to ask her yourself."

"That would not be polite," Ledacos said regretfully. He leaned close to Irona and whispered in her ear, "I never got a committee of my own on the Navy Board until my second term, and I was six years older than you are."

Evidently Fialovi had been blabbing to their mutual patron, although a topic classed as Absolute Secrecy was restricted to the members of the board, so he should not have revealed even that much.

Delighted by Ledacos's admission, Irona just shrugged. "You should shave your legs more often, darling."

Ledacos exploded in laughter and spilled his wine. He was more than slightly drunk, but probably everyone was by then. Irona was, and she had a hard day ahead. Not long after that encounter, she told Vlyplatin to take her home.

She always took the comfortable side of chair, the one that would most often face uphill, so she was at the front as their bearers ran down the endless hills and stairs from the First's Palace. For a while they sat in silence in the dark, listening to rain pounding on the roof, Irona tilted backward, Vlyplatin with his feet braced against her seat, his hands clasping straps to keep himself from sliding off his own bench. Vly, as she thought of him now, was incredibly attentive to her moods. If she did not speak, neither would he. If she wanted to talk, she chose the topic and he followed her lead. In fact, if Vly had a fault, it was that he was almost invisible, he so completely hid his own wishes.

"I love that tunic. You looked very dashing."

"Thank you. You outshone every girl there, of course. As usual."

"What was it that Chosen Ledacos wanted to know and I wouldn't tell you?"

"Why you never wear jewels." He spoke quite seriously, no hint of humor.

"You never asked me that."

"Of course not."

She was pleased. She always made sure that Vly was well deco-rated, as befitted a Chosen's escort. Tonight he wore gold bracelets, a jeweled belt, and the dagger she had given him on his twentieth birthday. It had been outrageously expensive, having a hilt of jade carved in the likeness of a dolphin. He was never seen without it, and she suspected he must sleep with it under his pillow.

"What else do you get asked about me?" she asked.

"How good you are in bed."

"No! Who asks that?"

"Lots of men, even a woman or two."

"And what do you say?"

"Incredible!"

"Right answer again," she muttered, but she spoke no more until they were home at Sebrat. Neither of them had mentioned sex since the day she offered him the job, but she had recently realized that Vly had no social life of his own. Whenever she wanted him, dawn or midnight, he was always available. Such total dedication was unheard of. Only slaves and Chosen worked like that, all day every day. It might be understandable if he was stupid or gauche, but he was certainly neither. What had she done to deserve such devotion? Given him trinkets?

The chair reversed its tilt on the stairs up to her door, making it her turn to hang on. Then it leveled out and they were in the porte cochere at Sebrat. She rang the doorbell as Vlyplatin paid off the bearers; her night porter let her in.

She knew that she was more than slightly tipsy. So was Vly, likely, but sober enough to catch her elbow and steady her when she stum-bled on the stairs. She pulled free of his grip when he seemed to want to hang on, and she was careful not to stumble again before they reached her bedroom door—where his duties ended, as she had told him at the beginning. He had never questioned or suggested other-wise. Always, it was there that he bade her good night and handed her the lantern.

Tonight was different. She was the youngest Chosen ever to serve on the Navy Board, she had been granted a committee in her first term, outperforming her patron. Such a day should end with a fanfare, a celebration, a breaking of rules. She surprised herself by ignoring the lantern and holding the door wide. Vly followed her in and set the lantern down on a table so he would have both hands free.

All he said was, "I have been going crazy, waiting for this to happen." That was as close as she had ever heard him come to complaining.

"Make it happen." She raised her lips to be kissed.

Life was suddenly full of surprises. She was amazed to learn in the embrace that he had an erection already, that the rest of his body was equally rock-hard, that kissing involved much more than lips, that having all the breath squeezed out of her was as enjoyable as being undressed in an indecent frenzy, that whole-body contact was heavenly, that a man could taste as nice as he smelled, that a tongue on nipples produced fantastic sensations all over, that a man without fuzz on his arms might have fur on his chest, that rough and tumble reverted to gentle, even delicate, when they got to the tricky part requiring insertion of part of the second party into part of the first party, which didn't hurt nearly as much as she had feared . . . slow and languid thrusting, becoming stronger, longer, fiercer, and finally a mad combined hammering like mating walruses. Then Vlyplatin collapsed on top of her.

Irona wailed. "Don't stop!"

"Sorry," he mumbled into the space between her breasts. "Couldn't hold back any longer. Wait until next time." He did have a wonderful growl; in this position she could *feel* it as well as hear it.

Now she knew why people worshipped Craver, the mad god.

"Who says there will be a next time?"

"I do. Soon."

Another surprise there: that an escort could be diffident, attentive, and obedient in public, but insistent, tyrannical, and irresistible in bed. Not that anyone seriously tried to resist.

Perhaps because she had grown up in a chicken coop, Irona disliked fluttering around like a trapped swallow in Sebrat's cavernous halls. Her favorite room, where she studied reports and ate most of her meals, was a small dressing room next to her bedroom, which she had converted into an office. It shared the ballroom's God's-eye view of the city, was easily heated in winter, and had windows on two sides to provide cross ventilation in summer. Usually she left the door open; when it was closed, she was not to be disturbed except for a Chosen in person or a courier from the Palace.

It was her custom to eat her morning snack there, and to let Vly-platin join her, so she could give him instructions for the day. That day he arrived a little later than usual and his smile seemed more beautiful than ever. But he closed the door.

"Open it!" she said.

He shook his head diffidently and came to sit at the table. "In a moment."

"I have no intention of acknowledging you as a gigolo. That would demean both of—"

"I agree. Have you ever seen one of these?"

On his palm lay a small medallion bearing a bas-relief of a face, a hideous face, apparently carved from some sort of brown stone.

"Ugh! No! Put it away. It's hideous."

"Of course. It's from Eldritch."

"Are you crazy? A fix? You must know what they do to people who own such things."

He shrugged. "Are you going to give me a son or a daughter? Have you decided?"

"I have no intention—" Oh, Goddess! It might already be too late for intentions.

"How many children did your mother have?" he asked.

Far too many. If his children were as beautiful as he was . . .

"Mine had only two," he said. "Soon after doing what we did last night, no more than half a day, you put this under your tongue and touch your toes three times. Then you don't conceive. Take it."

She just stared at the horrible thing as if it had petrified her.

Vly said, "Every rich man's wife in Benign owns something like this."

She wondered where he had gotten it. Almost certainly from his mother. Mustn't ask. She took it. The medallion felt cold and soapy, like lead. "Under my tongue?"

"Be careful! Watch you don't choke on it, because I'm told it gets very slippery. There are always dangers to using anything like this."

Irona did as he had told her and quickly spat the horrible thing out into her hand.

"You'd better keep it," he said, "if you're going to let me make love to you very often, as I hope you will. If you don't, I shall jump off a cliff."

"That will not be necessary. Thank you for the gift. Now open the door."

He did and returned to join her as if the earlier conversation had never happened. "Another terrible day, ma'am."

The rain was beating on the windows, and most of the city was hidden by fog. She did not comment, but it was an ideal day for what she planned. Again she felt the favor of the goddess.

Vly poured himself some water and flavored it with wine. "Orders, ma'am?" There was not a trace of a lover's twinkle in his eye now. He was a human octopus, coloring himself to match his background. At times in the night he had seemed to have eight hands, too. She wanted to drag him off to bed right away, but she mustn't.

"Order up a sedan chair for us. I want to go to the New Customs House, or near there. Just you and me. No escort."

His eyebrows shot up. He had beautiful eyebrows.

"Wear your sword, though," she said. "And a heavy cloak. From there we'll walk."

"To?"

"Brackish."

He did not question, just pursed his lips. He had beautiful—Goddess! She must stop behaving like a mawkish child bride. Craver had stolen her wits.

"In secret," she said. "As soon as you have finished eating."

He rose, clutching his bread roll. "I can eat and walk. By the way, Mother was asking if she can have the broken floor tiles in the hall repaired."

"Of course she may. Last night . . ."

He paused, eyebrows raised again.

"Was not your first time," she finished limply. She should not ask.

He smiled. "I was given a few lessons when I was younger."

"You can teach me everything you know. But, Vly—"

"Ma'am?"

"Always rumple your bed. I don't want the servants to know."

He looked at her pityingly. "They've known for months. I mean they've assumed it for months. I refuse to discuss it, but I am so gorgeous that they can't believe you could ever refuse me."

"Oh, you . . . ! Go!"

"And I don't abuse the slaves, so obviously—"

"Go, I said!"

Chuckling, he strode off to dispatch a slave runner.

He *was* gorgeous, and she was happy to hear that he had not been abusing the slave girls. Oddly, she believed him on that.

Still gulping the last of breakfast, she went to the strong room door near the fireplace. The keys lived in a box on the mantel—no point in hiding the keys, the Property Commission's flunky had said when instructing Irona in the strong room's operation, because then a burglar might try an ax instead. There were ten keys and ten keyholes, but you couldn't guess which key went in which lock, or which way to turn them, or even which needed to be unlocked. If you made a mistake, you locked instead of unlocking and finished up no better off than when you started.

The door opened inward, so its hinges were not exposed and vulnerable to attack, but behind all those safeguards, the strong room held little except dust, for Irona had long since returned all Podnelbi 681's jewels and other finery to the commission. She kept nothing in there except state documents and gold. She chose a bag holding ten whales, equal to a thousand dolphins, a sizable fortune. It was heavy, but Vlyplatin could carry it for her with some of those muscles she had so much admired in the night.

Locking the strong room was as tricky as unlocking it.

She rang for a slave to remove the remains of breakfast.

Irona was going to veer dangerously close to breaking the decree of Absolute Secrecy that Seven Knipry had laid upon the Irona Committee, but she had begun her inquiries before he issued it. A few days earlier she had asked the Geographical Section for a list of all the harbormasters on the island. Her assigned office in the First's Palace was a tiny nook, up in the attics where the most junior Chosen nested. It was furnished with a small table and one chair and illuminated by a single tiny window. The list was brought there by a young clerk with ugly buckteeth and ears as widespread as a cormorant's wings. He was undernourished, and his tunic looked like burlap. She thanked him and laid two silver dolphin coins on the table. He stared at them as if he had no idea what they were. His official monthly income was probably a few copper fish.

"What's your name?" she asked.

"Sazen Hostin, ma'am."

"I require some additional information, which may not be so easy to obtain."

"What's that, ma'am?" he asked warily. His job and even his neck might be on the line now.

"The outport of Brackish: the names of the guards, both day and night guards, their wives' names, the harbormaster's wife's name. . . ." She paused.

"No more than that, ma'am?"

She was pleased to learn that he was smart enough to know she was offering too high a price for what was close to public information.

"Plus the names of all the Section's informants there and a list of the evildoers they have reported in the last five years."

Again he said, "No more than that, ma'am?" But now he was back to staring at the coins.

"Ten more on delivery, and who knows what other needs I may have later."

"Ma'am." Sazen made the money disappear.

"Soon," Irona added.

He smiled those awful teeth at her and shuffled out the door.

The Geographical Section was the secret police, whose tentacles spread throughout the Empire. It reported only to the Seven, not to rank-and-file Chosen like Irona. Sazen Hostin might earn more by turning her in than by taking her money, but her attempt to bribe him risked only a reprimand and exclusion from well-paying jobs for a few years. A citizen would be charged with treason.

Sazen gave her the list she wanted the next morning. She paid him the rest of his bribe.

He smiled—oh, those vile teeth! "Very generous of you, ma'am. My mother mends clothes in the market outside the Source of Chiala, a blue stall. If a great lady such as yourself sent something to be mended, she would certainly notice."

"And if she found anything valuable in a pocket, you would get it?"

"By nightfall, ma'am. Certainly."

Irona wondered how many other clients the young scoundrel served.

∼

Even on a fine day, the walk from the Customs House to Brackish was a long trek. The downpour made it seem much longer, but only in such weather could Irona go muffled in her cloak of sea otter fur and thus keep her collar hidden. Vlyplatin was an anonymous pillar of sealskin plodding at her side, burdened with both his sword and the moneybag. He was fortunate to own stout boots. She had never thought to acquire any, but now intended to do so at the first possible opportunity.

There was almost no one else outdoors, and she had no fear of being recognized. The identity of the person she spoke with in Brackish would depend on who happened to be home on this dreary winter day. According to Sazen, none of the Republic's senior officers in Brackish had changed since her time—harbormaster, night guard captain, and so on. Harbormaster Dalb Broskev was still married to the same iron-jawed woman Irona remembered. Irona had not been in the least surprised to learn that one of the Geographical Section's senior snoops in Brackish was that same Beigas Broskev. The Broskevs lived in the grandest house in Brackish, and that was where Irona went first, with Vlyplatin at her side.

Drenched and half frozen, she halted to stare, horrified at how pathetic it seemed to her now, just one story and an attic, fronting right on the street, probably no more than four rooms in all. It was larger and better maintained than its neighbors, but that was all one could say of it. Suddenly she dithered close to panic at what she was about to do.

If she exposed a state secret, she would disgrace herself and ruin her career forevermore. Just as bad, she might find that her assumptions were all wrong and she had misled the Navy Board. She would be laughed to destruction. Nothing she ever said again would be believed.

"This's what we're looking for? Your orders?"

Even Vly's rumbling growl failed to steady her. She muttered a prayer.

"Irona!" Vlyplatin grabbed her shoulders and put his wet face close to hers, hood to hood. Never had he spoken her name before, and his grip was fierce. "Whatever it is you are planning to do, the goddess chose you to do it. Now give me my orders before we both freeze to death."

She pulled loose and forced a chuckle. "Thanks, but don't ravish me here. We have come to see Beigas Broskev. Knock softly, but put your boot in the door."

"We come in war, not peace?"

"In authority, not friendship."

"Good. Stand a little back of me so they don't notice you so much." He strode along to the door and thumped on it with his fist.

He was about to knock again when it opened a crack and a girl peered out. Vlyplatin seemed very large in his sealskin cloak and he *sounded* like an angry dragon.

"Open in the name of the Republic!"

The girl—one of very few household slaves in Brackish—fled, shrieking in terror. Vlyplatin thrust the door wide and entered, letting Irona follow. Then they were standing in the main room of the house, which was very luxurious by Brackish's standards, with a small woolen rug in the center, cushions on the chairs, and some ugly daubs of art on the walls. There was no fire in the grate just then, but no ashes, either.

As Irona bolted the outer door, the inner doorway was abruptly filled by the bulk of Beigas Broskev. She was a large, permanently menacing woman with hair dyed and face painted. Behind her hovered a male slave clutching a meat cleaver, although no slave would ever dare threaten a citizen. Irona had never liked Beigas and wished she could have dealt with someone more agreeable. She hated the thought of having to give the woman money. On the other hand, there could be no doubt of who held the upper hand now.

Vlyplatin, summing up his hostess in a glance, took two steps forward, so that he stood on the Broskev's precious rug. Then he stamped a few times and wiped his boots on it. The Street Cleaning Committee's mandate did not stretch to Brackish, where winter rains made the cesspits overflow, turning the streets into open sewers. Beigas glared down in horror as mud and feces reduced her treasure to garbage. This was a side of Vly that Irona had never seen before; as always, he had changed color to match her needs.

"Who are you?" Beigas roared. "How dare you force your way into my house?" She had a voice as domineering as Vlyplatin's own, possibly louder. Her face was inflamed like a setting sun.

"Give me the bag," Irona said. Vly fumbled under his cloak and passed it across, carefully not letting it jingle. "And see we are not interrupted."

He nodded, jostled roughly past their hostess, and went out. The slave backed away before him and the door closed, leaving the two women alone. It was better for his own safety that Vlyplatin not overhear the discussion to come.

"You know me." Irona pushed back her hood.

"Irona Matrinko! I might have . . ."

Then Beigas remembered what had happened to Irona Matrinko, and the red fury in her face ebbed away into an appalled pallor blotched with paint. Irona opened her cloak enough to expose the jade collar and watched without pity as Beigas Broskev subsided, sinking to her knees before the might of the goddess's Chosen.

It was a joyful moment. Beigas had always been the tyrant termagant of Brackish, scolding the children and snitching on them to their parents, denouncing adolescents as rapists or harlots, making trouble for adults in general and the sailors in particular, because through her mousy harbormaster husband she controlled the best anchorages and moorings. By Brackish standards she was wealthy, but every copper fish of it had been extracted by bribes, threats, and blackmail, and although she was easily the worst-hated woman in the village, no one ever dared speak against her lest he risk her spite.

It was entirely in character that Beigas was also a spy for the Geographical Section.

"What are you staring at, woman?"

Beigas was staring at her, but hastily lowered her eyes to regard the wreckage of her rug.

"I beg pardon, ma'am."

Nice! Caprice was kind to those who served her. "I come here for some information," Irona announced. "Swear by the goddess that you will not mention my name to anyone, or reveal that the Seventy have spoken to you; nor will you discuss with anyone else what I am about to tell you, except as I may give you permission later."

"Oh, I do so swear, ma'am!"

Anyone who trusted Beigas Broskev was dumber than a winkle. "And fear the wrath of the Seventy also."

"I am a loyal servant of the Republic, ma'am."

"Oh, I know that! And an upstanding citizen of Brackish, too—ask anyone. Ask Nos Pilulka, who babbled sedition in his cups one night, or Ledvin Vapmo, who was smuggling fixes and cheated you out of your cut, or . . ." Irona listed several more Brackish men who had been turned in to the Geographical Section by Beigas and had thereafter been seen no more.

The woman's face set in a rictus of terror.

"If you betray me," Irona said, "I will see that the news gets out in Brackish. Then I doubt that you will get out of Brackish, at least not alive. Now, can I trust you?"

Beigas groveled. "I swear!" This time she was more convincing.

"Good. So listen. The Republic needs to send some people to Vyada Kun. The matter is urgent and must be done in total secrecy. The navy's galleys are all laid up for the winter. Could you name . . . On second thought," Irona added, although this had always been her intention, "could you act as our agent in this and hire a boat for us? Probably several boats."

Now they were into bargaining, the older woman's face instantly registered greed instead of fear. "In this weather? The risk would be extreme."

"You forget I am a hunter's daughter."

"Alas, your poor father! It was just off Vyada Kun that his vessel foundered, you know. So many fine men . . ."

Irona had not known that. She had picked the name only because of Vyada Kun's proximity to Captain Shark's lair.

"But the hunters sail still. A boat that will carry at least a dozen men, better a score. How much to ship them there, as soon as possible?" Irona did not mention that she needed return tickets for the passengers, and captured pirate vessels might solve that problem.

Beigas registered dismay. "A boat so big? A reliable captain and crew who happen to be in port now?"

"How much?"

"Ten dolphins, maybe more, if you want the best." That probably included at least five for Beigas Broskev.

"I want the best, the very best. But the word must not get out, so only Brackish boats, Brackish men, you understand? No stealing from Sourport or Overock or any of the other harbors on the island. How many boats could you round up in Brackish, say, a week from now?"

Dreams of wealth roiled in Beigas's slimy brain. Her eyes shone. "Well, I would have to put them on retainer to keep them in port, ma'am. But if cost is no object, I could have ten or twelve by then. You'll want them provisioned. That would cost more, of course, because rations go off, and feeding so many passengers . . . Have to lay in fresh cables and sails for a long winter voyage like that, but Brackish men are the finest sailors and the bravest—"

"I know that," Irona said with a momentary vision of Sklom Uroveg's legendary arms. "So you think you could provide transport for two hundred people?"

"Even three hundred, at a pinch."

They would be sleeping in the stinking holds in heaps, and Irona recalled Knipry 640's scorn of the army brass. She was fairly certain that Beigas would offer leaky rowboats for that third hundred.

"Two hundred should suffice. Let me put it another way. How much per person?"

Beigas licked her lips. "A dolphin a head?"

Irona turned away to clink her bag of gold down on the table, but also to hide her excitement. It should be possible! Benign itself had by far the largest fleet on the island, but mostly trading ships, few of which would risk a winter voyage. There were five or six little fishing ports like Brackish around the inside of the bay and at least as many on the outside coast. Sea hunters and fishermen went out in all weathers, even knowing the risks. Supposing Beigas's boast that she could move two hundred men to the north meant only one hundred, then transporting an army of two thousand or so ought to be possible. Even allowing for a few hundred drowned on the way there, the Republic should still crush Captain Shark's gang quite easily.

Irona pulled open the purse and took out a fistful of gold, which she let Beigas see. "One hundred dolphins as an advance on transporting two hundred passengers. Of course, we shall require a detailed accounting later, but even if we decide not to go ahead, or the weather blocks us, then we shall allow you reasonable expenses."

Irona tossed a single whale down on the rug. She expected argument, but Beigas's meaty hand made the coin vanish before it had time to glitter.

"It is a great honor to serve the Republic, my lady!"

There was little to settle after that, except to agree how much Beigas could reveal to others. She demanded a code word to identify genuine messengers, a detail Irona would not have thought of.

"Sklom," she said. "You will hear from us within three days, then. Tell my guard I am ready to go."

She gave Vlyplatin the bag to carry again, and he must have

noticed that it seemed no lighter. They muffled up and went out to brave the storm; although the rain had tapered off, the wind was blowing as hard as ever. Bent into its blast, Irona waited for him to ask how her negotiations had gone, but he didn't. How many aides would be so discreet? How few lovers would?

"It went well," she said.

"Glad. Celebrate tonight?"

"I have a late meeting."

"Afternoon, then?"

How could they keep the servants from finding out?

Why did that matter?

"I'll think about it," she said.

"So will I. All the way home. It won't bother you if I mumble to myself about the curve of your breasts or the sweet taste of your nipples?"

"Not at all. I may make a few complimentary remarks about chest hair."

In fact they did not go straight home, because she went around by the harbor to admire the extended breakwater. Beigas had not thanked her for it, so perhaps nobody had made the connection. It didn't matter now.

Then they went home and celebrated.

That night, in her office, Irona confessed to Chosen Fialovi that she had already bent the secrecy rules by visiting Brackish. He admitted that he had cornered a couple of traders at the Naval Ball to ask if a delegation could be carried on an urgent mission to a northern destination. The answer had been a canny yes, as long as cost was no problem.

"So it's possible!" Irona showed him numbers she had worked out. "We can embark fifteen hundred men and have them in Udice in seven or eight days. Maybe sooner, maybe later."

"How much later?"

"Weeks. It all depends on the wind." Which depended on the goddess.

"We shouldn't need more than a thousand men."

"I said 'embark' not 'deliver.' There will be shrinkage."

He winced. "Sometimes I forget you're a woman."

There were so many possible retorts to that gibe that she ignored it.

"It all depends on Mother Caprice. If she stays her hand, we'll have a resounding triumph. If she turns against us, we may lose every man. . . . And woman."

Fialovi looked startled. "You expect to go with them?"

"It was my idea. I shall insist on going."

But no one insisted on anything to the Seven.

Old Knipry 640 was a master obstructionist, able to delay for years any proposal he disliked. When he saw a need for speed, though, he went straight to the heart of the matter like a war galley ramming a coracle. Two nights later, Irona found herself waiting in the anteroom of the Seven's chamber. Three elderly citizens she did not know were sitting there also, under the watchful eyes, and no doubt sensitive ears, of a couple of Palace guards. The citizens had knelt when she entered and she had bade them rise and resume their seats, but that was the limit of the discourse. She had no idea who they were; they could read her number on her collar.

The hour was very late, and she had been busy since before dawn. No doubt the Seven endured days like this all the time. Who would ever want to be a Seven? Not she. She would do her job as a Chosen and leave it at that. The shark-eat-shark world of higher politics was no place for her.

But she did want to show them that she could do as well as Nis Puol Dvure would have done.

She had collected all the information she needed for Operation Sklom. Knipry had taken her plan to the Seven. If they wanted to question her, they would. If they rejected it, she would be sent home—to Vly. She passed the time by thinking fondly of him, and the change he had already made in her life. As Trodelat had told her on the day she was chosen, a strong young man in attendance was a great bolster to one's self-esteem.

Her strong young man was waiting downstairs with the other servants and attendants. Irona was quite confident that he would change his octopus color to fit right in with them, and certainly never brag about how he slept with a Chosen every night. He might wait hours more, and yet he would never question or comment. How could she have been so cruel as to keep him waiting so long for acceptance as a lover? What a jewel he was! And she, who never wore jewels! She chuckled at the comparison.

The door between the guards opened and a flunky peered out. The three citizens had been waiting longer than the Chosen, but they would not be surprised to hear the Chosen called before them. Vainly trying to swallow the knot of fear in her throat, Irona went in to meet the council.

This room was the very heart of the Empire, and she had never seen it before. It was dominated by a huge eight-sided slate table, on which people had been scribbling with chalk. Above it hung golden lamps, and around it stood eight large chairs, seven purple and one red. One of the Seven was absent that evening, so Irona found herself facing a gap, and the First on the far side. There were no secretaries or other attendants.

The First gave her a faint smile. Knipry beamed reassuringly. Everyone else just stared, no doubt wondering how Nis Puol Dvure would be working out now had the seven-hundredth choosing gone according to plan.

The one to watch, Knipry had warned her, was Mallahle 669, who was senior on the Army Board. As soon as marines disembarked, they were under army orders. Mallahle was the one with the white eyebrows. He did not waste time on formalities.

"Welcome, 700," he growled. He did not invite her to sit. "Your numbers don't make sense, and the admiral over there can't explain them to us. You assume that seven hundred soldiers will be adequate to overcome the Shark's pirates. I want to know where you found that number. Then you want to embark twice that many. I assume you are planning to drown the extras before you get them there? And then you allow almost twice as many boats as you seem to require." He glanced briefly at notes he had chalked on the table. "You plan to load about a quarter of the food and water you will need. The total cost you estimate at two thousand four hundred dolphins, which again seems far too high. Can you explain for us simple landlubbers?"

Knipry certainly could have done so, had he pleased, but Irona had no time to worry about his motives.

"Your Reverence, Your Honors." She kept her speech slow and deliberate and was astonished to hear her voice sound quite normal, not the nervous squeak she had feared. "Navy estimates that Shark commands between two and three hundred fighting men. If Army feels that odds of three to one are inadequate, even with the advantage of surprise, then we can scale up accordingly. The extra men embarked are to allow for losses, but I would expect few of them to be drowned. Many boats will be separated from the fleet and fail to arrive on time. If the goddess wills, those aboard will return home safely. All boats should be lightly loaded in case they take on water in a storm." They might also have to pick survivors out of the sea when other vessels sank, but she did not mention that. "We estimate an eight- or ten-day journey there. Possibly longer coming back, but we can put in for fresh food and water at ports along the coast if we need." As galleys always must, because of their enormous crews, but she didn't say that, either.

"The weather is as dangerous as it can be at this time of year. Why not wait until spring?"

"Because the pirates may move out as soon as the weather improves and then we will have lost them. Because Navy believes

Shark keeps agents in Benign to report on profitable cargos. If we can send boats to Udice now, so can they. Again, the birds will fly."

Mallahle grunted. "This was all your idea?"

"Not at all, sir. The whole Navy Board and its staff, and especially Fialovi 694, all contrib—"

"Cesspits! That wasn't what 640 told us." Then he smiled and everyone else broke out laughing. "Irona 700, we are agreed that the idea is brilliant. The cost in gold and lives lost compares most favorably with a summer campaign against these vermin, which would require the entire navy and take months." The foamy eyebrows turned toward the First. "Your Reverence, I move that this plan be implemented immediately."

First Dostily smiled. "And it has already been approved unanimously. Congratulations, 700. We'll be dressing you in purple before you know it. Knipry 640 tells us you want to accompany the expedition?"

"Oh, yes!" Regrettably, that comment did come out as an excited squeak.

"We have agreed to appoint you vice admiral for this venture. Rasny 650 will be in charge. Go and sharpen your cutlass, Vice Admiral, and may the goddess bless your venture."

Triumph! Scorning a properly sedate withdrawal, Irona almost skipped from the Council Chamber. Fatigue forgotten, she was going to rush Vly straight home to bed, *rip* off his tunic, and *ravish* him.

Benesh warriors were marines. A war fleet was always led by a Chosen, called an admiral, with a professional sailor as his deputy, holding the rank of commodore. Each galley was commanded by a captain and a subordinate called a bosun. As soon as these men stepped ashore, they became, respectively, marshal, general, captain, and sergeant. The same hands that released the oars took up swords or spears.

By morning the army's efficient bureaucracy had been kicked awake from its winter sleep and told to have fifteen hundred marines with five days' supplies ready to embark at the naval docks in two days. Irona was barely to see her bed for the next two weeks.

Ten of the younger officers, men judged open to new ideas, were teamed up with officials from Treasury and agents of the Geographical Section and dispatched to various outposts scattered around the Island. Irona 700 and Rasny 650 accompanied the team that was rowed across the bay to Brackish.

It was a breezy but sunny morning. Navy galleys had closed off the mouth of the bay already, allowing ships in but not out, although there was little traffic in winter. Even if a spy guessed what was brewing, the wind was from the north, so it would be very difficult for any sailboat to reach Udice to warn Shark. If the wind stayed like that, Irona's mad expedition would never leave port.

She watched without guilt while her expert companions ground Beigas Broskev down to much less than she expected to be paid, but the Brackish boats were standing by for inspection.

The vice admiral had already decided to choose *Pelican* to be her flagship, if she were available. She was the largest hunter boat in Brackish, commanded by Captain Aporchal, who had been a friend of her father's, insofar as that disagreeable old tyrant had ever had friends. *Pelican* also boasted a second mast, an innovation that the old-timers scorned, while conceding that she was faster than anything else in the Brackish fleet. Who cared about speed when you were going after seals or dugong or stuff? Even with whales it was skill and experience that mattered.

Pelican was indeed in port, tied up at a jetty with her crew busily making her shipshape for the mysterious charter the Broskev woman promised. Captain Aporchal himself was sitting on the leeward side of the cabin, splicing a rope and keeping a weather eye on everyone else. He looked up in anger when a pretty-boy stranger with a sword came strutting up his gangplank. And behind him a woman? Girl? *That one?* Oh, Goddess!

Aporchal's knees hit the deck with a painful crack.

Irona laughed happily. "Permission to come aboard, Captain?"

"My lady!" He didn't dare look at her.

She told him to rise. He was a hulking bear of a man, much taller than she.

"You haven't changed a bit! How's your family?"

He mumbled that they were fine. Yes, grandchildren now. . . . Tragic about her father. . . . It took several questions and answers before he accepted that he was speaking to a person, and a person he had known all her life, not the goddess herself. Then he began to make more sense, but his hands never stopped fumbling with his hat, while the wind played with his white hair.

"We didn't believe it at first," he said. "But three days later men arrived to start working on the breakwater. . . ."

Her smile came easily. "It's nice to have important friends. Is there anything else Brackish needs?"

He raved about the honor of serving the goddess, and she made a mental note to find out more about Brackish later. They would have many days together. Admiral Rasny had let her go on ahead but now had tired of waiting and was coming aboard with his cloak open to show his collar.

Aporchal dropped to his knees again. Irona suggested he take the two Chosen into the cabin so they could benefit from his advice. There they swore him to secrecy and explained that the real objective was not Vyada Kun but Captain Shark in Udice. Aporchal barked like a harbor seal at that news. "Anything to clean up those . . . beg pardon, ma'am . . . pirates!"

Rasny began asking questions. If the old sea dog said that what they were planning was suicide, the expedition would die stillborn. But Aporchal had already guessed whose idea this had been.

"Nothing to it!" he said. "S' long as Caprice sends us good winds, it'll be easy as clubbing seals."

Irona had never appreciated before that excessive loyalty could kill you.

The ordeal of organizing had barely begun, though. In the next two days and nights, life was a blur of conferences and briefings. Irona's only relief came from the joy of seeing the expressions on the faces of bull-shouldered marine officers reporting to the vice admiral for the first time. That, and occasional encouraging pats on certain parts of her anatomy from the bodyguard behind her when no one was looking.

The only cloud in her sky was the thought that she would have to be parted from Vly. The men could not take wives or mistresses on a war mission, so how could she take her lover—or gigolo, as the sailors would see him? Surprising herself, she found a moment to seek out her old tutor, Trodelat 680, and put the question to her, woman to woman.

Easy, Trodelat said. A woman could not engage in martial arts and Chosen were not expected to. They were entitled to bodyguards. "Tie a sword on him and keep him close, even if you have to share a bunk with the sword."

Problem solved. Vly was in fact a skilled swordsman by then and was sure to be accepted once that information got around.

On the day planned for departure, Irona had an honored place close to the First at a very brief service in the temple, when the leaders asked for Caprice's blessing on their venture. Outside, the north wind had given way to fitful breezes that could resolve into anything, but Irona had faith in the goddess's favor. By then the whole city knew that something strange was happening, and when the worshippers returned to the docks, the bay was speckled with sails and hulls, with more still arriving from the outer ports.

Contingents of horrified and outraged marines were being embarked in what they saw as stinking little death traps. Few of them would ever have been to sea in anything other than a galley. They were rowers, many having arms that would have outbulged even Sklom Uroveg's. The company assigned to Irona's flagship, *Pelican*, was led by a squint-nosed, one-eared gorilla, Bosun Uvillas, perhaps the ugliest man she had ever seen. He and Captain Aporchal were already close to daggers drawn.

The wind veered into the west, a very good sign. As the last boats were loading, it strengthened. Admiral Rasny raised his flag on *Orca* and led the fleet out of the bay. The vice admiral's *Pelican* was to bring up the rear, but of course that instruction could not be followed too literally, or Irona would never arrive anywhere. Some stragglers would have to be left behind, although captain and crew would not then receive their promised bonuses. The marines they carried would miss out on battle pay, so disagreements would be inevitable.

After an hour or so, the wind turned into a strong sou'wester, as the goddess urged them onward, but this soon led to trouble. The sea grew rough and the tiny vessels began to roll excessively, in many cases being top-heavy because the living cargo refused to stay belowdecks like fish or whale flesh, which was what these boats were designed to carry.

The men's reluctance was understandable. Galleys never ventured out in winter, and marines were unaccustomed to small boat motion anyway. The owners could foresee their uncontrollable cargo bringing on disaster, but whether the sailors or the marines were to blame would not matter, for fear was contagious. Soon Irona, bringing up the rear, saw craft turning back. First one, then two . . . four. The great fleet was in danger of falling apart, and it would take her vocation as a Chosen with it.

"Captain, make all the sail you dare."

Aporchal looked at her as if she was out of her mind; perhaps she was, but a desperate situation required a desperate remedy.

"Take us forward to the van," she insisted. Then she borrowed Vly's dolphin-handled dagger to shorten her smock to the absolute limit of decency. As the gallant *Pelican* leaned into the wind, Irona scrambled up the foremast, to the accompaniment of lewd cheers and whistles from all aboard.

Fortunately the vice admiral's flagship had been provided with a bugler. With him continuously sounding the charge and the vice admiral herself waving a sword in full view aloft, the boat went surging forward through the fleet. The cheering and laughter spread.

When Aporchal had brought Irona almost to the admiral's boat in the van, he hove to and let the fleet go by, providing a second view of the exhibitionist hussy. Her bravado worked. The sight of a pretty girl brandishing a sword atop a wildly swaying mast shamed the men into remembering their duty. There were no more desertions, and the expedition was saved.

As an exhausted Irona flopped into Vlyplatin's arms later, she knew that she had created a legend. If the assault on Udice succeeded, she would be a national hero. If it didn't, she had just committed political suicide, and the Seventy would never take her seriously again.

Whatever their size, ships either anchored or beached at night, and in midwinter the days were short. The masters had been provided with a list of approved anchorages, most of them chosen because they were both virtually uninhabited and easily recognized, for maps were unreliable and place names could vary. Each boat carried at least one man who could read.

This system worked amazingly well, and the way the winds cooperated astonished everyone except Irona herself. Of the original ninety-eight vessels, only eighteen failed to report in at the last rendezvous. Only three were known to have foundered, and most of those aboard had been rescued. She had hopes that the absentees would turn up in due course.

The last rendezvous had to be at Vyada Kun, because there was no other adequate harbor near Udice. Vyada Kun was a sizable town controlling a large island of the same name, but it was a reluctant ally, only recently incorporated into the Empire and still nostalgic for the Good Old Days of being an independent republic. The pirates were bound to have agents and sympathizers there.

The harbor was a lagoon behind a long barrier island, easily large enough to hold the Benesh fleet but also easily secured. Commodore Lewommi took charge the moment he jumped ashore, ordering pickets set on the local boats, all of which were conveniently beached nearby on the windswept sand. No word of the army's arrival would be smuggled out of Vyada Kun that night, but that did not mean that the fleet had not been observed at sea and some other boat was not already carrying warnings to Udice.

A hundred boats arrived more or less together and two dozen more within an hour, but Admiral Rasny's was not among them. When a delegation came down from the city to find out who these newcomers were, Irona insisted that she would receive it, not Lewommi. After all, her vote had helped elect the governor, a Benesh appointee. She sent word back to him that he was to do all he could to keep news of the fleet's approach from spreading beyond the town. She doubted very much that this situation could last another day, though. If the marines did not attack tomorrow, they would find the pirates flown.

Before dawn she called the senior officers to a council of war aboard *Pelican*. Lewommi advised that they had sufficient manpower to risk an assault and the wind would probably serve. But it was Irona 700 who gave the order to proceed, and her flagship led the armada out. The wind was perfect, the sun rose into a cloudless sky: unbelievable weather for midwinter and a clear sign of the goddess's favor. Some marines began to sing, as they did when rowing, and soon the song spread throughout the fleet. They were still singing when they swept into the Udice fiord a couple of hours later, and their voices echoed back from the stark cliffs on either hand, as if the mountains were calling out a welcome.

But when Udice itself came in sight at the head of the fiord, the singing stopped and marines who owned armor began putting it on. The standard garment was an apron of sheep or goat leather clad with bronze plates. Irona thought its weight must put a serious strain on the men's necks.

Most of Shark's vessels were drawn up on the shingle for careening, as were the local fishing vessels. Only two ships were afloat, at anchor. They were lashed together, one of them dismasted for repairs and the other fitted with a derrick. The marines waded ashore and rushed the village. Not presuming to join in the fighting, Irona stood on deck with Vlyplatin and watched, but there was very little to see. The pirates who offered resistance were killed, but most did not, and soon about three hundred men were sitting in circles along the beach, facing outward, hands tied behind their backs. At the center of each circle stood a man with a drawn sword and orders to use it if he saw a need.

An estimated seventy pirates fled across the pasture behind the village and tried to escape up the cliffs that closed off the valley. Benesh archers used them for target practice.

A rather disappointed General Lewommi saluted the Chosen and announced that Udice had been secured with only two wounded, whose injuries were not serious: Now what? Irona had given no thought at all to *now what*. Nobody had, so far as she knew. Perhaps they had all assumed that the pirates would fight to the last drop. It had been too easy.

She called another council of war and included two graybeards from the village. Everyone agreed that to carry so many prisoners back to Benign for trial was impossible. To release them here, even without their ships, was unthinkable; the village had suffered enough already. But half of the captives were loudly complaining that they were innocent, either because they had been kidnapped, or because they were natives of either Udice or Benign.

Irona did not know what the law was, or even which law applied: naval, martial, or civil. But she was the ranking magistrate present, so she would have to make up her own law and hope that she would not later be impeached for exceeding her authority. Ledacos's maxim, that doing the least evil was better than doing the greatest good, was very little help when a whole army of philosophers might need a century to apply it to her present situation.

The only answer, and all those smirking bronze helmets were just waiting for her to admit it, was to kill the prisoners. But how to tell who was guilty and who wasn't?

"We'll hold a trial," she declared. "Commodore, collect a dozen or so women from the village. And don't leer at them like that or you'll scare them to death. At least we can be sure none of the women are pirates, and they'll know who isn't native and who's been abusing the villagers. You, there, clean out that dismasted ship, strip it of valuables. Commodore, we'll need a whole team of volunteers with good swords and strong right arms."

Lewommi snorted. "They all have two strong arms, and any man in the fleet will volunteer to kill pirates. Can't we just give them one each to play with?" But he stalked off to do as she said.

Irona was fighting a strong sense of unreality. This bloodthirsty tyrant was herself? She? The Irona she had known all her life? And she had barely started. Pirates, fine. Men from the Empire, probably fine. But if she beheaded a Benesh citizen, she would be impeached for certain.

"Bosun Uvillas? Collect a dozen or so men from Benign. Your team will question any prisoner who claims to be a Benesh citizen. Ask him to name the Sources or the street along the docks, and so on. Listen to how he speaks. If he's a citizen, tell him he can ask to be taken home for trial, but warn him that a guilty verdict there will mean the sea death. Here we're just going to cut off their heads."

The hog was even uglier when he grinned.

~

Irona had a vague memory that naval law was simpler than civil, so she set up her courtroom on the deck of *Stormdancer*, which was the seaworthy pirate ship afloat at the jetty. The twelve Udice women sat in a row, some knitting or spinning, others clutching babies, and all of them almost drooling at the thought of vengeance on the ruffians who had terrorized them for months. Vlyplatin was set to work as court reporter.

The first prisoner was marched up the plank. He was a fresh-faced, youngish man, who did not fit Irona's image of a monster.

Name? Plea?

But that was the last time Irona asked for a plea, for the women began screaming, "Pirate!" "Rapist!" and even "Child molester!"

"Guilty," she said.

His guards cut off his protests by forcing a horse's bit in his mouth and tying it there, so that he could scream all he wanted but speak no name to Bane with his dying breath. Then he was marched across to the dismasted hulk alongside, hauled over the rails, thrown down on the deck with his head over the open hatch. One swish of a cutlass was enough to silence his howls. His corpse was thrown after his head and by that time the next accused was arriving in court.

The fourth man claimed to be a citizen of Benign, and his accent sounded genuine.

"Why are you here, then?"

"Not guilty! I was being held for ransom."

The women all started yelling at once about rape and murder.

Irona raised a hand, and they fell silent. "You will be taken back to Benign for trial, but if the Naval Court there finds you guilty of piracy, you will be sentenced to the sea death."

Throughout that exchange his immediate predecessor had been screaming on the deck of the hulk. The noise stopped abruptly, being followed by two muffled thumps.

The accused smiled ruefully. "Bitch! All right, I change my plea. Guilty as the Dread Lands." He opened his mouth for the rope.

That one died without a scream.

About three hours later, when she was almost out of victims, Irona looked up and saw that the admiral had arrived, very late but not looking very repentant. Had he truly been delayed, or had he deliberately held back, whether to avoid involvement in a potential disaster, or to let Irona have all the credit for her proposal? His smile seemed genuine enough.

"I was going to ask if you need help," Rasny said, "but you obviously don't."

Irona stood up. "Take over, please. I've had enough."

She thought she would never sleep again, but in fact the massacre did not weigh long on her conscience. The accusations from the women jurors had confirmed the sort of scum she was exterminating, and the world was a cleaner place without them. There was nothing romantic about piracy.

The next day the mass hearse was towed well out to sea and set afire, sending roasted pirates to feed the hagfish and lobsters. Rasny left a large contingent of marines at Udice to refurbish the pirate vessels and defend the inhabitants from any pirates who had managed to escape inland, but the villagers predicted they would soon freeze there, or die of thirst.

The sun shone, and Caprice sent a north wind to speed the expedition's triumphant return to Benign. Those captains whose craft no longer carried marines were talking of seeking other cargoes. It was a good time for seals, and the humpback whale migration was almost due.

As *Pelican* neared the mouth of the fiord with Captain Aporchal at the tiller, he turned a regretful eye on his distinguished passenger, who was leaning on the rail talking with her pretty-boy guard.

"You'll be in haste to get back, ma'am?" he asked tentatively.

Irona could guess exactly what the big old rogue was thinking: it was a great honor to have her aboard, but there was a lot to be said for a hold full of baby seal pelts.

"I'd love to skin a walrus or two again for old times' sake, Captain. But I'm afraid I must report to the Seventy as soon as possible. However," she added thoughtfully, "I was going to ask if we could make a brief detour. I'd like to visit Kadowan."

Aporchal's expression changed as if he had been kicked in the crotch. "Can't advise that, ma'am. No, no. A long way off our course. Very dangerous shore there. Bad currents, lot of fog."

Irona felt Vly bristle at this defiance, and nudged him into silence with her elbow. "I'm sure your advice is good, Captain."

A few minutes later, when they had moved forward and thus downwind and out of earshot, Vly angrily demanded, "What was all that about?"

"Kadowan Island. It's small, very rocky, no water, no inhabitants, no really safe landing."

"But why did he react like that?"

The trouble with keeping secrets from Vly, which she was forced to do sometimes, was that he knew her very well. Better than anyone else did, certainly.

"I'd rather not tell you, lover. It really doesn't matter."

He smiled forgiveness, but she knew her evasion rankled. The secret of Kadowan Island could explain how Irona Matrinko had become Irona 700 and it was better that nobody else know that.

*E*ffort begot success and success begot jealousy. Udice made Irona 700 a hero in the eyes of the younger Chosen and the people, but the establishment subtly closed ranks against any more wild adventures. Children simply could not be trusted with authority—given her head, she had callously chopped off more than two hundred heads. For the next few years Irona was loaded up with well-paying but routine offices: Fish Markets, Education, Harbors, Night Watch, Property Commission, Morality, and so on. She always did her best and never complained.

Time was on her side. Dostily 631's tide ebbed at last and he was succeeded as First by Knipry 640. More and more younger faces were gathering around Irona at meetings of the Seventy and, although she was careful to continue deferring to Ledacos 692 as her patron, she could deliver almost as many votes as he could without her. She played the game, never making enemies, always collecting IOUs against the future. In 707, she won a hotly contested seat on the Treaty Board and spent the entire summer inspecting allied ports on the mainland.

In 708, she was elected to several offices, including a seat on the Treason Court, which was an honor, but an empty one, because the Treason Court heard few cases, and in most years none at all. The stipend was correspondingly low. A few days before her term would end,

*the Republic was appalled to hear that a Chosen had been murdered.
The victim was Trodelat 680, Irona's former tutor, and the chief suspect
was her majordomo, freedman Jamarko.*

For the two days that elapsed between the announcement and the
trial, Irona agonized over her responsibility in the matter. Her former relationship with the deceased offered a slim chance that she
might persuade the First to excuse her from participating. For three
nights she barely slept, tossing and turning, thrashing in nightmares,
and keeping Vlyplatin awake also.

"I do not understand," he said, clutching her to him as if she were
a wild animal trying to escape, "why your former friendship—which
I hardly believe in anyway, from some of the stories you tell of her—
should exclude you. I would have thought you would want to see her
killer punished."

That was precisely the problem. Justices of the Treason Court
were required to witness the executions they ordered.

"I knew Jamarko, too."

"But you always told me you disliked and distrusted him. Sounds
like your judgment was better than Trodelat's. Of course, I've always
thought it was." Vlyplatin tried nibbling her ear.

"But he isn't a citizen!"

"So?"

"So they don't just hang him!"

"Serves him right." Ear nibbling did no good. "Would it help if I
sexually violated you now?"

"No!"

"Oh?" he said judiciously. "I think I will anyway."

Of course Irona had known from the start that it was her duty to
serve. She never evaded a duty and didn't in this case. The Treason
Court always comprised the First, two Sevens, and two other Chosen. As the most junior, Irona sat at the far left.

The prisoner was led in, clattering his chains. Irona had never seen Jamarko except in armor, and now he wore only a slave's sack. Somehow he seemed more of a man in it, or perhaps that illusion sprang from the way he held his head up in spite of his captors' efforts to humble him. He had been savagely beaten. He recognized her and smiled, but his smile was a toothless grimace that must have hurt his battered face.

He admitted his name, heard the charge, and mumbled that he pled guilty.

The First frowned. "You realize that the punishment for murdering a Chosen is the sea death?"

Jamarko sneered. "It was worth it." His speech was slurred.

"Has the accused been tortured?"

The chief bailiff said, "No, Your Reverence. He never denied his guilt and there were several witnesses."

Elevation to head of state had not sweetened old Knipry's acidulous humor. "No torture, but he has fallen down several flights of stairs recently and landed on a hot stove every time?"

"He was questioned about his motive and possible accomplices, Your Reverence."

"Defendant, you admit you killed a Chosen of the goddess?"

"I broke her neck with my bare hands," Jamarko said proudly.

"Why do such a terrible thing?"

Another gaping smile. "To be a man again," he said, his mutilated mouth mangling his speech. "For twelve years she used me as a toy—me, once a cadet captain of the Havrani! Three days ago she dismissed me. Told me to turn in my weapons and armor and leave. Turned me out in the street with not so much as a crust. She had put a *boy* in my place!"

The worm had turned at last, but it had turned into a serpent.

"Questions?" Knipry glanced along the bench and met only silence. He turned his disk to black. The four others concurred. He spoke the legal formula: "You are sent to the goddess for her justice." Then he added, "Don't ask me for mercy, because you won't get it."

The prisoner spat at him and was clubbed down by the guards.

"Bailiff, what time is low tide today?"

"Right about now, Your Reverence."

"Then the execution will be held three days from now. We decree the usual public holiday."

On the appointed day, Irona and the other judges—plus most of the rest of the Seventy—were rowed in the state galley to Execution Bridge, which was close to the northern entrance to the bay, across from Brackish. Huge crowds from the city were already in place, with more streaming in by land and water.

The site of the execution was a gully that cut through the headland, dry at low tide, an arm of the sea at the flood. When the Chosen arrived, the grassy slopes on either side of the gap were already packed with spectators, many of whom must have been there all night. None of the thousands still on their way were going to find good vantage points, but those who had were in no small danger. There were many records of human avalanches on those slopes, with hundreds of people swept down to join the condemned. When the goddess was being especially capricious, she would smash boatloads of bloodthirsty spectators on the rocks. "The Cruel One" was well named.

The five justices sat in an official gallery of black basalt, whose benches were well cushioned, and whose roof provided welcome shade and protection from the view of gawking spectators. As soon as the justices were seated in their places, with the other Chosen standing around it, the prisoner was marched out to the center of the pass and chained there by the ankles. Naked except for the cruel iron branks around his head that would prevent him from uttering a death curse, he was left to wait upon the mercy of the goddess.

Having studied reports of previous executions, Irona knew that sometimes the spectators cheered these human sacrifices, sometimes mocked them, and sometimes wailed or threatened riot. So far this crowd remained ominously silent. Jamarko turned painfully until he faced the judges, then urinated in their direction. Still the crowd neither cheered nor booed.

He had hours to wait until the full tide swept through there, and even then it might not be deep enough to drown him. There were records of tall men surviving virtually unharmed, unable to swim because of the weight of chain on their ankles, but standing with their faces raised above a mirror-calm sea. Such survivors were deemed to have been pardoned by the goddess. The horror was barnacles, which completely covered the rocks and even the chains. Jamarko's feet and ankles were already bleeding and he could not sit down without increasing his torment. The sea looked deceptively calm at present, but the swell was quite enough to send breakers foaming through the gap when the tide rose. No man could stand against the might of the waves. At first he would be able to cling to rocks, but they would abrade him. Eventually, he must be torn free and dragged back and forth on his tethers. The stronger he was, the longer he would suffer.

A man's hand settled on Irona's knee; Ledacos 692 was kneeling beside her. She edged away from the hand, and it was withdrawn. He never stopped hinting, but he treated all women that way. She bent her head to hear what he wanted. Her neighbor on her right was chatting with the First and probably wouldn't care what she discussed with her patron.

Ledacos whispered. "I'm thinking of trying to succeed Rasny. How do you rate my chances?"

Rasny 650's term as a Seven was due to expire in a couple of weeks, and he would be ineligible for reelection for a year. But already? Ledacos was only thirty-three.

"I thought forty was the minimum. Are there precedents?"

He chuckled. "I want to set one. There were a couple of thirty-eight-year-olds, back a century or so. How many hands could you deliver?"

She stopped short of saying she would need time to think. Anything that would distract her at the moment would be better than sitting staring at a man waiting to be rasped down to bare bones. So think!

There were eight Chosen junior to her now, although two were still in tutelage. Pavouk 708 had promised to fasten his flag to her mast, but he would not be free of his tutor until after the election. He seemed such a cunning young rascal that she was flattered he considered her worthy of his support. The other six would follow her lead, especially in a vote as important as the election of a Seven.

"Seven for certain," she said, "including me. Another four possibly, depending on your competition."

"You can do better than that!"

"If I put my back into it, maybe another three," she said. "You know how reluctant some men are to be led by a woman. But a lot of mine will support you anyway. I won't waste my credit chasing mermaids. Who's going to run against you?"

Ledacos smiled cryptically. "I estimate sixty-two Chosen voting in a three-way race, so anything over about twenty-six on the first ballot has a good chance of winning."

"The old guard will make it a two-way fight just to keep you from collecting votes on a second ballot, sonny."

He nodded, not taking offense. "Maybe. What do you have your eye on next?"

She shrugged. "I remind you that I am presently warming three benches. My ass is not wide enough for more."

"It's a beautiful ass. You can be promoted!"

A Chosen could not refuse election to anything, but almost all of them held several offices, and when two positions could not be reconciled, resignation was permitted. Another Chosen would then have to be brought in, often resulting in a cascade of replacements. The length of term remained the same, counted from the day of election, so elections happened all year round. Only the goddess's choosing had a fixed date.

"To what?" Irona asked warily. She felt she was about due for something prestigious, but she would never say so.

Ledacos chuckled. "In four days we elect a new governor for Vult. Two-year term. Go for that!"

"Vult? Why on earth should I want Vult?" Vult was a fortress in the far north, at the end of the Benesh Empire. Even *South Wind* had never gone that close to the Dread Lands. Grim, cold, and remote, yuck! "I suppose the gratuity is enormous, so I will be able to buy basketfuls of jewels?"

"The gratuity is a miserable pittance."

"Huh?" That made no sense.

Ledacos was smirking, definitely up to something. "You want a worthy cause? You're always looking for causes. Go to Vult and clean it up! You know how much. . . . Or perhaps you aren't aren't familiar with the market in black magic?"

"Of course not! Are you?"

Ledacos smiled. He always knew everything. He must be aware that she had slept with a human billy goat for years without conceiving. Twice she had been forced to replace the Malefic talisman she used to ward off babies. But when it grew too smooth to make out the grotesque face engraving, it would stop working, so said the legend. The first time Vly had obtained a replacement for her, it had cost thousands, but the second time much less.

"Believe me, then," Ledacos said, "a torrent of fixes is flowing south these days, rivers of evil spreading all through the Empire. Vult is supposed to keep it out. It doesn't, anymore."

"Why not?"

"The present governor is Zajic 677. The next one will probably be Redkev 676, who was the previous governor, having succeeded Zajic two years ago. The pair of them have been playing catch with it for the last dozen years."

Irona wondered why she had never noticed that strange alternation in the governorship of Vult during her nine years as a Chosen. Lower price meant larger supply and therefore more customers. It was obvious; why did it take a political genius like Ledacos to see a wrong that screamed for righting?

"What happens if anyone runs against them?"

"Nobody wants to, because the money is terrible, the weather appalling, and the sky turns purple and green. Not to mention the ghouls."

"Tell me about the ghouls."

Ledacos stopped smiling. "The army prefers to call them the Shapeless. They haven't been seen since Eboga 500 whipped their asses. They cannot get into the rock of Vult itself, and they shun daylight. As long as you don't go for long walks at night, you should be safe."

"You believe in them?" She had thought the ghouls were just bogeymen to scare children.

"I believe Maleficence rules the Dread Lands and the evil must be contained. It's a vitally important job, Irona, and it is not being done properly. The Empire is being poisoned with fixes."

He had given her the bones and she could add the flesh for herself. It was not true that the goddess's Chosen could never be bought. They lacked for nothing, but most of them had children or other family who could benefit. The kickbacks from an illicit trade in Eldritch fixes would be mountainous.

"You guarantee that I won't find moray eels in my bed or succumb to terminal dandruff the moment I announce my candidacy?"

"The point is this," Ledacos said, choosing not to answer that question. "You and I are known to be partners—political partners, not bedmates, unfortunately, although I keep hoping. If we put ourselves about, twist all the arms, call in all the favors owed us, promise the moon, we can beat Redkev and elect you governor of Vult. *Then* I run for Rasny's seat on the Seven! The waverers will jump aboard our bandwagon."

And Irona would earn two delightful years on the edge of the Dread Lands itself, being stalked by Shapeless. She said, "Not today, thank you."

"It is your duty, Irona 700! The frontier of evil there was set by Eldborg 300 and reestablished by Eboga 500. This is why the goddess chose you on that special turn-of-the-century year. Both of those men went on to be First, and great Firsts they were, too."

"Nice try, but the answer is still no."

The crowd sighed with a sound like a spouting whale. The first ripples had reached Jamarko's feet.

"It's started," she said.

Ledacos never gave up. "He's got a couple of hours yet. He won't start screaming until he has to move his feet. Tell me who you have for certain . . ."

"No! Tell me how many other people have tried to get these two thieves out and have died in their beds before the vote."

"Don't know of any deaths," he insisted. "Several have withdrawn because of ill health, which may just mean threats. But we can get around that by not revealing your name. You and I and a couple of other patrons will campaign for a Candidate X, whom we praise as a man of incomparable honesty. Your name is never mentioned until I nominate you. By then it's too late to curse or threaten you, and we shoot you out of town as fast as possible to take up your post."

So it wasn't going to be *our* bandwagon, as he had said earlier. It would be the Ledacos 692 bandwagon. He would round up forty or so votes with this story, using danger to keep his collaborators' names secret, and establish himself as a potent power broker. Granted, he would be taking some risk himself if the Maleficence dealers got word of the plan.

"The answer is still no," she said. "But I will try to line up as many votes as I can for whoever you nominate."

He sighed. "That's what they all say. So tell me who I should ask next."

"You could volunteer yourself, clean up Vult, and be a shoo-in at the next Seven election."

He sighed. "I may have to, but field commands are not my forte."

The water was surging above the condemned man's knees before Ledacos finally accepted defeat and left Irona in peace. Soon she wished she had kept him there to continue distracting her.

Jamarko was a very strong man, and Caprice punished him in full measure for his crime.

As the state galley returned to Benign, the Chosen aboard divided into two groups. One, including Irona, stood under the stern awning in a numb silence broken only by the creak of oars and the tap of the coxswain's hammer. Even little Dychat 702 was not chattering, for the first time since he was chosen. The rest, connoisseurs of the grisly spectacle, gathered at the bow to discuss the finer points of the traitor's death. Most agreed that Jamarko had put on the best such show in years.

The navy docks were crammed with sedan chairs and their bearers. Vlyplatin had thought to order Irona's house guards to meet them there with a hired chair. It was a single. That was good thinking, too, for a double would be slower in such a crowd.

Vly appraised her expression. "Home, ma'am?"

"Straight home, double time." Never in her life before had she felt an urge to drink herself senseless.

She collapsed into the chair and Vly closed the drape. Even with the guards clearing the way, the bearers made slow progress at first, but once they left the docks, the streets and stairways were fairly clear on the holiday, and Vly could shout for double time. And shout. And again. Irona realized how hot it was, even for a Midsummer noon. She should not have asked for double time.

When the chair was set down at Sebrat House, she went straight in, to the welcome shade and comparative coolness. Vly stayed to pay off the team, but he was right behind her as she entered her bedroom. She went and sat on the edge of the bed; he closed the door.

"Water!" she said.

He brought it. His tunic clung to him as if he had swum in it, his hair was plastered to his forehead. His face was brick red, and his shoulders still heaved. In fact, he looked aroused, but she had more tact than to say so.

She drank. He just stood there and panted.

"It was ghastly," she said. "Did you see?"

"No. I went back to the barge."

"At the end he was a lump of raw meat with bones showing, and he was still trying to breathe! Why didn't they just hang him?"

"Why didn't they just let him go?"

She had raised the goblet for a second drink when she realized what he had said. It was totally unlike Vly.

"He murdered a Chosen! He killed a woman with his bare hands!"

"I don't suppose he owned gloves. The bitch deserved it."

"*Vly!*"

"Yes, she did! She treated him like a dog. I watched her do it a hundred times—taunting him, belittling him, telling her friends he was sterile when he was standing right beside her."

"That does not excuse murder!"

"What she did at the end did!"

Irona tried to tell him to stop, and he shouted her down.

". . . threw him out to starve. No money. Nowhere to go. No education or skill except fighting, and he was too old for that. You wouldn't do that to a dog."

Hand trembling, she set the beaker down on the bedside table. "I hope I do not treat you like a dog?"

"No. Furniture, yes, but not a dog."

Dismay! "Furniture?" she whispered.

"You dust me once in a while. Take a rest and recover from your ordeal. I have to bathe." He turned to the door.

"Vlyplatin Lavice, you come right back here. If you have complaints, then please state them."

He looked back but left his feet where they were. "I've tried. You don't hear me."

Goddess! This was much worse than she had realized. "What have you ever asked me for that I refused you?"

"Children."

Her mouth opened and closed and said nothing. Maybe he had. Yes, he had. She had not taken him seriously. Did men really want children? Her father had merely tolerated his as the price of pleasure. She had thought only women really cared about children and that she was odd in having other ambitions.

"I am mortal," Vly said, "and proud of my heritage. I wish to leave something behind me when I go. It is not a rare desire." He opened the door.

"Wait!" she cried. "Close it. Let me think a moment."

"You have had years to think. I have done my best for you. I am a very efficient, well-trained, and obedient gigolo and escort. But if I now fail to give satisfaction, you can do what your friend did. I promise not to break your neck for it. There is not a wide market for my skills, but I still have most of my hair and all of my teeth, so—"

"Stop!" She shut her eyes. How could she possibly serve the goddess and rear a child at the same time?

Or was this the hand of the goddess again at last? The butchery at Execution Point, Ledacos's plotting, and now this sudden lovers' quarrel, all on the same day. The first hard words between them in six years! Capricious, very capricious!

"I am sorry," Vly said softly. He had come to kneel in front of her, silent on the rug. He took her hands in his. She could smell his sweat. "I should not have said any of those horrible things, ma'am. Not when you were so upset. May I please go and make myself respectable, as befits the majordomo of a Chosen, an office I am honored to hold?"

She opened her eyes. She gripped his arms.

"I want you to do something first. Run next door and see Ledacos 692. If he isn't home, you must find him. Tell them it's very urgent, because it is. It is also very secret, so you tell only him."

"And the message, ma'am?"

"Tell him I will take the job he suggested. That's all."

Her lover wanted a child, and Vult would solve her conflict of interest. Pregnancy and childbirth while attending three or four meetings a day would be too much for anyone, but her duties at Vult should leave her lots of time for a private life, plus welcome privacy from the carnivorous gossips of Benign.

Vly did not know what was involved. He said, "Yes, ma'am," in the same cold tones. "And then may I bathe?"

"Yes, but as soon as you'd done that, come back here and put a baby in me."

"Oh, yes!" He grinned like a baby himself. "I hear and obey, My Queen!"

"I have told you never to call me that."

"But you are my queen and I will give you a prince if it kills me."

The tension in the Scandal Market was almost as oppressive as the lingering heat of the day. Leaves and flowers drooped; people clung together in clusters, not circulating as usual. There was almost no laughter.

Irona had sensed the same mood a few times before, when a hard-fought election for Seven was scheduled. Yet tonight's agenda seemed bland, and normally the only worry about a vote to determine the next governor of Vult would be the danger of winning such a horrible honor. In theory, Chosen who refused election or scrimped on their duties could be stripped of everything except their jade collars and exiled to Maasok, a barely habitable islet far out in the ocean. In practice, everyone tried to be fair because they all knew that someday it might be their turn. If Redkev 676 were to protest that Vult had been foisted on him three times already, he would certainly be excused and the curse laid on someone else.

But now that Ledacos's campaign had drawn attention to the Redkev-Zajic juggling act, the stakes were much higher. In the end, Irona had approached only six people, because the others she had suggested were either on Ledacos's own list or on other lists that he knew of. To all six she had pointed out this sinister alternation of one highly undesirable posting and the possible connection with the illicit trade in fixes. Ledacos 692, she had explained, had obtained the willing consent of an honest and effective candidate, who would accept the election as a chance to investigate affairs in Vult and root out any corruption uncovered. A candidate, in short, who would accept the posting as an important challenge, not an unfair exile. All six had agreed that it was wise to leave the white knight unnamed at present in case the dealers struck at him before the vote; they had all promised to support the man Ledacos nominated. They could always renege, of course, if they didn't like the candidate in question. No one dreamed of sending a woman to Vult.

Redkev 676 himself was there, standing on the outskirts and happily chatting with Seven Kapalny, who had solemnly promised Irona he would vote for Ledacos's nominee. Redkev was a huge man, a seagreen bear bulging inside his gown. His collar probably contained twice as many plates as Irona's and was half buried in jowls. Stooped and silver haired, he looked older than his number warranted, but long residences in Vult would have deprived him of the benefits of Source Water, for beneficial springs could not exist so close to the Dread Lands. His decay emphasized how well preserved other Chosen were.

Ledacos was not there! Alarmed, Irona walked across the sunshriveled grass to a different vantage point, but still could not see him. She looked for Dychat 702 instead. That was trickier, because he was much shorter than most of the Chosen and even some of the bushes. Six years of good food and Source Water had worked marvels on the rachitic child who had wept on being chosen, but he had never salvaged the growth he had missed. Ledacos had been his tutor and thereafter his patron, and he remained Ledacos's shadow, a chatterbox shadow, although Ledacos excused him by reporting that he never spilled secrets.

Dychat was not there either.

The gong sounded to summon the Chosen to the council. Redkev was one of the first to respond, walking alone, his face giving away nothing. It seemed likely that he or his backers had learned of the conspiracy against him and had found a good way to block it, for the opposition was sworn to vote for Ledacos's nominee: no Ledacos, no nominee. Irona could ask someone else to nominate her, but she was not certain that she was the only "volunteer" the wily Ledacos had enlisted. He never let his thumbs know what his fingers were doing.

The Chosen filed into the Assembly Hall, relieved to be out of the sun. First Knipry strode in with a train of six Sevens, the last of whom was tonight's chairman, Byakal 633. He was incredibly old, but still as sharp as his sword had been in the service of the Republic, many long years ago.

There was shouting at the back. Heads turned. The great door slammed, but Dychat 702 had talked his way in at the last possible instant. He ran forward to take a seat, bowed hastily to the First, and raked the crowd with nervous eyes until he located Irona.

Secretaries conferred, double-checked numbers, and submitted a slate to the chairman. Byakal cleared his throat and excused the three Sevens and two Chosen who were absent from the city on state business. Ledacos 692, however, had not requested permission to absent himself and was not in attendance.

Dychat sprang to his feet, almost dancing in his need to be recognized. Byakal's neighbor drew the chairman's attention to the lad and whispered his number.

"Chosen 702?"

"Your Reverence, honored Chosen—" His voice was a squeak. "I regret to inform you that Ledacos 692 was taken suddenly ill about an hour ago. He is chuck . . . er, vomiting, and has the, um, bowel disorder. *It started when he found a black feather on his dressing table!*"

All eyes went to Redkev 676, who frowned at this silent accusation. If he had not foreseen trouble earlier, he must do so now.

Old Byakal called the meeting to order with a cough. "Then we excuse Ledacos 692's absence and wish him a quick recovery. The first item on—"

Dychat sat down.

The First had risen. This was the first time since his election that Knipry had intervened in a debate of the Assembly.

"Honored 702, did the honorable Ledacos give you any instructions regarding tonight's business?"

Suddenly Irona was certain that the originator of the Vult plot had not been Ledacos, but Knipry himself. It had his tooth marks on it.

Dychat stood up, pale at being singled out by the First. He nodded, then found his voice again. "He asked me to nominate . . . a certain person . . . Your Reverence. . . ."

Knipry gave him a grandfatherly nod and smile. "In that case, Honored Chairman, I ask that the Assembly go at once to Item Seven on the order tablet." Gathering his red robes, he sat down.

Byakal's air of surprise was not convincing. "The Assembly thanks His Reverence for this guidance. Item Seven: Election of a governor for the fortress at Vult, a term of two years or until relieved, the stipend to be ten—Goddess, is that all? I call for nominations."

Young Dychat bounced up again like a leaping dolphin and screamed, "I nominate Irona 700!"

Nominations were neither applauded nor jeered. In the expectant hush, Irona rose and walked to the front, wondering why being posted to the barren Dread Lands of the north for two whole years should feel like a triumph. She bowed to the First and then to the Assembly.

Redkev was frantically trying to signal to Seven Kapalny, but Kapalny had been struck with inexplicable impairment of vision. He nominated Redkev 676, who then had no choice but to heave up his bulk and proceed to the front.

There were no more nominations. No one, even Kapalny, raised a hand for Redkev.

Everyone else voted for his opponent. That was the moment for applause; it rolled and echoed around the chamber.

Again the First intervened, this time requesting immediate consideration of Items Ten and Eleven, neither of which was clearly explained on the order slate. Item Ten turned out to be a brief notice, read by the chairman, that the Seven had approved certain recommendations from the Army Board, one of which was a new commander for Vult. Item Eleven was a joint request from the Geographical Section and the Office of Decency—respectively, the secret police and the witch-hunters—for permission to question Chosen Redkev and, when available, Zajic 677. This was approved without dissent.

As the fat man slunk out to meet whatever fate awaited him, Irona noticed the First beaming his best grandfatherly smile at her. She had been a Knipry favorite ever since she announced her plan to deal with Captain Shark. She had gone to Udice for him, and now he was sending her to Vult.

By then Irona had graduated to an office one floor down from the attics, with two chairs and a larger table. When she arrived there the following morning, whom should she find waiting but Sazen Hostin, her gnomish agent in the Geographical Section. He smiled his rabbity teeth at her but did not quite wiggle his ears. She did not invite him to sit.

He offered her a report, a stack of four wooden tablets, whose tiny, cramped writing would require at least two hours' study.

"A report on recent increases in the fixes trade in the Empire, ma'am."

"I think I have already read that," she said.

"Chosen Ledacos's copy, I expect? Virtually identical, but we always insert very slight changes, so that we can trace any leaks back to their source."

She had not known that. What she did know now was that almost every Chosen used bribery to milk information out of the Geographical Section and she was grossly overpaying Sazen. The Seven knew what was happening, because they had all done it themselves in the past, and it saved them having to pay the clerks much. In a sense, the corruption kept the clerks honest, because they did not wish to risk losing such incredibly profitable employment. The Seven might even decide which secrets could be leaked and which couldn't. But now Sazen had just volunteered something, which was a first, perhaps a sign of Irona's growing status.

She pointed at a chair, the first time she had ever given him leave to sit in her presence. "Now tell me about the ghouls. Not the legends or the bogeyman stories, the truth behind them. What did Eboga and Eldborg really fight?"

He sat and folded his hands on his lap. He did not ask why she had helped to engineer her own election to the governorship without finding out about the enemy first. The reason, of course, was that such questions would have advertised her candidacy.

"The records support the legends, ma'am. They were called the Shapeless because witnesses often disagreed. One man might see a great serpent and another a corpse riding on a dog's back. Giant spiders or carpets of rats. Beautiful naked women with fangs were a popular choice. They never appeared in direct sunlight, rarely in daytime at all."

"But they were real, not just illusions?"

"Oh, yes. Real enough to bite chunks out of men, or tear them apart. Swords and spears and fire would kill them, and then they often crumbled to dust."

Irona said, "Mm," and put that information aside to discuss with the Office of Decency, the experts on Maleficence.

"When I got home last night, I found Sebrat House surrounded by grizzlies of the Palace Guard. Who ordered that?"

"Sounds like the sort of thing we might do," Sazen said thoughtfully. "We weren't good enough to protect Chosen Ledacos completely, though, so please be careful."

"So my election was organized by the First and the Geographical Section, with Ledacos and me as joint puppets?"

The little man looked profoundly shocked. "Oh, I wouldn't say that, ma'am!"

Irona was amused. This Vult enterprise was the most important and dangerous assignment of her life so far, and already she was enjoying the thrill and the challenge. She was descending into a world of bats and spiders, the shadowy landscape patrolled by the Geographical Section. "Not an approved crime? Well, what can I do for you?"

"I feel the need for a change of air, ma'am. You will need a reliable secretary during your tenure, will you not?"

"Not just the governor and commander? You're saying that even the Section's resident spies have been corrupted by Eldritch?"

"Oh, I wouldn't say that, ma'am!"

In his world of keyholes and whispers, that sometimes meant yes, sometimes no.

"I don't believe my nit-sized stipend will let me hire any staff at all."

"I am confident that, at your meeting today, the First himself will offer you a substantial contribution from his discretionary funds to tide you over, plus a guarantee that Sebrat House will be preserved and guarded during your absence, and so on . . . ma'am."

A bribe to uphold the law must be something new.

"I wasn't aware that I had an audience with the First scheduled."

Sazen's remarkably outstanding ears did wiggle then. That happened, Irona had decided, whenever he felt pleased with himself. "At midmorning, ma'am. *Sea Dragon* will depart on the noon ebb, so we have taken the liberty of warning your majordomo that your baggage should be ready well before then. Once you are at sea, the malefactors will be unable to get at you."

"I have promised my vote—"

"For Ledacos 692's election as Seven? He will be a shoo-in now, ma'am."

That was going too far, much too far! The Seventy prided themselves on being inscrutable and utterly independent. Having a minor clerk from the depths of the government dare to predict one of their decisions was intolerable.

"You seem remarkably sure of that!"

Sazen flashed his buckteeth at her. "But there was an attempt on his life! That hasn't happened for eighty-nine years, not since—"

"I suppose," Irona barked, "that there can be no doubt that the evil magic peddlers were truly responsible for Honorable Ledacos's sudden indisposition? It was not, perhaps, sleight of hand by the Section to make certain I would be elected? And now him also?"

"Oh, I wouldn't say that, ma'am!" The little man frowned. "I cannot recall anyone ever being elected by diarrhea."

Sea Dragon was one of the navy's newest biremes, powered by a crew of two hundred. She led a flotilla of three, the others being her sister ships *Sea Dog* and *Sea Demon*. Irona felt flattered that she inspired so much hard work by twelve hundred male biceps. *Sea Danger* and *Sea Death* were to follow later in case reinforcements were needed. The Navy Board was not noted for imagination when it came to names.

It was good to go to sea again, to feel the salty wind in her hair, to sleep, often, on beaches and listen to the cry of gulls and the rush of surf on shingle.

In addition to Governor-Elect Irona, *Dragon* also carried Vlyplatin, Sazen Hostin, and the new marine commander of the Vult station, Quebrada Bericha, ranking as both general and commodore. He was probably little older than Irona herself, but he weighed twice as much and looked as if he might wrestle walruses for recreation. He had coarse features and no detectable sense of humor. She knew at a glance that she was going to have trouble with him.

During the five-week voyage, though, he was rarely in evidence. He rowed like a common marine all day, every day, just for the exercise, albeit wearing his bronze helmet so everyone would notice. When *Sea Dragon* beached, as happened roughly every second night, he went for an hour's run or swim. On nights when the flotilla pulled into a port to top up its stores—six hundred hardworking men went through incredible quantities of food and fresh water—the local magistrates always invited the visiting Chosen to a hastily prepared banquet. Then Bericha had to accompany her, but he did so unwillingly and displayed few social graces.

The goddess sent calm seas appropriate for galley travel, and Irona enjoyed herself thoroughly. She had Sazen Hostin to entertain her by day with long and detailed histories of the Empire's struggle against Maleficence. Vult was the limit of imperial power, a permanent blockade to the importation of evil.

By night she had Vlyplatin Lavice for company, whether in a tent or the guest suite in a succession of mansions. At first Vly seemed convinced that with enough effort they could produce nine babies in one month. Gradually, though, as the voyage continued, a change came over him; his mood darkened and even his lovemaking faltered, which had never happened since they had become lovers that epic night of the Naval Ball in 703. He wouldn't say what troubled him, but she suspected he was starting to learn just what they were in for and blamed himself for it.

Irona's Vult mission would be a total failure in her own eyes if she didn't produce a baby there.

On what she expected to be the third-last day of the voyage, Irona paraded along the catwalk between the upper ranks of rowers. She had waited for a water break, when the men were given a chance to rest on their oars and enjoy a drink. That many of them used the opportunity to do another sort of watering did not bother her; they were all facing outboard and nobody shouted rude things at a Chosen. She reached the bow and came back, stopping at Quebrada Bericha's cushion.

"Tonight," she said, "right after the meal, I want you at a council."

He feigned ignorance. "About what, ma'am?"

"If you have to ask, I have more problems than I thought." She went back aft, to the canopied area where she could sit in comfort and admire all those arms.

"You should have sent me to tell him," Vly said accusingly.

"Oh, I enjoyed it!" In truth, the crew would have called him nasty names, which would have embarrassed her.

By evening, the weather was changing, the sky cloudy, rain spitting, a sign that they were drawing close to their objective. The marines pitched Irona's tent on the only decent patch of grass in sight, between the shingle beach and the inland scrub. She had just finished her meal in her tent when Bericha loomed huge outside the doorway. He wore a simple smock and carried his helmet under his arm. She wondered if he slept in it.

She sent Sazen and Vly away. They both frowned at this dismissal, but she wanted no witnesses to the coming confrontation.

The commander-elect settled on the stool Vly had just vacated. It creaked ominously. He smiled, which made his face even more gruesome. "Now, ma'am, what's worrying you?"

"Nothing except the weather, which we can't do anything about. But we must agree on what will happen when we arrive at Vult. The fortress cannot be approached unseen, I am informed. So the garrison will know we are coming."

He nodded. "But we outnumber them. They won't give us any trouble."

A promising draft text for an epitaph, that. "The fortress is reputed to be invincible. Better to avoid the use of force if possible, yes?"

"Of course," he said, looking as if he didn't agree at all. Peaceful transactions won no medals.

"And it is normal for the new governor to arrive in one galley, not three."

"Ah!" He leaned back as far as he could on the stool and crossed one massive thigh over the other. "But my orders are to protect you, ma'am, so if you are going to suggest that I don't go in with my full complement, then I will have to disagree."

She was tempted to squelch him right there, but she would have to work with this muscle-bound dugong for the next year.

"What happens after, Commodore? You land your men on the beach and . . . ?"

"First I relieve General Gabulla of command and place him under arrest. Then I proceed to locate Governor Zajic and arrest him, also. And after that, I report to you, ma'am, that the post has been secured and you can disembark and take over." He beamed reassuringly. Nothing to worry her pretty little head about.

"The only problem with that, Commander, is that you have no authority until I have read myself in as governor. Suppose this Gabulla man arrests you instead?"

Bericha colored. "That is an absurd suggestion, ma'am! I have my orders!"

"So do I," she said. "Have your orders, I mean. I have a copy of them, and they clearly state that you are under my command unless and until your men come under attack. Only in the face of armed rebellion or breakdown of civil authority can you overrule me. Correct?"

He nodded, redder than ever.

"Then we'll do it this way. Zajic and his men will be expecting Redkev, coming to take over as usual in their continuing dance. So you and I go in on *Sea Dragon*, leaving the other galleys out of sight. We will be taken at once to the governor, and I will read myself in. At that point you serve your warrants, legally and probably peacefully. They ought to be too surprised to object."

He tried to bluster. "Absolutely not! Your safety is my primary directive."

"It comes third in your list of priorities. Are we to have this same argument every day for two years, Commander, or is it understood that I can give you orders?"

He took some time to answer, perhaps trying to find words that he could later weasel out of, but in the end he just muttered, "Yes, ma'am."

"Good. Then we are agreed, and I hope that together we can give Vult two years of fair and honest government, while cutting off the flow of fixes into the Empire. Now if you would be so kind as to ask Sazen Hostin to come in, he can brief us on the geography of Vult and Eldritch." Irona already knew it by heart, but she suspected that Bericha did not, and the questions he subsequently threw at Sazen confirmed that.

The next night, the last night before Vult, the flotilla anchored at Fueguino, a small town with a good harbor. Irona dined with the mayor, a local appointed by the Treaty Commission. He was a rough frontier man, the son of a former marine who had retired to the north after his service ended, probably to farm or fish. So the mayor was an imperial citizen, even if he spoke Benesh with an accent so impenetrable that she wished she had Zard 699 there to translate. He seemed honest enough, but she reserved judgment. There were many such people in the town, some of them former marines who had served in the Vult garrison.

One question she had was answered there, in Fueguino. She had wondered how much faith to put in the general belief that Eldritch's only access to the Empire was by sea. Her first glimpse of the icy Rampart Range to the north settled her doubts. Nothing, human or not, was going to cross that. She had never dreamed that such mountains existed.

Fueguino was Vult's market. Its fishing fleet and farmland kept the garrison fed, and it was the only town with which Vult had legitimate trade. If Eldritch's export of fixes came through Vult, it likely continued by way of Fueguino. Irona's writ ran there, also. In a pinch, she could hang the mayor by his chain of office.

The mayor's guest room was tiny and homely, but comfortable enough for a woman who had been raised in a shed. And the down mattress was soft as a summer cloud, stuffed with local feathers, no doubt.

"This is your last chance," Irona said as she slid naked into bed, "to father those triplets you promised in reasonably civilized surroundings. You can have three tries."

Vly blew out the candle. The mattress billowed as he joined her. "I can't. Not tonight."

"Rubbish. I've known you to score four." Not recently, of course, but he still managed three if sufficiently provoked during a long winter night.

"Good night, Irona."

"Not yet it isn't." She cuddled closer and groped for that infallible apparatus he sported—except that what she found was small and limp and pathetic. Erectile dysfunction had never been Vly's problem before. At times in their association she would have welcomed it.

He removed her hand. "Good night, Irona."

"What's wrong?" she whispered. "Tell me." He had been surprised that she had not become pregnant right away, and she had explained that this was nothing to be alarmed about. Perhaps he was suffering from delusions of inadequacy.

"You just found out what's wrong. Keep your hands to yourself, woman!"

"Forget about babies then. Just fuck me."

No answer.

"I need it. Please, Vly?"

"Go to sleep," he said.

The Vunuwer River flowed southward out of the Dread Lands into a wide delta of marsh and brush, infested with snakes and poisonous reptiles. Nothing remotely human lived there, so far as was known. Every squall of rain that came marching over the desolate landscape was welcome, because it brought some relief from the fog of gnats and the overpowering stench of rotting swamp. Blustery winds made even the nimble galleys hard to control, and sailing boats would have been hard put to traverse the twisting channel at all.

Admiral Bericha had abandoned his oarsman masquerade. Clad in a jangling armored apron, he had joined the civilians, coxswain, and steersman under the aft canopy, but his monosyllabic conversation did little to lift the prevailing gloom. Everyone aboard was facing at least one year's miserable exile in this bleak and blighted land.

The only man aboard who might have welcomed the prospect was Vly, for he would have Irona all to himself for the next two years. But Vly had turned a lurid green color and hung on the rail like a dying man, barely speaking even in monosyllables.

Around midmorning, Vult itself came into sight, an isolated monolith of black rock shaped like some great sea lion asleep across the river's path. *Sea Demon* and *Sea Dog* pulled in to the edge of the channel and dropped anchor. At noon they would follow, with their actions on arrival to be dictated by the reception *Sea Dragon* had encountered.

"I had not expected it to be so big," Irona muttered as the great rock loomed ever larger.

"Well, it does not compare with the Mountain, of course." Sazen had never been to Vult, but he always enjoyed being the expert. Knowing everything was his job, and he welcomed any chance to show it. "About a third as high. The habitable portions are at the top. I expect there will be transportation for you, ma'am; the rest of us will be glad of our Benesh leg muscles. The lower portions are still being, um, excavated, and are not safe. One day the worms will eat it all away and it will collapse into dust."

"You chatter too much," Bericha growled.

The spy ignored him. "I believe I can hear the falls already. The weir was built by Eboga 500, when he was governor here. That was long before he became First, of course."

"They don't banish senior Chosen here, you mean?" Irona asked sweetly.

"Usually not until they're at least forty," Sazen countered, slickly turning a perceived insult into a compliment. "Eboga was thirty. It is said that there was a chain of reefs and islets extending right across the delta, east and west from Vult Rock itself. He had the higher islets quarried for building stone, so he could dam up the channels and raise a weir across the width of the delta. The Two League Waterfall, he called it, and it bars access to the interior. No oceangoing vessels can navigate the Vunuwer above Vult."

"Which means that we can't just bring in the army and sack Eldritch to stop their crap," Bericha said.

No one commented on that. Eldritch had originally been Eldborg, named after its founder. It had fallen to the Shapeless in 490. At least three times the Empire had tried to retake Eldritch, meeting worse disaster every time.

Suddenly Irona's arm was gripped in steel claws.

"Irona! Don't!"

She turned to find Vly staring at her, eyes wide with horror, lips curled back, traces of foam on his teeth.

"Let me go!" she snapped. "What are you doing?" He had never behaved like this before.

"Don't go there, Irona! Can't you feel the evil? You mustn't go on! Don't you see what this is doing to me already?"

"To you? You're breaking my arm, you idiot."

Bericha stepped forward, broke Vly's grip without effort, and threw him aside. He fell flat on the deck.

"Sorry about that, ma'am," the commodore said happily. "Civilians, you know." He meant *weaklings*.

Vly had rolled over and appeared to be sobbing. If guilt was his problem, there was nothing Irona could do to change it now.

"And there it is!" Sazen announced triumphantly.

He might mean the great rock itself, now fully revealed to their left, but more likely the Eboga Weir on the right. The channel the galley had been following opened up into a muddy lake, which extended from the base of the Vult rock far off to the east, winding along the base of the man-made wall. If not a thousand waterfalls, at least several dozen fed the lake, dropping about half a man's height, far enough to dig out the mud and excavate a shallow basin.

"You see?" Sazen continued. "The galley can go no farther, and the tribes inland cannot enter the delta to trade."

Irona did not believe the second statement. "Surely any reasonably agile man with a bag of fixes on his shoulder could jump over that wall? There are dry places where he could scramble back up again." She could do it herself.

"There are good and toothy reasons not to swim in this water, ma'am—I believe they call it the moat. The garrison is supposed to patrol it in small boats."

Irona looked quizzically at the commander-elect. "So if the garrison turns a blind eye, oceangoing ships can come up the river and meet dealers from inland right here?"

"And if that is how it's done," Bericha said, "then every manjack of them must know it. I still think you should bring up all your forces, ma'am."

Irona shook her head. The garrison was changed every year, so they couldn't all be guilty, or the racket would be common knowledge throughout the Empire and men would clamor to be posted to Vult. On the contrary, it was almost a penal station; a tour at Vult on a man's record counted against him. The corruption must be limited to those at the top and perhaps a few lower down. The rank and file might suspect, but no more than that. She would have to investigate all this in due course; that was the task that had brought her here.

And "here" was rapidly becoming a steep gray beach that fringed the rock. Two galleys were pulled up on it, both of them smaller than *Sea Dragon*. The present garrison, Sazen had told her, comprised those two ships and their crews, totaling about six score men. Even without the two support vessels lurking downstream, Quebrada Bericha should have no trouble taking control if push came to thrust.

The rock itself, she now saw, was visible only in its upper two-thirds or so, the lower part being mantled in long slopes of the same gray gravel that made up the beach.

On the beach were shacks, catwalks, a line of rowboats, and what seemed to be ramparts built of rough boulders. Behind all those, a wooden staircase rose about twenty or thirty feet up the rock before disappearing around a spur. Men were hurrying down to meet the new arrivals, but not in large enough numbers to oppose a landing.

It had started raining again.

"Take her in," Bericha ordered.

The coxswain beat a signal on his drum, oars were shipped, and a moment later *Sea Dragon* shuddered to a halt, her keel grating on shingle. In a frenzy of well-disciplined movement, the crew vaulted over the sides to drag the galley higher up the beach, but this beach was unusually steep, and they did not, or could not, raise her very far.

The rain shower was becoming a downpour. Irona huddled her robe around her and set off along the ship's catwalk, leaning into the wind. Her tour of duty was about to begin. It would make or break her career as a Chosen.

"Irona, don't go there!" Vly called after her. "Please, please!"

She pretended not to hear.

The only concession the navy made to a Chosen's dignity was a ladder for embarking and disembarking. She clambered down until her feet reached a very odd beach. Shingle should consist of rounded pebbles, but these were angular chips, hard to walk on, sharp through her sandals.

"Worm poop, ma'am," Sazen explained, right behind her.

Not wanting another lecture just yet, she crunched over to where Quebrada Bericha stood at the start of a boardwalk. He was glowering like an adolescent thunderstorm.

"What's wrong?" she asked.

"Everything in sight. Look at those galleys' hulls! When were they last careened? Look at the cables! Half the strakes in those rowboats are rotten. The boardwalks are falling apart. Moss everywhere. See those hairy apes? Beards down to their waists!"

The men in question wore bronze helmets and carried spears, but they did look more anthropoid than marines should. They were lining up at the foot of the staircase as a farcical honor guard.

Then Quebrada Bericha released a thunderclap of profanity such as Irona had not heard since she was sentencing pirates at Udice. Clearly his normal reticence was not caused by a shortage of vocabulary. The subject of his abuse was a procession that had come into view descending the staircase: four men carrying a fifth in a sedan chair. The passenger wore an ornate brass helmet that marked him as Commander Gabulla. Even at a distance, he could be seen to be enormously fat. Irona felt a touch of dread. A very nasty pattern was emerging.

Converting from mariners to warriors, the crew of *Sea Dragon* had donned armor and were lining up behind their leader. Irona pulled forward the hood on her cloak and clasped her hands behind her, so that her arms would not give her away too soon. Gabulla would be expecting Redkev 676 and she wanted the general closer before he discovered his error.

But then she was distracted by the sight of his companions. The guards who had annoyed Quebrada Bericha were merely slovenly, while Gabulla's bearers were not even human. They might have been assembled from a random collection of body parts, but not by any well-intentioned deity, and some parts were more animal-like than human. They were asymmetric and misshapen; the jaws below their piggy snouts hung open, slobbering and displaying flat teeth like millstones; their eyes were as dead as eyes painted on masks. One man had gigantic arms and tiny, twisted legs. Another was a muscular hulk, and yet a hunchback. All four sprouted seemingly random patches of mangy fur, and none of them wore more than two squares of cloth hung on a string around their hips.

Were these the dreaded Shapeless? If they were capable of changing form, why look like horrible mistakes? They seemed more ludicrous or pitiable than dangerous. Then she wondered if that was the idea.

"Stop!" the fat man shouted. "Halt!" He whacked at the front pair with a cane, and the chair came to a stop. "Now put me down. *Down*, I said."

The chair went down one corner at a time. Gabulla heaved himself upright and stepped forward, leaning heavily on his cane.

"Broken ankle," he muttered. "Damned thing won't heal. I suppose—"

"*What are those?*" Bericha bellowed, pointing at the bearers.

"What those? Oh, those are trogs, General. From Svinhofdarhrauk. Useful. Work for food and eat anything. You are . . .?"

Bericha recalled the correct drill, presented both himself and Irona. By then the fat man had had time to appraise her, so he was not taken unaware. She looked in vain for guilt, surprise, mockery, dismay, or any of the other emotions she expected. What she thought she saw instead was *pity*. Gabulla smiled sadly and attempted a bow, so far as one of his shape could bow while balanced on one foot and a cane resting on greasy wooden slats.

"Your Honor is the Chosen who dealt with Captain Shark." It was a statement, not a question.

"I am. So what?" She could foresee several possible responses, but the one he used was not one of them.

"You deserved better than this."

She could not disagree with that, but she did not want to agree with him either.

Bericha broke in. "I am sure the commander will lend you his chair for the climb, ma'am."

Irona didn't want it. Even indirect contact with that human fungus was a repellent thought. And she dearly wanted out of the rain.

"He needs it more than I do." She walked around him, crunching on the shingle, and headed along the walkway to the ragamuffin honor guard, which watched her approach with alarm. She picked out the youngest, a wiry youth with skimpy whiskers. The others looked more asleep than awake, but his eyes were as bright as a bird's.

"Do you know where Governor Zajic is, or is likely to be?"

He nodded nervously.

"I am the new governor. Take me to him. *Now!*" she barked as he looked to his squad leader for confirmation.

Bericha shouted for her to wait, but she kept going. Her appointed guide padded along at her side, and she guessed that the slapping sandals behind her belonged to Sazen, hurrying to catch up. Even the staircase, which appeared to be the main entrance to the Vult fortress, was in poor repair. It canted sideways in places and changed pitch without warning, so that she was continually stumbling. Her young guide was not doing much better. She heard a curse or two from her secretary.

"Your name, marine?"

"Daun Bukit, ma'am, oar five, lower starboard watch, Royal Genodesan Galley *Swiftest*."

"You're from Benign, though." What was a Benesh citizen doing on a tribute ship from Genodesa? The manpower traffic was usually the other way.

"Yes, ma'am. Overock."

"Then we're neighbors. I'm from Brackish." She glanced at him and saw a glaze of wonder. A *Chosen* calling him neighbor? A Chosen just speaking to him was marvel enough.

Would the damnable stair never end, never get her out of the wind and rain? As if the gods heard her wish, the steps rounded a corner to the north face, which was more sheltered. Irona paused, mostly to catch her breath, but also to inspect the view. Yes, her follower was Sazen. No signs of the military, and that was good. She began to hope that she could get to Governor Zajic before Bericha and his army arrived and made civilized conversation impossible.

Whatever had happened to Vly? Usually in a strange place he stayed as close as her shadow.

Except for a few low, bare islands, all the land to the north had been flooded by the weir. There were hills in the far distance, with hints of mountains beyond, while gaps in the clouds showed a sickly green sky. The closest island looked inhabited, being completely covered with low shacks, some of which were trailing smoke. Four or five boats were tethered there.

"That is Eldritch?"

"Oh, no, ma'am! That's just Svinhofdarhrauk. Eldritch's back in the hills somewhere."

Irona began to move again, but at a slower pace. Her guide seemed less puffed than she was, so she threw more questions.

"Nobody ever goes to Eldritch?"

"Nobody ever goes inland at all, ma'am."

"Tell me about that other place."

"Svinhofdarhrauk? It's where the trogs live. A really, er, messy place."

Coming from a resident of Vult, that was probably a gross understatement. "People from here do go there?"

Silence. Lip biting. Flush showing under whiskers.

"Good fucking there?" she asked.

Gulp.

"Talk freely, Daun. I know all the dirty words."

"Some men go there for that, ma'am. I never, see? Honest! Wait and do it with a real woman, back home. Did go there once, but just to drink and dice and stuff, not that other. Have to be home before dark."

She did not ask for details. "And the trogs work here, in Vult?"

"Yes, ma'am. Do stupid work."

"They're not dangerous?"

He hesitated several heartbeats before he said, "Officially not, ma'am. They're all sent away at night and we lock the rock up tight. But men have disappeared."

After another hundred or so treads, she had learned that a few dozen trogs came over from the unspellable place every morning and did whatever they were told and could understand. They were sent home at sunset with the day's trash as payment.

The staircase had climbed above the slopes of gray gravel and was now more or less attached to bare rock, although in a few places it swayed and sagged alarmingly. Then it ended at a perfectly round hole in a cliff face. A massive bronze door was chained open. It had bolts the size of a man's arm on the inside.

"One at a time, ma'am," Bukit said. "You gotta stoop."

"Lead the way."

He had to stoop even more and carry his spear at an angle.

She followed him in. At first she advanced very slowly, feeling her way, but the tunnel was smooth and as round as a chicken's gizzard. After a few moments, as her eyes adjusted, she realized that the walls glowed with an eerie green light and she could just make out the marine's pale limbs ahead of her. His smock was too dark to show.

A low scratching sound puzzled her. "What's that noise?"

"The worms, ma'am. Never stops. Hear 'em all through the rock."

"Tell me about the rock worms."

"Eat rock, ma'am." The tunnel seemed to swallow Bukit's voice; it did not echo. "Spit out gravel. Nobody knows if it's puke or shit, 'cos both ends have teeth. And they like their food damp. Upper half of the rock's too dry for them now."

"So they're not dangerous?"

"Not much. One broke through in the winter and ate a man. Half of him, anyway. Can hear them coming, usually. Watch your step, ma'am. Is a grating."

The bronze grille in the floor emitted a cool, damp draft with an unpleasant, sulfurous odor. A few paces farther along, a similar grating showed in the left-hand wall.

"Keeps worms from backing up, ma'am," he explained.

"Would that stop a rock worm?" Irona asked.

"Hope it would, ma'am."

Behind her, Sazen chuckled. "Likely not, but it provides confidence. The glow on the walls is some sort of fungus."

Irona's back was aching already, and this tunnel seemed to be angling more down than up. "I wish the worms were fatter."

"Just a little way," Bukit said, and in a moment they emerged in a much larger, but still tubular, tunnel, high enough to walk upright, two abreast. It sloped steeply, and they headed upward. The floor had been leveled with a layer of rock worm gravel.

Irona made a decision. She suspected the goddess was dropping hints again. "How long have you been here, Bukit?"

"A year, ma'am."

"Looking forward to going home?"

He glanced at her briefly and made a quizzical noise. Why in the world would a Chosen want to know that about a junior oar puller in a tribute ship? Which confirmed Irona's suspicion that she had stumbled onto a smarter-than-average oar puller.

"How did you make Benign too hot for you? You have no brand."

"A girl." His eyes stayed forward. "Her brothers came looking for me."

"If you could stand another year or even two here, I need someone who knows his way around this place. Two dolphins a month plus your board. I'll go higher if you turn out well."

His eyes went wide. "Doing what?"

"Answering my questions truthfully. Relaying my orders. A bit of spying for me, although no one else will trust you, so you won't have to betray confidences. Nothing dishonorable, in other words."

He thought for a while, which raised her estimate of him even higher. Then he nodded.

"I could write and ask her if she's married and if she had the baby and . . . And all that?"

"And send her money so she can wait for you. If you can read and write, I'll make it four dolphins right now."

He smiled into the darkness ahead. "You just bought yourself a trog, ma'am."

That dark humor made Irona's skin crawl. Whether the trogs were human-monster hybrids or massively deformed people, that a healthy young man would compare himself with one, even in jest, showed how low the morale of the garrison had sunk. Although the priests claimed that Maleficence was a malevolent god, many Benesh saw maleficence more as a disease. In that view, all of Vult had been infected.

The higher Irona climbed in the rock, the more the labyrinth confused her. The posted signs made no sense. She passed slouching, ill-kempt marines and brutish trogs carrying loads. She passed side tunnels hung with hammocks or furnished as messes. Every one of them was a stinking pigsty. Now and again she caught glimpses of daylight along laterals, until eventually they came to another whale-strength door. Beyond that, Bukit led her up a short flight of stairs into fresh air and a real building, with stone walls. She blinked in a brightness that seemed as dazzling as if the sun were shining, which it wasn't.

She was on top of the rock, and the nearest window looked southward, over the delta, where *Sea Dog* and *Sea Demon* were advancing up the channel with banks of oars moving in a stately dance. She crossed the floor—which needed a good sweep and scrub but was the cleanest she had seen yet—and looked out again over the interior lake. The closest islet, Svinhofdarhrauk, was hidden by yet another rain squall.

Bukit was waiting patiently by the door, so she followed him out to a small, almost flat, area at the summit, a storm-swept yard within a coronet of buildings. He led the way across to the largest, whose grandiose doorway and the faded emblem above it proclaimed it to be the governor's reception hall. She entered what should have been an impressive chamber, for the floor was well tiled, the walls plastered, the roof supported by massive rafters. But the floor was dirty, the plaster peeling, the roof leaking, all with the same air of decay and neglect that she had seen throughout the fortress.

In proper republican fashion the interior lacked the dais and throne that royalty would require. The only furniture was a row of half a dozen chairs at the far end. The only person present sat on one of the chairs and wore a blue-green tunic. So Irona's wish had been granted, and she could have at least a brief talk with Zajic before the talons of justice carried him away.

"You," she told Bukit, "go and bathe and shave and make yourself respectable. In the name of the goddess, clean your fingernails! I hope you have a decent tunic to wear. If not, borrow or steal one. If anyone asks, you are personal aide to Governor Irona. Sazen, wait here."

She marched off along the hall and Zajic 677 just sat, awkwardly slumped on his chair, watching her approach. She had liked him back in Benign. She had enjoyed his wry humor when they had served on the Harbor Board together. He rarely spoke in the Assembly, and then usually as a peacemaker, proposing some middle ground between factions.

He had always been cadaverously thin. As she drew close, she saw that his limbs were dangerously wasted, his skin sallow, his eyes deeply sunk in a face like a skull. Even when she stopped in front of him, he did not rise to greet her.

"Irona 700!" he murmured, seemingly more to himself than to her.

"Governor?" she said.

He nodded and murmured her name again, as if he was deciding that her presence was surprising at first, but made sense on consideration. "If she can't, who can?"

She pulled a chair around to face him and sat down. "Tell me, please. What do I have to expect?"

Still he did not meet her eyes. "It's spreading," he whispered to the empty hall. "Keeps spreading, you know."

Like a contagion? "Were you bribed? Terrorized? Or did they warp you with fixes?"

"Even Eboga couldn't roll it back at Eldritch, and it's much stronger now." He twisted as if his back hurt, which it probably should from the way he was sitting.

"What is stronger?"

"Even stronger than it was two years ago."

"Maleficence, you mean?"

"Redkev warned me before he left."

"*Zajic!*" she snapped. "We have only a few moments to talk. Look at me."

His eyes turned in their sockets to stare at her, peering out of dungeon windows. "You will have to live with it, Irona. All your life you will have to live with it."

"Live with *what*?"

"Maleficence."

Well, at least he had answered a question. But the door at the far end creaked open, and Quebrada Bericha marched in with marines at his back.

"Did they bribe you?" Irona demanded.

The governor was staring past her. "It seeks out your weakest point."

"It? What? *Who*, for Holy Caprice's sake? Evil works through people. Who threatened you? Bribed you? Tormented you? For the sake of the goddess, Zajic! You are one of her Chosen. Why did you desert her? Maleficence is behind this. How did it twist you from your duty?"

"It doesn't *force* you to be evil. It makes you *want* to be evil." He closed his eyes. "The world grows heavy. Life is most confusing sometimes. Nothing makes sense in the end."

And for him it might well be the end. He needed Source Water urgently.

Irona stood up as her commander came to a halt. The carrying chair with former commander Gabulla had arrived also, and Sazen had come along ahead of the military and was waiting at the side. She held out a hand to him and he brought her the warrant, two wooden tablets the size of a man's hand.

She untied the ribbon binding them and the room hushed.

The dying man whispered, "Irona 700?"

She looked down. "Zajik 677?"

"If I knew, why wouldn't I tell you?"

Not knowing what to say to that, she began to read: "In the name of the Goddess and by order of her Chosen . . ."

The rest of that day was a nightmare. Irona ordered Zajic dosed with Source Water from the galley's medicine chests, but he retched at the smell of it and screamed when given it, as if it burned his lips. Moving him south for proper treatment was obviously urgent. That turned out to be easier ordered than done.

The newly relieved garrison had a nominal strength of 120 tribute marines, mostly Genodesan and Nedokon, as those two allies had contributed the galleys, but imperial policy was always to divide and rule, so other client states were certainly represented. Normally, the ships would now be released to return to their respective home ports, but suspicion that Vult had become involved in fix trading made every man suspect. Bericha's orders required him to deliver all the old garrison to Benign for interrogation. Every one of them was to be strip-searched for evidence of unexplained wealth before he boarded. That was why the much larger *Sea Demon* and *Sea Dog* had escorted Irona's flagship north and two more Benesh galleys would be arriving soon. The departing marines would be divided among five ships, so there could be no unpleasant accidents on the way home.

When the roll was called, twenty-two men reported in sick or disabled, including their commander, and thirty-seven failed to respond at all. No one seemed to know where the absentees had gone, or when. They might have been eaten by rock worms or the giant eels in the moat, although such disasters had been rare in the past. Even Daun Bukit was puzzled, but he muttered that Svinhofdar-hrauk might be involved, also that there was a trog with a mark on its arm that looked very like a birthmark he had noticed on one of the missing men. Trogs were too stupid to be dangerous, of course.

Of course? Irona always distrusted those words. If the Shapeless shape-shifters could look terrifying, why could they not make themselves seem harmless and repulsive?

The oar pullers who powered the navy and battled the Empire's foes were rough men, never finicky or self-indulgent, but the new garrison came close to mutiny when they saw the quarters they would have to inhabit: filth, rotting hammocks, pestiferous kitchens.

Clearly Vult was deeply infested by Maleficence, from the governor to the lowest scullions, who were not even human. Eldborg 300 had founded the city now known as Eldritch to rule the Dread Lands. Maleficence had taken it. Eboga 500 had tried to recover Eldritch for the Empire and failed. He had withdrawn the frontier to Vult. Would Irona 700 now have to abandon Vult? She spent the rest of the day on an exhausting orientation tour with Daun Bukit and ended feeling more lost than ever. The buildings on top of the rock were in sad disrepair. Many of the tunnels inside it were less inviting than sewers.

Sazen Hostin, who could usually answer any question she cared to ask, had vanished as completely as the missing marines. She finally tracked him down by telling Bukit to take her to the fortress's archives. There she was relieved to find her secretary, sitting on a box in a gruesome tunnel stinking of rats. The floor was heaped and piled with hundreds of the little wooden tablets that were used for any document intended to be permanent—slates were only for temporary notes. He was trying to read by the light of a single candle.

"Look at it," he wheezed. "All that's left of the archives. Dry rot, mildew, woodworm, death watch beetle. And rats."

"It's late," she said. "You can't read it all tonight."

"It's in here somewhere. The answer. It must be."

"Leave it now. Come back tomorrow."

The little man looked up at her blearily. "Tomorrow may be too late. Go away."

The quarters used by ex-governor Zajic were near the top of the rock, but too squalid for Irona's use. She explored the buildings outside, on the summit. Apart from the reception hall, she identified a dovecote, a henhouse, a wine store, several abandoned sheds that looked as if they hadn't been entered in years, the guardhouse over the entrance to the rock, and what she decided had been built as a governor's bedchamber. It had a fireplace, a stout oaken door, and windows with both bars and shutters. The rafters were massive beams, still solid, and she could see no slates missing. The door was held by a latch that could be opened from either side, but the stout brass bolts were on the inside. There was no furniture, and not even much in the way of litter: no dead leaves, bat droppings, or even dead birds on the hearth, so the chimney probably had bars on it also. If the rain ever stopped, the view would be spectacular.

"This will do," she said. "Find General Bericha and tell him I want this scrubbed out right away. I'll need a roaring fire. Have my bags and camping supplies brought up from the galley. Vly can tell you which—"

"*Ma'am!*" Bukit had turned corpse white. "You can't sleep up here!"

"And why not?"

"Because nobody goes outside the rock in the dark, ma'am! Nobody! Both doors are locked—up here and down at the beach. They're guarded on the inside by six men apiece. Standing orders are to kill anyone who tries to open them at night, for any reason."

Irona went over to the shack door to inspect it again. The hinges were monster size and the timbers a handbreadth thick. It would stop a charging war galley.

"You're telling me that trogs will climb up here to kill me? That Shapeless will break in?"

He just shook his head, still aghast. Perversely, Irona felt that she might have stumbled onto something. These had once been the governor's quarters, but Zajic had not been using them. True, she would be cut off from the garrison, but if no one went out or in at night, then any problem that arose would have to wait until morning anyway. And her instincts said that she might be safer in isolation up here than down in that maze, where all sorts of nastiness could lurk in dark corners.

Also, it wouldn't hurt to signal to the garrison that she wasn't afraid of ghouls in the night.

She looked to Vly for support. He just stared back. Vly, she realized, had been following her like a shadow for some time without saying a word. She was so used to him just being there that she had not noticed his return. He was holding a wine bottle that she recognized as one she had brought with her.

"What do you think, love?" she asked.

"Go home," he said. "Don't stay here. Vult's a leper house."

His voice was slurred, but he had always taken his guard duties so seriously that she could not recall ever seeing him anywhere close to drunk. Mere merriness was his limit.

"Citizen Lavice and I will sleep here," she told Bukit.

Vly shook his head, mumbling. "You can't do any good here, Irona. It will destroy you."

"It's making a good start on you," she said, and took the bottle away from him.

Bericha came to inspect later. He made sure she understood about the lockout at curfew but raised no objection to her choice of quarters. Perhaps he hoped the Shapeless would come and get her off his back. As the setting sun made a brief appearance in a slit between clouds and horizon, Irona ate an insipid meal of cold fish and hard bread, washed down by navy-issue wine. Vly barely ate anything, but he put away most of the wine.

When taps were sounded, Irona took him with her to watch the summit door closing ceremony, and then to inspect all the other buildings so she could be certain they were unoccupied. Vly showed no interest in any of it and had found another bottle by the time she bolted them in for the night.

She planned no baby-making efforts tonight. Tomorrow would be soon enough to begin serious procreation, after she had organized a proper bed in place of a thin straw pallet between her back and a floor of bare rock.

It was not much of a bedroom, with rain dripping and hissing in the fireplace, wind howling in around the shutters, bare floors, minimum furnishings, and baggage piled along one wall, but it was probably the cleanest place north of Fueguino. She thought it was trying to seem homely, with the fire crackling and candle flames dancing. In a week or so she would transform it, Irona promised herself, with rugs and hangings and some of the quite attractive pottery she had seen the previous day. If she couldn't find what she needed in Vult itself, she would go to Fueguino for it, give those rowers' arms some exercise.

On her second attempt, she identified a bag containing some of her clothes—Vly had done the packing and in great haste, so she had no idea what all he had brought. And she struck lucky, finding a warm woolen nightgown in there. Dropping her tunic, she slipped it on and turned toward the mattress in front of the fire.

"Take it off," growled a low voice behind her.

She spun around in alarm to find Vly with his eyes unfocused, his mouth pulled down in an ugly pout, already naked—and with a fully erect penis.

"What?" she asked automatically, but she knew instantly what was going to happen. She wasn't going to enjoy it, either.

"Shut up," he said. He took her neckband in both hands and ripped the gown wide open, then pushed it down until it dropped. "You want a fucking baby. I'll put a fucking baby in you."

"Slow down . . ."

"Shut up." He slapped her face just as she remembered her father doing. But then he forced her down to her knees.

"At least the mattress . . ."

Another slap, hard enough to make her head spin. She tried to put the remains of her nightgown under her, but he pulled it away and pushed her back down on the bare rock, hard and cold and gritty. Vly had always been strong, but now he seemed incredibly so, pushing her legs apart as if she wasn't resisting at all. She cried out, remembering her mother's protests when this was done to her. Her pleas went unanswered and her efforts to respond in the hope of turning deliberate rape into some sort of lovemaking merely provoked him to even greater violence, nipping and punching. She screamed when he thrust his phallus into her like a sword.

"Good," he said, and did it again. And again.

Irona closed her eyes and tried to believe that this wasn't her lover Vlyplatin doing these awful things to her. It was a shape-shifter who had taken his form. It was Maleficence himself, or itself. *It doesn't force you to be evil. It makes you want to be evil.* But why Vly? Why him so soon? All her struggles were useless against his strength.

It seeks out your weakest point. Had Vly been so desperate for a child that he would descend to this, taking by force what would be so willingly given?

Several times she thought it was over, he had finished. But each time he was just resting, or gloating, then the torment would begin again. After an age, he achieved his climax and sighed at the sense of release. He did not even roll off her, as he usually did. He scrambled to his feet without a word or a glance, walked over to the mattress before the fire, rolled himself up in a blanket, and seemed to go to sleep instantly.

"The next time you need to empty that thing," she said, "I hope you'll use the other bucket, the one by the door with a lid on it."

There was no reply.

Bruised, frozen, and bleeding, Irona sat up and wrapped the remains of her nightgown around her, trying to stanch the blood oozing between her legs. She took an edge of the cloth in both hands and tugged it as he had done, but it wouldn't rip for her. Her back and elbows were bleeding, too. She shivered convulsively, from cold and shock.

Even if it had been Vly and not something else masquerading in his likeness, even if the two of them had gone through much the same process hundreds of times, she still felt defiled, mutilated, and degraded.

She crawled over to the bedding and found the other blanket. Vly was lying on a corner of it, but did not stir as she hauled it free. However much the prospect appalled her, she knew she must lie down there beside him because it was the only warm place in the room; she could not remember if Akanagure Matrinko had ever raped his wife twice in a night. She thought not, and the question was irrelevant anyway. Precedents did not apply. Irona 700 was shut up until dawn with a monster in human shape, and short of murdering it in its sleep, there was nothing she could do about it.

"What?" she said, starting awake. The room was dark, and the wind still wailed. Lightning flashed through the chinks. She thought a voice had wakened her. She could hear rainwater trickling somewhere, and the door rattled. She rolled over, wishing for that down-filled mattress she had enjoyed the previous night in Fueguino.

The door rattled again. The candles had burned out. The storm was still wailing as loud as ever. Remembering that the door had not rattled before, she sat up.

"Vly!" She reached out a hand for him and found no one.

She hit the door running, grabbed the bolts, slammed them home. That stopped the rattling. Goddess, Goddess, why would he have gone outside in the middle of the night?

Or had he? If what had raped her earlier had been a Shapeless, then it must now have gone home to Svinhofdarhrauk and Vly might have been dead for hours.

But she could not know that.

If it had been a doppelgänger, it had been a very convincing one—not behaving in the least like the real Vly, but looking like him, smelling like him, sweating like him. Vly blaming himself for her decision to come here, crazy with guilt, drunk out of his mind for the first time in his life . . . But Vly had always been so protective! The least hint of an insult, a hand reaching out to her from a crowd, anything, and he had reacted to draw his sword and defend her.

Irona took a log from the scuttle, poked up the fire, threw some fragments of bark and kindling on the embers. As flames flickered, as darkness retreated, she made out his sandals and smock lying where he had dropped them. His sword was not in evidence anywhere, but his precious dagger was there by his sandals. Armed with that, she went all around the room, accompanied by her monster shadow, but together they found nothing, not a mouse.

Shivering, she wrapped herself in a blanket and sat close to the fire, with the dagger beside her. She could not go back to sleep while Vly was out there. She was certainly not going out to look for him.

Wail . . . Howl . . . Moan . . . *Iro-o-o-na* . . . It was only the wind. Not Vly's voice. She would know his subterranean growl anywhere. She realized that she did not expect to ever hear it again. If the Shapeless had not gotten him, or he had not fallen over the edge, he would soon freeze to death out there. But she must stay awake, must keep vigil until morning. Vly had never walked in his sleep before, so far as she knew. He had never mentioned doing so. He couldn't have gone down into the rock. He had either fallen over the parapet, or his corpse was lying out there in the yard.

Something scratched on the door. A dog might do that. A man half dead with cold might crawl close and just have enough strength left to . . . No. She remembered the thickness of the timbers. No human hand could scratch hard enough to be heard through that.

From time to time she put another driftwood log on the fire.

How had her life gone so terribly wrong? Obviously Maleficence had corrupted Zajic and most of his garrison, although not all of them. Why had Vly succumbed so quickly and tragically? He had been unhappy about her decision to accept the appointment, but it had been her choice, not his. If anyone was to blame for Vly's death, it was Ledacos 692, who had tricked her into it. Had there been any truth behind the stories of black feathers and efforts to poison him? No doubt he was now stalking around Benign in a Seven's purple—at her expense.

There was nothing she could do about Ledacos now, but she would survive. She would live to fight another day. *Revenge needs a well-sharpened knife*, said the proverb.

～

When morning light peeked through chinks in the shutters, Irona dressed and prepared to face the worst. She cleaned the blood from the floor and burned the stained nightgown.

The wind still gusted, but the rain had stopped. The predawn sky was lurid green and purple, especially to the north. She could see a silhouette of hills that way, the hills around Eldritch. What she couldn't see, not anywhere, was Vly. A bugler emerged from the guardhouse and blew the reveille, as if anyone up there needed it or anyone below would hear it. The rest of the night guard followed him out, surly and unshaven, but obviously relieved to find her still alive. They insisted they had not heard Vly—and couldn't have done unless he'd beaten on the bronze door with a sledge. No one had gone in. No Vly.

A few wisps of smoke were rising from Svinhofdarhrauk. . . . Irona's brief glance suddenly became a stare of wonder. There were trogs in the water, a line of them, up to their waists. Barely visible in the half-light, they were heading west, but in a few moments the leader turned south and the rest followed. She had assumed they came and went between islet and rock by boat. No one had told her that Lake Eboga was fordable, but she had never asked. It might have silted up since Eboga's time. She filed the fact away for later action and continued her hunt for Vly. Nothing else mattered, and yet cold reason insisted that he had gone; she was never going to find him alive.

The parapet around the edge of the compound was in just as bad repair as everything else. A man could step over it in most places, scramble over it anywhere. The sides of the rock were nowhere truly vertical, so a falling body would bounce and roll and eventually slide down steep slopes of sharp gravel. Nowhere would it have landed in water, neither in the moat to the south nor Lake Eboga to the north, so his body must be down there somewhere. If he were still alive, he must be horribly injured. She ran back to the sentries and told them to sound the alarm.

Quebrada Bericha was furious. Morale was already dismal and now the governor's boy toy had fallen or jumped—driven over the edge by monsters from the Dread Lands, no doubt. After what she had heard in the night, Irona herself was inclined to believe something along those lines, except that she thought the monsters had been inside his head.

Eventually they found where he had gone over. Daun's sharp eyes noticed a smear of blood on the edge of the low parapet, at a spot where it was barely knee-high. Another smear of blood on the first rock below showed where he must have struck, and bounced. If he had jumped to his death, he would have first stepped up on the wall. Instead, he must have walked into it, barked his shin, and toppled. After that he could only have tumbled and rolled all the way to the ground, arriving both dead and shredded by the sharp gravel of the scree slope. His corpse was not there now, nor was his sword.

Whose name had he screamed to Bane in his death curse?

Morale sank even lower. Irona's efforts to belittle the ghouls and banshees had failed utterly. The only reason the governor was not interrogating her on suspicion of murder was that she *was* the governor. That, and the lack of a body.

But when Commander Bericha suggested she choose new quarters, the cross-grained stubbornness she had inherited from her father reared up like a grizzly bear. "Never!" she said. "I have made my choice and here I stay. I do not walk in my sleep. And I am not scared by banshees."

The thought that Vly's rotting corpse might return some other night was not to be considered.

All day Bericha kept both garrisons, old and new, feverishly cleaning up the base. Crews gathered reeds from the delta to make brooms, which served until they fell to pieces. Much of the bedding, and even furniture, was only good for burning, and some of it made a handy contribution to the governor's woodpile.

Irona chose a barren little shed next to the reception hall to be her study. That might have been its original purpose, for it had a fireplace and parchment-covered windows that provided more light than the fungus down in the tunnels. Except in very heavy rainstorms, she could see well enough to write and was reasonably, if not comfortably, warm when she wore her furs.

She had set Daun Bukit to work packing the departing governor's possessions, because Zajic seemed incapable of doing anything now. Sazen Hostin was still grubbing among the rats in the archives. She could procrastinate no longer.

She ought to write to Velny Lavice, Vly's mother, but she had nothing to tell her except that Vly had disappeared. *Sea Dog* would leave on the morrow, because the fortress was grossly overcrowded, but *Sea Death* and *Sea Danger* would arrive soon, so that letter could wait until there was more definite news.

Nothing should be harder to write than a letter telling a mother her son was dead, but Irona's obligatory report to the Seven came close. She had arrived and assumed her post. What else was she to say? That Maleficence had infected the fortress with an epidemic of idiocy? That after a few weeks here both she and the men under her command would probably succumb to the same? That her mission was doomed to fail before it even began? She did not know how to fight an evil as deadly and insubstantial as the north wind.

The door flew open. Sazen and the wind entered together. He was filthy, unshaven, and red-eyed. He had probably not eaten, slept, or even drunk since the day before, but he was croaking in triumph, waving a tablet.

"Sit down!" Irona commanded, striding across to the door to shut it. "What have you found?"

Sazen took her chair, as it was the only seat in sight. "It had to have started in Redkev's first term, right? Whatever it was, that was when the change took place. Twelve years ago."

Irona leaned against an empty bookcase. "Makes sense."

"I found this. It's part of a journal the governors used to keep. It says, 'Although they are not human, the trogs' pitiful deaths upset the men and are bad for morale. I ordered that the garbage and offal be tipped into Lake Eboga instead of the moat, so the trogs can retrieve it without going near the moat eels.' That's it!"

"It is?"

He turned the slab over and peered at the minute writing. "Almost. There's this, a few months earlier. 'Trogs have been seen on an islet about three hundred paces north of the fortress, in Lake Eboga. The men call it Svinhofdarhrauk, which apparently means something funny in Osopan.'"

Yes, yes, yes! Sense at last!

"Oh, well done! We must find you something to eat. Have a drink first." Irona handed him a bottle of wine she had just unpacked from her luggage. Then she took him out into the wind and down to the former governor's quarters, where she found Daun Bukit stuffing dirty clothing into a chest. Zajic had been confined in a cell, deeper in the rock, and was reported to be almost catatonic.

"Leave that for now," she said. "Sazen desperately needs something to eat and a place to catch up on his sleep and he doesn't know his way around yet. Will you help him, please? And get word to Commander Bericha that I need to speak with him urgently."

Daun said "Yes, ma'am!" very happily. He looked as if he were about to add something about what he had been doing, then changed his mind, repeated, "Yes, ma'am!" and dashed out.

Irona was back on the summit making notes for her report to the Seven when Bericha banged on the door, walked in, and slammed it behind him. Her face must have given her away because his lit up at once.

"You've found him?"

"What? No, not Vlyplatin. But Sazen's discovered what happened. Back in Redkev's first term, twelve years ago, trogs turned up and settled on that tongue-twister sandbank. The garrison used to throw its trash in the moat—so the river would carry it away, I suppose—and the trogs would try to scavenge it and get eaten by the eels. So Redkev told the men to throw it into the lake."

The commander was not as stupid as he looked. He nodded approvingly. "Then the brutes started making themselves useful, the marines were happy to let them do the grunt work, and pretty soon the Empire's finest were lying around, rotting, doing nothing all day long!"

No doubt human laziness had been part of it, but Irona was certain that there had been other, more sinister, influences at work also. "Do you know how the trogs come to work in the morning?"

Bericha opened his mouth and then shut it again. There had been no canoes or coracles lying on the shingle yesterday. "No, ma'am."

"They wade. The Eboga wall is only a couple of feet high. There will be deep channels, I'm sure, but most of the lake must be very shallow. This place is not as secure as we thought, Commander."

"So what are you ordering me to do, ma'am?" His smile was menacing, but she did not feel that the threat was directed at her.

"Drive out the trogs. Kill them if they won't go. Burn that settlement of theirs down to the mud. Patrol the lake to make sure they don't return." She was encouraged by his grudging nods of approval. "Dump the daily trash in the moat or, even better, somewhere far away down the channel. Double-check every grating to make sure trogs aren't feeding people to the worms, or even nesting here under our feet."

"Done that. We found one loose grill, only one. It's tight now."

One would be enough.

"And then, I think, we should give this place the most thorough cleaning it's ever had. Before we left I asked the Office of Decency what fixes actually looked like, and they said almost anything: lotions, ointment, nonsensical writing, bats' nests, drawings on a wall, dirt in a corner, rat shit . . ."

The commander shrugged bull shoulders. "Polish till it shines, then? Aye, ma'am." He saluted her, which was a first, and spun around to leave.

"And, Commander?"

He turned.

"I suspect that strip-searching the departing garrison is not going to find anything. I don't think they've been bribed, I think they've mostly been stupefied until they don't care. The fixes probably aren't *sold* at all."

He looked at her as if she had gone insane.

"Don't you see?" she said. "Whatever horrors live at Eldritch or anywhere else in the Dread Lands don't want our money. Why would Shapeless need money? They leave their vileness somewhere as a free gift for someone. When the supply boats from Fueguino arrive, watch to see if they make any detours coming through the delta. You might even organize a hunt for marked caches before they get here. Or fishing boats, coming in to sell their catch. If there's smuggling going on, I think that's how it has to be done."

Quebrada Bericha barked, "Aye, ma'am! Brilliant, if I may say so." He marched out, looking happier than she could ever recall seeing him. She had given him something for his hands to do.

Irona turned back to her own work.

The tablet on top said:

You gave me a promise. You are forgetting how grateful you were. I told you I might ask a favor in return some day, and you said you would do anything I asked. "Anything" was the word you used.

Whatever did that mean? Irona had no memory of writing it, and it wasn't in her handwriting.

The report she ultimately sent to the Seven was cautiously optimistic. Already the fortress was a functional military base again. The trogs had been driven away, excepting a few who had refused to go and had been slaughtered and fed to the giant eels of the delta.

After Svinhofdarhrauk had been burned, bones had been found in the ashes. While some trogs' bones were hard to distinguish from human, others were so deformed that their origin was obvious; trogs' teeth were more like dogs' or pigs', but some skulls and jawbones were definitely human. Weapons and fragments of armor had been recovered, also, so marines had certainly died on the islet. Vly's sword had been a standard issue, without distinguishing marks.

She mentioned her theory that there had been no treason in Vult, only folly, which Maleficence had exploited. She suggested that dealers received their wares for free and profiteering started downstream. She recommended that the Geographical Section investigate the traders who brought in the station's supplies from Fueguino. While she had authority to do that herself, she could not turn up there in a galley full of marines without alerting the culprits, if any.

She wrote to Velny Lavice, too, and that sad news also went south on *Sea Death*.

About a week after the galley left, Irona awoke one morning certain that she was pregnant. It was far too early to tell by most women's standards, but her mother had always known, and Irona had no doubts. Of course she had wondered ever since the night Vly died whether that had been the whole purpose of that brutal attack. Was she carrying her dead lover's child or a monster? The priests claimed that maleficent creations could not themselves create life. Time would tell in this case.

Two days after that, while Irona and Sazen were reviewing tablets in her office, Daun Bukit appeared with word that the commander requested the governor's presence in the reception hall. Could be a breakthrough, he said. Without bothering to wrap up in a cloak, Irona dodged out one door and in the next, doubled over against the wind and rain; Daun and Sazen came scampering at her heels.

Quebrada Bericha was there already, looking ominously pleased with himself. So was the bosun of *Sea Dragon*, plus two dozen of his oar pullers, looking even more so. The marines were grouped in fours, and each group contained a prisoner, hands bound and mouth stuffed with rags: four men and two youths. Their expressions varied from defiant to terrified, and it must be hard to feel otherwise in such circumstances.

"Pursuant to your instructions, ma'am," the commander boomed, "the delta has been kept under close surveillance. Yesterday a red rag that had been tied to driftwood above high-water mark at the mouth of a minor channel was observed, ma'am. The vicinity was then explored and a heap of eight bulging bags was discovered stacked on the eastern bank. This location was staked out, and this morning, a fishing smack was observed approaching under cover of a rainsquall. The galley was summoned and these individuals were apprehended while loading the bags aboard. Upon questioning, the suspects refused to say who they were or where they came from, ma'am."

This, indeed, was a breakthrough! Caught red-handed!

"Very good work, Commander! There will be bonuses for all concerned. Where are the bags?"

"Still in the fishing boat, ma'am. Eight bags. One of them moves a bit; must be something 'live in it."

"And any sign of gold or silver for payment?"

"None at all, ma'am." Bericha had hesitated a bit there. It would be asking a lot of common seamen to turn in the prisoners, the loot, *and* the money, if any had been found. Even two out of three was good.

Irona looked over the prisoners and chose the hairiest. "Remove his gag! Now, you, what's your name?"

The result was a flood of gibberish, of which she understood about one word in four.

"We think that's meant to be Benesh with a Genodesan accent," the bosun said. "He won't speak good Benesh, but he understands it well enough. I told him I was going to stuff a marline spike up his . . . um, nose, ma'am, and he understood me well 'nuff."

"He said they're all honest fisherman and they come into the delta for catfish." The quiet voice belonged to Daun Bukit. He had served on the Genodesan galley *Swiftest*.

More gibberish. "And the bags were just flotsam they found, washed up by the waves."

"Crab shit," said the bosun. "Begging your pardon, ma'am. No waves there. And they were well above high-water mark."

"They will have to be interrogated separately," Irona declared. Her stomach cringed at the implications of what she was saying. She looked apologetically at her aide. "Daun, since you can understand them, will you head up the inquisition?"

"Yes, ma'am." No hesitation. "If Citizen Hostin will advise me on technique?" He looked to Sazen, formerly of the Geographical Section.

"Happy to, ma'am," Sazen said. "Quick or slow?"

"What's the difference?"

"About a month. Three days for the quick way, but the damage is permanent." The victims were listening, of course. The softening up had begun.

"It's getting late in the shipping season. Do it the quick way."

"General," Bukit said, "have I your permission to call for volunteer torturers?"

Hands shot up all over. *It makes you want to be evil.*

Three days later, as Irona was nibbling her normal breakfast of black bread and watered wine, her team returned, Daun and Sazen. She had not seen them since they went off with the prisoners. In fact, she had hardly seen anyone except the marines repairing the stonework on the summit.

Daun and Sazen were both unshaven, red eyed, and haggard, but they could not have slept much while conducting six interrogations at once and maintaining pressure on the victims.

"Guilty," Daun said, handing her some tablets. "All six gulls singing like canaries."

"From the same songbook," Sazen added. "Naming names and placing places."

"Lots of names!"

"They don't know what's in the bags. Were warned not to open them. They all agreed on that much right at the start! They come every full moon, and they're paid ten dolphins per bag on delivery."

So whatever inside was much more than old clothes.

Irona said, "Very well done! One of the galleys will have to rush these statements straight back to Benign." Quebrada Bericha would be outraged at losing half his force. Why should that worry her? "Are the prisoners fit to travel?"

Daun shook his head.

"Gangrene setting in already," Sazen murmured sadly. "Internal bleeding . . . You know how it is."

So Irona would have to hang six dying men and confiscate their boat. She had already burned the evidence, as too dangerous to keep. "Very well done," she repeated. "You both look like you have some sleep to catch up on."

"Yes, ma'am," Sazen said.

Daun muttered, "That's going to be another problem."

With the possible exception of the penal island of Maasok, Vult must be the worst place in the Empire to live. For Irona, in her aerie atop the rock, the wind never stopped, howling in every pitch and discord, speaking with the voice of every bird or beast. When the clouds weren't pouring down rain, they threw hail, or sleet, or snow. Thunder and lightning came with all those, and clear sky could be any color except blue. Conditions within the rock were no more cheerful, for the rock itself seemed to speak as the wind boomed through the tunnels, and the constant *scritch-scritch* of the worms drove some men to distraction.

Irona never went anywhere without Vly's jade-handled dagger, because she was always convinced that there was someone close behind her. She thought this was her own personal weakness, but a chance remark from Daun led her to question him about it, then others, and it seemed that everyone felt it. No matter how much Quebrada Bericha had the troops sweep and scrub—even when every corner of the entire base was spotless—that one spiteful taint of Maleficence lingered. You were never alone.

Despite that, Daun insisted that conditions were much better now than they had been under Governor Zajic. Bericha's strict discipline, his rigid standards of hygiene and order, and the capture of the smugglers had all improved morale enormously; the men now felt that they were doing well and keeping Maleficence at bay.

Soon there were two of Irona. Someone kept kicking her from the inside. A strong kicker meant a boy, her mother had insisted, and she should certainly have known. Apart from that, Irona's pregnancy went smoothly. She was never nauseated. Her only complaints were minor back pains.

Vult could boast of one small advantage, its beaches. Bathing in the delta was suicide, but out where the surf rolled in on clean sand, even a brief dip was exhilarating. The sea was cold, but it never froze. Bericha decreed that every man must wash all over at least once every two days, either in the sea or in a good downpour, and most men's preference was for both, to wrestle with the surf and then rinse off the salt. Irona herself enjoyed the sea until her balance became uncertain, but rain was never in short supply. She was convinced that insistence on cleanliness helped keep Maleficence away.

By the time the winter storms were tapering off, Sazen, Bukit, and the commander were begging Irona to bring in a midwife from Fueguino. She refused, fearing that fixers in the town might seek a chance to strike at her, for she was the only person in Vult who might have need of such services. When the time came, she bolted the door and delivered the child herself.

She had watched her mother give birth many times, and it had seemed easy. She had underestimated the travail of a first-time delivery. A night of fear and pain gave way to a day of agony, but as the second night dawned, the wailing of the storm was joined by the howls of a large and loud boy. Fittingly, she cut the cord with Vly's dagger.

A second anonymous message arrived at the same time, but this one was more easily explained. When Irona was cleaning up, she found the word *Podakan* written in blood on the floor beside her pallet. It was traditional in Benign to name a firstborn son after his grandfathers, in this case Podnelbi 681 and Akanagure Matrinko. Irona had considered the Podakan combination, of course, but had decided on Akanelbi. She might have written the other name on the floor in her travail, although she did not recall doing so and she would have had to shape the letters upside down. It wasn't her handwriting, either, but she knew whose it had been. She looked down at the little red-faced scrap asleep in his basket.

"Forget what I just told you, son," she said. "Your name is Podakan."

THE YEAR 711

Quebrada Bericha and his men were relieved around Midsummer, having completed their one-year term. In the report that Irona sent back to Benign with them, she suggested that the tours of duty were too long. They had been established two centuries ago, but newer galleys were swifter and more seaworthy. She suggested that governors should serve a single year and garrisons only six months, with relief in spring and fall. If Vult were regarded as a hardship posting, instead of a penal one, it might be better served. She added that men with better motivation and briefer exposure would be less likely to succumb to Maleficence.

The new commander was Mandalagan Furnas, a jovial, quickwitted young man, and a big improvement on Bericha. The dispatches he brought informed her that both former governors had died, Zajic on the voyage home and Redkev soon after his arrest. Sazen suggested that they had been poisoned years ago and been kept alive since by regular supplies of antidote, which had been cut off as soon as their involvement with the dealers was compromised. As usual, what he said made sense. She was amused to learn that Ledacos 692 had failed to win his coveted election to the Seven, being defeated by Obnosa 658, who had finally achieved her lifelong ambition.

At times Irona longed for some female company, but Podakan took up so much of her life that she had hardly had time to attend to her minimal gubernatorial duties.

Spring came early, more welcome than ever it was in Benign, and Irona could start looking forward to her return.

Podakan was growing fast and no one could deny that he had inherited his father's good looks, but also much of Grandfather Akanagure's vicious temper. On the very day that Podakan took his first bipedal steps, Daun Bukit put his head around the door to announce that a war galley was in sight.

"Flying the Benesh flag!" he added with a grin. He, too, would be heading home now, after almost three years. The garrison had not expected their relief yet, for midsummer was still a couple of months away. Clearly the Seventy had changed the schedule, and therefore had adopted at least some of Irona's suggestions.

The weather was so fine for once that she dared to sit outside her quarters to await her replacement, watching Podakan amuse himself in the sandbox the men had built for him. Her son had only two tricks: he was either so soundly asleep that an earthquake wouldn't waken him, or he was a whirlwind of noisy activity. And now he was only days away from proper walking! How by the goddess was she ever going to control him on the galley going home without putting a chain on his ankle?

Then a man in a sea-green tunic and jade collar emerged from the guardhouse and she learned that her replacement was Minasguil 697. He was saturnine, cheerless, and rather friendless, much given to sarcasm. A Ledacos client, she recalled, but she couldn't attribute his posting to Vult to a lack of popularity without condemning herself.

They went to meet each other, hands outstretched and hypocritical smiles firmly in place. They discussed everything except politics. She was not going to seek gossip from Minasguil, and he did not volunteer any.

The next day, Irona and Podakan sailed away on *Sea Dragon*. As she watched the rock dwindle behind her, she reflected that if she never saw it again, that would still be much too soon.

The weather was capricious on the voyage home, but as *Sea Dragon* left Vyada Kun, the winds dropped and the sky turned blue. Irona told Furnas she wished to visit Kadowan Island. It was a long detour, but the crew was willing to do anything she wanted, for she had shortened their stint in Vult. When she reached the ill-reputed and uninhabited island, the sea was as smooth as a puddle, so Caprice must favor what her Chosen had in mind. *Sea Dragon* was able to beach. Irona went exploring with a small keg and a hammer that she had brought along just in case. After half an hour, she had completed her task, and two strong marines carried the keg back to the ship for her. Master and crew both assumed she was crazy, but whatever this Chosen wanted was divine command for them. Irona 700 wasn't quite sure how she did it, but she knew she had a remarkable ability to inspire men.

They were east of Genodesa when a westerly blew in. The crew could not row in the swell, so Furnas could only raise sail and run before the storm. For a couple of days, they bore down on a lee shore with their prospects looking very grim indeed. Fortunately, the storm died before they did, and they found shelter in the estuary of the Tombe River. Needing repairs, *Sea Dragon* went on to Tombe itself, where the work could be done. Irona and son enjoyed a two-week vacation. Tombe was not a hotbed of excitement, but anywhere would have been an improvement over Vult, and it did have a wonderful beach where a one-year-old could run himself to exhaustion instead of his mother.

It was a few days short of Midsummer when *Sea Dragon* rowed into the great harbor of Benign.

Sebrat House had been maintained just as Irona left it, even to the same documents stacked beside her bed. But Sebrat without

Vly was going to seem very strange, almost lonelier than Vult. She thought she would ask the Property Commission for another home.

Velny Lavice was still there, although her hair had turned white; she wept tears of joy on meeting her grandson, who callously ignored her. After the welcoming hugs and lamentation, the two women settled down in the familiar ballroom to look at the view and talk of their loss. Irona did not mention that Vly's body had never been found. Nor did she mention those gnawed bones on Svinhofdarhrauk, some of which could have been his.

"Did he ever sleepwalk as a child?"

Velny nodded. "Several times, but only when he was very worried about something. The last time was when his father was dying and we had no future."

"He was worried at Vult. It was in appalling condition when we arrived, and we had to stay two years, so we thought. The parapet was in bad disrepair. *Oh, no! Podakan!"*

Podakan had discovered a fine pottery vase that he could lift, and he knew what pottery did when dropped on a stone floor. It did. Joyfully displaying all four teeth, he then reached for an alabaster bowl. Irona swept him up in her arms before he could plant a bare foot on a splinter. He yelled in protest. His grandmother roared with laughter, which was definitely not the correct response. She rang for a slave to clean up.

"Perhaps we should take him out on the terrace, ma'am? Nothing breakable there."

"You think so? He will turn the grounds into a desert in no time."

They went out to the terrace, to the shady end under the chestnut trees, and there resumed their conversation. Podakan went after the pigeons. For two years, Irona had been starved of political news, but Velny could tell her little. Knipry 640 was still First, still hearty and active. Their neighbor, Ledacos 692, had tried again to win election to the Seven and had lost to Waesche 623, who was literally the oldest of the old guard. Last year's Chosen was Haruna 710, the first woman since Irona.

She would eventually learn all the details from Sazen Hostin, who had agreed to continue as her secretary, but had gone to visit old friends in the Geographical Section for an exchange of news. Irona had no doubts that her affairs would be an open book to the snoops if Sazen was handling them for her, but he would keep her well informed in return.

Daun Bukit had headed home to Overock to discover what had happened to the girl he loved. His letters to her had not been answered, but that was hardly surprising. Much more surprising was that he still cared, after more than three years. Whatever the minstrels sang, not all men were fickle.

"Oh, not the roses!" Velny exclaimed. Podakan had been joyfully ripping apart all the blossoms he could reach and had now spotted new targets.

"Why not the roses?"

"Roses have thorns!"

"Life is a learning experience," Irona murmured. Podakan was training her how to be a mother.

But then a shadow fell over the scene, quite literally, as a man came striding up the grass toward the terrace. Chosen changed little in two years, and Ledacos seemed just as Irona remembered him. The hem of his sea-green tunic was a little lower, the bracelets and rings a little flashier, but nothing unusual. Velny, of course, dropped to her knees. Podakan thought she wanted to play and came running to her, waving a stick.

Irona remained seated. *Revenge needs a well-sharpened knife*, but now was not the time to produce it. She smiled.

"Very like his father," Ledacos said. "He will grow up as beautiful as both his parents." He raised Irona's hand to kiss it. "I have already told Velny of my sympathy. Believe me, that was the worst news I heard all the time you were gone."

Worse than two failures to join the Seven? Irona thanked him, bade him be seated. Now she was certainly going to hear all the news. Velny muttered excuses and carried Podakan off with promises of cookies.

Ledacos leaned back and regarded Irona with a warm glow of admiration. "Magnificent! You rank now with Eldborg and Eboga as destroyers of evil. The Seven are planning a public celebration of your return, thanksgiving to Caprice and other rigmarole."

"I have a funeral to attend that day, whenever it is."

"You won't escape so easily," he laughed, but his eyes were puzzled. He would love to be feted like that. He was, of course, male.

"When I left so hurriedly," Irona said, "you were poised to become the youngest Seven in the history of Benign. What went wrong?"

His eyes glinted. "You used to be a client of Obnosa 658."

"Not really. My tutor, Trodelat, was. After I tied my ship to your star, they discarded me as a traitor to the cause of womanhood." *And look where it got me.*

Ledacos smiled wolfishly. "Then I may safely describe her as a vicious old sow? As you predicted, my dear, the old guard made a two-way race out of it, and the candidate they rallied around was Obnosa. She was the ideal compromise candidate because she has never had enough principles to belong to any faction except her own. The vote split predictably. The kiddies voted for me, but we weren't enough."

"Time is on your side, then!" Obnosa's term must be about to end. Irona had forgotten how addictive politics was.

"And I may still count on your support?"

"Of course. Whatever I may have achieved—and it really wasn't much—I owe to your help and encouragement." What a proficient liar she had become! How strange that the ground did not open and swallow her up.

"What you achieved was spectacular. The price of a love fix—which is a rape tool, of course—has gone up a hundredfold since you left!" He chuckled. "That information comes from the Office of Decency, not personal experience."

A Chosen did not need maleficent sex aids. Power and wealth would do the trick every time, aided by robust health from imbibing ample Source Water.

"And we only ever intercepted one shipment at Vult," Irona said. "The word went out, which suggests that there is a single dark intelligence lurking in the Dread Lands."

"But you defeated it! We must consider what you are to do next. The choosing is coming up, and the female tutelage is yours for the asking. There is a seat on the Treaty Commission that offers good opportunities for travel." His smile added that the opportunities for graft were even better. "Or the Property Commission? I did sort of agree to support a client for that, but I can fob him off with something else."

She was not going to let him stampede her into hasty decisions. She had her own agenda.

"I need time to think. The ground is still going up and down like a ship for me."

"Yes, but . . . But it looks like you are summoned."

Indeed, blessed relief came striding across the terrace in guise of a young man in the scarlet livery of the First's heralds.

"Irona," Ledacos said hurriedly. "Obnosa's term ends very shortly. I lost to Waesche by only three votes, and all my supporters are urging me to try again. If I decide to do so this time, will you do me the honor of nominating me?"

Obviously that question had been the main reason for his calling on her so soon. It was a trick question, of course, a means of taking a potential opponent out of the running, or at least of learning whether that person was a potential opponent. But he couldn't truly believe that she was a rival for that job. She wasn't even twenty-seven yet. It would be ten or twenty years before she could try for the Seven, if she ever wanted to.

"I am sure you can find dozens of more senior Chosen whose sponsorship would do you far more good than mine."

"I doubt it very much. You are a state hero. Please, as a very special favor?"

"Yes, of course I would be honored," she said. *Never make enemies.* The goddess did not strike her dead.

The herald arrived and went down on one knee to deliver the First's summons.

The chair the First had sent for her was ornamented in red and gilt, and luxuriously cushioned. Eight bearers carried it, sprinting the entire way up the Mountain, with the accompanying honor guard racing alongside.

Much to Irona's surprise, she was shown into the Treaty Hall and advised that the First would be with her shortly. The Treaty Hall was the showpiece of the First's Palace. This was where he received allied kings and princes, or the elected magistrates of the handful of other republics in the Empire. At one end stood the red throne, seven purple thrones, and the appropriate number of sea-green chairs for the Chosen. Opposite that was a magnificent pillared balcony overlooking the mansions of the rich, which descended in a frozen cascade of roofs and fine gardens to the Old City, whose slums and squalor were safely obscured by distance. And beyond them all shone the great bay, with its sails and galleys.

More intriguing for Irona were the portraits along the south wall. Although she had seen them often enough, she had never had a chance to study them properly. Here hung all the Sevens for the last three hundred years. Before that date, portraiture had been too primitive, or else the Seven had not acquired the importance they later achieved in the structure of the Republic. There were no names, only the numbers on the collars. The parade began with seven old men; stolid, face-on, and bearded. All seven had probably been rendered by the same artist, in a single commission. Beards disappeared a couple of generations later and faces grew younger when it was decided that the likeness should be taken upon first election. She found Eboga 500, uglier and meaner than most. So few women! She found Knipry 640, at around forty, looking a great deal more dangerous than he looked now; he had learned to dissemble in the last fifty years, that was all. The latest was Obnosa 658.

Then Knipry himself was striding across the hall to her, beaming and extending both hands in welcome. He brought no one else with him, which was a signal honor. He was still the jovial old gentleman with a loving smile and the virulence of a spitting cobra, and he could have passed for twenty years less than his tally of eighty-seven. He forbade her to kneel, ushered her to a table and two chairs set up in the great window. He poured wine for both of them.

"Magnificent! Simply magnificent! Do you know that the price of a death fix was down to three dolphins? That's less than the cost of having someone stabbed in the streets. Now the assassins are back in business, and all the Night Watch has to do is follow the bloodstains." He raised his beaker. "To your past success and future glory!"

She took a sip before protesting that she had done nothing much.

"Yes, you did! The Office of Decency was obsessed with tracing the money back to the source. It was you who saw that whatever lurks in the Dread Lands was giving fixes away for free. The evidence you sent south broke the ring in Genodesa, and after some gentle persuasion, they led us to half a dozen other cities. Now tell me what really happened to your consort."

"I don't know." She told him what she did know, even mentioning the bones they had found on Svinhofdarhrauk. If all the blabbermouths and gossips in the Empire were listed in order, Knipry would be the last. She did not tell him of Vlyplatin's madness or the mysterious messages that seemed to be written by his ghost, but she described his disappearance.

Knipry stared at her for a long moment when she was done, and then took a swallow of his wine. "That frightens me more than anything I have heard yet: that evil could reach right in and steal a man away without trace, almost out of his lover's arms."

"In some ways, I think he . . . I'm tempted to say he cooperated, but I don't really mean that. He didn't resist hard enough! Vlyplatin was a very sensitive and gentle man. The thought of two years in that awful place wounded him deeply and he felt guilty that he had tricked me into it."

The snowy eyebrows rose. "How so?"

She shrugged. "Water under the bridge now."

"Or bloodstains under the rug?" The old man's wits were as sharp as ever, and his eyes as bright. How much did he know, or guess?

"Possibly."

He smiled contentedly. "You were studying the rogues' gallery when I came in. What did you decide?"

"Too few women and all too old."

He nodded, and she could guess then why she had been left alone in this hall, out of a dozen rooms he could have chosen.

"What are you going to do now?" he asked. "Obnosa 658's term ends in a few days. She is strongly of the opinion that there should always be a woman among the Seven."

"And what do the rest of the Seventy think of that idea?"

Knipry chuckled. "Tell me what you want them to think."

"I think I should bide my time. I'm too young; I have too much still to learn." And female, which was an even worse handicap. Obnosa hadn't made Seven until she was forty years older. "They keep refusing Ledacos."

Knipry had a curious trick of folding wrinkles down to hide his eyes, so that they disappeared without actually closing. He used it now.

"Ledacos 692 tries too hard. He serves himself before he serves the goddess. Why don't we elect you to the Seven instead of him? Have some more wine while we plan your campaign."

"He has already asked me to nominate him, Your Reverence."

"That sleazy rascal! He wasted no time, did he?" The First chuckled knowingly. "Well, have some more wine anyway. And tell me why you never wear jewelry."

"Because I am the one who never wears jewelry."

"That's a very good reason," he said seriously. "I suspected that."

The day seemed endless. The Seventy met at sundown, and Irona had to attend. In the Scandal Market, everyone—literally everyone—wanted to fawn over her and congratulate her on conquering Maleficence at Vult. She insisted that it was not conquered and never would be. The only advantage to being mobbed was that Ledacos could not manage to corner her and pin her down on anything else. He hovered on the outskirts, looking vaguely worried at her enormous popularity. He ought to be pleased that his sponsor in the coming election was so well thought of.

Very little of substance happened at the actual meeting. The main excitement was a verbal report by Irona 700 on her tour of duty at Vult, which was followed by a standing ovation. If they kept up this flattery, she was going to start believing it.

She breakfasted alone, thinking of Vly.

Sharpening her knife.

As soon as she was finished, she sent for Sazen and Daun Bukit to plan the day. Sazen was his usual toothy, puckish self. He seemed to grow smaller, not larger, although he was definitely starting to show a grotesque potbelly on his otherwise tiny frame. Daun looked as if he were about to be hung, drawn, and divided into eighths. Irona exchanged glances with Sazen and then told Daun, "Report!"

"I can't stay in your service, ma'am. Now they know I'm back, they'll come after me. They never forget."

"Did you get to see her?"

He nodded, glummer than ever. "I found out where she lived.

She answered the door herself. When she saw me, she burst into tears. . . . It was terrible!"

Daun was a very clever, competent aide. In Vult, he had done everything she asked while backed up by no more authority than his own word that this was what the Chosen wanted. He had handled the smugglers' interrogation with a fearfully cold-blooded efficiency. As a former marine, he was no milksop, and he had rowed his share of watches on the way home. Once or twice in Vult, men had made jokes about the governor's gigolo, and Daun had won most of the resulting punch-ups. Yet when it came to his own affairs, and especially his blighted love life, he seemed to fall apart. Irona had never pressed him for details before, but now she snapped at him to get on with the story. Who were these "they" he kept talking about?

"Kanaga's brothers, six of them! The Nisyro family . . . they had a rich marriage planned for her and when we . . . when she . . . then they had to settle for a lot less and he's old and she really hates him and he came to the door to see who was there and I never even got to see my son but he swore he would tell them I was back and they would see to me he said so I can't stay—"

"Stop, stop! You have only two speeds, don't you? Like Podakan. Tell me about these Nisyro goons."

"They're timber importers. They work for the Dvure family. They're bad enough themselves and they have dozens of longshore-men working for them. . . . You must know how rough Overock is, ma'am! They filter corpses out of the harbor every morning."

"So I've heard, but I assure you that I can be a lot rougher. Are you absolutely certain that, er, Kanaga, would rather be married to you than to her present husband?"

"She was begging me to take her away, ma'am!"

Irona disapproved of the goddess's Chosen using their god-given powers to further their own ends, but this sounded like a serious injustice needing to be righted, and conventional law could not prevent crimes before the fact, only punish them after, which might be much too late for Daun. "Sazen, how long will my meeting with the Office of Decency take?"

"No more than an hour, ma'am."

"Then will you invite Nis Puol Dvure to meet with me right after?"

It was rare for Sazen Hostin to look surprised. He asked her to repeat the name.

"An old friend," Irona explained.

Her new office was larger than she had expected and two floors lower, which was a sign of approval from on high. That it was flanked on either side by Sevens' offices was even less subtle. It was furnished with four stools around a table and a separate group of two chairs, plus some impressive artwork that she had not yet had time to study. She was late getting back to it, because the meeting with the Maleficence hunters had taken much longer than predicted. Daun was sitting in the anteroom. He jumped up and confirmed that her visitor was waiting.

Nis Puol Dvure was standing with his back to the door, staring out the window. He spun around as she entered. Irona walked over to the group of chairs, then nodded to acknowledge him.

For a moment he just stared at her collar, the very collar he had expected to wear around his neck. He had hardly changed at all, but if a Dvure could not afford Source Water, nobody could. His tunic was still youthfully brief, to display his shapely legs. He wore rings on his fingers, his wrists, and even around his upper arms, which was the latest affectation of rich youth.

Daun followed Irona in and closed the door. Only then did Nis Poul walk over and kneel to her, eyes lowered.

"Good of you to come, citizen," she said. "I am sorry to have kept you waiting."

"My honor," he informed her feet.

"Please rise. And sit there. You look well. And your family?"

He still did not meet her eye, which was correct protocol at this stage. He had been trained in such things since he was born. "They are all well, ma'am, and will be honored to hear that you asked after them."

Were they talking about the entire Dvure clan, or were they discussing his wife and children, if he had either or both? Irona should have done more research on him. Nil Puol might be a totally unimportant tadpole in the great Dvure pond, unable to provide what she wanted. Somehow she did not think that. If the family had been willing to pay a huge bribe to rig a choosing for him, then he must have ability, and rich merchant families did not waste ability. His adolescent arrogance had not diminished by a single freckle.

"I invited you here to listen to a fairy tale, citizen. This is my aide, Daun Bukit."

Dvure turned his shapely, arrogant head to inspect the insignificant Daun. "A fairy tale, ma'am?"

"Tell him, Daun." She had coached him in what she wanted, and she could rely on his knack of completely suppressing his own personality to become the perfect servant. He spoke up with no emotion at all.

"Yes, ma'am. Once upon a time a boy and a girl fell in love. She was a great beauty and her brothers planned to marry her to a certain very rich man. She conceived a child by her lover and the brothers vowed to kill him, so he had to flee for his life. The proposed bridegroom backed out, and the brothers were forced to marry her to a much older man, not as rich as they had wanted. She bore her lover's son, but had no other children, and she was very unhappy. Her name was Kanaga Nisyro."

Dvure waited a moment to see if that was all, and then looked inquiringly at Irona.

"Your family employs the Nisyro brothers, I believe?" she said.

"We employ a family by that name in Overock, yes." He had detected Daun's accent. But he was still being no more than politely attentive. It must, of course, be infinitely galling to be summoned like this by the backwater slut who had cheated him out of his due. Had the priests refunded his family's bribe money?

"I disapprove of threats of physical violence."

"So do I, ma'am. The Overock docks are a rough area. You wish me to have the Nisyros warned?"

"I do."

"What was the name of the proposed victim?"

"Daun Bukit."

Dvure nodded. "I will see it is done. There will be no further menaces or violence. Anything more you require of me, Your Honor?"

Irona drew a deep breath. "Yes. I want the Kanaga woman delivered to my residence before sunset today, with her infant son. I want her free to remarry."

He raised shapely eyebrows. "Divorced or widowed?"

His insolence took her breath away. "Divorced, certainly."

Immediate divorce was legally possible but expensive, and the husband would have to be bought off—or just invited to choose between the alternatives?

Dvure paused a moment to let her know that her first request had been legitimate law enforcement, but this was over the skyline. Or was he calculating how big a favor he could demand in return?

Then he nodded. "I am sure that can be arranged."

"You are very kind, citizen!" Irona rose, so of course he jumped up too. There was a glint in his eye, though. She was going to owe him big after this one, but what could anyone offer a Dvure?

"By the way," she said. "I have just returned from a tour of duty at Vult, the Empire's remotest and most vital outpost. The First is organizing a parade and banquet in my honor—diplomatic corps, march past, state barge, and so on and so on. Would you and your wife care to join us as my personal guests?"

He actually colored. Some Dvures would be invited, of course; certainly the supreme patriarch, whoever he was, and probably a few others, but no one of Nis Poul's age. And Irona was hinting at reception line and head table. If his wife was any sort of socialite, this would be the triumph of the decade for her.

"We should be honored beyond words, ma'am!"

"I will see that you receive an invitation." She offered her fingers to be kissed again. Daun showed the visitor out, then came back in and tried to kiss her toes.

Kanaga and her child arrived at Sebrat House before sunset, and Irona officiated at her marriage to Daun Bukit. Their son, Kao, was a year older than Podakan, so that was all right by everyone except Podakan, who threw a temper tantrum.

A couple of days after her return, Irona was elected female tutor for the next choosing. It was intended as a token honor, because Caprice never chose girls twice in a row. On Midsummer morning, Irona spent an entertaining hour in the temple with Komev 701, who was still as gangly, red-haired, and brash as he had been ten years earlier, when she swore him in. He had not lacked confidence then, and now he brazenly flirted with her. He was a lot better at it than Ledacos, and she made a mental note to keep him in mind if she ever felt the need for a refresher course in bedroom athletics. He was the first person since she returned who did not pester her with questions about Vult. Mostly he passed on all the amusing gossip she had missed, and she noted that his stories were never malicious, unlike Ledacos's.

Their tête-à-tête was interrupted by the roar that always greeted Caprice's decision. Together they peered through the slatted window. Last year's Chosen, Haruna 710, was walking out to greet the newcomer—another girl.

"Two in a row?" Komev said. "Either the goddess has gone crazy, or she's showing she approves of your performance."

"I hope this new one likes children," Irona retorted, thinking that she really did not need more household complications.

A few minutes later, she went down to greet her protégée, Puchuldiza 711, who was plump, plain, and quite short. She was also starry eyed, showing none of the terror and resentment that Irona had endured at her own choosing.

"Congratulations. I'm Irona 700, and I've been appointed your—"

"Yes, yes, I know! Haruna just told me." Puchuldiza bubbled like a Source Water spring. "And you're going to have a parade! That's how I get to ride in the imperial barge with you! I dreamed it, you see. I've been dreaming for weeks of the goddess choosing me, and lately I've been dreaming of riding in the state coach with you and the First and I told my sisters but they wouldn't believe me."

"Then you're not surprised?" Irona tried not to look at Haruna, who was pulling outrageous faces in the background.

"Oh, not surprised at all," Puchuldiza said. "I often dream things before they happen. But do I *have* to wear that terrible green? It absolutely is not my color."

The tension in the Scandal Market the next day seemed greater than Irona ever remembered. Possibly she had forgotten how it could be, or perhaps she was just imagining it. For days Chosen had been wishing her luck in the coming elections. Most had been too polite to mention any specific election they had in mind, and to those who did she had merely said she would be nominating Ledacos 692 for the Seven. She suspected that some of them had been sent to check on her and would report her answer back to him.

The First was above politics and never meddled in them, and yet she had a strong suspicion that Knipry had been warning her that he was going to arrange for her to be drafted. And that would be embarrassing for both of them. She really, *really* could not expect to be elected to the Seven at her age. Ledacos's ambitions were well known, and it would be a brutal blow to him to be passed yet again, and in favor of a woman eight years younger. The smart money—and half the citizenry of Benign gambled on elections to the Seven—would be on Gamchen 642, who had served a dozen times before and was well respected. He was elderly, true, but Chosen did not decay. The seat was almost certainly his if he wanted it, not least because he was known to be a close friend of the First, so voting against him might have unfortunate results later.

Obnosa 658 was there, back in sea green because her term had ended at dawn. She made no effort to speak with Irona. Unlike other magistrates, retiring Sevens never nominated candidates to be their replacements.

Irona had her protégée with her, and Puchuldiza's endless chatter was a good pest repellant. A gap opened around them.

"When do I get to wear jewels?" Puchuldiza demanded, scanning the glittering throng.

"Any time you like," Irona said. "I'll show you where the Property Commission's office is. They'll lay out trays of gold and silver and gems for you. Pick out whatever you want."

"Why don't you wear jewelry?"

"I think my collar is ornament enough. Money can't buy one like it."

"Oh, that's sweet!"

Sweet or not, it was a safe bet that by tomorrow Puchuldiza would outglitter the midnight sky.

The gong sounded, and the Chosen headed for the Assembly Hall.

The election of a Seven was always placed at the end of the agenda, because it was traditionally followed by a party. Kapalny 664 called the meeting to order, and they all settled down to a long grind of routine business. The first two counts confirmed that there were sixty-two Chosen voting. Kapalny had just announced the second decision when Knipry rose from his throne. Kapalny sat down.

"I ask the Assembly to proceed to Item Ten." The First chuckled with the joy of an expert making an unexpected move in some intricate board game.

"The-Assembly-thanks-His-Reverence-for-this-guidance-Item-Ten-election-of-a-Seven-the-chair-calls-for-nominations-Chosen-642?"

The recognition came even before old Gamchen rose from his seat. Irona's scalp prickled. If Gamchen was going to nominate, then he was not himself a candidate. Then she realized that he had spoken her name.

So it had happened! Knipry had followed through and was indicating his own preference by asking his old crony to nominate her. That would swing a lot of the old guard. Her own nomination of Ledacos had been preempted.

As Irona rose, her heart began beating very fast. A first election to the Seven meant far more than just one two-year term. In practice, the Republic and its Empire were run by the First and a dozen or so senior Chosen. With elections scattered around the calendar and a compulsory one-year leave between terms, there were always former Sevens waiting in the wings, eager to return. These were jocularly known as the Six, although their number varied. First election to the Seven meant admittance to the inner circle. It was almost never granted before a Chosen reached forty, and very rarely withdrawn later. Four-fifths of the Chosen were never admitted at all.

She walked forward and turned to face the gathering. Instinctively, she met Ledacos's eye. He was sneering at her betrayal, but his expression quickly became one of dismay as Suretamatai 683 jumped up to nominate him. That was unwanted support from an ally, who did not see, as Ledacos himself clearly must, that Irona was almost certain to win in the prevailing mood. Having no choice, Ledacos stalked forward and took his place on Irona's left, ignoring her.

After a brief pause, the chair asked if there were any more nominations, and up shot Azalka 660. She nominated Pavouk 708, who was only a year out of tutelage. He strode forward, grinning from ear to ear. Obviously he had been forewarned and knew that he was not a serious candidate, but he was popular and his juvenile amusement was reflected back in more smiles. Ledacos bit his lip, knowing now that he had run into a well-organized conspiracy.

The number of candidates could be critical. A third candidate, often a mere stalking horse, could deny either of the main factions a first ballot win and allow them to assess each other's strength—and also see who was in what camp, which was even more important. Most patrons did not bind their clients to more than the first ballot, so many votes would be freed to switch.

There being no further nominations, the honorable Chosen wishing to vote for Pavouk 708 must raise their right hands. . . .

The First never voted except to break a tie, but the Sevens did, so Irona could not be sure of the total without blatantly turning around to look at them, which was bad form. She saw eleven hands, and the chair decreed twelve—candidates were deemed to vote for themselves. So no Seven had supported the brash kid. His was a good showing for a stalking horse, though, and now there would almost certainly be a second ballot.

For Ledacos 692? Eighteen hands that she could see, plus Ledacos himself, and evidently three Sevens, because Kapalny announced a total of twenty-two. That left twenty-eight for Irona, which was what she got.

Pavouk was excused. He bowed to the First and returned to his seat, being awarded a round of applause that made his grin stretch superhumanly wide. If all his votes went to Ledacos, Ledacos would win.

But they didn't. On the second ballot, Irona scored forty-seven and Ledacos only fifteen. It was a staggering defeat. His bow to the First was barely perceptible, and the round of applause he received as a consolation prize was thin.

So Irona 700 stepped up to take her place among the Seven and received a standing ovation. All for torturing six smugglers? But Ledacos had been thoroughly snubbed, thanks to the well-meaning efforts of one of his own supporters, and she had been given her revenge without having to lift a finger for it. After all that knife sharpening, too! Never had the goddess so clearly shown her favor.

The rest of the agenda was run through roughshod, so the Chosen could adjourn to the upper reaches of the Palace. First Knipry never stinted on parties. Young Pavouk received much mock commiseration and good wishes for his next try. Of course he promised to run again next time. He could not realistically expect to be elected for another twenty years, unless Irona's breakthrough had permanently changed the rules.

Ledacos was conspicuously absent. How long would he have to wait before he tried a fourth time?

The reception was held in the Treaty Hall, and after all the congratulations had been passed and several flagons of wine consumed, they made Irona stand at the end of the line of portraits so they could agree how much she would improve the quality of the display. Obnosa protested loudly, of course. An argument then developed over the best portrait painter in the city. Irona had no opinion. Four or five names were tossed around, until the First stated his views quite strongly and that settled that. The name he suggested was Veer Machin.

When Irona arrived home that night, Ledacos was waiting for her. Velny Lavice was keeping him company but was very happy to make her excuses and leave him to her employer. Irona told Daun to remain.

"Send your ape away!" Ledacos was more than a little drunk. "What I have to say to you, bitch, is private."

"Daun is my confidential aide and I keep no secrets from him. What is your problem?"

"You betrayed me! You agreed to help me get elected. You promised to nominate me." Much more than a little drunk.

Irona sat down on the most comfortable chair without inviting her visitor to try another.

"I did agree to nominate you. I would have done so had I not been nominated before I could speak. A nominated candidate cannot nominate an opponent, as you well know. I did not campaign on your behalf because you never asked me to. I wouldn't have done so, anyway."

"Two-faced, conniving, scheming slut!"

Daun came closer. Irona waved him back.

"You have the finest political instincts in the Seventy, Ledacos 692, but this time you let ambition overrule it. Three tries in two years is unheard of. It stinks of greed."

"And going back on your sworn words doesn't?"

"I gave you my word, yes. I told anyone who asked me that I had agreed to nominate you. I did not seek the nomination; I did not campaign for the office. You, on the other hand, were campaigning ferociously. Don't tell me you didn't pick up on the fact that I was being touted as a national hero. You didn't let that worry you because I had promised to put your name forward. You thought you had blocked me. But some people more powerful than you didn't like it, and they blocked you."

"Bitch!"

That was enough. Ledacos was making a complete fool of himself, and the longer she let him go on, the worse he would feel about it in the morning, if he remembered this scene in the morning.

"You have outstayed your welcome. Daun, show His Honor out, and send a porter with a lantern to make sure he manages to find his way safely home."

"Your Honor?" Daun moved close again.

Ledacos turned his rage on him. "I'm a Chosen, you ape. Lay one finger on me and you'll die the sea death!"

"And I am a Seven," Irona said, her own temper flaring. "Leave my home this instant, or I'll see you posted to Maasok for the next five years!"

Ledacos threw down his beaker and stormed out of the room, with Daun at his heels like a terrier.

Her promotion buried Irona under a rockslide of work—reports to read, committees to chair, staff to hire, social invitations by the score, and umpteen meaningless civic or ceremonial duties. About a score of Chosen wanted her as a patron and her protégée desperately needed guidance, not least because Puchuldiza herself did not see the need.

Irona had not even yet organized her home life, for she needed more staff to look after Podakan, who barely ever saw his mother now. She fell into bed exhausted and could barely drag herself out again at dawn. One morning she arrived at her office in the Palace and was less than pleased to learn that her first task was to interview half a dozen people for secretarial help. It had to be done, for Sazen and Daun were grossly overworked. Her patience began to show cracks when Sazen coughed his you-won't-like-this-but-think-before-you-explode signal.

"I ventured to inform Citizen Machin that you might spare him some time also, ma'am."

"Citizen who?"

"Veer Machin, the artist hired by the Seven to—"

"Don't be ridiculous! Tell him to come back next year."

Sazen did not move, which was a bad sign. "The Seven's resolution set a deadline on completion, ma'am." And quickly: "He says he needs to spend an hour or two just watching you, studying your face and gestures, and so on."

"Oh, very well. As long as he doesn't smell too bad, bring him in."

The man who lumbered in seemed clean and inoffensive, unlike most artisans. He was young and large, a sort of amiable bear of a man, with a thick tangle of fairish hair, a passable brown smock, and fingers all the colors of the rainbow. His movements were clumsy; dropping to his knees, he almost overbalanced.

"Do rise, citizen. Veer Machin, I understand."

"Yes, ma'am."

He took up a lot of space standing there, with his face lowered, nervously rubbing his hands together. Not fat like a rich man, not muscular like a rower, just big.

"And what is it you require of me?"

"To watch you, ma'am. Study the way your face moves. The play of light on your skin. How the color of your eyes changes."

"I am not aware that my eyes change color!"

"No, ma'am. But they do. Everyone's do."

Interesting! "Don't you need to draw me?"

"No, ma'am. I remember everything I see."

The Geographical Section might be interested in Veer Machin.

"Well, sit over there. I'm going to be interviewing some clerks. I prefer that you do not interrupt."

Soon she forgot all about him. Only when all the interviews were over and she was due to leave for a meeting of the Customs Board did she realize that he was still sitting there, hands on knees, staring stonily at her.

"Anything more? Seen all you need?"

"All I need to start, ma'am. But I need for you to sit for me when I do the waxing itself."

Oh, did he? "And how long does that take?"

"About six or seven sessions, ma'am. An hour or so each. You'll get tired if it's longer."

She almost laughed in his face. But it was a comely, honest, well-meaning face that did not deserve to be laughed in. She had expected a laborer, like a tiler or a bricklayer, but he didn't really look like one. He didn't look at her the way an artisan would.

"Have you any idea . . ." Of course he didn't. She couldn't possibly waste that much time just to put her face on the Palace wall. But if he could do his waxing sitting in that same corner and she could continue her own work at the same time, doing non-confidential things . . . "Talk to my aides, and they'll find you a corner—"

"It has to be at my place, ma'am. I have waxes and colors and boards and easels . . . I'd fill your office and turn it into a . . . midden . . ." His voice tailed away uncertainly.

Irona was giving him her look for crushing admirals.

"And where is your place?"

"Corner of Gutter Road and Suicide, ma'am."

That was surprisingly close to Sebrat House, not down among the docks and slums. "How on earth can you afford to live there?"

"Selling portraits, ma'am."

Come to think of it, Veer Machin did not speak like a laborer. He spoke like people who lived on the Mountain; the First had recommended him. Irona was suddenly intrigued.

"Suppose I stop by for an hour this evening on my way home? I may not—"

He beamed. "That would be splendid, ma'am!"

She had meant to say that she could not promise more than two or at the most three sittings. . . . Well, she would see what his place looked like and what sort of portraits he produced.

The Machin residence appeared to be on the flat roof of a six-story building, but the ground was very close to vertical there, and the entrance was at the rear, a gate at the top of a single flight of stairs. As a Seven, Irona had to tolerate an official escort from the Palace guard wherever she went, which made her personal guards furious and surly—another problem to sort out. The chief guard inspected the premises before he would let her enter, and then he wanted to post men inside with her. Irona smote him with thunder and lightning. He and his men could wait on the steps if they wanted to; her chair could return in an hour. Then she stalked up the stairs and shut the gate firmly behind her.

She was in a small yard with whitewashed walls, three of the four sides overhung by projecting roofs. A door and a single window opposite the gate led into a shed, which could not possibly contain more than one small room. The ground was almost invisible under jars, boxes, wood shavings, work benches, stacks of panels, easels, braziers, sacks, bottles, and other miscellaneous clutter. Machin must work outdoors as much as he could, which in Benign would be most of the year. As she entered, he was adjusting a large easel. He spun around and tried to kneel without finishing what he was doing. The easel collapsed, knocking over another, and dislodging a stack of wooden panels. He finished sitting among the ruins, looking dismayed.

Irona had put in a long hard day, but the big man's expression was so pathetic that she laughed aloud. Scrambling to his feet, he sent a jar flying off a table. It shattered in an explosion of red powder. He looked at her doubtfully, then suddenly grinned, reassured.

"My mother used to tell me I'd never make a juggler, ma'am."

"I can't think why you'd want to. Show me . . . show me this!" She picked her way through the chaos to one of the sheltering overhangs. The First himself was sitting there in his red robes, three-quarter length. His eyes watched her approach and he looked ready to speak. Irona had not known there could be portraits like that. Compared to this, the portraits in the Treaty Hall were daubs.

She turned to the artist, who was waiting anxiously for her reaction.

"Did First Knipry tell you to let me see this?"

He nodded, looking as shy as a small boy.

She said, "And did he come here to pose for it?"

Another nod.

"He's a sly old devil. Now, where do you want me to sit?"

"Oh, here, ma'am!" Machin grabbed up a chair. The back came off in his hand, and his elbow knocked over another easel.

So it began. Irona stopped by every evening on her way home, as close to the same sun height as possible. She sat on a very hard stool and stared at the same swallows' nest under the eaves. He talked while he worked. She talked, too, smiled when he asked

her to, and often when he didn't, for he had a dry, self-depre-
cating humor. It was a wonderfully relaxing break in the day, as
long as she didn't think about the child at home, waiting on his
mother's return.

Machin had strange ideas about the social gulf between a dauber
and a Seven. During the second session, he suddenly said, "Stop
talking."

Indeed? She stopped, mostly because she was speechless.

"And don't look at me like that!" he barked. "You want to sneer at
the Treaty Hall for the next thousand years?"

He refused to let her see his work. He worked in encaustic, spreading colored wax with a spatula. Encaustic was never
impressive until it was finished, he said. It was lumpy and ugly,
but at the end he would smooth it out with a hot iron, and then
it would be complete. But he seemed to be working on more than
one panel, often discarding one halfway through a sitting and
grabbing up another.

The six or seven sittings stretched into nine, then ten. And one
evening he stopped work altogether to stare straight at her with an
expression of extreme frustration.

"What's wrong?" she asked.

"What the shit did you do to Vlyplatin Lavice?"

What? Irona drew a deep breath. . . .

"That's it!" he yelled. "Hold that! Yes, yes!" Like a madman, he
began slashing and scraping at her portrait, sending shreds and curls
of wax flying everywhere.

"What are you doing?" For a moment she thought he had gone
crazy. She sprang from the stool and ran to him. She was far too late.
The portrait had vanished, reduced to a faint and lumpy ghost.

But Machin was leering triumphantly down at her. "You never
were the grinning jackanapes I was trying to paint. Putting spotty
boys and giggling girls at ease in your office? 'Do please relax and
tell me why you want to work for the Republic. . . .' But Governor

Irona 700 about to send me to the gallows? That's the Irona I needed to see!"

"What do you know about Vlyplatin?"

"Nothing. Just public gossip and I don't care if I never know. I wanted to make the lioness roar, that's all." That lopsided, boyish grin again. . . . "For a moment there, I really thought you were going to have my head."

"You are crazy!"

He shrugged. "Probably. Do you ever wear jewelry?"

"Never."

"Why not?"

"Only my collar, which the goddess gave me. I own nothing else in the world, not even the clothes on my back."

He nodded. "That's good. I'll paint that in, too." He hurled the panel across the yard and picked up a fresh one. "Now we start over."

Every morning—or almost every morning, because a Seven had many duties—Irona met after breakfast with Daun Bukit and Sazen Hostin to plan her day and other days ahead. They were a good team, those two, a matched pair of opposites: Daun as honest and straight-forward as a javelin, Sazen as ugly and devious as a spider.

One of Sazen's task was to keep track of the votes coming up in the next week or so. One day he said, "Election of a Seven. Taulevu 666's term is ending."

Ah! Irona thought for a moment. "When we get to the Palace, would you ask Chosen Ledacos to drop by my office sometime? At his convenience, of course."

Daun looked appalled. "You're not thinking of voting for that rodent, are you?"

Sazen chuckled. "Of course she is. After three losses, he will never get elected to the Seven. But she'll offer to nominate him, and in their present mood, the Seventy will certainly give her whatever she wants. He still has a stable of fifteen or twenty clients, and this way he'll have to tell them to follow her lead or he'll be seen as a monstrous ingrate. Combining his clients and hers will let her run the Empire for the next two years."

"Sazen," Irona grumbled, "you are too fornicating sneaky for your own good."

Before she even left Sebrat House, though, Irona had to receive Velny Lavice, who was waiting outside the study door. She was clearly in great distress. Perched on the edge of the stool, she had great trouble getting to the point, gabbling about trivialities, while all the time her hands clawed at the lace apron that was the formal symbol of her housekeeper status.

Eventually Irona had to prompt her. "Is this about Puchuldiza again?" Her protégée was more trouble than a whole shipload of trogs.

Velny nodded, biting her lip. "She's been upsetting, I mean asking . . . Hayk and now Sopoetan. . . ."

Sopoetan was a footman. "Who's Hayk?"

"The new garden slave, ma'am. He didn't feel he could refuse her, and now he's terrified what you may do to him."

"I shall do nothing to him. Praise him for telling you, but instruct him that if she tries it again, he must report it to you right away. Did Sopoetan 'fess up too?"

"Um . . . when I asked him, ma'am. He looked so guilty."

Velny sighed. She had an empire to run and that was easier than handling a stupid, spoiled, oversexed child.

"Where is she now?"

"Still in bed, I believe."

"Then I will go and see her myself," Irona said. "I shall need a bucket of cold water and a stout leather belt."

An hour or so later, at the Palace, Ledacos 692 entered Irona's office with his chin high and a smile that could have been waxed on his face by Veer Machin.

"Goddess bless, Your Honor! Purple suits you. You look lovelier than ever." His eyes flickered around the big room appraisingly.

Irona offered him a chair, which he accepted, and wine, which he declined. Then he asked what he might do for her.

Grovel was one possibility. *Vly, I am doing this for you.*

"Taulevu 666's term is ending in a few days."

Ledacos's smile vanished. He had known perfectly well why she sent for him. "And you are gathering votes for . . . ?"

"I am willing to nominate you."

He scowled. She had been his client and was now offering to be his patron. "You cheated me last time, so why should I trust you now?"

"Don't be childish, '92. I did not cheat you; I was drafted without prior warning. But I promised to nominate you then, and I am willing to stand by my promise now."

"You have the seat in your gift, don't you? You have the Seventy eating out of your hand."

"Probably, but it won't last long. I suspect that they'll give me a chance to bring an ally on board to keep me company, just this once. Soon there'll be a new leader to follow over the cliff."

"Two baby Sevens at the same time? The old guard will—"

"The old guard will not dare provoke an open split between the old and the young, because then their power will inevitably start to dwindle. I can deliver enough votes. Do I ask my clients to cast them for you or Dilivost 678?"

Ledacos looked as if he had just bitten into a maggoty samosa. He must know, as she did, that a candidate rejected three times would almost certainly never succeed. This was his last and only chance to make the inner circle.

"All right. Yes, I want to wear purple, even if I must accept it as Irona's gift. Now can we celebrate our reconciliation by going to bed together?"

"No. I find hairy men too ticklish."

He left without a word of thanks.

She hoped that Vly would have approved. She would give Ledacos his heart's desire and make it worthless to him, because it had been a gift from her.

Days like that one seemed never-ending. More and more Irona found she was counting the hours until she could go to sit for Veer Machin.

His father was senior designer in the Republic's shipyards. Not surprisingly, his paternal grandfather had been a Chosen. Veer was the Vlyplatin Lavice story one generation on, son of a child who had been educated with the gentry but left without inheritance. Irona probed gently: unmarried, no children, casual affairs that never lasted long. He owned a slave, he explained, who boarded with a family downstairs, brought up meals for him, and kept his room tidy. Irona did not ask the slave's gender.

Veer was incredibly clumsy. Anything that could fall over would do so as soon as he entered the room. He was, Irona decided, so intent on looking at the world that he became a disembodied point of view.

It was easy for a Seven to learn that Machin was probably the only portraitist in the Empire who could earn more than an artisan's meager wages. Now he had caught the attention and patronage of the First himself, but he still wasn't rich, and probably never would be. He seemed to want little more than his art. Music, perhaps. He spoke lovingly of music, of the temple choir and the rare free concerts he could attend. The really worthwhile performances were privately sponsored, admittance by invitation only.

Irona also enjoyed music, when she could find the time. So the seed was sown. By showing favor to Nis Poul Dvure, she had created a problem. Now other rich families were clamoring for her attention, but she no longer had Vly to be the escort that social convention required. She could buy herself a male animal, like Trodelat's Jamarko, but the prospect sickened her. She could pick up some cultivated idle rich boy, but his relatives would swarm on her like ants, wanting preferment. So why not Veer? His manners were passable, and he had his own career, which she could neither make nor break. Recommending his art was not going to cheat the Republic of anything, not like granting building contracts to a gigolo's cousins.

"The king of Genodesa's personal orchestra is in the city," she remarked.

"I wish," Veer muttered, with his nose very close to his spatula.

"I'm invited to a concert at the Castovets," she said. "But I have no one to escort me."

Pause . . . Then Veer's left eye scowled around the edge of the panel on the easel. "Is that an offer or an order?"

"Which do you want?"

"Either. But what happens when some grande dame asks, 'And what do you *do*, citizen?' What then?"

"Say you're an artist."

"Why not say I'm a drain cleaner?"

"Wouldn't be true." Irona knew she was grinning and didn't care. "Besides, I'm looking forward to her reaction just as much as you are. Tomorrow evening? I'll send a chair to pick you up. Sevens get the best seats in the house."

His behavior at the concert was very close to perfect. He did knock over one statue but managed to catch it before it hit the floor. His lack of jewelry was understandable when Irona wore none.

When she arrived at his yard two days later, he let her see what his second attempt had produced. It was complete, all smooth and perfect. It was breathtaking. Her chin was raised, her lips tight together, so the lioness was not truly roaring, but the glare in her eyes ought to have melted the wax right off the wood—there were hints of flame in the background. Her neckline was far lower than she ever wore it, which showed up the jade collar, and Caprice herself could not have seemed more terrifying.

It would dominate the entire Treaty Hall, now and forever.

Irona stared for a long time, and finally whispered, "It's . . . it's incredible! I really look like that?"

"Sometimes. I could paint you as a mother, talking of your child. Or just a very beautiful woman, laughing. Or a seductress to drive men out of their minds."

She was aware that he was standing very close. He had performed a miracle for her, and sunlight sprinkled his big arms with gold dust.

"I don't think I have that much bosom."

"Yes, you do. What I would really like to do is to paint you in the nude."

"Go ahead," she said. "I'll be interested to see what you've got."

He held her gaze for one beat to make sure he understood. Then he grabbed his smock with both hands and hauled it off over his head.

"Couldn't ask for more," she said. "I assume you have a bed where I can pose?"

He ran to open the door to the shed. The slave's work showed, for it was not the pigpen she had feared, but clean, tidy, simply furnished, and decorated in excellent taste. Thick stone walls had kept it comparatively cool. The bed was narrow for two, but that was not going to matter. She shed her tunic and sandals.

"How do you want me?"

His face was flushed scarlet, but he was grinning. "I prefer to be on top, but you decide." He wrapped those big furry arms around her and kissed her. By the end of that kiss, they were both on the bed and he was on top.

It had been a long time for her, but she hadn't forgotten how.

"I needed that very much," she murmured eventually. "In fact, I need it often. I can offer you a studio in my house." She pushed herself up on one elbow to look down on him. "Or build one on the grounds."

"Wouldn't work. I go crazy if anything keeps me from my work."

"And I could not tolerate a consort who kept trying to use my power to do favors for his friends and relatives. But you have your own career and I have mine. I offer you a home, a workplace, and the best food I can buy. My only claim on you would be that you do what you have just done frequently, and sometimes escort me to concerts, balls, temple services. We can set a limit on how many evenings I claim.

"I'm not asking for a gigolo," she added, suddenly worried. "It would be a partnership of equals."

He nodded, still doubtful. "I'd hold you to that. I won't be made to feel like a servant."

"You feel like a great hunk of man," she said. "And if we're equal partners, it must be my turn on top."

Late in the fall, when Irona had caught up with her duties, she was able to deal with a few things she had been putting off. One of them required a private audience with the First.

Knipry received her in a private sitting room she had never seen before. A fire crackled on the hearth although the sun shone in the windows and the air was not especially chill. His appearance shocked her, for he seemed to have shrunk in the three days since she had last seen him. His face was pasty, his collar hung loose on his neck. He noticed her reaction and smiled without comment.

The Benesh were fatalistic about death and generally spoke of it as the ebb tide, because they gave their dead to the sea. Some poets sang that the tide would return them in another incarnation, others that it would bear them to a better land. The bulk of the people just seemed to trust their goddess to do whatever was best for them.

"Purple suits you, my dear. Sit, sit!"

"Thank you, but what I want to show you, Your Reverence, would be seen best on a table."

"Well, I haven't quite washed away yet," he said, and heaved himself out of his chair. It was clearly an effort, though, and he kept a hand on her shoulder as he shuffled across to the table. A Chosen's life, supported for many years by Source Water, ebbed in a riptide.

A servant entered with the bowl Irona had requested, followed by another with the jug of water. They put the bowl on the table and filled it, and then they departed. Knipry watched with interest.

"I am intrigued," he murmured. "Party tricks? Proceed!"

"When I went to Udice," Irona said, "in the dead of winter, some of our little boats were scattered by the wind. That happens, but almost all of them turned up safe in the end. When I was coming back from Vult in one of the navy's best galleys, we spent four days on a beach and almost starved. Because of fog."

He waited, smiling at her recital.

"My father was a sea hunter. Sea hunters and fishermen know a secret that the navy does not."

"Indeed? I assume you have convincing evidence?"

"Watch!"

She produced the crude little wooden boat that she had made. Veer had tried to help her and inevitably had cut his finger. She laid the model on the water and it slowly turned through a right angle. She turned it back again. It repeated its trick.

Knipry was showing his teeth in a grimace of fear. "A fix!"

"No, Reverence! This does not come from Vult or the Dread Lands. There is a little island called Kadowan, west of Vyada Kun. The fishermen pick up black pebbles there. They call them 'mating rocks' and they play some odd tricks, but a black stone is just a black stone, like copper ore, nothing to do with Maleficence."

She had brought along a few pieces to let Knipry play with, but his reaction was not what she had expected.

"It's a fix! Maleficence!"

"Your Reverence, the sea hunters use it in boats! Fixes won't work over water."

"Ha! Prove that. I never believed that and I don't believe it now. Get rid of the horrible—" His voice broke off in a spasm of coughing.

"It does good!" she protested, feebly. "It saves hundreds of lives. Every sea hunter and I suppose every fishing boat, carries one of these little floats with a scrap of the black rock inside it, and it always points to the north! That is how they can find their way in the dead of winter, when they cannot see the sun or stars."

"Put it away!"

"But the navy needs—"

"No! No! No! Put it away. Show that around Benign and they will send you to the sea death, Chosen or not. Even a Seven!" Then he fell to coughing horribly.

If Knipry 640 could not believe, then there was no hope. The men whose lives were at stake might feel otherwise, but it was people like Knipry who made decisions for the fleet.

That was the last time she saw him.

She had never wept in public before, but the wind was sharp and would have put tears in her eyes on any occasion. Grief did the rest. Knipry had been more than a patron to her. At her first assembly, he had given her a breakwater for Brackish. He had promoted her career more than Trodelat or Ledacos had. He had recognized the hand of the goddess upon her.

In the mouth of the bay, centered in Main Channel, the state barge rocked and tugged impatiently at the anchor cable slung over its stern. The motion was clumsy and made Irona queasy. Waves slapped at it, and another rainsquall was sweeping in around the Mountain across the bay. All the Chosen were aboard, paying their last respects, and dozens of other craft had braved the weather to join in the farewell.

The ebbing tide had turned the barge to face seaward, eastward, so the time had come. Rasny 650, the most senior Seven, and likely to be the next First, gave the captain the signal. Drums and trumpets struck up a slow march as marines lowered the coffin over the bow, then tossed the cords in after it. It floated, but Irona knew, as few people did, that it was designed so that it would sink in an hour or so.

The current drew it seaward, rocking gently in the lead-gray waters, bearing Knipry out to sea for the last time, to the waiting arms of his goddess. When it was out of sight, the crew raised the anchors, dipped oars, and the state barge headed back to the city.

THE YEAR 719

Irona did not, as Sazen had predicted, rule the Empire during her first term as a Seven, but she performed well enough to be reelected unopposed as soon as her one-year deferral was up. By then she was recognized as a leader within the inner circle. Running the Empire turned out to be child's play compared to running her child. Podakan did not improve with age except in the sense that he grew better at doing what he enjoyed doing.

Less than two weeks after she completed her third term as a Seven and could look forward to having a little spare time again, the various threads of her life suddenly came together and tied her in knots. Career, motherhood, love, and even the painful memories of her failure as a tutor all seemed to reach out to tangle her emotions.

"The court will come to order," announced First Rudakov.

Irona raised a hand. "As I was once the accused's tutor and may therefore be considered an interested party, I ask the court to recuse me from this case."

"This court considers such cases so rarely that we have no precedents to guide us," the First said, having been warned that Irona planned to raise the matter. "I ask guidance from the other learned judges."

One of the two Sevens required to sit on the board was Ledacos 692, wearing his sympathetic smile, of course. "It is my understanding that all the charges against the accused relate to the period after her tutelage ended, and therefore the point seems irrelevant. Was she ever our honorable friend's client?"

"Never." Irona sighed. No one had ever accepted Puchuldiza as a client.

"Then I think the decreed makeup of the court must be preserved," Ledacos said, keeping most of the snide out of his voice. "An odd number is vital in case of a split decision."

Four black disks appeared, so it was unanimous.

The First, two Sevens, and two other Chosen: Irona had just completed her third term as a Seven and was therefore a "Six." The other green tunic on the board enclosed the brawny form of Vakat 716, barely a year out of tutelage himself, a junior to balance all the elders.

"Request denied," the First announced. "The accused will rise. . . ."

The Treason Court convened rarely, most often in secret, and always in secret when the Chosen had to judge one of their own. In this case, the verdict was a foregone conclusion, and that evening it was read out by the First at a special meeting of the Seventy in the Assembly Hall. Irona had joined in the unanimous decision. She was present when the verdict was announced, sitting in the front row, which was her right as a Six, but that evening she placed herself at the extreme end.

First Rudakov's face bore an expression of extreme distaste as he rose to address the congregation.

"Pavouk 708 . . . Vakat 716 . . . step forward, please."

The men named had been forewarned and they looked as grim as First Rudakov as they advanced to the front.

"You have been appointed bailiffs to enforce the orders that the court issued in the name of the goddess. You will not fail."

They shook their heads in glum silence.

"Chosen 711, come forward."

Swinging her hips, Puchuldiza sashayed out from the shadows at the far side of the hall from Irona. It would be blasphemy to hint that Caprice had made a mistake when she chose 711, but the thought was very hard to shake. During her trial, Puchuldiza had dressed as a demure, wronged maiden, none of which she was. That evening, either because she still expected to be acquitted or just to show defiance, she was playing the tramp to absurdity, with her hair dyed scarlet, her face painted, and flashing half her weight in gold and gems.

Ledacos whispered, very softly, "At least she has the courage of her conviction." For once, Irona agreed with one of his sneers.

"Chosen Puchuldiza 711, on the First Count, namely that you have deliberately and on numerous occasions failed to perform duties assigned to you by way of absenting yourself from meetings and failing to prepare for meetings, the Court found you: Guilty.

"On the Second Count, namely that you have on numerous occasions appeared in public in an inebriated condition and have in diverse other ways failed to maintain a standard of conduct befitting a Chosen of the goddess, the Court found you: Guilty.

"On the Third Count, namely that you have sold or pawned property of the state, namely jewelry and other valuable items entrusted to you by the Property Commission for your personal use, the Court found you: Guilty.

"The Court therefore sentenced you, firstly, to forfeiture of all property presently entrusted to you other than a necessary minimum of clothing, secondly, to two years' exile on the island of Maasok, and thirdly, to the sea death if you fail to remain in that place until your sentence is completed. Sergeants, remove the prisoner."

Pavouk and Vakat moved in on her. She tried to back away from their menace, but Vakat seized her and held her as Pavouk methodically unpinned her finery, dropping it on the floor as if it were trash. When he took the jeweled combs from her hair and her coiffure collapsed, she began to scream.

By then Irona had risen and headed out of the Assembly Hall; the rest of the Chosen followed.

A chair scraped on the tiles in the dark, and a male voice made noises appropriate for a man who has just stubbed a toe. Irona rolled over on her back. She had grave doubts about that chair. How often could a man who remembered everything he ever saw down to the tiniest detail keep stubbing that long-suffering toe on that same chair every time he came home late and horny? But what he wanted was probably about what she needed.

"You're very late."

"Sorry to waken you." Having lied to her, he scrambled in to lie beside her. In the process, he managed to kick her leg and bang her breast with his elbow. Veer seemed to have no idea of how much space he occupied, and she adored him anyway. They argued sometimes, but never fought. She sometimes wondered how much longer she could have tolerated the unquestioning doggy loyalty of Vlyplatin Lavice.

"I wasn't asleep. Did you get the commission?"

Veer had been negotiating to paint murals for the temple. He had insisted that Irona not meddle, so she hadn't. Much.

"Eventually. Those baldies are crazy. Why are you still awake?"

"Had a bad day," she said. "What are you going to do about it?"

He wrapped thick arms around her. "In a moment. Tell me what's wrong."

A second Treason Court case in two days was part of it. A band of drunken juveniles had been caught shouting out seditious lies about the Chosen being tyrants. Standard practice was to flog their fathers. In a doomed quest for mercy, Irona had pointed out that their fathers were all marines and absent from home a lot, serving the goddess. The rest of the court had then voted to whip their mothers instead. Sometimes she thought that being governor of Maasok would be preferable to being a Chosen in Benign.

"Podakan has been beating up Kao Bukit again."

Veer sighed. "Kao is more than a year older."

"Pod is bigger."

"Why tell me? You're his mother."

But she was no more successful as Podakan's mother than she had been as a tutor for Puchuldiza 711. And it was not hard to imagine Podakan in a gang of blaspheming rebels within a very few years. He would probably be the ringleader.

"I want you to talk to him. You're his foster father."

"Not if you mean that I put the food on his plate. You do that and he knows it. He had you all to himself until you brought him to Benign and promptly disappeared from his life. Then I came on the scene and he has to share your love with me. I can't talk to him. He hates me."

"That's absurd! He doesn't even remember Vult. He doesn't hate you."

"He certainly doesn't listen to me, except to do the opposite. I should tell him to keep after Kao and batter the little shit every chance he gets. He might leave him alone then."

"That's ridiculous. Stop talking and do something. Give him a baby brother."

"Then he'd really get homicidal."

"Just do it."

The following morning Daun Bukit announced that he and Kanaga were moving to a home of their own, and of course taking their children with them. That was hardly surprising, but it was an inconvenience. Forced to admit that her son was practically running her household, Irona made an appointment to meet with the Heritage Committee.

Heritage was one of the most obscure arms of the government. Its members were appointed by the First instead of being elected and reported only to him; few Chosen outside the Sevens and Sixes even knew that the committee existed, because its sole function was to keep an eye on the next generation. The Chosen prided themselves on being incorruptible, but almost all of them had families, and pressure might be brought to bear on them through their children. *Evil seeks out your weakest point.*

It had been the Heritage Committee that had arranged for Podnelbi 681's son, Vlyplatin Lavice, to be articled to a lawyer in the city. It might well have arranged other employment for him when that fell through after his father's early death. Had Vly or his mother even known such a body existed, Ledacos might not have intervened and so brought Vly and Irona together.

The only current member of the committee, Irona discovered, was Azalka 660, who had arranged for her to lease Sebrat House so long ago. The old harpy had never made the inner circle and could barely conceal her delight at having a Six come calling on her in her poky office, nor her contempt for a mother who could not control a ten-year-old boy. She didn't say she had been expecting Irona, but she had probably heard tell of the hellion son and had certainly made Irona wait a few days for the privilege of a consultation.

Having accepted that she must seek help or at least advice, Irona was willing to bare all. "Just this morning," she said, "we discovered he had somehow broken into Veer's studio and trashed it. He had tipped out boxes of dye powder, so the floor was covered. He had ribbed gouges in completed paintings and smeared them with red ochre. He had even urinated on the mess. Veer estimated the damage, just to the paintings, must be six or seven hundred dolphins."

Azalka blinked at that news. "The boy admits it?"

"Of course not. He blames the slaves. But his footprints were on the floor and he had wax under his nails. In that sense, he was caught red handed *and* red footed. Now I am worried that someone may tell him about the latest Treason Court decision, in which case Podakan will start running through the streets shouting antigovernment slogans in order to get me flogged."

Worse even than that was the possibility that Pod, having managed to drive Kao and his parents away, would succeed in getting rid of Veer also.

Now Azalka looked more sympathetic. "I do see that you have a problem. Of course there are many tutors and schools . . ."

"I have tried them all," Irona said, and reeled off a dozen names. "The longest any of them stood him was three weeks."

"The boy was born in Vult, wasn't he?"

"Just what has that got to do with it? Are you suggesting that I send him back there?"

For a moment the old hag looked as if she might, but then she said, "Of course not. There are two other men who come to mind. Fagatele Fiucha has had some success with hard cases. You could see if he's available. He does not come cheap, because he acts as day-and-night jailer, never letting his charge out of his sight—chaining him to the bedpost at night, going to the privy together, and so on. Usually, a few weeks of that will bring them to their senses. Failing Fagatele, there is always Akhtang Korovin, but his methods . . ." She looked up in annoyance as the door opened unbidden.

One of the First's heralds bowed.

"Begging your pardon, Your Honors, but the Seven are in session and request that Irona 700 attend them."

"It never stops." Irona sighed. "Thank you, Azalka. I will follow up on your suggestions. Pray excuse me." Whatever problems that Sevens' meeting was going to pose, Irona was quite relieved to leave this one.

Two Sevens had left town, leading a punitive expedition against Genodesa, which had been skimping on its manpower levy again, so only six of the eight chairs were occupied as Irona was ushered in to the Sevens' room. First Rudakov motioned her to take one of the others. The mood, she saw right away, was grim.

"Welcome back, 700," he said. "I know you haven't been gone long enough to catch up on your grocery shopping, but it seems we have a job for you, as I am sure you have already guessed. What do you know about Achelone?"

"I can see its name written all over this table," she said, regarding the doodles on the slate. "Apart from that, nothing. I've never been that far inland."

"Achelone is farther from the sea than any of our other allies."

Irona nodded. An ally was a client state, and Benign's power depended on its navy. A Six was a tried and trusted, all-purpose emissary.

"We depend heavily on Achelone as our main supplier of timber," the First continued. "And now Achelone is having trouble with raiders from the deserts to the east of it. It claims they are not human and has appealed for our aid."

As it was entitled to do by the treaty, but at the moment the navy was not available. Irona did not point out that she had strongly opposed the Genodesan mission just before her term among the Seven ended.

"Which you can't supply."

"We can send Irona 700," Rudakov retorted, "who is mightier than a thousand marines. Navy?"

"Three galleys only," said Seven Ranau. "All we can spare at short notice. Small ones, I'm afraid, but they'll have less trouble in the river. Low water in summer."

Did they think she was Caprice herself, able to work miracles? "How many men does that mean?"

"Less than two hundred."

That was barely more than a personal bodyguard. Irona wondered if Ledacos had suggested her for this impossible job. On the surface he was her friend and colleague, but any debt he had owed her for his first election to the Seven had long ago been paid off and forgotten. Some day they would be rivals for the top office, and neither could ever forget that.

She even thought briefly of refusing. It seemed that all the threads of her life—her profession, her son, her lover, even her performance as a tutor and a judge—had become hopelessly knotted. She needed time to get them untangled, but if she let down the system by refusing, she might find herself shut out of the inner circle forever.

"They can't be ready before sunset," the First said, "so we'll run it by the Seventy tonight, and you can sail at dawn."

"And my commission?"

"Carte blanche. The report hints that these Gren, as they're called, may be open to peaceful trading. Promise them the world now and we'll hang their hides on the wall next year. In other words, do or say whatever it takes."

"You cannot," remarked Ledacos 692, "do much damage with less than two hundred men."

The others, all at least twenty years older than he, frowned at his unseemly levity. Irona smiled with a confidence she was very far from feeling.

"Just watch me," she said.

Irona left the room graciously enough, but she was practically running by the time she reached the stairs. Sazen Hostin was caring for his dying mother. Daun was moving house, and his wife was close to term with their third child. It looked as if she would have to make this journey without her usual support.

She stuck her head in the door of the Geographical Section. "I want to be briefed on Achelone in my office an hour before the Seventy meet."

The clerk on duty began to say they were ready for that now, but she was already gone.

Likewise at her own office. "Find a tutor called Fagatele Fiucha and have him come to Sebrat House right away. I am going home to pack, leaving town at dawn."

At home, she found Veer Machin morosely trying to clean up the shambles that one hateful child had made of his studio. It had never been tidy since the day he moved in, but disorder was a long way from deliberate devastation. Veer's emotions ran very deep, yet he never let them escape his control. A lesser man might have given way to rage and hurt; Veer would suppress those feelings until they emerged in a portrait. There was one such portrait prominently displayed on an easel in the center of the room now. Irona had never seen it before, but she knew it was no spur-of-the-moment creation; it must have taken many days of work.

The first thing she said was, "When did you make that?"

He shrugged his heavy shoulders. "About a year ago. After the dead-cat-in-the-bed incident."

It was an incredible three-quarter likeness of Podakan. The background was dark, inchoate, and menacing, but the brilliantly lit child in the foreground was more lifelike than any other artist could ever hope to achieve. The image almost seemed to lean out of the panel to her. It captured Pod's angelic good looks perfectly, but his smile was predatory, pure serpentine evil. His teeth were not portrayed as pointed, yet they were fangs. So that was how her lover saw her son? She had never seen him that way herself, or had never admitted to herself that she did.

"Didn't show you," Veer said. "Didn't think you'd like it."

"I hate it. But it's horribly, horribly true to life!" She tore her eyes away from it to explain why she had come home some hours earlier than usual. "I have to go out of town."

What she had been dreading since she learned that news herself was that Veer would say it didn't matter, because he was leaving too. He didn't.

"Sorry. How long?"

She could breathe easy again. "Six, eight weeks."

He pouted. "I may strangle . . ." He gestured at the portrait. "Before you get back."

"I'm going to take him with me. I can't trust him out of my sight now."

"Watch you don't strangle him yourself then." Veer dropped the spatula he had been holding and closed in on her. "I will miss you." Then he administered one of his all-consuming panacean embraces that banished all the troubles of the world except the hours to wait until bedtime.

Irona's next priority had to be the terror himself, who had been locked in his room all morning. He had been staring out through the bars on the window, but looked around as she entered, and she searched in vain for any sign of guilt or apprehension in his expression. He was big, more like a teenager than a ten-year-old. He stayed where he was while she went to sit on the bed.

"Well? Are you ready to tell Citizen Machin that you're sorry?"

"You always tell me not to tell lies."

"Why aren't you sorry for what you did?"

Pause. He was still young enough that she could see him considering whether to continue denying that he'd done the damage. But he said, "'Cos I don't like him."

"Why? He's a very kind, clever man. He would be your friend if you would let him."

"He hates me."

"Not surprising, considering how you treat him. He'll be in charge of the house for the next eight or nine weeks. I'm going away to the mainland."

That did produce a hint of alarm. He was old enough to know that she was his only defender. "Why?"

"To try to stop a war."

"Why can't I come with you?"

"Because I can't trust you to do as you're told."

"I promise I'll behave."

"You've told me that a hundred times before."

"But this time I really mean it." He probably did—just then.

She pretended to think about it. "I'd have to find a grown-up to look after you. Would you do what he says, always?"

Podakan solemnly nodded.

"I don't want a nod. I want a promise."

"I promise."

"Promise what?"

"I promise to behave and do as I'm told while we're away."

Fair enough. "I'm hoping to hire a new tutor for you. His name is Fagatele Fiucha. If he can't come, then I'll take Tidore."

A former bosun, Tidore was her chief house guard and slave master, and Podakan probably hated him more than anyone. He snarled, but didn't withdraw his promise.

"Where to, Y'r Honor?" the commodore asked.

The query was a formality, because he knew perfectly well where *Scamper* was heading as the crew swept oar blades through the surface of a mirror-smooth bay. What he meant was that the little flotilla had now officially left port and was Irona's to command. The sun was barely up, dazzling bright in the northeast.

"Sodore and Achelone, Commodore, if you please."

The commodore was Irona's old colleague, Mandalagan Furnas, who had been with her at Vult and on the voyage home. He was one of Benign's senior military men now, and the fact that his left arm was in a sling explained why he had been available for this makeshift expedition, instead of away up north, helping to loot Genodesa. His misfortune, her good luck.

Beside them on the steersman's deck were the steersman himself, plus Podakan and Fagatele Fiucha, who was a thin, balding man, with a disagreeably smarmy manner. Irona had taken a dislike to him on sight and was quite sure that Podakan had too, but the tutor came with good references and had assured her that he could straighten out "the lad" in a matter of weeks. She had been desperate enough to agree to his outrageous fees.

He and Podakan were currently attached, wrist to wrist, by a length of silver chain. Fiucha had explained that he was a strong swimmer and would make sure "the lad" did not drown if he fell overboard. Irona was fairly certain that Podakan would be able to pull his handcuff off whenever he wanted, because it had been intended for much larger troublemakers than he, although no larger troublemaker could make any larger trouble than her dear little boy could. If Fiucha kept referring to him as "the lad," he might find that out sooner rather than later. At the moment, though, Pod was totally entranced by being on a galley and watching the bare-chested rowers at work.

And she was already starting to relax with a long voyage ahead of her and no responsibilities other than keeping a careful eye on Podakan, which she had to do all the time anyway and would until he legally came of age in 725, Caprice preserve us!

"You appear to have started the war early, Commodore?"

"Broken collarbone, Y'r Honor," Furnas said with much disgust.

"What happened to the other guy?"

"Nothing—yet. We were loading to ship out on *Sea Eagle* at dawn and a couple of men bringing a bundle of oars misjudged a turn and knocked me off the dock. Hit the deck. Just a silly accident."

Irona had served on enough judicial benches to know hornswoggle when she heard it.

"And what will happen to those men when you meet them the next time?"

"One of them's going to lose half his teeth and the other a knee-cap, ma'am."

"*Really?*" Podakan had turned to stare up at the commodore with a glow of hero worship in his eyes.

"Really. You got ears in the back of your head, boy."

Podakan felt the back of his head with his free hand. "Have not!" he said indignantly.

The sea stayed as smooth as glass for them, ideal water for galleys, whose rowers had trouble with even a low swell. Podakan behaved better than Irona had known him to since he got his first two teeth and learned to bite her breast. She wondered how long he could keep it up and knew it could not be very long.

Neither Purace nor Severny, the two largest cities on their route, had anything new to add to the stories of lizard men raiding in Achelone. Sodore, though, at the mouth of the Huequi River, had been invaded by scores of refugees, who spoke of the Gren as monsters that couldn't be killed and ate human flesh. The holiday mood vanished. The flotilla lingered a few days there, partly because even Benesh marines needed a rest once in a while, and partly to prepare for the journey upriver. Two hundred men would eat whole shiploads of food in the ten days or so to Achelone, and the fleeing human locusts would have stripped the countryside. Fortunately, the galleys would not need to carry water on a river, and there was a salmon migration under way, so Commodore Furnas had bought fishing nets. The banks of the Huequi were well stocked with driftwood for campfires.

It was a dangerous road for shipping, though, because Achelone's great export was timber, and the logs were floated downstream. They were supposed to be chained together in rafts and marked by flags, but there were always strays. Galleys' bows were reinforced for ramming, so they were in less danger than other craft, but a large log fouling a bank of oars could injure half the crew. Furnas put the flotilla in line ahead and insisted that Irona not travel in the lead ship.

She spent her time studying the bagful of record tablets she had been given by the Geographical Section. On other missions she had been able to rely on Sazen Hostin to brief her, but she could almost hear his dry, sly tones in the words, as if he had written what she was reading.

Achelone was a fairly poor province, bounded by the Rampart Range to the north and the unexplored wasteland of Grensdalur to the east. The lowlands supported large cattle ranches and the foothills provided timber, which was cut by the same slaves who provided the muscle power to haul the logs to the rivers for transport. A few Achelonians were very rich, and everyone else very poor. With much of the Empire now deforested, the colony was vital as Benign's principal source of lumber and also an important provider of leather. The Gren, whoever or whatever they were, must not be allowed to interfere with trade.

Achelone was officially a republic, but in practice a tyranny run by, and for the personal benefit of, the longtime vice president, Sakar Semeru, who was propped up by Benesh arms. Reading behind the words, Irona gathered that he was about as unsavory a character as the Empire possessed. She had been part of the inner circle for years, so why had she never learned that imperial troops were being used to support such a horror? Because, perhaps, none of the Seventy had ever bothered to investigate: Achelone was a long way from the sea.

In theory, Semeru ought to be kept in line by the Benesh representative, but the Seventy never wasted anyone with real ability on such a posting; and the current representative, Ambassador Golovnin, sounded fairly typical. In practice, nobody would ever squander Benesh lives to support a revolution that could do very little to better the lot of serfs and slaves in what was very much a foreign land. Now the problems had all been dumped on Irona 700.

Just keep the timber and leather coming, darling.

Refugees were still trudging tediously along the dusty trail that flanked the river, or coming dangerously downstream on rafts or in cockleshells. Each evening, when the flotilla made camp, Irona had a few of these wretches rounded up so she could buy their evidence with a good meal. None of them convincingly claimed to have seen Gren with their own eyes, but almost all the stories agreed: the raiders weren't human and couldn't be killed. No one could tell her how far east the Rampart Range extended, but she was seriously wondering if the Shapeless had found another way out of the Dread Lands. If that idea had been suggested in Benign, it would explain why she had been selected to investigate: she was the Empire's expert in dealing with Maleficence. Her term at Vult had been a curse she would never shake off.

She wished now that she had not brought her son with her. If Maleficence was roaming Achelone, he would know her and seek revenge. None of the human participants in this, whether Achelonian or Benesh, would see any advantage in killing the Empire's commissioner, but she discussed the problem with Furnas, and he agreed that she must be very careful.

The capital, Achelone City, was a dusty, dilapidated scattering of shacks set on a baking hot plain for no evident reason except that two rivers met there. Several great palaces towered above the shanties like swans among pond scum, and the largest of all must belong to the current figurehead president. The second largest, and closest to the river, was flying the Benesh flag and could be presumed to be the ambassador's residence. Although *Scamper* was displaying a Chosen's standard, there was no sign of a guard of honor at the jetty. There was no sign of anything much happening anywhere. Granted it was noon, and stupefyingly hot, with a wind like a skinner's knife, but Irona was in no mood to make allowances.

"General," she said, giving Furnas his onshore title, "send forty men to that red building, and bring me Ambassador Golovnin." She did not add "dead or alive," but she was thinking it.

"Aye, Marshal!" He had a ferocious bare-knuckle fighter's gap-toothed leer.

Golovnin arrived at a run, bleary and unshaven, wearing a rumpled, sweat-stained tunic and, with his remaining tufts of white hair awry, generally looking as if he had been dragged out of bed, which he probably had. He was florid, corpulent, jowly, pompous, and stank of wine. Coming down the gangplank from the quay, he stumbled, and a marine caught him just before he fell flat on the gratings. Everyone from Podakan up was grinning by then.

Irona received him under an awning at the stern, having dismissed everyone else to what had to count as a respectful distance, but was certainly not out of earshot aboard a small galley. She read out her commission, which handily overrode his, but her jade collar alone did that. Then she invited him to sit down. He did, glowering at her resentfully.

"Report," she said. "Where are the Gren?"

"Last I heard, Your Honor, they were three days' walk from here. But they could be here in a half a day. They ride on the backs of these giant lizards of theirs, far faster than people can run."

"And what are they doing?"

"Think they're waiting for you, ma'am. . . . I mean, Your Honor. They were told that you're coming."

"So you can converse with them?" This was like skinning a live bull with your teeth.

Yes, he said, some of the Gren understood Benesh. He couldn't explain how they had learned it, since no one had ever heard of a Gren until this summer, when they came storming in from the Grensdalur desert. No, he did not know how far east the Ramparts extended. Yes, it was true that the Gren ate human flesh. They had been seen doing so, and leftovers had been found.

"What are they eating now?" she asked with distaste.

Cattle, he said. They were being provided with cattle.

And what do they look like? Tall, gray, scaly. No, not human. Swords just bounced off their hides. No one knew how to kill them. Golovnin did not say he had seen any with his own eyes, and Irona would have bet her collar that he had never been closer to them than he was now.

"You can provide accommodation in your palace for me?"

Her Honor would be most welcome in the Benesh embassy.

Her Honor was heartily sick of living on a galley and camping on seashores and riverbanks. "I shall require a suite of four rooms, close together. And inform Vice President Semeru that I shall expect him at sunset."

Um . . . protocol . . . invitation from the president . . .

"Arrange it," she snapped. "Expect me at the embassy within the hour. Dismissed."

If this wretch was the best the Empire could find to look after its interests, then the Empire was growing dangerously complacent.

Achelone "City" was almost as repellent as Vult, if not worse. There were serpents and scorpions on land, snakes and alligators in the river. The nights were hot and the days hotter, with a vicious wind. The palace was airless, although the accommodation provided for Irona was acceptable once it had been cleaned to her standards. She took Podakan and Fiucha with her and put them in the room next to hers. She used the other two to billet some of Furnas's men, who manned a checkpoint in the corridor. No one could approach her unbidden.

Fortunately her stay seemed likely to be short, although whether she would depart alive or dead was still to be determined. On the very first night, runners were sent to inform the Gren that the imperial commissioner had arrived. The Gren rode in the following evening—causing a panic in the town—and agreed to meet with her the next morning.

If the lizard men knew anything about acoustics, Irona decided, they would not have demanded that their leader's entrance be preceded by a fanfare of war horns. Or perhaps they did know and were deliberately trying to stun her. The cacophony seemed endless, echoes bouncing around the marble senate chamber like clouds of bats. The senators pulled faces and covered their ears. There were at least two hundred of them, an absurdly large number for a thinly populated land.

Mercifully the clamor died. The trumpeters marched out, their robes swirling around their ankles, and for a moment there was blessed silence. Irona had been given the throne, which she assumed was where the president—Sakar Semeru's current puppet and future scapegoat—normally sat. Semeru himself was humbly seated down on the front bench, among the lowliest senators. As he had nominated them all himself and arranged their elections, they could hardly object. Even Golovnin agreed in private that he was a revolting man to support, and that the Geographical Section's reports of his personal habits were more flattering than exaggerated.

A pair of Gren came striding in and took up positions on either side of the doorway. The agreed terms were that no weapons would be worn, but who knew what was hidden under those robes? Irona chuckled to herself, thinking how Veer would respond to that question. Goddess, but they were tall! And the trumpeters had been tall, too. Had their leader, reportedly named Hayklopevi, combed his tribe for giants, or were the lizard men all that size?

Or bigger. A group of three had halted just beyond the doorway, shadows against sunlight behind. The one in front was likely Hayklopevi himself, standing a head taller than the two behind him. He spoke to one of them, who came marching forward, stopping in the middle of the circular chamber. He might be even taller than Veer Machin.

"The noble Beru bids me say that he does not negotiate with women."

He? The Achelonians did not regard the Gren as human. To them, Hayklopevi was an *it* not a *he*. Irona was reserving judgment. She glanced down at the back of Sakar Semeru's head, for he had warned her that there would be endless quibbling and posturing. The vice president did not look around.

She said, "You may tell the Beru that he will not be negotiating with a woman, he will be negotiating with the Benesh Empire and its choice of negotiator is not negotiable."

The interpreter turned and stalked back to report.

And returned to the center again.

"The noble Beru bids me say that he does not negotiate with people sitting higher than himself."

"Tell him I will meet him on level ground if he promises to kneel, so that our eyes will be level."

The senators cackled like squirrels. The interpreter started to turn, then changed his mind—probably a wise decision. Judging by the atrocities attributed to him, the Beru had a very bizarre sense of humor.

"That is an insulting and ridiculous answer."

Irona was not going to play this game all day. She stood up, and the chamber seemed to hush, although it had been quiet before. She walked slowly down the stairway until she was on the second step, which put her eyes not much above the interpreter's, in so far as she could judge at that distance.

"This should make us about level. Tell him to approach now and talk, or go back to his desert and eat rats."

Hayklopevi took the bait. He emerged into the light, although very little of him was visible in the swirling gray robes. Long sleeves hid his hands, and his hood came forward to shadow his face. Two companions followed him, but even they could hardly match his stride. He slowed for a moment at the center but, as Irona had guessed, he could not resist coming all the way forward to the bottom of the steps, so that he could show how much higher his eyes were than hers. She now had the option of backing up a step, but then he might follow her as far as she wanted to go and make a mockery of the meeting. He was easily a cubit taller than Veer.

The face inside the cowl was gray hued, hairless, and inhumanly narrow, as if his head had been squeezed in a vise—or it was a normal human width and he had been stretched lengthwise. The nose was prominent, but as narrow as an ax blade, and his eyes were set deep in his skull. The irises were yellow, the pupils slitted, not human at all. The tips of his upper canine teeth showed over his lower lip, but were much closer together than they should be. The effect was very disturbing. She could almost believe the Achelonian claim that the Gren were hybrids of men and the giant lizards they rode.

But the sheer hatred in that face . . . If ever she must look into the face of Maleficence himself, it was now.

She forced herself to ignore that burning gaze. "I am Irona 700, of the Seventy chosen by our goddess to rule our city in her name, and I am plenipotentiary for the First and the Seven."

The interpreter translated into the Beru's lisping speech, then his reply.

"His Magnificence says, 'I am Hayklopevi, Beru of the Gren.'"

"Define *Beru.*"

"Warlord," the interpreter said, "speaker to the spirits, father, protector. All of these. He speaks for the Gren."

"And I for the Empire. Let us not waste words. Shall we speak here, or send for chairs?"

While that was being translated, the Beru folded his arms and she caught a brief glimpse of a gray hand with taloned fingers, but his sleeve covered it before she could count the fingers.

"I can stand as long as you can," the Beru said, and together they lapsed into the platitudes that began all such conferences: We seek only peace . . . You oppress/massacre our people . . . You started it . . . No, you did . . . Let us heal the wounds and bind in friendship . . . Trade is good, because partners do not fight.

And at last: What will you trade?

Fine rugs and dragon hides, the lizard man offered.

"I will send for merchants from the Empire who will examine your wares. If they think they will sell, then the traders of Achelone will transport them and all will benefit. And in return?"

Before the interpreter had even caught up, the giant spat words at him.

Translation: "Live cattle; swords and spears."

"We shall be happy to sell cattle," Irona said, "but the Empire does not trade weapons to any who may plan to use them against us."

A torrent of words from the Beru almost overwhelmed his interpreter. "His Nobility . . . He says your weapons are good against animals. We, the Gren, do not fear them. The Gren are strong. You are few and, um, feeble. He says we, that is the Gren, can take what we want and eat you instead of cattle. You taste better."

"Tell the Beru that he may see us as few here and now. Tell him that Achelone is a big land, but one grain of sand in the great river of the Empire. He counts his followers in hundreds. The Empire has thousands and hundreds of thousands. The Empire never loses. Any more killing and the Empire will come against him in numbers greater than he can imagine."

"He asks what these multitudes will do to us? Your weapons cannot harm us."

"We have other weapons that we have never needed to bring here." Now she was bluffing. A human opponent might be able to tell that, so she must just hope the lizard men did not read human faces well. If they were Shapeless, they might read minds. "The choice is yours: Will you have trade or war?"

"We will trade for weapons or kill you all and take yours."

"No swords. Spearheads. Knives no longer than my forearm." Shields could stop spears, and Irona had plans for the knives.

The Beru asked how many, so the dickering was about to begin.

"How many can you use?" she countered. "Tell the Beru that he must withdraw to the first oasis he attacked and we will send our samples there at the time of the new moon. . . ."

She had known negotiations to be more heated and last much longer. As soon as the meeting was over and the Gren had departed to prepare for a trading session in four weeks' time, Irona interrupted Vice President Sakar Semeru's congratulations to ask how many bronze workers there were in Achelone. It had been too much to expect that he would know, but by evening he had located six, to her surprise.

She ordered a hundred knives of the requisite length and three hundred spearheads, but with enough extra copper in the alloy to make them incapable of holding an edge for long. The spearheads would bend. The Seven had told her to postpone the problem until next year, and she could but hope that this would do it. She could see no permanent solution until some clever human discovered a way to kill Gren.

If war did break out between the impoverished desert nomads and the comparatively rich folk of the Empire, she knew who would win. It was a reliable maxim that those with nothing to lose would always beat those who had nothing to gain.

She ordered Furnas to prepare for an early departure in the morning. Then she went back to the embassy to comfort a boy who was bored to insanity because he wasn't allowed to do *anything*—not poke the scorpions with sticks, nor even go close enough to the river to throw stones at it, because there were snakes in the reeds.

Irona spent the hours until bedtime with Pod, playing board games, eating a lackluster meal, and describing the horrible Beru and his Gren. That part was more to his gruesome juvenile taste.

Eventually she saw him to bed and put Fagatele Fiucha back in charge of him. Then she went to her own room to pack her small personal bag and have an early night, her last chance to sleep in a bed until they reached Sodore. It wasn't much of a bed and would have been seriously cramped by the presence of Veer Machin in it—seriously cramped, but infinitely improved. She fell asleep gloating over the prospect of getting back to cohabitation in a few weeks.

She thought she had barely closed her eyes before she was awakened by screams and the crash of her door hitting the wall. Then Podakan was all over her, babbling and terrified. The corridor came alive with lantern light and guards' voices, which rapidly rose in alarm.

"Citizen Fiucha, Your . . . Oh, beg pardon. . . ." The guard hastily turned his back. "The citizen is taken sick, Your Honor. Convulsions."

"He's gone crazy," Podakan whimpered.

"I'll be right there," she said, extracting herself from Podakan's grip with difficulty. "Close the door! I have to go and see, Pod. You tell me while I get dressed."

"He started making funny noises, woke me. I asked what was wrong. . . . He didn't answer. . . ."

"Here, catch." She found a towel. "Wrap yourself in this, and we'll go and see."

His hand was icy and trembling as she led him back to his own room, which was now full of very worried marines. The tutor's face was almost black in the lantern light. His lips were everted and flecked with foam, and he was curled backward, twitching and choking.

"Send for a healer!" she said.

"Did that already, ma'am."

It was obvious that Fiucha was dying. The best thing Irona could do was get Podakan away before it happened.

"Give me that lantern. Keep me informed; I'll be in my room."

She took Pod back next door, to her room. "Now, you help me search in here."

His eyes looked huge in that chalky face. "What for?"

"Snakes? Scorpions. Anything that could be dangerous."

They peered under the bed, in the bed, behind the chest, everywhere, and found nothing. Because there was only one chair, she sat them both on the bed. Pod was still in shock, very far from the fractious, defiant rebel she knew best. When she put an arm around him, he actually cuddled close, as he had not done in years. Fagatele Fiucha had brought them closer, if not in the way intended.

"I expect Citizen Fiucha ate something bad in his supper tonight," she said.

Just for a moment, she thought that Podakan shook his head. He said, "Snakes and spiders could come in the window, couldn't they?"

"Perhaps spiders could, and we should have known to watch out for them. The bars are only to keep people out. I don't think snakes could climb up from the ground." But someone, or even some*thing*, could have arranged their arrival. If assassination had been the game, then the culprit had mistaken the window.

Or it might have been an accident. . . . "I thought," she said, "that Citizen Fiucha fastened your chain to the bed at night."

"I was so frightened that I pulled the bracelet off, Mom. It hurt, but I was too frightened to notice." Pod wriggled the fingers on his left hand. She couldn't see any scrapes or bruises—but the light was bad.

A knock on the door announced one of Ambassador Golovnin's aides, whose name she had never been told. She had gathered from chance remarks that the ambassador was not generally available after he had gone to—or been put to—bed.

The aide glanced at Podakan, then said, "Bad news, Your Honor."

She nodded to show her understanding, but she knew that Pod would have caught the message.

"It was a spider, Your Honor. The sort called a malice spinner. We do get them in the palace, but not often, and they very rarely bite people."

She felt Podakan shudder, which was not an unreasonable reaction, perhaps, when he had been sleeping in the next bed.

"I didn't know spiders could bite people," he whispered.

He had been the first to mention spiders, she recalled.

"Yes, they can," she said, wondering if he meant, *I didn't know spiders could bite people or I wouldn't have picked it up and put it in his bed.* After all, an admittedly spiteful ten-year-old might reasonably consider vermin in a bed to be a harmless and hilarious prank. How could an oath to behave oneself possibly last any longer than five or six weeks anyway? To a child that was half a lifetime.

Irona said, "Thank you, citizen. Please tell the guards that my son will be sleeping with me tonight."

She went back to bed, letting Podakan snuggle in beside her, under the covers. They lay like that for a long while, neither of them speaking, neither sleeping.

Had he put the spider in Fiucha's bed? She ought to ask him out-right—but what if he confessed? He had certainly wriggled out of his manacle after the attack; he could have done so before it. Seeing the spider, perhaps? Fiucha snoring, sound asleep . . . It was just the sort of nasty prank Pod enjoyed. He was just barely ten, an age at which he could be tried for murder. If he were, he would probably not be executed, because he could not have known that spiders bit people; Fiucha had been in charge of him and should have done a better job of controlling him. But he might still be found guilty and brutally punished. That wouldn't bring Fiucha back. If the boy was guilty, he knew it, and maybe, just maybe, he would be shocked into mending his ways?

A very cute rationalization, Your Honor. You wouldn't accept it from anyone else. You swore to obey the laws, remember?

No, she couldn't betray her son, Vly's son. She wasn't going to mention her suspicions to anyone. But, Irona vowed, when she got back to Benign, she would take her son up to the palace to witness some sessions of the Juvenile Court so he might start to understand the stakes in his chosen sport of raising hell.

THE YEAR 721

Nothing seemed to help. To Podakan, the defendants in Juvenile Court were merely losers, and thus beneath contempt. Irona took him to watch some public floggings. He enjoyed them. He found a public hanging hilarious, screaming with mirth as the dying man jerked and twisted on the end of his rope. Admittedly most of the other spectators were doing the same.

Akhtang Korovin was a large, ungainly man, with too-long gray hair and wrinkles set in a perpetual glower; a man accustomed to respect and instant obedience. It was not easy for him to be on his knees before a woman, but Irona left him there out of sheer fury.

"I chose your establishment, citizen," she said, "because you have a reputation for harsh methods and strict discipline. You assured me you had never met a boy you could not train. The word you used was 'break,' I believe."

"I am confessing to you now, ma'am, that I have met my match in your son."

"You let a mere child defeat you so easily?"

"I have tried everything I know! I beat him every day, because the other boys dare him to see how many strokes I will give him. It does no good. He smiles in triumph when I tell him to return to his seat, and he often goes right back to doing whatever I forbade him to do. If I ignore his rudeness and disobedience, he attacks one of the others. He smashes things. A few days ago I was beating him and he . . . defecated on the floor! He looks five or six years older than his age and behaves like a two-year-old."

"Are you saying he is stupid? Or insane?"

"Not stupid! Never that, ma'am. Yesterday I set the boys an assignment to memorize ten lines of the *Apremiad*. I have learned not to call on Podakan to recite, but today he jumped up when I would have passed over him and rattled off not just the ten lines I had set but twenty, or thirty. . . . I had to shout at him to get him to stop. I don't know how long he would have gone on. And of course the rest of the class was screaming with laughter . . ."

With a big effort, Irona managed to keep a straight face at that story. Obviously the battle was no longer to educate Podakan but to keep Podakan from making the teacher look a goat in front of the class.

And Podakan was making her look a fool, too. He would certainly know that his tutor had come calling on her and would guess why. Not funny, tragic.

"I am sorry," she said. "I accept that you have tried. And you were my last resort. Tell me, what else can I try?"

"Ma'am, I would not presume—"

"Do presume! I will not take offense. What would you do with him if he were your son?"

The teacher winced at the thought and shook his head.

"Please? Any ideas at all?"

Very reluctantly, the old man said, "Only the last resort."

"Meaning?"

"Apply to the courts to have him declared incorrigible."

"And sold into slavery?"

"You did ask me, ma'am."

The following day, Irona took Podakan down to the slave market to watch the pathetic wares in their chains. That sobered him up for a couple of months. Then he started randomly beating her own slaves, who dared not even defend themselves. If he was like this at twelve, how would he be at fifteen?

Putting her political mind to the problem, she devised a possible compromise. She had the petition to the court drawn up and called in a notary to explain it to Podakan. Still not certain whether she was about to sign it or not, she had to go as far as to ink her seal and poise it over the tablet before he cracked and fell on his knees.

"No!" he screamed. "I'll behave!"

"You've promised me that before, hundreds of times."

He looked up at her with his father's eyes, flooding tears.

"Dam," he whimpered. "*I can't help it!*"

Which was what she had already concluded. "And I can't put up with it. So what else can I do with you?"

"Make me a slave just sometimes?"

So it was agreed. After each outbreak of spite, vandalism, or cruelty, Podakan would be turned over to Tidore, to dig, weed, saw wood, scrub floors, clean out latrines, sleep on straw, eat slave food. Only when Tidore testified that he was doing everything required of him and Irona was satisfied that he had been punished enough would Podakan be released. He accepted that arrangement. Often he would come straight to Irona and confess his sins in a voice that soon became astonishingly like his father's.

THE YEAR 724

The Gren, it seemed, had disappeared. Nothing had been heard of them for almost five years.

On the last day of 723, First Rudakov 670 sent for Seven Irona. She was not surprised, because rumors had been circulating all day, and there wasn't a rumor in the world that Sazen Hostin hadn't either heard or started. What she had not expected was to be shown into the cozy, intimate room where she had tried to convince First Knipry that the mating rocks of Kadowan were not fixes, on her last meeting with him. Rudakov used it as his personal office, and there was no one else present.

He smiled wearily when she entered and gestured to the chair on the opposite side of his table, which was piled high with report tablets. He looked worried and bowed. Of the four Firsts she had known, Rudakov was the least impressive, and not improving as the years mounted.

Formalities first, of course. . . .

"Glad you could come, 700," he said. "I expect you were just about to go home and prepare for the festivities."

"Not yet, Your Reverence. What can I do for you?"

"Bad news, I'm afraid. The Gren are back."

Sazen had told her so just before noon. She was the expert on Gren, so why had she not been sent for sooner? Why had the Seven not been called into emergency session?

"Trading or raiding?"

"Raiding," he said. According to Sazen, it was more like an invasion in force. "Reports read a bit hysterical, probably exaggerated."

"They haven't told anyone what they've been doing for the last five years, have they?"

The Gren had traded some hideous rugs and rotting hides for Irona's flexible weapons, and then just vanished back into the desert. Since then, the only sign that anything lived out there had been a negative one: an army exploratory expedition, which Irona had recommended and the Seventy approved, had vanished without trace. So had a second, sent to find the first.

"Breeding lizard children on lizard women, from the sound of it." The First sighed. "And now they are all full-grown already? I told you it sounded fishy."

"We knew it was only a matter of time."

"You did. You warned us. Some of us kept our fingers in our ears. I don't doubt for a moment that both the Seven and the Seventy will want you to lead the response, 700. I'm calling an emergency meeting of the Seven for Day Two. I thought you should be forewarned so you could have some recommendations in mind."

If Irona were wearing the crimson instead of him, the Seven would have met hours ago, the entire government staff would have been told to cancel their holiday plans, and everyone would have begun working day and night to mobilize the entire Empire. She said, "Thank you, Your Reverence. Thoughtful of you."

Irona was not at all surprised that bad news about the Empire was soon followed by bad news about Podakan, news bad enough to ruin the Midsummer Festival for her.

Day Two was likely to be worse. It began soon after sunrise with Irona and Veer sharing a very glum breakfast.

"Let's get it over with," she said.

"He won't be awake for hours."

"If I say so, he will be."

Veer sighed and got up, knocking over his chair. He pulled the bell rope beside the fireplace and managed to resume his place at the table without further accidents. In a moment, the door was opened by Tiatia, one of the house slaves. She was barely more than a child, and yet she looked as if she felt the bony hands of death around her throat already. In fact she must be suffering from a severe hangover and near-mortal terror. She flopped down on her knees.

"About last night," Irona said. "If I ever find you in bed with a man again you will go to the slave market with no reserve price. Understand?"

"Oh, yes, ma'am, and thank you, ma'am, it won't ever—"

"Now tell our son to come here at once. If he won't wake up, warn him I will send the porters with buckets of well water."

Greatly relieved that nothing terrible was going to happen to her soon, Tiatia scrambled up and fled.

Our son. Irona did not look at Veer. She knew how much he disliked being classed as Podakan's father. He admitted to hating Podakan, and there were times when she almost did so herself. This was one of them. Vly's child would have broken his heart.

"How can you prevent it happening again?" Veer asked. "If she won't consent, he'll rape her."

"As far as I'm concerned he already has. And he won't, because he isn't going to be here."

Veer guessed at once what she had in mind. "Is that wise?"

"He's going to be the Empire's secret weapon." Irona wasn't sure how much she was joking.

Without a knock, the door flew open and in walked the problem, with one hand behind his back. Newly turned fifteen,

Podakan Lavice was already taller than most grown men, although not quite a match for Veer yet. His oversized hands and feet suggested that he still had more growing to do, quite apart from filling out his adolescent lankness with bulk. He took after his grandfather, Akanagure Matrinko, having inherited much of his brutishness as well as his size. He was barefoot, clad only in yesterday's stained smock, and his hair looked like kelp on a rock. Long hair was the style now, so his had to be longer than anyone's. His eyes were scarlet and his head must be pounding, but he made an effort to look cheerful.

"Greetings, Dam. And you, Machin. Lovely morning."

Irona pointed at the floor in front of her.

He shrugged, walked over, and knelt. Then he produced the bucket he had brought and set it between them. At least it hadn't been used yet.

"Just in case," he said. "Where do you get that awful wine, Machin?"

"Last night you abused one of my slaves," Irona said.

"Not abused, Dam. She loves it."

"So that she can bear a freeborn child, which you will have to raise?"

He shrugged, but the smile had gone. "We're still only kids. No problem yet."

"Do you believe that or is it just what you tell her?"

He shrugged again. As long as the girl believed it, he could get what he wanted, so what else mattered?

"You remember our agreement?"

"Agreement, my ass. You're going to sell your fifteen-year-old son into slavery for humping one of your slave girls?"

He was right, of course. No judge would agree.

"Oh, Podakan, we haven't had to paint the slave mark on your shoulder for months. I was really hoping that you had started to behave like an adult."

"That's exactly what I was doing last night. It's fun!" He glanced at Veer as he said that. He didn't need to mention that Veer had failed to father any children with Irona in more than a dozen years.

"Silence! She is my slave and I will decide who sleeps with her, if anyone. I am going to have you stripped and tied up in the courtyard, and have Tidore give you five strokes of a rod on your buttocks, with the entire household watching. I'm sure he won't hold back."

Podakan didn't speak, but his irises slid up until white showed under them, so he looked blind. She knew it as a sign of suppressed rage and thought of it as his killer look. Given the chance, he would now go away to smash something or hurt someone.

"Irona," Veer said, "I think you'd better leave his tunic on. He's one of those twisted people who enjoy pain. You exhibit him naked and he's likely to display an erection, just to embarrass you."

"Blabbermouth!" Podakan said. "I was saving that as a treat for her, fat man."

"Thanks, Veer," Irona said. "Earlier yesterday, Podakan, where were you?"

He blinked a few times until his eyes returned to normal. "It was Festival, remember? Down in the Old City, celebrating with the guys. Who got chosen?"

"Some boy from the Old Town."

His mouth opened and then closed. He knew she was lying.

"Come to think of it," Irona said, "it was a girl, Apolima. Seems promising, I hear. Kao Bukit was there, of course. And his father."

Silence.

"Daun saw you, Podakan."

"Didn't see him. Saw Kao, though. He was a little slug five years ago. He's still a slug and not much bigger."

"Podakan, I have told you before that you are not eligible to go to the choosing, because you were not born in Benign. A year from now, I will—"

"—will certify to the priests that you're a citizen and I'm your little boy. Then I swear to obey the laws and it's done. I'll be a citizen, but I can't be a Chosen. I think I've got it now, Dam."

"But you went to the choosing anyway, when you're only fifteen. That is sacrilege! Do you know what would have—"

"Didn't!" the boy snapped. "Didn't try to go in that side. Liado's dad's off on the mainland; he'd no one to take him, so I said I'd go with him and pretend to be his uncle."

"No! Oh, Podakan, that's as bad, almost."

He smirked. "Didn't have to. The priests didn't even ask."

It was plausible. He certainly looked like an adult, if a baby-faced one, and there was no rule against a friend or older brother escorting a pilgrim.

"So you didn't break the law. That is good, Podakan Lavice, because do you know what I was planning to do? I was planning another ten strokes of that rod. That is absolutely nothing compared to what the court would give you, and brand you as well. So you escape that, but you still get the five. And you and I still have to get through one more year before I stop being legally responsible for your actions. Do you want to get me flogged?"

"You mean usually or just right now?"

"I'll add one more stroke for insolence. And we'd best get it over with now, because we'll be leaving in a few days."

"Going where?" he growled suspiciously.

"To Achelone. There's a war on, and I expect to be appointed admiral."

His face lit up, and he flexed the muscles in his arms. "Can I row this time?"

Two frantic days later, Irona embarked on her flagship, *Foam Racer*. For commodore she had recruited her old associate, Mandalagan Furnas. This was to be no token force of a couple of hundred marines. The Seventy had insisted on mobilizing the entire Empire against the Gren, although Irona had argued that there was no way Achelone could feed an army of tens of thousands. Her advice had been ignored in a panic of war fever. Now her only hope was to get there first and organize some sort of a reception for everyone else. If Caprice favored her, she might manage to defeat the invaders before the allies' forces arrived, so she could send them straight home again. The worm in the apple was that nobody had yet discovered how to kill Gren.

With her was Daun Bukit, still her trusted chief of staff. Sazen Hostin was traveling on another galley, but he would join her when they reached the front, and then it would be quite like old times. She had made sure there was room on *Foam Racer* for Podakan, who was a much bigger handful than he had been on her last trip to Achelone. She could count the days until she would wash her hands of him, although Caprice alone knew what would happen to him then.

He had gone on ahead, either childishly eager to watch the preparations or unwilling to trust his badly bruised buttocks in a sedan chair. She had given him a pass to enter the naval docks and found him down there, gaping around in glee at the bustle of marines and porters, chandlers and carpenters, and dozens more. Momentarily, he was a kid again.

But the first thing he said was, "I wanna row!"

As tactfully as she could, Irona said, "Rowers sit on sealskin cushions, dear. They slide back and forth with every stroke. I doubt if your backside is in good enough shape to do that all day."

"Pain never stops me, you know that. It's a test of manhood. I bought an oarsman's cushion. I wanna row!"

"I'm proud of your courage, but if you lose the stroke and tangle the others, you may injure other men as well as yourself." Seeing his stubborn look, she added. "Ask Commodore Furnas if you want. Just don't say I order it!" She foresaw no problem, because she had warned Furnas the previous day.

By the time she boarded, though, Podakan was proudly sitting on a rower's bench, surrounded by grown men no taller than he and parrying their lewd banter like a veteran. Somehow he had acquired the correct attire of leather shorts. Apart from a lack of hair on chin or chest, he didn't look at all out of place, and she felt an absurd knot of pride in her throat, as if she had created him the way Veer created a portrait. At times Podakan seemed to go from five years old to twenty-five and back again between breaths.

Commodore Furnas had trouble meeting Irona's eye. "You didn't tell me he'd be one of the biggest men aboard, ma'am."

"He's a child, Commodore. He can't row all day!"

"I've doubled him up with Sturge, there. He's a good hand, ma'am. He'll keep his arms folded until he sees trouble coming, then take over the oar. You ought to be proud of yon lad! Grown a lot since the last time we went to Achelone."

In some ways he had. He still had to learn that other people mattered.

She was more open with Daun as they stood on the steersman's deck waiting for something to happen. *Foam Racer* was at anchor. Furnas was being rowed around her, checking the trim. The hands were shifting stores as the bosun bellowed orders. No one was listening to the passengers.

"He didn't try to pass himself off as sixteen at the temple," she said. "He was waved in through the adult gate."

Daun said nothing, just stared at the man in question, heaving bales and barrels around with the crew, playing at being one of them. Marines had to accept discipline, and Irona could not imagine Pod ever doing that.

"You saw?" she asked.

"Didn't see that, ma'am."

Oh, Goddess! So Pod had not merely walked through the adult side, he had passed himself off as Benign born, lying about this age, pretended to be one of the pilgrims. She did not wonder which one was lying. She had trusted Daun since before Podakan was born.

"Did Kao see him there?"

"He hasn't mentioned it. I didn't ask."

"Thank you," she said. "I should know better by now than to take his word on anything." If Kao had seen, then the worm could bite back now; the childhood victim could report his former tormentor for perjury and sacrilege and watch Podakan go to the sea death, and Irona with him, likely. "I don't know where I went wrong with Podakan. I suppose I neglected my son to serve the goddess. His grandmother tried to fill the gap, but she died when he was still small, and the women I hired kept leaving. He drove them away."

"The damage probably happened before all that, ma'am."

"Meaning?"

"He was born at Vult."

"I can't blame Vult for all of it."

"That place destroyed some men faster than others." Daun pulled a face at the memories. "The worst of them just disappeared. I had a couple of friends who . . . withered. It didn't change you at all, ma'am, not so far as I could see."

"Nor you. That was the first thing I noticed about you, that you didn't have the dead look your companions did."

"I was determined to survive and come back to Kanaga. I think her love saved me."

"And I had my duty, and my child." Vly had succumbed faster than anyone, because Irona would not have had to endure the ordeal of Vulk had he not asked her for a child. His sense of guilt had driven him crazy.

"It was better after I got the trogs out," she said.

"It was better," Daun agreed.

But that had been too late to save Vly. Was a child of rape contaminated from conception? That seemed like a sleazy excuse for bad parenting.

"How long do you imagine he'll last rowing?"

"Until he's told to stop," Daun said confidently.

"But he hasn't got an oar puller's hands." She was more worried by the pain of the bruises she mustn't mention. That beating had been a terrible mistake, of course. Podakan had taken his punishment without a murmur—with his smock on—and had then had the nerve to tell her the sex had been worth it.

"But he won't stop. All respect, ma'am, he gets that from you. You never admit defeat, nor will he. Once, after he hurt Kao real bad, I took my belt to him. I knew I shouldn't, but I just couldn't stand it any longer. I hit him as often as I dared. He was only about five, but he didn't make a sound. Did he tell you about that?"

"No. I suppose he took it out on Kao later?"

Daun nodded glumly.

The commodore was coming aboard again. The bosun was ordering the men back to their benches.

"I may lie about his age myself," Irona said. "I'm not going to rest easy until he's been sworn in as a marine. Maybe the Republic can tame him better than I ever have."

The flagship upped anchor eventually. Oars dipped and swayed, oarlocks creaked. Irona watched Podakan work and sweat. His minder, Sturge, sat beside him, waiting to take over when he gave up, and no doubt expecting that to be soon. But Daun had predicted he would never stop, and Daun knew Pod well. Not for the first time, Irona wondered whether her son did not feel pain as other people did, or felt it and enjoyed it, as Veer believed. No other form of discipline worked any better on him.

One by one the other galleys followed in line—ten of them in all, almost two thousand men going to war. Her vice admiral, Dilivost 678, would bring up the rear. Dilivost was more than twenty years her senior and had more experience of action, although even he had not seen much real fighting, for the Empire had long been at peace. Age had not reduced his pomposity or increased his chin, but when his name was mentioned for the command, he had shown enough sense to refuse, claiming that he was too old. Unfortunately, he had not refused to serve as her deputy. He would not have been her choice. Dilivost was competent and hardworking, but seriously lacking in imagination—a good adjutant but a poor chief. If anything happened to Irona, anything might happen under Dilivost.

The bay was full of sailboats as people came to watch the fleet depart. Benign had not sent out such a force of its own troops in thirty years, and never under a woman's command. Others would join them before they reached Achelone: tribute forces, perhaps fifteen thousand in all. The Empire was going off to war again.

Execution Bridge on one hand, Brackish on the other, and ahead the long swell of the sea. *Foam Racer* was leaving the bay. Predictably, Commodore Furnas was standing close, watching the other ships line up before he formally asked for orders.

Irona smiled teasingly. "What does the wine shop scuttlebutt say about our objective?"

"Says we're going south, Y'r Honor, going after the Three Kingdoms. Teach them a lesson, pick up some loot and slaves."

If only it were that simple! Any marine who turned a slave over to the dealers in good condition was instantly rich. But who would want to buy a Gren?

"I'm happy to hear that for once they've got it wrong. Set course for Achelone, if you please, Commodore."

"Aye, aye, ma'am." He need do nothing more than hold his easterly course and let the rest of the ships follow. In an hour or so, he would veer to the northeast. But he glanced back at the great fleet still emerging from the bay and pursed his lips.

"Yes," Irona said, speaking softly so that the coxswain and steersman would not hear. "It's more than Gren raiding this time. It's a full-fledged invasion. The latest news was that Sakar Semeru was hung up by his heels and skinned alive. And that was before the enemy even got there."

"Ah!" said Mandalagan Furnas. "They do say there's a pearl in every oyster if you look long enough. Overnight at Shellong, ma'am?"

"I leave that to your judgment. I'll address the troops when we beach."

The galley was starting to pitch in the swell, which made the rowing harder. Sturge took a grip of the oar and said something to Podakan, who nodded impatiently. After a few strokes, he got the knack and Sturge left him on his own again.

At the first watering break, the commodore inspected his volunteer help and allowed him to continue. At the second rest, he took one look at Podakan's bloody hands and ordered him aft. The boy obeyed as meekly as any veteran marine, as he never did for his mother. She noticed that the rest of the crew didn't jeer him for quitting. They didn't cheer him either, but their silence sounded like respect.

Shellong was a rock barely worth the name of island, about a third of the way to the mainland, a convenient place for a ship to make its first landfall and scratch its first-day itches: find misplaced gear, grease squeaky oarlocks, caulk minor leaks, rearrange shifting cargo. Shellong lacked water or arable land, but it had a long shingle beach on the leeward side. There the fleet pulled up for the night to pitch camp. And there Irona made a speech.

She had done this many times now, and her initial terror had long since been overcome and forgotten. She stood on a rock with her back to the breeze, well away from the noisy waves. Her captains stood close around her with their bosuns behind them, looking over their shoulders. The rest of the two thousand jammed in tight, older men in front, youngsters with sharper ears on the outskirts.

"We sail for the Bight and the Huequi River. I hear your moans! But it is Midsummer and the current should not be too strong. And before the river is Sodore. Some of you were there with me before. Good food, I know, and good beer, and from the stories I heard of the girls, they were even better."

She waited for the cheering to end. "Achelone is an ally of Benign. They are friends of Benign, part of the Empire. One of us. We have never been at war with Achelone. It asked to join the Empire almost a hundred years ago and the Seventy voted to admit it."

She wondered how big the bribes had been, and if Sakar Semeru's great-grandfather had been as murderous as he.

"Those oars you pulled today came from Achelone. The planks of the ships you rowed today came from Achelone. The wood of the benches you sat on came from Achelone. Your homes are built of Achelonian timber. Achelonians are our friends and partners! A few years ago, they were attacked without warning. Attacked by the lizard men of Grensdalur, which is a desert land to the east. The Achelonian senate asked for imperial help. I was sent with a small force. I met with Hayklopevi, their warlord."

She paused a moment.

"The Gren are not human. Hayklopevi is not human! He—it—is taller than anyone here, its skin is gray, and it has six fingers on each hand. The Gren ride on the backs of lizards, and the Achelonians believe that they breed with them, too."

Irona did not say that their hides were sword-proof. Instead she told them of the atrocities: pregnant women disemboweled, babies impaled, men flayed, towns sacked, prisoners massacred. Those tales—and sometimes truths—were as much a part of warfare as blisters and belly fever. She also mentioned another possibility, a horror unique to the Gren, a liking for raw meat. Specifically there were tales of people being eaten alive by a dinner party of Gren, even babies snatched from their mothers' breasts and passed around as snacks.

"There was a garrison of Empire troops there. At least a hundred of them were native-born Benesh, like you. Your brothers. So far as we know, they are all dead now. The honor of Benign is at stake, and it is up to us to save it!"

At the end she swore retribution, and they cheered her. It was a good cheer, although she had known better. She turned to dismount from her rock and two oversized, bandaged hands gripped her and lifted her. She was about to explode at this disrespect when she realized they belonged to her son. He swung her down easily.

And then he grabbed her tight and hugged her. He had not done that since he was an infant.

"Great speech, Dam," he muttered. The lads had cheered his mother! Had he only just realized how special she was, or was he merely flattering her?

"Thank you. And a good hug. I enjoyed that more than the cheers."

Podakan spun around and walked away.

Later, when the meals had been eaten and tired rowers were spreading their bedrolls, she called the captains and bosuns to a conference around a fire. On land, these men would be her warriors. If she gave them a fair chance, they could win the war for her. If they lost, it would be her fault. She had Dilivost beside her, of course, plus Sazen, Daun, and a darkly suspicious Podakan. Overhead the stars were starting to appear.

She worked her way around the group, naming when she could, asking when she couldn't. She knew about a quarter of them, and they were pleased to be remembered.

"It's worse than I told the troops," she told them. "Five years ago, when the Gren first emerged from the desert, they said they wanted to trade. We had one exchange of goods and then they disappeared. This year they have come again, not in bands as before, but in hundreds. They have leveled villages, burned crops, wasted the land. Maleficence is back and we go to battle monsters, as our ancestors did."

She was asked how that could have happened.

"We don't know. We do not know the interior. Because our goddess rules the sea, not the land, we never venture there. What happens to the Rampart Range farther inland? It is possible that Maleficence bypassed the range on the east and found its way into Grensdalur."

"You mean the Gren were spawned in the Dread Lands?" asked a voice with a Brackish accent.

"It is possible. We must beat them and drive the survivors back where they came from, wherever that is. We must discuss tactics while we travel and study how our ancestors fought Maleficence." She might have some clues after Sazen finished working through the sacks of historical tablets he had brought along.

The questions died away. They all had hard days ahead, for most captains and bosuns rowed at least half watches on a long journey. She asked Dilivost if he wanted to speak and 678 loyally said she had said it all much better than he could have done.

"Then, finally," Irona said, "please note my son. Stand up, Podakan. This is Podakan Lavice, my son. Despite his size, he is not yet a citizen, so he will not be fighting. I hope you all understand that very clearly: Podakan will *not* be fighting! If you see him with a weapon, take it away from him instantly. He can row if he wants, although why he thinks he needs any more muscles than he already has, I can't imagine. I will employ him as a runner, so he will have to learn all your names. Excuse him if he comes up to you and asks you who you are."

She held her breath for a moment, wondering how he would react. Just as Veer could recall exactly what he saw, Podakan never seemed to forget what he heard. She did not doubt that he could already reel off all those twenty names correctly, all the way around the circle.

But he didn't. He just sat down. Perhaps he doubted that real men would be impressed by a party trick. Or perhaps he would rather do his own showing off than be spoon-fed by his mother.

Two nights later they beached at a small fishing village on the mainland and were met by even worse rumors of disaster. Achelone had been overrun, the survivors were streaming south and west, the Gren were heading south, toward Kasuga.

The mood of the fleet grew grimmer, but no one deserted yet. By the time it reached Purace, second-largest city in the Empire and guardian of the mouth of the Bight, Podakan was rowing a full day's watch—and eating as much as all the rest of the crew put together, according to the bosun.

At Purace the expedition was due to be reinforced by eight more galleys. The governor passed along the locals' excuses for not being ready yet. Irona told him not to worry, she wasn't leaving until dawn, so they had plenty of time to get organized. And if the full levy of eight ships and seven hundred men was not ready by then, the governor and all his council were going to be going along to feed the Gren.

Some other allied contingents ought to have reached Purace already, but none had. Irona did not wait for them. She anchored offshore that night and made the crews stay aboard, but half a dozen good swimmers disappeared into the dark. At Purace she spoke with Achelonian refugees, who talked of monsters—deadly, but never clearly seen. The Gren fought only at night. That report agreed with the descriptions of the Shapeless on the cracked and faded wooden tablets Sazen had found in the Benesh archives.

"So we'd better beat them while the days are long," Dilivost said.

As they headed deeper into the Bight, the mood began to change. The locals feared for their own survival now and were ready to join in the fight. Finding themselves hailed as saviors, the Benesh began to brag. More and more tales of atrocities turned the mission into a cause, a path to glory, history in the making. The fleet grew, as did the difficulty of feeding it, until Irona had to divide it into squadrons, traveling a day apart.

There seemed little doubt that Achelone was past saving and the Gren had moved south, into Kasuga. Rowing up the Huequi

River would be pointless, for it would put her behind them, and she could not hope to match their speed overland. At all costs Irona must position her army ahead of them, so they would come to her. At the great fork in the Bight, she turned southward and set course for the Visoke, leaving word for the other contingents to follow.

The Visoke was a fast stream, a test of the men's endurance, but armies had gone that way in the past. At times the channel was so narrow or swift that the crew had to ship oars and haul the galleys along with ropes, even in some places wading alongside and pushing. Twice they had to strip the vessels down to empty hulls, manhandle them over shoals with levers and brute strength, then reload them again on the upstream side. Podakan never questioned an order and worked till he dropped. At long last she began to see a future for him; for the first time she could even respect him.

One evening she told him so.

"Then stop smothering me," he said, and walked away.

When they reached Didicas, their voyage was over. They had been traveling for almost a month, but wherever they went from there they must walk. Didicas was a small town, overrun by refugees, mainly women and children. Achelone menfolk had stayed behind to fight the invaders, but nobody knew how many still survived. Nobody knew anything, and that was Irona's second-biggest worry, after provisions.

She would have to allow at least ten days for the rest of her army to catch up. Dashing ahead in contingents of a few hundred men would be a recipe for serial massacre. Her problem now was to feed and maintain her army until it was big enough to seek out battle, when she didn't know how big the enemy's forces were, or where they were. She requisitioned the largest house in the town to be her headquarters and settled in to run her war.

The first thing she did was send out teams of scouts. Too late she realized that she should have started by chaining Podakan to a rock.

Her son was nowhere to be found. Did he expect to defeat the Gren single-handedly?

A stream of warships flowed up the Visoke. In the next few days, the remainder of the Benesh fleet arrived, with a dozen allied galleys too. The camp around the town grew steadily larger. Many smaller boats returned, part of the ferry service Irona had organized to clear the refugees out of Didicas and ease the food shortage. Those boats were promptly sent back downstream with more evacuees.

A runner could cover two days' march in one day, but to return with his report doubled his journey, so the first scouts, limping back at sunset on the second day, could tell her only that the Gren were at least two days' march away, which might be only one night's ride for them. They admitted that Podakan had left with them. He had been unarmed and marines must obey orders, so no one had even tried to send him back. Two days later, the second troop returned with much the same information. By then Irona had set up advance warning posts, manned and provisioned.

The Gren lizards could move much faster than a marine carrying rations and weapons, but it seemed the monsters' sprinting range was limited and they shunned sunlight. Most refugees were able to stay ahead of them, as long as their food lasted. If hunger slowed them, or they stopped to forage, then they got caught.

Irona had been in Didicas a full eight days before she gained some meaningful military intelligence. A young marine named Jailolo Jingbo, a survivor of the Benesh force once stationed in Achelone, staggered into town, haggard and starving.

By then the lack of allied support was becoming obvious. Many mainland cities like Purace and Severny were responding—slowly but convincingly. Support from the islands was conspicuously scanty. Irona summoned a council of war, packing all the allied commanders available into the ground floor of her quarters, a dozen men sitting on the floor, knees up. She sat on one stool and put Jailolo on the other, for he could barely stand. He gave his report in a painful croak. The Benesh and a thousand or so Achelonian troops had opposed the Gren advance and been savagely mauled. The survivors had fallen back on the capital and tried again, three days later. He thought he was the only Benesh to have escaped the massacre that resulted. Irona was inclined to believe him.

What mattered most was that Jailolo gave a warrior's account of the fighting. He told of the lizards' speed, which was far greater than a man could run, but only in short spurts. He had seen the lizards' scaly hides deflect Benesh spears like raindrops, and their jaws bite off men's heads, helmets and all. He estimated their numbers at between five and six hundred, no more.

"We were told thousands," Irona said.

"Begging your pardon, ma'am, we decided that their speed confused people. They move around so fast that the Achelonians thought there must be several armies."

"Will anything kill a lizard?"

"Think lances might, ma'am. I saw a couple of men charge one with a galley oar. They hit it in the throat, and it went down. I don't know if it was dead, but all its riders fell off."

Until then, Irona had not even known that a lizard could carry more than one rider. Then she asked the question that had worried her for years.

"What kills the Gren themselves?"

"Hammers, Your Honor. Their hides are as tough as armor, but hit 'em with a sledge and their bones break."

Her sigh of relief was echoed throughout the room.

The Gren themselves rode into battle on their steeds' backs, lying prone, so that they were very hard to hit with anything. On foot they fought with their talons, which were poisoned. One scratch sent a man into agonized convulsions, with death following very soon after. Either they had never needed the bronze weapons they had demanded, or they had found a better alternative.

Poison might explain why they shunned dead bodies and ate only the living.

Most important, Jailolo reported that the invaders were heading in the direction of Didicas, simply because they were following their food supply and this was where most of the refugees were heading. Irona's scouts had already identified a possible ambush site half a day's march to the north. She must stand and fight somewhere, and that would be as good a battlefield as she could hope to find, where the road came through a wide expanse of olive trees.

The Empire had bought off human invaders in the past, granting them lands in return for oaths of loyalty and an annual tribute of fighting men. But the Gren were inhuman, Maleficence incarnate, inspired only by hatred and a yearning to destroy. Never before had such great evil come in force south of the Rampart Range. Irona held the fate of the Empire itself in her hands and tried not to think about that.

"Citizen Jingbo," she told Jailolo, "you are hereby promoted to sergeant, with back pay due from the first battle against the Gren. We'll put together a watch for you as soon as you're well enough to take command."

Dilivost, as loyal adjutant, called for cheers for the new sergeant. Irona dismissed the meeting and sent Jailolo off with Sazen to be fed, billeted, and interrogated in more depth. Then she looked around the grim-smiling faces.

"What do you think, gentlemen?"

"Lances!" they chorused. They had been shown a slim edge of hope. Two men with an oar had knocked over a lizard—once—and that was all. But no one had seriously tried lances in the Achelonian battles, and hope was what they needed more than anything.

"Go back to your contingents, then," Irona said. "Put your carpenters and bronze casters to work, and turn some oars into lances. And don't forget sledges and poleaxes! Bring your best tries here tomorrow at noon, and we'll compare designs. Also, Vice Marshal

Dilivost, I appoint you to work out the tactics and drill we'll need to use these, and what the men should do when they manage to disable a lizard and have to face dismounted riders. Dismissed!"

She gestured for her deputy to stay and called in Daun Bukit, who had been waiting outside with the day's figures. He estimated that they now had between eleven and twelve thousand men in the camp. Yesterday's arrivals had mentioned no other contingents close behind. She might have to fight with what she had now. But if twelve thousand men could not destroy five hundred lizards, then surely nothing could.

"Two ships only from Biarni," Daun concluded. "Three from Brandur. No word yet from Vyada Kun, or Lenoch. There are rumors that the Genodesan fleet put to sea and was recalled." Those three major islands all had much larger populations than Benign itself. They could field as many men as their fleets could deliver.

Dilivost could never resist a chance to belabor the obvious. "Perhaps they're hoping the lizard men can't cross the sea to get at them."

"Well, we still can!" Irona said. She could tell from Daun's expression that he was thinking, as she was, that Benign itself was now dangerously stripped of fighting men. Any two or three of the missing allies acting together would easily overwhelm any defense the Seven would be able to raise. Dilivost wouldn't think of that in ten years.

"But let's deal with the Gren first and the traitors later," she said.

A man walked through the open door and dropped to all fours before pushing himself up to a kneeling position.

It was Podakan, and she hardly knew him. He had his dandy's hair tied back out of the way, and his face and arms were dark brown. His smock was in tatters, his legs all scratched and bruised. Nagging worry was washed away by a rush of relief that he was still alive and well, followed instantly by illogical fury.

"Rise!" she said.

He struggled to his feet with some help from Dilivost. She resisted conflicting urges to hug him and have him flogged. He seemed both taller and thinner. She gestured him to the stool Jailolo had recently quit, and he slumped down on it. He had a somber, worried air that seemed new, but might only be extreme fatigue.

Daun quietly walked out. He hated to be anywhere near Podakan.

"I've been worried sick, of course," she said.

Her baby giant nodded. "Don't punish anyone but me, Dam. The others told me to go back but I just did what I wanted to and they couldn't stop me running along beside them."

"So they told me. I won't punish anyone. You've punished me enough, and yourself too. Was it worth it?"

"They'll be here in eight or nine days."

Her heart stopped for a moment. "You've *seen* them?"

He found that funny and glanced at Dilivost to see if he did. "No one sees them and lives to tell of it, Dam."

Not true, but almost true. "What did you learn then?"

"I got as far as a ridge they call Height of Land, and I could see the smoke from there. By then I could understand a bit of what the rabble were saying when they tried to speak Benesh, telling me where they were from and when they had left and so on. Putting it all together, it looks like eight or nine days." Then he repeated a lot of hearsay that she had heard before, and some that Jailolo had witnessed. He was telling her very little new, but it had been a worthy effort and she was absurdly proud of him. She had waited a long time for that sensation.

"Then you need to eat and rest. But you have to choose first. Either you give me your word that you will obey my orders from now on and not try any more mad escapades without my permission, or I'm going to put you on a refugee boat right now and send you back to the sea."

He shrugged. "I'll obey. I was stupid to run off like that and I'm sorry."

Wonder of the ages, a Podakan apology!

"Thank you. You are forgiven and I'm very proud of you, stupid or not. It's against the law for a child to bear arms, but I made a mockery of that law when I let you row. So I'm going to give you a sword and a job." Swords were useless against the Gren, but there could not possibly be enough hammers to go around. "As soon as you're rested, pick out three nimble youngsters and a veteran who knows some sword fighting to train you all. I'll be leading this army from the front, and I'll need a personal bodyguard. You'll be in charge. Now go and do it!"

That was better. He actually smiled!

And hugged her! Then he limped out the door and was gone.

"Am I crazy?" she asked Dilivost. "A dottily doting dam?"

He thought for a moment, rubbing the place where his chin should be, then said tactfully, "No one can call you crazy for putting your next of kin in charge of your bodyguard, 700. Don't suppose they'll do much good if the lizard men come for you, though."

"No," she said. "But then nothing will." And until then she could keep her eye on Podakan.

The wide, gentle valley of the Visoke carried on eastward past Didicas, but the Achelone trail turned north, over gentle hills. On the upward slopes it wound through olive groves, but farther up, the trees gave way to pasture. This was where Irona wanted to fight, and nobody spoke up against her plan. They could hide their thousands in the trees flanking the road, and also along the uphill edge, in case some lizards tried to outflank the ambush.

Sergeant Jailolo Jingbo, once he had recovered from the worst of his trauma, turned out to be an unpleasantly cocksure chatterbox, not nearly as convincing as he had been when he first arrived, two-thirds dead. He clearly regarded himself as the Empire's expert on the Gren, which he might be, but Irona did not enjoy being pelted with banalities. The choice of time would be vital, he said. The Gren could see in the dark much better than people, he insisted, and the moon was in the last quarter now, available only after midnight. Their lizards did not like daylight, so at dawn they holed up in dark places: forests or buildings. So he said, but Irona, remembering Hayklopevi in an all-enveloping gray cloak, suspected it might be the Gren themselves who shunned daylight, like the Shapeless of the Dread Lands.

She had no choice of time or date. The army would fight when the enemy arrived. That was likely to be about dawn, when the Gren were finishing a night's trek. Admittedly at dawn the quarter moon would be high and the lizards likely tired. Although that was a very bad time to ask men to fight, after a night on the bare ground with no fires or hot food, Irona had no choice.

Or so she thought. But a solution came from Sazen Hostin, with his batwing ears and devious Geographical mind. It happened when Irona was eating a drab dinner of beans and squash in her headquarters with her personal staff and, in one case, family. Podakan was in an especially grumpy mood. Apparently there was a lot more to sword fighting than he had expected.

"Citizen . . ." Sazen began.

"I am not a citizen."

"Boy, then. What lies north of the proposed battlefield, boy?"

"Grass and goat shit."

"And beyond that? Advise us. You have been there, and the rest of us have not."

Slightly mollified, Podakan said, "Land slopes down to a stream. There's a village."

"Ah! How many buildings, and what are they made of?"

Podakan screwed up his face in a scowl. He lacked Veer's visual memory. "Ten or so. Lath and plaster. Roofs made of thatched reeds."

Sazen flashed his heron's nest teeth in a smile.

Irona thought she could see what he was thinking. "So the Gren will camp there the day before they come here?" They could be attacked there, maybe?

"The Gren might like to camp there. Tell us more, boy. What other choices will they have?"

The "boy"—who stood head, shoulders, and some chest taller than Sazen—caught on also. His eyes gleamed. "None. A few trees along the river, but not enough to give much shade. So we burn it before they get there?"

Irona had not seen that, but Sazen had even more ideas.

"We burn it *just* before they get there. The smoke tells us they're coming and the ashes will still be too hot to sleep on."

"Can't see the smoke from here," Podakan objected.

"But you can from the outpost at the top of the hill, and we have built a signal beacon there, which will be visible from down here, in Didicas. We may need a third fire somewhere. . . . We should know when the Gren are approaching the village—around dawn I hope— only to find it burning. They either sleep outdoors in bright sunlight, or they keep coming, looking for somewhere better."

Would the Gren be alerted by that so-inconvenient fire? Would they notice the signal fire and guess what it was? Or would they just be tired and hungry? There were very few refugees coming down the trail now. Irona decided that she had nothing to lose by putting Sazen's suggestion to her council.

Pray the goddess not to send fog or heavy rain.

Podakan's estimate of eight or nine days turned out to be optimistic. Possibly the Gren ran out of food and increased their speed. But the signal fires were set in time, and they flared up very early one morning. If Irona waited too long to set up her ambush, the Gren might be into Didicas before she knew it. If she put her men in place too soon . . . It didn't take long for a stationary army to start stinking, and she credited the enemy with enough sense to wonder why olive trees smelled like that.

She ordered the army to battle stations.

Benign provided every marine with a bronze helmet, a sword, and a throwing spear. After that they were on their own. Some owned armor, others had only wooden shields, and a few lacked even those.

Every contingent had been assigned a place and had already marked it. Irona had put her most reliable troops, her own Benesh, at the south end of the sack, because that was where the trap must close once the Gren were inside it, and they would try to break through in that direction. Allied contingents lined the road back to the mouth of the trap, and along the northern limits of the orchards. After that there was nothing to do but sit down and wait through the longest hours of their lives.

There were farmhouses among the groves, and Irona had chosen a cabin at the south end for her headquarters. It was small and dark, smelling of mildew, with wicker walls and a floor of packed dirt. The door swung loosely on a pivot, and a wicker shutter could be tied over the window. The furniture comprised a slightly raised earth platform covered with rushes for sleeping, a rickety table, and two stools; the one she chose was extremely uncomfortable, threatening to give her splinters. It almost made her homesick for Brackish, and the days when the juvenile Irona would have accepted all this as normal.

She waited there with her bodyguard, meaning Podakan and three citizens from the Benesh contingent, whom he might have chosen because they all looked younger than he did. Biam and Silay wore armor, Dofen had only a shield, while Podakan had neither. Every unit wore some identifying badge, so Podakan had equipped Irona's bodyguard with purple neckbands. They were all pretending to be in a furious sulk at being kept out of the battle, of course. No doubt each of them was hugely relieved and absolutely determined not to show it. She couldn't resist telling them about her meetings with the Beru, Hayklopevi.

Mentioning the Grenish poison claws, of course.

And their habit of eating people alive.

Silay, Dofen, and Biam just got madder. Then she took pity on them.

"Listen, heroes. We have twelve thousand troops against five hundred lizards and maybe a thousand Gren. Even if everything goes as planned—and I admit that in warfare it never does—then very few of your buddies are going to have the satisfaction of sticking a lance or a sword into anyone or anything. And I chose this hovel because I expect the heaviest fighting to happen right about here."

They pretended to be happy at that news and Silay said, "Why?"

"Because, if the plan does work, the enemy will come charging down the road until their rearguard is into the trees. Then the Purace marines up there will sound the charge and close the trap. Spears start flying. The Gren guess what's happening and try to ram their way through. But the Benesh marines are lined up across their path, right here. Crunch!"

"Hot turds!" Dofen said.

After that they had nothing to do but wait.

Evidently Podakan's solitary scouting mission had proved his manhood to his own satisfaction, because he strutted over to the bed, unbuckled his sword, and threw it down. Then he took a second look at the bed and decided that the better part of valor was not to put himself in that zoo. Instead he settled on the floor in an empty corner behind the door, leaned his head back against the wall, and pretended to go to sleep. Perhaps he did sleep, because he looked much too uncomfortable to be faking.

Irona kept thinking of all the things that could go wrong. The lizard men might guess that they were being set up for an ambush. Would they not wonder who had fired the shepherds' village? Did they really believe that the Empire would never retaliate? They could turn aside and go somewhere else. Or they could detour a thousand paces east or west, for there were many lesser trails through the orchards; then they could wheel around and attack the army from the rear. Or they might wait until nightfall, when her army was worn out with waiting and couldn't see in the darkness—it was gloomy enough under the olive trees even at noon.

A bugle call in the distance was to be the signal that the Grenish column was fully into the trap. When it came, faint on the wind, she needed a moment to realize what it was. Then the signal was relayed three times, each call closer.

Irona and Dofen collided at the tiny window, trying to see. Biam and Silay dashed to the door.

Irona yelled, "No!" and they stopped. "You stay here or I'll have your balls for earrings."

Surly faces glowered back at her. Podakan muttered angrily in his sleep and twisted into another position.

"You may open the door if you stay right outside," Irona conceded, because the doorway itself did not give a clear view of the road. The boys opened the door. She turned back to the window.

Her view was chopped into strips by olive trees, but she could see men sprinting in from both sides. It seemed there must have been a whole century hiding right behind the cottage. More were hurrying past, going uphill. There was some shouting, some screaming, most of it far off, although the dense foliage would muffle sound. If this was a defining moment in the history of the Empire, it was a very quiet one.

The storm broke as a lizard came roaring down the road, a monstrous thing, far larger than Irona had expected, with a nightmare, bloodstained muzzle. Its gait made the ground tremble, its hide was the same gray shade as the Grenish robes, its legs spread out sideways, and a double frill ran along its back to the tip of its tail. At least two Gren were riding it, prostrate between the two frills, so that little could be seen of them except their six-clawed hands hanging on.

Biam yelled, "Flaming shit!" No one disagreed.

A hail of spears bounced off the monster's sides and head, having no effect except to cause it to roar even louder. Men scattered out of its path, those who did not move fast enough being trampled or hurled aside. It looked as if this lizard at least was going to smash its way through the Benesh blockade.

The lancers! Where were the lancers?

Four lancers came trotting up the road, right in the monster's path, each pair clutching a lance. They had barely started their run at it before the lizard impaled itself on the barbed bronze blades. One struck its leathery gizzard and the other ran into its gaping mouth. It bellowed and tossed its great head, snapping the lances like twigs and flipping the lancers through the air. The monster stumbled. Two more lance teams charged into it from the side, buying their blades in its thorax. Blood spurted. The lizard toppled over, tipping its riders off on the far side from Irona, but cheers from that direction suggested that the Gren over there were being well hammered.

Dofen screamed in triumph right in her ear, but she was doing the same in his. Thank the goddess for the two marines who had died in Achelone using an oar against a lizard! And more thanks for Jailolo Jingbo, who had seen and reported their valiant deaths.

Even now, the monster in the orchard was not dead, still thrashing weakly as a score of men jabbed and slashed at it, and presumably also at its former passengers. They were all yelling like madmen. Its corpse blocked the road and would slow down any others following. Judging by the noise and the way the marines were turning their attention, there was another lizard on its way.

Biam shrieked in agony.

Silay cried, "Holy Caprice, preserve me!"

"Not a hope," lisped a new voice.

Silay hurtled backward into the cottage, propelled by Biam, who was continuing to scream and was himself being forced back by a gray-robed Gren, which had a taloned hand around his throat. The Gren crouched almost double to clear the door lintel, then kicked the door shut. It dropped Biam and reached Silay before he could draw his sword. A single slash of its taloned hand ripped the flesh from his face. He screamed and collapsed in a heap: whimpering, thrashing, and bleeding.

Dofen roared out an oath and struggled to draw, but he was not fast enough. The Gren raked his chest with its talons. He toppled on the others, so then there were three young men writhing on the floor in their death throes. Biam had gone into convulsions already. Dofen began turning purple. Silay was spurting blood in jets between his fingers. Appallingly, all three still seemed to be conscious.

Irona was hard against the wall, clutching Vly's jade-handled dagger, which she always wore on campaign.

The Gren was too huge for the tiny cottage, bent over under the beams. It threw back its hood to reveal a grotesquely narrow head and elongated features. It had no external ears and no hair, only a sort of fleshy crest like a gray cockscomb.

"Seven 700, you have risen since we saw each other last."

It was the Beru itself, Hayklopevi.

Irona was edging away along the wall, knowing that there was nowhere to go. The three dying boys had sunk from screaming to whimpering, although they were still thrashing in terrible spasms. Judging by the noise outside, the battle was raging hotter than ever, so no one was going to walk in here and rescue her.

Podakan was awake in the background. She dared not look at him in case she alerted the Gren to his presence. Very slowly, Podakan had risen to his feet. His sword lay on the bed, beyond the intruder, out of reach. Would he have the sense to dive out the door and run? Irona was beyond help. *Run, my baby, run! Save yourself!*

"How did you find me?" she asked, amazed that her voice worked as usual. The Gren warlord had certainly not been riding on the lead lizard.

That was a smile? "Easy. I tasted you as soon as we crested the slope." Hayklopevi's black tongue flickered out briefly, like a serpent's, although it was not forked. "A faculty you cannot understand."

"The last time we met you didn't speak Benesh." She edged farther away.

It followed, eyes glittering with joy or hatred. "I consumed a man who did." It opened its mouth, the narrow jaws spreading as wide as a lion's. It had at least two banks of teeth in each jaw, and she looked away quickly.

She could no longer see what Podakan was doing, because Hayklopevi was in the way. Pod hadn't fled, either because he had dreams of killing the Beru and rescuing his mother or because Silay's body was preventing the door being opened. Nor could he get at the monster, for the floor was covered with thrashing bodies.

"You can't hope to escape from here, you know," she told the Beru. It had thrust her back until her heels were against the edge of the sleeping platform.

"An insignificant detail." Threads of slobber hung from its lips. "What happens to this vessel is of no importance, to me or anyone." Fast as a snake, its hand shot out and hooked its talons in her jade collar. She felt the claws cold against her throat, but the points had not pierced her skin.

Irona rammed the dagger into the monster's chest. The blade broke off near the tip.

"That tickles," Hayklopevi growled. "You cannot injure me, woman. But you are dangerous in other ways. You have acquired some immunity. Do you know what we do to prisoners, Seven 700?"

"You eat them."

"Certainly. And the first thing we do is make certain they cannot run away. We need to keep the meat fresh, you see?"

It pushed, so she tilted backward, flailing her arms for balance, but supported by its grip. It tightened its hold, pushing its fingers into the collar to throttle her and make her panic.

"Thus!" It stomped down hard on her left knee.

She heard the bones break, the tendons snap. As the Gren let go, she crashed down on the platform screaming in an inferno of mind-destroying agony that drowned out everything else in the world. Even childbirth did not compare with that instant, unexpected torment.

In a few moments, terror overcame the pain enough for her to look up at the gloating monster looming above her. There was only one thought in her mind: that nothing must move or touch her leg, absolutely nothing. If she lay completely still, she could survive, but rather death than the least motion of her shattered knee.

Hayklopevi knew what she was thinking. "So you shan't escape," it said. "Sadly, we have a long way to go before I can safely feast. I will carry you."

"No!" she screamed as it stooped to lift her. "Don't touch me!"

Podakan rammed the point of Silay's sword into the Gren's back in a mighty two-handed thrust that would have gone right through a man, killing him easily. The bronze blade caught in the scaly hide and snapped. Podakan cried out in dismay. The Beru roared and spun around. The boy leaped on it. Together they fell on Irona, with Podakan on top.

They did not land on her injured leg, but the jolt was enough to make her scream and see swirling darkness. Hayklopevi heaved Podakan off with no apparent effort and rolled free of Irona. She heard cloth rip and her son scream, but he still managed to roll his opponent back again, and this time Irona fainted.

Pain had taken her away, pain brought her back: steady, nauseating hammer blows of pain in her knee to warn her that she was still alive and capable of suffering. She seemed to be alone. Only silence, both inside and outside the hovel. The poles and thatch of the roof were above her, with no leering monster faces in the way.

Then she heard a sound of tearing cloth, and very carefully turned her head. The first thing she saw was the Gren, obviously dead, with a sword hilt jammed in its jaws and green blood everywhere. Her son was sitting cross-legged on the dirt floor beside it, apparently wearing nothing except the purple ribbon around his neck. His chest was caked in blood—red, black, and some green. He had what seemed to be the Gren's gray robe spread over his lap. He raised it and ripped again. He saw that her eyes were open.

He smiled vaguely. "Oh, you're alive?"

"You won!" That seemed unbelievable, as if she were hallucinating. A boy against that giant *thing*?

"Clever! You noticed. Had enough blade left to get to its brain, or whatever was inside its skull."

"You killed Hayklopevi! Oh, Podakan, I can't start to tell you how proud I am!"

"It ruined my smock." Producing a brown-and-red bundle that must be all that was left of that garment, he dabbed cautiously at the six parallel scars on his chest. Then he inspected the cloth and frowned at the results. "Almost stopped bleeding."

Joy and fear and pain all jangled together in her mind.

"Why didn't those scratches kill you?"

He shrugged and winced as if that had not been a good idea. "Ran out of venom? Glad you aren't. Dead either, I mean." He sounded confused, understandably. She couldn't be thinking very straight herself.

"The other boys? They're dead?"

Podakan regarded the corpses for a moment. "They're turning a sort of blue color. Phew! They stink worse than the lizard." He ripped the gray cloth again. "Losers."

"Your father would have been—"

"What happened to Vlyplatin?"

"What?"

"My father. What happened to him?"

"I've told you. Over and over, I've told you."

"I'm grown up now. I want the truth."

He didn't sound grown up. He sounded like a bewildered child, except that he had inherited his father's deep, melodic voice.

"I've never told you anything but the truth." She needed Source Water to ease the pain. But the Source at Didicas was tiny, and there must be many wounded marines who needed succor more than she did. "He walked in his sleep and fell over the cliff."

"Loser."

"No! He was worried about me, and even more about you." That wasn't entirely a lie, for although Vly had never known that he had fathered a child, if he ever had come to his senses that terrible night, he would at once have been consumed with guilt for what he had done. He might have sleepwalked, as she had always insisted, or he might have fled from the cabin in horror and tripped over the parapet in the dark.

"Loser," Podakan repeated, and wrenched at the tough cloth again. He held up a piece. "This should cover the essentials."

Holding the gray cloth around himself, he struggled to his knees. He tied the ends and twisted the knot around to the back. He looked down at Irona.

"I'm not a loser."

"No, son. You're a hero. I'm proud of you!"

He grunted. "Wanna be feared, not admired. You ready to go?"

"I need a litter." Her heart shriveled at the thought of being lifted onto it.

"Don't have one. I'll carry you."

"*No!*" She smiled and calmed her voice. "Every move hurts."

Wincing, he managed to stand up. "I'll go, then. Need a woman."

"You what?"

"Should have brought Tiatia." He began stepping over the bodies. "Losers."

"You will send help?"

He mumbled something that sounded like, "Later," and went out, leaving the door open.

It was probably an hour before she heard voices outside and a marine peered in the door. He blasphemed loudly, then asked if she was hurt.

"No, just resting. I enjoy the stench of rotting bodies, you bonehead!"

He vanished. In a few minutes, a sergeant arrived with more men and a medical kit. He wet a bandage with Source Water and spread it over her grossly swollen knee. Then he gave her a bottle of something and told her not more than two swallows. She took three, and the world soon faded away.

Life and pain were still there in the morning, when Irona found herself abed, back in her headquarters in Didicas. Her leg was splinted, and two nurses flitted about, trying to be supportive. Her world had shrunk to this single, poky room and would probably remain so for weeks. The sun was warm, so the shutters were open, but most days it would be dark, and it still stank of the sulfur they had burned to fumigate it for her. She wondered if the stench had killed whatever spun the webs among the low rafters, or everything that inhabited the mattress.

The sick room was a strange place to receive a report of a glorious victory from a jubilant Dilivost 678. The battle had been truly historic. The human death toll was 802, less than the count of 1,324 dead lizards. Only 925 Gren corpses had been found, so it seemed that many must have escaped, but several witnesses insisted they had seen them vanish like bubbles on a stream. No one could be sure if they had all been real to start with.

"I've told the lads we'll have them home in a month!" Dilivost laughed. "On the optimistic side, maybe, but it cheers them up."

In some ways, Dilivost was an idiot.

"Of course, you can rest here for as long as you want, ma'am. I've ordered kegs of Source Water brought upstream for you alone. We'll have you as good as new in no time."

In most ways, Dilivost was an idiot.

"I am sure the Seventy will vote rewards for all the heroes," he said. "Ten dolphins, maybe?"

"Considering that they may have saved the mainland Empire, I'd be more generous. And I'd pay the same to the families of the dead."

He looked puzzled. "Corpses can't spend it." Imagination was not his forte.

"No, but it will motivate other men, next time. Where is my son, do you know?" Her heart sank when she saw the expression her question had provoked. "Tell me the worst."

"There was trouble in the refugee camps, ma'am. The lads are not allowed in there, of course . . . Thirty-two men have been convicted of rape. There were more complaints, but we lack evidence on the rest."

Oh, Vly, Vly, what would you have said to this?

"Sentence?"

"Under the circumstances, ma'am, the court-martial officers felt that ten lashes would be sufficient. Subject to your approval, of course. Thirty would be normal, but after such a victory . . ."

"I agree. Ten."

"You confirm the sentence, ma'am? There may be some heroes in there who might be treated more leniently, pardoned even, under the—"

"*No!* Those women were under our protection, not defeated enemies." Personally, she did not believe that even conquest excused rape, but war was no respecter of ethics. Podakan had practically told her what he was going to do when he left her.

Dilivost shook his head. "There are men there with open wounds, ma'am. It won't look good to add more. At least let me reduce the lashes by the number of scars. In every case."

She nodded reluctantly. "If they were strong enough to rape women, they should be strong enough to pay the penalty. But my son is not to be treated any less harshly than the others, you hear? If you try, he will probably refuse and make a scene. And mention no names!"

Dilivost 678 just shrugged. The news would get around. Everyone would hear of Irona the Terrible, who flogged her own hero son, right after he had won the war and saved her life.

The next day she was feeling better, but she could not have felt worse. The swelling had eased a little, so the splints were more comfortable, even if the pain was still bad. About midafternoon, when she was almost well enough to feel bored, she had her nurses prop her up on pillows and fetch Daun Bukit, so she could start dictating her report to the Seventy. She had hardly begun when the toothy gnome face of Sazen Hostin peered in around the door.

"A citizen downstairs, ma'am, says he has urgent business with you."

"No!"

"Nis Puol Dvure, ma'am."

"Goddess! The vultures are gathering already? Bring him up. Daun, you stay."

Smirking, Sazen went off to fetch the vulture.

The years had done little to change Dvure. His hair was thinner, his neck fatter. His waist might have grown a little; his arrogance couldn't. He and Irona were old partners now, veterans of many joint ventures to enrich the Dvures and profit the Republic. She was careful never to gain anything for herself, except a reputation for getting things done. Dvure's motives were the exact reverse, but she usually kept his bloodsucking within reason. He provided good mercantile advice, and his wife threw wonderful parties.

He knelt and offered polite hopes for Irona's speedy et cetera. He did not fit in a peasant cottage. His tunic was as finely cut as ever, his chin shaved as smooth as glass, his hair perfection. He had the sense not to sport much jewelry in a war zone: the army might decide to liberate it. She told Daun to bring the citizen a stool, offered wine, which he declined, then asked Nis what brought him to Didicas.

He smiled as if she ought to know, but what he said was, "Timber, ma'am. Or the lack of. Achelone was the city's main supplier, as you know. What is the situation now in Achelone? The government was overthrown, of course, but have all the inhabitants fled? Are the Gren in control there now? Are they preparing another assault? Where else can Benign find its lumber? Are the old contracts still in force or void?"

Irona realized that she could not answer even one of those

questions. It was typical of Nis Puol to arrive at the heart of the situation before anyone else even started.

"I regret that I cannot comment on such matters until I have reported to the Seventy, citizen. If you have any thoughts on the affair, I am sure they would be of value."

Dvure smiled. He looked at Daun and Sazen. Then smiled again at Irona.

Irona nodded; the other two departed, closing the door.

"Talk," she said. "And to the point. I am still too weak for chatter."

"The rumor in Didicas is that you are going to send the army home. But Achelone has collapsed. The government there was always a rancid affair, and now there is none. March north, put Achelone under martial law, and turn it into a protectorate."

"And loot it, of course?"

He shrugged. "You need to install a garrison sufficient to repel the Gren if they should try again. The people should pay for their own defense. Pay in timber, of course. The country will have to be reorganized."

Meaning *looted*. What Dvure said was hypocritical, nauseating, and true. She should have seen this. In a protectorate, the people had no rights whatsoever. They were ruled by an overseer without even a council to temper his decisions. The Seventy often awarded the office to the highest bidder.

"You see yourself as autocrat?"

"I would be interested."

Of course he would be. "I will mention your interest to Dilivost 678. As you say, he will be marching north to restore order. Forgive me if I cut our conversation short. Anything else?"

"Several allies were slow to answer the Empire's call for troops and ships."

"That is a matter for the full Seventy," Irona said wearily. "It is not within my mandate." It was certainly not something she would discuss with an outsider.

"If I may presume, ma'am . . . Don't let them flood the market. Take them one at a time."

"I don't understand," she said, and for once she didn't.

"Too much art, too much gold, too many slaves . . . No matter what commodities Benign demands in penalty will drive down the price. Allow time for the markets to adjust. Take, say, Genodesa this year, Lenoch next year." Nis Puol Dvure smiled, as well he might at such a prospect. "Not all at once."

"Certainly not all at once."

How could he have been so right about Achelone and be so terribly wrong about the missing allies? She sent him off with her thanks, and Daun must have shown him downstairs, because Sazen came in right away. His odious smirk showed that he had been eavesdropping.

"Tell Chosen Dilivost that I need to speak with him as soon as possible," Irona said. The navy would have to descend the Visoke River and then row up the Huequi to Achelone. She must hurry back to Benign as fast as possible. If the Seventy's thinking was anything like Nis Puol Dvure's, then the Empire was in serious danger.

As Irona had feared, Podakan continued to make trouble. He refused to accept less than the full ten lashes, yelling insulting remarks about his mother so there could be no doubt of his identity. Even when the guards untied his wrists after four strokes, he would not leave the whipping post. When the onlookers began to cheer, the sergeant in charge told the marine with the knout to oblige him. He fainted on the ninth stroke, or pretended to.

Irona did not send for him, but left word that he was to be admitted if he came. He had not done so when she departed from Didicas. She was miserably aware that she was washing her hands of her only child, and that whatever success she might claim as a magistrate, she was admitting to utter failure as a mother.

～

She made a fast trip home, but even she could not triumph completely over human weakness. Attending meetings of the Seventy was still beyond her strength. In an unprecedented honor, the Seven assembled in her home to hail her triumph over the Gren.

Edziza, who had been Irona's seneschal since the death of Velny Lavice, was a portly, dignified man, normally as imperturbable as a two-day corpse, but even he seemed impressed by the solemnity of this event. He announced each guest as if he wished he had drums and trumpets available. Irona received them in the ballroom, which Veer Machin had long since redecorated in inimitable style. There she sat in state on a couch, like some barbarian potentate, an effect ruined by the ugly plaster cast on her leg.

Viewing the current collection of jewels in the Empire's crown for the first time in several months, Irona noticed how overripe most of them were. It was time to start bringing in fresh blood. As the youngest Seven and unquestioned leader of the younger Chosen, she ought to regard that as her responsibility. The next youngest, of course, was Ledacos 692, once her mentor, later a resentful protégé, and now unspoken rival. They tended to favor the same policies, so they were often partners in government business, but they both knew that one day they must be rivals for the top job, and they were close enough in age that only one of them was likely to serve as First. Not unexpectedly, Ledacos was the only visitor crass enough to ask how her hero son fared. She answered, truthfully, that she thought he was with the army, and if he had not yet reached legal manhood, he had certainly demonstrated enough of the real thing in practice. There was no possible reply to that except agreement.

The First was last to arrive, of course, so that everyone except Irona could rise and bow to him. Rudakov 670 had never been the most vigorous of men, and now, after her long absence, Irona noticed even more how he rambled and forgot things. That morning he did manage to mumble through the preliminaries without consulting notes. He announced that the only items on the agenda were

to accept Irona 700's excellent report on her campaign, to congratulate her on her historic victory, and to determine what monument
should be raised in her honor.

A quick glance around the circle of faces confirmed Irona's suspicion that there were some things they did not want to discuss in
her presence.

She then listened politely to much the same words repeated over
and over. Their congratulations seemed subdued, shadowed by her
new reputation as the monster mother. At the end she thanked them
for giving her the opportunity to serve the goddess, and the goddess
for blessing the army's efforts. All routine so far.

Rudakov asked her to choose a monument, mentioning that she
had earned the right to a statue in the temple of Caprice. She suggested
instead an aqueduct to deliver clean water from the Mountain to the
southern outports as far as Brackish, replacing the local supply that
had given the hamlet its name. But she insisted it be called the Didicas
Aqueduct, to commemorate the battle, not named after her. They all
seemed happy with that and agreed to call for design proposals.

Then the First began to show signs of announcing adjournment,
for the meeting had achieved everything it intended. Irona had not,
and Ledacos had given her the opening she needed.

"One detail remains, Your Reverence," she said. "Honorable 692
referred in his remarks to your army having 'some allied support'
and I dealt with the same matter in my report. In fact, a great many
'allies' failed to answer the Empire's call. I believe this is relevant to
today's business?"

The old man dithered for a moment. Then, to her dismay, he
referred the question to Banahaw 688. Banahaw was third youngest
of the Sevens, after Ledacos, but he was a blustering firebrand, and
even less reliable than Dilivost. If he had the file, then the results
might be even worse than she feared.

"Genodesa, Lenoch, and Vyada Kun," he proclaimed, "were the
most egregious renegades. A few minor entities offered various

excuses, but those three must be dealt with first. Lenoch and Vyada Kun did not respond at all. The king of Genodesa sailed, then had second thoughts and returned to port. Lenoch is the easiest nut to crack, so naturally we shall deal with it first. Zard 699 is already on his way there with our final terms."

"Which are?"

"One thousand boys and twelve hundred girls, plus ten members of their council, chosen at random."

Irona shuddered. "You expect them to send their children into slavery without a struggle? Or their rulers to surrender themselves to the 'mercy' for which we are so famous?"

"Of course not." The idiot smirked. Others must have supported him so far, but they were leaving the defense to him.

"So next you declare open rebellion? You invade, loot, pillage, and raze?"

"That is putting it too harshly, but the cowards must learn the cost of betrayal. We cannot tolerate such insubordination. The whole concept of empire is founded on—"

"Is founded on bluff!" she shouted, and the effort brought a stab of pain from her knee.

The rest of the company remained silent. Ledacos was smiling innocently at the ceiling. Did no one else see the precipice ahead?

"You are provoking civil war when our army and those of our truly loyal allies are far inland, at Achelone."

Idiot Banahaw swelled like a pouter pigeon. "We have other allies. The smaller states and cities that did not respond or did so halfheartedly will be eager to make amends by aiding us in putting down the rebels."

"Why should they?" Irona asked softly, and for a moment the silence was deafening. Ledacos pursed his lips.

Irona charged ahead. "Do you think either the king of Genodesa or the senate of Vyada Kun is too stupid to see that they must be next, after Lenoch? Those nations love their children too. They will combine against us, all of them, and the next thing you know there will be an assault on Benign itself and overthrow of the Empire."

Protests erupted, both pro and con her statements. The First made clucking noises like a broody hen, but failed to obtain order. It was Banahaw himself who got it, red-faced and bellowing that he had the floor and had the right to respond to the slurs.

"This action was approved by the Seventy, by a large majority. What else would you do? Ignore this insult to our Empire and our goddess?"

"Have you finished?" Irona asked, and waited until he grumpily resumed his seat. When the honor of the Empire was in question, the Seventy would support any idiotic measures trumpeted by tub-thumping patriots. That did not make them right, though.

"No, I would not ignore the insult. But I would not punish the innocent along with the guilty. I would demand that the senators in Lenoch who voted against helping the Empire be handed over to us for trial, although I might guarantee that they would not have to face the death penalty. If the city fails to conform—which it probably will, because the same senate must decide on its response—then I would blockade their harbors and embargo their trade. After that, when the guilty were eventually handed over, I would put them to the sea death. And after that I would demand an explanation from the king of Genodesa . . . and so on. Persons are a lot easier to punish than states or cities, '88."

They promised to think it over and departed, in their litters or sedan chairs, all except Ledacos, who left on foot and doubled back as soon as the rest had gone. Irona had been expecting him.

"They are insane," he said. "We have had our differences in the past, 700, but we've got to pull together on this. They shouted me down, but they'll have to listen to you."

"Let's hope so," she said. "Give me a couple of days."

~

Three days and a dozen meetings later, Irona had matters under control. She had called in every Chosen whom she could by any stretch regard as a client or who just owed her a favor, and she had convinced them that beating up your most powerful allies when your own forces were far away was a very bad idea. Ledacos himself was dispatched with fresh orders for Zard.

Few people would have agreed with her, but Irona was convinced that she had just saved the Empire for the second time that year.

As fall wore on, news drifted in that Dilivost 678 had arrived in Achelone to find that it was making a good recovery from the Gren invasion. The citizens had begun setting up a republic that would be more genuinely democratic than the rule of the unlamented Sakar Semeru. Dilivost typically failed to adjust his thinking to an unexpected situation. Bullheadedly following Irona's orders, he proclaimed a protectorate with himself as overseer. When the locals objected, he began slaughtering them for their own good.

This was too much even for the hotheads in the Seventy. Fialovi 694 was sent over to repair as much of the damage as possible, and Dilivost slunk home in disgrace. At the first meeting of the Seventy after his return, he was elected in short order to three totally insignificant jobs. Aware that there were a dozen more such horrors on the agenda, he took the hint and begged leave to resign from the Seven, "to devote the necessary time to these important responsibilities." He would never be trusted with significant office again.

It was winter by the time the ships began to return. Husbands, lovers, brothers, and sons were awarded their bonus gold and sent home to their families. Not all were accounted for. Irona was not the only mother worrying about a lost son.

Late on an especially foul winter evening, when Irona and Veer were sitting by a crackling fire, chatting with Komev 701 and his consort—were in fact trying to persuade them to stay the night—Edziza came in to whisper in Irona's ear that she had an important visitor. By then she could hobble on a crutch, so Veer helped her rise and she went out to see who could possibly have come calling without notice in such weather.

He was filthy, with hair tangled and patchy stubble on his lip. His tunic was tattered, and he was in urgent need of a bathtub.

He rumbled, "Blessings on you, Dam!" in his father's basso.

She hurled down the crutch to embrace him with both arms. She had not expected him to return her kiss, but he did, and the rowers' hands clutching her shoulders were rough as pumice stone.

"You've grown," she said. "Not just taller, but thicker and broader. Oh, these arms! My boy has become a man." And he was a man, warm blooded, breathing, not the walking corpse who haunted her worst nightmares.

"Yes. Want to see my scars? Up and down in front, crosswise on my back."

"No! Never! Oh, I am so happy to see you home, love! Your room is all ready. Edziza, have a fire lit in there, please, and the hot bricks in the bed."

"Hot bricks and Tiatia," Podakan said, in tones that implied an ultimatum.

Irona was not surprised. "Provided she agrees. Even a slave is a person, dear, not an animal to be ordered out to stud. Edziza," she called after the seneschal, "would you first ask Tiatia if she would like to be reassigned as my son's concubine."

Although Edziza's face remained expressionless, it somehow confirmed Irona's opinion that the question was a formality. He stalked off in the direction of the servant stairs.

"I can't legally give her to you until you come of age, dear, but I'll have her assigned then, if she's still willing. Have you eaten? Why don't you clean up and get . . . I'll find one of Veer's tunics to fit you. None of your old ones will now. It's a good thing that I have another giant in the house! Then come and tell us all your news. Chosen Komev and his lady are here and we'd love . . ."

"Tomorrow," Podakan said. "Tonight it's bathe, eat, and then Tiatia, Tiatia, Tiatia. I haven't had any tail in a week."

"That's boy talk, trying to shock me. Men don't speak that way."

"The men I fight alongside do." Podakan retrieved her crutch from the corner where Edziza had stood it; he handed it to her. "See you tomorrow, Dam. Go and break the bad news to Fat Man Machin."

In some ways he hadn't changed a bit.

It was just over a week later that Veer wandered into Irona's study while she was reading reports and said, "He's gone."

She felt sorrow, but not surprise. "Podakan?"

"And the girl. With their belongings, such as they are."

She sighed and went back to her homework. She was fairly sure that Tiatia had been the only reason her son had come home at all.

Unfortunately, she was wrong.

THE YEAR 725

By summer Irona was working as hard as ever. She had no strength in her crippled knee but had adjusted to walking with a staff and wearing a bronze brace on her leg.

Her current term as a Seven would end soon after Midsummer, and she was giving thought to which offices she might enjoy during her year's sabbatical as a Six. It was a measure of her status now that she could choose and be confident of getting whatever she wanted. A place on the Treaty Commission would be coming vacant in a month and would be a new venture for her. The present holder, Zard 699, would make a good Seven if the old guard among the Chosen could be persuaded to elect a stripling of forty-two. So many ancients had died off during the winter that there were now as many Chosen younger than she as there were older. Irona found this disturbing, and she wasn't the only one to have noticed the increased workload.

She wore long gowns to hide her brace. It occurred to her during one interminable meeting that she would soon be changing back from Seven purple to Chosen sea green and must order a suitable wardrobe. While she had let her attention wander—another sign of advancing age!—Ledacos nominated her for something.

She had the Chosens' permission to remain seated during meetings, but did not use it. She heaved herself to her feet and bowed to the First. What was Ledacos up to? She was not allowed to nominate an opponent, although she could easily signal to a follower to do so, but she daren't do that until she knew what office was being filled. *Definitely* senile!

Nobody rose to oppose her, so she graciously accepted election by acclamation. Mallahle 669, the evening's chair, announced that the next item was election of a male tutor for the choosing, which informed Irona that she had just been appointed female tutor. That was a very minor office, not normally awarded to Sevens, but a fine example of Ledacos's malicious humor, a gibe that she might thus gain a daughter to replace her lost son.

Irona promptly nominated Zard 699 for male tutor, as this should give them a couple of hours together, when she could broach the subject of his potential promotion. He looked peeved at not having been consulted beforehand, but dutifully came to the front and bowed to Rudakov on his throne. He was plump now, Zard, and a grandfather, a long way from the skinny boy who had clipped the collar around Irona's neck a quarter of a century ago. He, too, was elected by acclamation.

They met in the temple, early on Midsummer Day, and Irona was able to explain to him why she had sprung the tutor job on him without warning.

"A Seven?" Zard's eyes, always prominent, now bulged. "Me?"

She laughed. "Don't tell me you haven't thought about it! But when Ledacos sprang this vigil on me, I decided it offered an excellent chance for you and me to spend a few undisturbed hours discussing how we get you elected, and for you to advise me on the Treaty Board. I can't speak nine hundred languages, you know." The standard joke among the Chosen was that 699 was growing suicidal trying to find another language to learn, because he knew them all.

"The Treaty Board may not be the best use of your abilities, Irona. This Elbrus thing is—"

In rushed last year's Chosen, Apolima 724, all a-fluster. Irona explained that she had to wait downstairs and would find the 725 collar ready for her there. Zard summoned a junior priest to guide her.

Then Irona and Zard sat down to wait for the priests to bring them breakfast.

"As I was saying," Zard continued, "the dispute with Elbrus is going to need a special—"

Trumpets sounded.

"Sounds like they're starting." Zard rose and wandered over to the window. "Goddess! Look at them, Irona. They're only kids. When I put that collar on you, I saw a gorgeous young woman, not a child!"

She had seen him as an owlish youth, she recalled, but girls of sixteen preferred mature men, at least two years older than themselves. She thanked him for the compliment and went to join him, just as the boy at the head of the first group of pilgrims reached into the coffer and brought out his token.

"Mind you," Zard remarked. "Some of the lads there are too hefty to argue with. Like that one in the second group, see?"

Irona swallowed a few times before she managed to agree. She had completely forgotten that this would have been Podakan's year to make the pilgrimage, were he eligible. If he had truly masqueraded as a pilgrim last year, as Daun had said, wasn't he terrified of being recognized by the priests? Well, no. With thousands of adolescents marching by every year, they could not possibly remember every face.

But he wasn't eligible, so why was he here? When had he ever turned up early for anything before? He must have been waiting at the temple gate for hours.

She watched in dread as the boys progressed through the

ritual—not many girls had shown up so early. All her fears were realized when that year's fourteenth candidate's token stopped on the same spot hers had, so many years ago. The spectators yelled in astonishment, and it took the trumpeters a moment to realize they had to blow the final fanfare already.

"Looks like we'll have to postpone our discussion, Irona," Zard said.

She mumbled, "Yes." There was nothing she could do about the latest Chosen. He was an adult now. Not being native-born, he wasn't eligible to be chosen, but Lavice was a common Benesh family name, so the priests would not have thought to ask unless they had reason to, and they couldn't ask now. *The goddess would not make a mistake!* Apolima 724 came running out on the stage—that girl never just walked anywhere—and reached up to fasten the collar around Podakan's already burly neck.

Irona said, "I hope it chokes him."

Zard spun around. "*What?*"

She had not intended to speak aloud. "You are going to have your hands full with that one, Tutor."

Not for Podakan the terror or hysterics of most Chosen. The crowd cheered as he waved fists above his head in triumph. Then he grabbed Apolima in both arms and kissed her. The crowd gasped in horror, before managing an uncertain second cheer.

"I see what you mean."

"I never managed to teach him much," Irona said. "He wears the scars of the knout on his back and Gren claws on his chest. He has his own concubine, by the way."

Zard's eyes looked ready to fall out altogether. "Your son? This is incredible! Caprice has never been known to choose a Chosen's child before."

She hadn't this time, either. Why, oh why, had Irona not foreseen this? "Let's go down and congratulate him, shall we?" *Oh, Goddess, Goddess!*

In the recovery room, they found Apolima still chalky white with rage at the way Podakan had shamed her in public, and the villain himself enjoying a draft of Source Water. A flash of apprehension crossed his face when he saw Irona, but then he leered triumphantly. She could not denounce his deception now without dooming them both to the sea death.

"Bless you, Dam! Didn't expect to see you here. Are you to be my tutor, Your Honor?"

Then Apolima had to be told. "Your son? The one you . . . er . . ."

"Flogged," Podakan finished for her. "Yes. Took the flesh off my back. I'll show you my scars if you want. Oh, here, Dam, this is yours. I borrowed it." He handed Irona his empty water bottle. She had never seen it before. He was so smug that she wished somebody would throttle him.

Apolima clapped her hands. "So Holy Caprice is showing her appreciation of . . ." She hesitated.

"Her appreciation of my son or her disapproval of me?" Irona asked ironically.

Podakan found that even funnier. Revenge was proverbially sweet, and he had totally outwitted the mother who had shamed him. "Now I'm a grown-up, so I'll send Tia over for the assignment paper, Dam."

"That's up to your tutor," Irona said, and was pleased to see her son at a loss, even if momentarily.

"Tia is the concubine?" Zard asked. "I think you should assign her to me, 700. I can decide what her duties will be."

"Yes, I'll do that," Irona said. Ownership of Tiatia would give Zard some hold over his diabolical protégé.

Veer hated to be interrupted when he was working, but the moment Irona got home she thumped into his studio and insisted he stop what he was doing, find a lantern, and escort her down to the cellar.

He gave her an odd look. "May I reserve judgment on your sanity?"

"The new Chosen is Podakan 725."

"*What?*"

"And I should have guessed. Come along."

The cellar was fairly small, for Sebrat House was built on a steep hillside, where cellars tended to leak during winter rains, causing anything stored in them to rot and fall apart. It had been a dozen years since Irona hid the bucket she was searching for, and much had changed since then in the way of furniture brought down to be stored or removed to be disposed of. When she did find it, the evidence was obvious.

"Look at the dust!" she said. "Someone moved these tapestries to get at whatever was underneath. Over there, where things have not been disturbed, the dust is thicker. And there are fingermarks."

"Not very recent ones." Veer was being wonderfully patient, considering that she had still not explained.

"He grew up in this house. You can't have a small boy not explore a cellar."

"Of course not. Darling—"

"But he was here last winter. When he came to stay for a week, remember? He knew exactly what he wanted and where to find it." And that was what she should have foreseen. "It's full of black pebbles. Give me one and bring another."

"You've been overworking. A Source Water poultice on the forehead . . ."

"Stop trying to be funny. This is deadly serious."

"They're sticky," Veer complained, but he did as he was told.

Irona hobbled back to the stair and hauled herself up, one step at a time, all the way to the second floor and her study. She sat down. Her hands were filthy and she might have cobwebs in her hair. Veer pulled up a chair and tossed the black pebble from one hand to the other. She gave him the one she had brought, so he had two to play with.

He shouted, "*Goddess!*" and dropped them both as if they were hot coals. They stuck together even after they hit the rug. "It's maleficence. A fix!"

"No." She explained as she had explained to old Knipry a dozen years ago—not the Dread Lands, but tiny Kadowan Island, mating rocks, how sea hunters and fishermen used a piece of such stone to find north. Veer took some persuading, but eventually he picked them up and examined them again.

"You see that they will only mate one way?" she said. "The other way they repel each other. The effect works even through cloth or a thin board. They're not interested in other types of stone. Nor metal. I've tried every kind I could get my hands on: lead, copper, silver, gold, tin, even quicksilver. The mating rocks mate only with each other."

"Or quarrel with each other. Are you hinting that Podakan stole a piece of this and . . . and what, Irona?"

The sudden anger in his eyes made her wonder if even Veer might denounce her to the Seventy as a witch.

"When I was a child, I found a few tiny pieces my father had hidden away, just as my child must have found these. I discovered what they did, and my father swore me to secrecy, telling me he would be sent to the sea death if I talked and I might go with him. But I remembered, and even on the day I was chosen, twenty-six years ago, I wondered if the miracle was faked."

She had mentioned it then to Zard 699, she remembered. She hoped that he didn't, or he might start wondering what had happened today.

"How?" Veer asked.

"A big piece of black stone underneath the goddess's bowl, and one special token with another piece inside it. Think back to when you made your pilgrimage; you reached in the coffer to find a token, and what happened?"

"What do you mean, 'what happened?' I picked up a token from a heap of them in there. What else could happen?"

"Hands inside the box forced mine on me, love. My tutor said that the priests had simply been refilling the basket at that moment, which could be true, but I suspected that a special token had been intended for the boy in front of me. A girl had fainted and thrown the count off. The priests had taken a bribe. . . . Perhaps only two priests, or a few of them. One priest identified Dvure and somehow signaled to another in the coffer. They daren't cry foul, of course. And they won't today, either. But now they have two 'special' tokens."

Veer had turned pale. "First you, by accident. . . . Then you faked it for your son?"

"I certainly did not, but that's what they'll all think. If the priests denounce Podakan or me, they'll bring the whole Empire tumbling down. No miracles. Caprice is a fake. They are charlatans. The Seventy are frauds. Total disaster."

She could see his mind rejecting what he was hearing, building walls of denial.

"I think you're misjudging your son, Irona. You drive yourself hard, and you've always been too hard on him. The goddess knew what she was doing when she chose you to guide her city. Today she chose him."

Irona shook her head and produced the canteen that Podakan had given her. "Ever seen this before?"

Veer did not bother to take it from her. "Don't think so. But there are thousands like that, made from a tube of hide off an animal's leg. Tan it, turn up one end, sew it tight, seal it with wax. Put a mouthpiece in the other end, add a cord. . . . Thousands."

"And cut a slit in one side to make a pocket out of it? You can slide your hand inside it, see—what sort of water bottle is that? He went to the choosing last year, remember. We all thought he was trying to bluff his way in at fifteen, but he went to see exactly how it was done. He has very large hands, so he probably took two tokens from the box, tossed one out to the goddess, and palmed the other. Then he hollowed it out, or something, and glued a black stone in it. He made this fake water bottle to smuggle it into the temple. When his turn came, he pulled the token out, again hidden in one of those big hands of his, and pretended to take it from the coffer. And finally he couldn't resist giving me this evidence because he wanted me to know how he'd outsmarted Caprice and the Empire."

Veer sat silent for a while, playing with the pebbles.

"How is it done, Irona? If there's a mating rock under the bowl somewhere, then the token may come to it wrong-side down. Then it won't stick. It'll just about jump off, but it won't stop."

For a moment she was stumped. Then she saw. "It will work if the rock underneath is big enough. If the one in the token is the right way up to stick, it will stick. If it's the other way up, it will stop and not slide any farther. So it stops either way."

No, he just could not believe that everything he had been taught to believe was a lie. And she could not stop believing it.

"Or perhaps," he said, "the goddess set the device up centuries ago and nobody knows how it works except you. Or you may be completely wrong and the choosing has nothing to do with black rock. Caprice made a good choice when she chose you, and today she chose Podakan. His efforts to cheat may have amused her. She is capricious above all. And, while your son has been a pain in my ass for years, I can admit that he may make a very good Chosen, and perhaps one day even a great First for Benign."

"*Podakan?*" She thought Veer must be joking, then saw that he wasn't.

"He is quite a lad, Irona. He was a hero before he was even a man. Now he's a Chosen, and you had best respect the goddess's decision." Veer stood up, laid the two black stones on the table, and left the room.

She wanted to scream. Now it was all so obvious! Obsessed by guilt that he was the cause of Irona's two-year exile in the hellhole of Vult, Vlyplatin had succumbed to Maleficence and had passed the curse on to her in his seed. In Didicas, whatever sentience had possessed the Beru had willingly abandoned that "vessel" so it could occupy Podakan. That was why the boy had lived and the monster had died. Now Maleficence was one of the Seventy.

Irona 700 met Chosen Podakan 725 again the following evening in the Scandal Market and was relieved to see that he was on his best behavior, accepting congratulations graciously and modestly, *Your Honor*ing everyone. She hardly recognized him, all scrubbed and close-shaven, wearing a newly made, large-size sea-green tunic. Of course she received congratulations also, but they were guarded: Had the goddess just given her a reward or a reprimand? No one was sure.

In the meeting that followed, the novice listened intently, said nothing, and voted as his tutor did. Long may that last! Just once he caught Irona's eye with a knowing look. She made an effort and smiled in acknowledgment.

At the last meeting of the Seven that Irona would attend during her term, Ledacos presented a report from the Treaty Commission regarding the Elbrus problem. Navy had been concerned for years that pirates were openly using ports there as bases, and lately had taken to preying on shipping almost as far north as Benign itself. The Seven had referred the matter to the Commission, which now responded that Elbrus, being part of the Three Kingdoms, was not within its mandate, which bore only on treaty lands within the Benesh Empire itself. Relations with sovereign states, it added, were historically handled by the Seventy, on the advice of the Seven. But, it concluded, if the Seventy should decide to send a special emissary to the ruling satrap of Elbrus, then he, or she, ought to be backed up by a significant show of strength.

That "or she" was a pretty broad hint as to which "he or" they had in mind. Somehow Irona 700 had become the Empire's hunting dog. But a summer voyage to Elbrus was not without appeal. She might even drag Veer along with her and stop worrying about Podakan.

Suretamatai 683, a Ledacos crony, pointed out that Seven Irona would be laying down her current office tomorrow and would be an excellent choice for emissary.

Hands slapped the table in applause.

Ha! "Your Honors, grateful as I am for this flattering show of confidence, I must point out that men of the Three Kingdoms treat their women as fine jewels. A woman is never even seen by any man other than her father, her husband, and her juvenile sons. To send a woman, and a crippled woman at that, will be interpreted as an insult of the highest order."

"Excellent!" boomed Banahaw 688. "That is exactly the message you can convey."

A recommendation to the Seventy was approved unanimously, and so was Irona's nomination for the post. She could look forward to visiting that fabled land and receiving quasi-royal honors as Benign's emissary.

The realm that the Benesh contemptuously dismissed as the Three Kingdoms was in fact an empire both larger and richer than their own, an amalgam of many peoples and races. The two had clashed several times in the past, but a maritime power and a continental one could never deliver decisive blows on each other. All their conflicts had ended in mutual recognition that the border between them must run through the Gulf of Berutarube, although this agreement had rarely been stated in formal treaties.

When Irona got home that evening, she found Veer relaxing on a chaise longue out on the terrace, with one hand clutching a goblet of wine and the other vaguely beating time to music drifting over from the neighbor's. A private orchestra had been the price that Ledacos's latest mistress, a buxom singer, had demanded as compensation for the loss of her virtue. In fact, a spell as a Seven's doxy would advance her subsequent earning potential tremendously.

Veer was probably not concentrating on the melody, though, for his thoughts rarely strayed far from painting.

"Ah!" he said as Irona sat down where his feet had been an instant before. "Good meeting?"

"Interesting." She held out her hand for the wine and took a long draft. What she needed for her ambassadorial state was a convivial escort. Veer, regrettably, boasted of never having left the shores of Benign and never wanting to do so. "I am about to undertake an ambassadorial visit to Nabro."

"Where's that?"

"It is the capital city of Elbrus."

Veer reached under the couch for the wine flask. "Which is?"

"The most westerly of the many provinces of the Three Kingdoms. Nabro is an ancient city famous for the beauty of its setting and the grace of its art and architecture. Especially its many towers."

He knew what she wanted. "Give it my love, love."

Hopeless! Veer was a very atypical Benesh, completely uninterested in politics or war. But she knew the endless trouble other female Chosen had with consorts trying to meddle. Veer was a pure diamond and she must not complain.

"It will be a long voyage but should be very pleasant in summer." Coming home close to winter might be less appealing.

He raised the flask to his mouth again and then lowered it. He frowned. "And I suppose you will enlist some husky sailor to help you on and off with your leg brace?"

Irona sighed. "I thought of that, but it won't work. The navy is very fussy about watches and time off and so on. I shall need more than one. I fancy a husky, hairy-chested type to assist me in the mornings, and another—probably of the lithe, youthful, nimble sort—for evenings."

Veer took a drink, then wiped his mouth with his wrist. "When do we sail?"

~

Thanks largely to Irona's nagging over the years, the fleet now included sailing ships of several types, all classified as barques. Some were small, but some were as long as galleys, because length brought speed. They were less maneuverable than oared craft, but could travel in rougher weather and carry more cargo, making provisioning the fleet less dependent on unreliable local sources. A week after her appointment as admiral-ambassador, Irona raised her flag on the galley *Invincible* and led out a fleet of fifteen war galleys and a dozen support craft. Keeping such a collection together would be impossible, and she did not even want to try, lest word of the approaching force reach Elbrus ahead of her. She ordered all vessels to rendezvous at Aoba, the most southerly city in the Empire, and promised bonuses for the first to arrive.

Daun Bukit went with her, of course, and even Sazen Hostin, who had officially retired to enjoy the remarkable fortune he had amassed in thirty years of working for starvation wages. It would be just like old times, and even better with Veer to brighten her nights. But the goddess was still capricious. Eager as Irona was to see the shining towers of Nabro, she was fated never to set eyes on them.

She came within a few hours of Aoba, one blazing afternoon, when sunlight glittered off a sea of blue silver too bright for human eyes. The smoke-toned hills of Hertali lining the northern skyline had not seen a cloud in weeks. Irona sat in her personal chair beside the steersman, under a canopy on the afterdeck, talking strategy with Commodore Chagulak, who was standing. Veer was stretched out on a blanket, leaning back on his elbows, and seemingly engrossed in a staring match with a white seabird on the rail.

Indomitable had caught up with *Invincible* a couple of days earlier and was following, hull down. Both bosuns were setting a fiendish pace in this, the final leg of the race.

Chagulak was a heavyset man with arms as thick as his legs and a head like a granite bollard. He stopped speaking in midsentence, gazing ahead. "Bosun, is that a sail off the port bow?"

"Aye, sir, it is!" The younger man—his name was Turfan—sprinted along the catwalk to the mast and raced up it like a squirrel. In a moment he shouted down, "Friend, sir. Benesh galley under sail." If she was under sail, then she was heading roughly in their direction. In a moment, he added, "She's seen us, sir. Turning our way."

The commodore said, "Permission to clear for action, ma'am?"

"Granted."

Veer sat up as pipes began to shrill. "I thought he said it was one of ours?"

"He meant that it *looks* like one of ours," Irona said. "We'll believe it when we're close enough to smell them."

Veer pulled a face, as if to say that he was currently downwind of *Invincible*'s own overheated crew.

The newcomer was indeed another ship of the fleet, *Insurmountable*. By the time she was identified, *Indomitable* was hove to a couple of oar lengths aft of *Invincible* and the race to Aoba had been suspended.

Bringing two galleys alongside in the open sea was tricky, but well within the navy's competence when the sea was as calm as it was that day. *Insurmountable*'s Captain Garbes leaped across the gap easily, but a younger man who followed him almost fell back and had to be grabbed by hasty hands and hauled aboard. The two then headed aft toward Irona, while three crews waited to hear their fates.

Garbes was the most junior of the captains and thus very eager to prove himself, although he already had a reputation for being sharp and ever eager for a fight. He saluted. His younger companion dropped to his knees.

"Report, Captain," Chagulak said, meaning he must explain why he had disobeyed orders by either leaving the rendezvous without permission or turning back before reaching it.

Seemingly unworried, Garbes told how he had taken *Insurmountable* into Aoba the previous day, only to find two of the supply ships already there. Later that evening, a third barque had arrived, having rescued a man adrift in the sea, clinging to an oar and in great distress. This, Captain Garbes confidently announced, must be the hand of the goddess at work. He nudged his companion with a horny toe.

He was, the lad recited in a nasal Lenochian accent, Jalua Fayal, deckhand on the trading ship *Albatross*. Two days ago, they had been chased and boarded by pirates. Knowing that their fate would be death or slavery, the crew had resisted. Most of them and some pirates had died in the fight. Fayal himself had been disarmed but had jumped overboard with an oar, preferring to face sharks or drowning rather than the pirates' vengeance.

Commodore Chagulak looked thoughtfully at Irona. "Miraculous! This indeed sounds like the hand of the goddess, ma'am."

She nodded and waited to hear more.

He turned back to Fayal. "You don't happen to know where they planned to take their prize, do you, sailor?"

"Kell, sir. I heard them say so. That's a big pirate port and slave market, sir."

More questions: Describe the pirate. Describe *Albatross*. When could a skeleton crew bring her into Kell . . . ?

Back to Garbes, who was wearing a very satisfied expression.

"You did think to bring a local who knows Kell?"

"Two of them, sir. Both good pilots."

"Kell is one of the smaller islands, is it not?"

"Yes, sir. They tell me there's only one port. On the southeast coast."

That pretty much decided it. From his look of alarm, even Veer could tell how the wind was blowing, and Irona knew it was set fair for Kell. She hated giving orders sitting down, but she was not steady enough to stand on a rolling deck. "Your recommendation, Commodore?"

"Commend Captain Garbes for his initiative and clear thinking. All three galleys to proceed at once in hot pursuit, mission to intercept *Albatross* and engage the raider if found, Your Honor."

"And if not?"

"Go in and cut 'em out, ma'am."

"Captain Garbes, I agree with the commodore that your actions were commendable, and I appoint you acting deputy commodore, effective yesterday. You agree with Commodore Chagulak's proposals?"

"Aye, ma'am."

"So ordered. Proceed, Commodore."

Chagulak began barking orders through a speaking trumpet, and all three crews obediently cheered at the prospect of action.

Veer rose on his knees for a private word with Irona. "My sweetest turtledove, my rose without a thorn, are you seriously planning to take war galleys into a foreign port to seize two ships?"

"If necessary."

"Did the Seventy authorize you to start a war?"

"Not in so many words," she admitted, "but that's what they're hoping for. And now the goddess has sent us a perfect excuse."

Early in the morning of the second day, Irona's tiny flotilla rowed along the eastern coast of Kell. They passed a lush and fertile land, green with unfamiliar crops and trees, sprinkled with grand white villas. Kell was a jewel, and Irona 700 began to rethink her strategy for dealing with Elbrus.

Even if the town of Kell was the only port on the island of Kell, it was a good one, with a superb natural harbor protected by a long, curved spit. Although scores of vessels were anchored there, or tied up at the single pier, or dragged up on the beaches, it could have taken Irona's entire fleet as well without crowding. Most of the current residents were fishing boats, but some were obviously more, especially one obvious war galley. It posed no threat in itself because it was currently lying out of the water, being careened, but its crew must be around somewhere.

The town stood on the landward side of the harbor within walls of pale stone. Above the battlement showed tiled roofs of many colors, a few narrow towers, and a high building that must be either a temple or the governor's palace.

Invincible and *Insurmountable* rowed boldly in, while *Indomitable* waited in the harbor entrance. The intruders were recognized at once for what they were. Trumpets sounded, drums beat, and torrents of people fled from the harbor to the safety of the town walls. Sunlight flashed on bronze as armed men arrived on the ramparts.

"There's *Albatross*!" Jalua Fayal cried. The prize had been beached for unloading and was tipped over by the low tide. "And that's the pirate!" He pointed to the vessel he had described, a rakish, two-masted craft at anchor. *Insurmountable* was already heading for that one. Bosun Turfan steered *Invincible* toward *Albatross*.

One ship, a small galley, must have been ready to leave, with its crew aboard, because it tried to escape. Oars dipped and swung in perfect unison as it made a dash for the open sea. *Indomitable* turned to face it, then surged forward to ram. The crash was loud enough to echo off the city wall. Captain Onikobe did not try to board. He had his men back water, leaving the other craft to founder and its crew to swim. When no others tried to make a break, he headed into the harbor and went in search of pirates.

Irona and the naval officers had talked for hours about every possible eventuality, and she did not meddle in tactics during action. Chagulak gently beached his galley just one fishing boat away from *Albatross*.

Veer had been standing by the rail as if turned to stone, no doubt loading his prodigious memory with exotic alien images. He staggered as the galley grounded, then turned to Irona with revulsion written all over his homely face. "There's bloodstains all over the deck!" He meant *Albatross*'s deck, of course.

"You'll see more of that before the day is out, dear." Having him along had made the voyage a treat, but she wished that he could have been spared this violence. Veer had an artist's fragile soul.

Armed marines waded ashore and ran to the prize ship. As soon as they had confirmed that there was no one aboard, Bosun Turfan, now Sergeant Turfan, ran off along the beach toward the town. He was unarmed, wearing only rower's leather breeches and carrying a flag.

"Where's he going?" Veer asked.

"Flag of truce. He's our herald, gone to demand that *Albatross* survivors and the pirates be turned over to us."

"You expect them to agree to that?"

"Depends on the state of the governor's liver," Irona said flippantly. But a governor who caved before a mere three galleys would find himself looking down from a high spike very soon after word reached the satrap in Nabro.

Sounds of battle rolled in over the water as *Insurmountable*'s crew overpowered the watch on the raider. Three men dived overboard and were used for target practice by Benesh archers; another four were killed on deck and thrown in the water.

Eager to enjoy some exercise on a stable surface, Irona pulled herself upright and began pacing, thumping with her staff. She was wearing her jade-handled dagger again. It was a little shorter than before, because it had been reground to replace the point that had broken off when she tried to stab the Beru, but that didn't show in the scabbard. Veer stood with his arms folded and glowered every time she passed him.

"The worst part of war is always the waiting," she said.

"Waiting for what?"

"Waiting for our herald to return with an answer."

Chagulak clambered over the bow and came marching along to the afterdeck. "It'll be three hours or more before we can float her, ma'am. I told the lads to prepare her for burning."

"But hold off until we hear from the city. They may give her up freely."

He nodded doubtfully.

"Then what?" Veer asked.

"If enough of the crew have survived to man her," Irona said, "they can sail her to Aoba with a few of our men as deckhands. Otherwise, we'll have to tow her."

"And we head to Aoba?"

Possibly. Irona was starting to have better ideas. The rest of her fleet would be now be in Aoba and wondering where its admiral had gone. It would take two days for her to summon it and two more for it to arrive.

"Commodore, crenellating a town is illegal in our Empire, but a couple of exceptions are allowed, and I have seen their walls. I have also seen remnants of ancient castles' walls, too. None is less than five times a man's height. I don't think much of Kell's defenses. Do you?"

Pugnacity glinted in the commodore's eye. "Three man-heights, maybe? No, ma'am, I agree. Just for show! They look old and weathered, too. If enough mortar has fallen out, a good lad might be able to climb up, given time."

"You must have a man who could throw a grapnel that high?"

"I could throw the man himself that high," Chagulak said with a straight face. "But the defenders would cut the ropes before we could climb up, ma'am."

Irona nodded a maybe, thinking of nighttime. First man up a rope could pull up a rope ladder. The next four or five could defend the bridgehead while the rest followed to take the city.

Turfan was still standing outside the city gate, looking up. A few guards on the balcony were staring down, and no doubt the two sides were bandying insults. The governor might be considering his options, or he might have already decided. The town must have a population of several thousand, of which a quarter would be potential fighting men. He might be lining up hundreds of them for a counterattack.

Out in the lagoon, smoke was rising from the original raider. Garbes had recovered his men and was heading for another likely victim.

Indomitable had already set one ship aflame and was inspecting another. It would be easy enough to identify pirates after boarding them. They would certainly carry grappling hooks, probably shackles and extra weapons. They might have slave pens for prisoners, although slaving itself was not illegal. Onikobe's orders were to burn all the raiders he could.

A crowd's roar drew everyone's attention back to the city gate. For a few minutes the noise continued without explanation. Then more heads appeared on the battlements. One rose higher than the others and quickly vanished.

Veer swore luridly. "They're returning the prisoners the quick way."

Twice more the invisible crowd cheered, and each time another victim followed the first, hurled down to injury or death.

"Recommend fast withdrawal, ma'am," said Chagulak, scarlet with rage.

"Granted."

He told the bugler to sound the retreat.

Now four pirate vessels were burning in the lagoon, and curls of smoke were rising from the beached *Albatross* as the boarding party waded out to their galley. The last man to board was Bosun Turfan. He was a seasoned fighter, who had earned promotion in fierce fighting at Achelone, but his face was still green with horror when he came aft to report to the commodore.

"Three prisoners," he said. "They blinded them, castrated them, then threw them off the battlements."

"You made sure they were dead?"

"Aye, sir."

A herald went unarmed, but even a herald carried a knife at his belt, like any other man. Turfan's right hand was bloody.

"This is all?" screamed Jalua Fayal, the last *Albatross* survivor. "They do that and you just sail away and let them be?"

"That's all for now, citizen," Irona said. "But only for now, believe me."

"Kell was caught with its smock up," Irona explained to Veer as the island slid below the horizon. "Its governor must be either young and inexperienced, old and debauched, or a highborn gink. He—obviously he, because the Three Kingdoms never let women out of the bedroom—clearly failed to consult men who could have advised him. Or else he has none to consult. He will probably now be working his people day and night reinforcing the defenses of the harbor against more Beñesh attacks."

"So?"

"So we shall not attack the harbor again."

Five nights later, shortly before dawn, grapnels flew over the walls on the landward side of the city. A thousand men followed. Kill any who resisted, Irona had ordered. Looting was permitted—that was certain to include slaving and rape, which she did not try to forbid—but not burning. She directed, "Save the town itself. We need it."

Three galleys blocked the harbor mouth, although two of them were grossly undermanned and just for show. Another fifteen galleys—Irona's entire force plus some from the Aoba station—lay on a beach a mile or so along the shore from the town and would have been vulnerable had the governor thought to have the coast patrolled, which he hadn't. Irona nervously limped back and forth on *Invincible*'s deck, waiting for news. Within an hour of the assault, word arrived that resistance in the town had collapsed, and Kell was hers.

$\sim$

That evening Irona held court in the town's palace, seated on a gran-diose gilt throne. Kell was a remote provincial backwater of empire, and yet the hall was as grand as any in Benign, a showpiece of bril-liant tiles, mosaics, and gilt—overblown and almost grotesque to her taste.

The former governor was brought before her. He still wore finely embroidered silks decorated with lace, but they were soiled and crumpled after a few hours in jail, and his complicated coiffure had collapsed. Although he was too young and shrill to bluster convinc-ingly, he did try, folding his arms and spreading his feet. The guards kicked the back of his knees to drop him into a more suitable posi-tion and then stepped on his outspread robes, forcing him to stay there.

Irona addressed him through an interpreter. "We have a proverb in Benign," she said. "*Do not hit a lion with a fly whisk.* By mutilat-ing and murdering helpless captives, you were fighting me with a fly whisk. You violated all civilized standards to no gain."

"You don't look much like a lion to me."

"I give you another proverb, then. *The lion does the roaring; the lioness makes the kill.*" Her guards smirked.

"Don't you threaten me, whore! I am a fourth cousin of the king of kings."

"You really should not have mentioned that." Irona could tolerate ruthlessness if it served a purpose and was backed up by courage, but pointless sadism was unacceptable. "Sergeant, take this toad away, blind him, spay him, and see he is delivered to the satrap in Nabro with my compliments."

That night Irona sent a brief report home to Benign, justifying her action. Kell was a rich island for its size and had been very poorly defended. As soon as she had made it secure, she planned to assault one of its neighbors, either Ilimuda or Agrigan. Whatever lands she conquered could either serve as valuable additions to the Empire or be ransomed back to the satrap. Ships were being loaded with booty,

and the most promising slaves were already on their way to Aoba.
She could use more galleys and men. Praise the goddess.

*There was dancing in the streets when the news reached Benign. Not
for decades had the Empire had a good infusion of loot. The price of
slaves dropped at once; dealers in all sorts of commodities booked passage for Kell. The Seventy ordered holidays and thanksgiving. It sent
out Empire-wide appeals for men and ships to head for Kell. A statue
of Irona was erected by public subscription.*

Irona herself moved with dispatch. A quick reconnaissance of the
island found no signs of resistance, and she assured the rest of the
population that there would be no further violence as long as they
behaved. She waived taxes for a year.

Satrap Karkar would be a much deadlier opponent than the
deposed governor. He would start reinforcing the other islands
as soon as the news reached him, and his resources were vastly
greater than hers. Time was not on her side. She used her advantage in sea power to blockade Agrigan. For two weeks, her galleys
rammed and sank innumerable smaller craft trying to ferry men
across the strait from the mainland. She more or less ignored the
crossing to Ilimuda. The satrap swallowed the lure and concen-
trated on Agrigan.

Irona attacked Ilimuda. This time the fight was bloodier. She
must keep control of the strait to block transport of Elbrusian forces,
but men working oars afloat could not be wielding weapons ashore
at the same time. She would have been thrown back into the sea
had not fresh troops started flowing in from the southern portions
of the Empire: Lenoch, Hertali, and others. They held the battle to
a stalemate until men from Benign and the north could arrive, just
before winter closed the ocean. With her army approaching twenty
thousand strong, Irona prevailed, and added a second conquest to
the Empire.

~

Again the news was greeted with hysterical joy in Benign. General Chagulak was voted a Hero of the Empire, which entitled him to a statue in the temple.

His report on the death toll did not arrive until spring, and the Seven never released it.

When winter arrived in the north, Irona was cut off from Benign. The south's equivalent rainy season hampered the satrap also, for his forces must travel overland. Irona's fleet still ruled the sea and seized a dozen or so minor islets. Those were of little value in themselves, but their loss would hamper the Elbrusians' counterattack.

"Agrigan!" General Chagulak would proclaim. "Everything depends on Agrigan. If we can take that in the spring, then we can keep those grass-eating slinkies at bay forever."

"There are a lot more of them than there are of us," Irona would reply.

"Bah! They're slugs—slow and slimy and they can't swim."

Irona worried more about ants than slugs. Poke a twig in an ants' nest and they would come at you by the million.

Sazen Hostin had organized an intelligence unit, although he warned that it depended on locals and must not be trusted too far. He said that the king of kings, although far away in Acigol-Nevsehir, would certainly know by now of the Benesh invasion. He would regard even the loss of two tiny islands as an intolerable insult to his imperial glory. Sazen thought Irona had made a serious mistake, but he was too loyal to say so.

Irona 700 tried to play the role of an imperial potentate but always had too much work to do. Without Source Water, which was never found outside the Empire, her skin dried up and her hair began turning gray, like a peasant's. She missed friends, the zest of the Seventy, the cultural glitter of Benign.

Veer Machin worried her. She had never intended to keep him away from his art for so long. He pined. He went for walks by himself until he narrowly escaped death, sustaining a cut along his ribs and a bad bruise on the fist that smashed the would-be assassin's nose. Irona had written to Edziza, telling him to collect and dispatch everything Veer would need to set up a new studio, on the advice of a couple of Veer's former apprentices. She did not expect to see the results before spring or early summer, but she had underestimated her majordomo's superhuman efficiency. The Seven could not get a letter to her, but Edziza's eight chests of cargo arrived. Instantly rejuvenated, Veer went into a frenzy of waxing saturnine, menacing Elbrusian faces. His appetite returned, all of his appetites.

In the worst of the rainy season, when deluges drowned the moon and fog dimmed the sun, Sazen Hostin reported that the satrap had begun moving troops across to Agrigan. Sazen refused to reveal his sources, as always, but Irona had never known him be wrong. She called a council meeting.

At first Chagulak refused to believe it. They would sink, be wrecked, get lost, be blown out to sea. It was impossible to sail in dense fog or pitch darkness.

Irona knew better. Now, more than ever, the navy needed the direction-finding black stones she had collected on Kadowan, but they were all safely at the bottom of the sea, thrown overboard on her way south. "What do we do about it?"

"I still believe that Agrigan is the key to this war," Chagulak said. "If Benign takes that, the king of kings will be forced to negotiate."

"Then you had better act now," Irona said. No one disagreed, although Sazen rolled his eyes. When, he would often ask her, did you ever hear military recommend anything except fighting?

Fifty galleys and twenty-one barques, almost the entire fleet, set out from Kell on the next reasonably calm day. The vanguard managed to land unopposed, but natives rushed the news to the governor. The long and bloody battle for Agrigan had begun.

THE YEAR 726

Midsummer brought a new year, but not the end of the war. The body count was a daily nightmare. The ships needed overhaul. The troops had been away from their families too long; allied contingents especially were growing restless. The Seventy ignored Irona's appeals for more reinforcements and showed no inclination to relieve her. As they would be saying in the Scandal Market, "Her spike, her head."

In the dark of the night Irona herself wondered if she had made a fearful mistake.

According to Sazen, Satrap Karkar had been given permission to commit suicide. His replacement had arrived from Acigol-Nevsehir—to see that he had done it properly, Veer suggested. To march the Benesh invaders back to Acigol-Nevsehir in chains, more likely.

In early fall, the navy's blockade won the battle. The people of Agrigan, with their homes and crops ruined, and close to starving because their defenders had emptied the larders, rose in revolt. The satrap's forces were forced to surrender, so Benign held the whole of the offshore archipelago, and it was Elbrusian troops who went off to slavery in chains. Irona hoped she might be a hero again, but no message of recall arrived before a second winter closed the seas.

Sazen Hostin reported that the king of kings was preparing to march west in the spring with an army of four hundred thousand men.

The first imperial ships to arrive in the spring were a dozen galleys, whose varied styles and colors showed that they had been assembled from all over the Empire. They were greeted by wild cheering as they rowed into the harbor at Kell one airless, sticky afternoon. Their very freshness showed how badly the garrison's ships needed refitting, and every marine in port began dreaming of the road home. Irona had just retired for her customary siesta in the heat of the day, but she heard the cheering and forgot about that. The most important news, for her, was that the lead ship flew an admiral's flag, so there were Chosen aboard.

Most visitors were greeted in the throne room, but not these, not yet. Although there might be a formal ceremony of welcome later, the first meeting must be more intimate. She ordered refreshments laid out on her favorite rooftop terrace, which was private, shaded, reasonably airy even on a windless day like that one, and high enough to have a view of the harbor. She watched the forecourt from overhead as the dignitaries dismounted from the litters she had sent: one Seven and two Chosen, too foreshortened for her to recognize them. She made sure Daun Bukit was standing by in the anteroom to maintain security and pass on orders.

Then she could only wait to find out who had been sent. Just the choice of messenger would be the message. Who had been sent would give her a very good idea of her current standing in Benign.

She felt as nervous as she had on the day Trodelat 680 first took her to the Scandal Market, which was ridiculous. She was the first Chosen in sixty years to expand the boundaries of the Empire. True, the cost in blood had been high. Also true, the king of kings had not yet sued for peace and was assembling enormous forces. Sazen had also heard stories of a great fleet being built, but he cautioned that those rumors might have been planted.

Voices in the anteroom . . . Daun's and one she could not at first believe. Then a man in jade collar and Chosen green strolled out, all alone.

"Blessings on you, Dam."

"Podakan?"

"Aren't you sure? Have I changed so much?" He accepted her embrace and let her kiss his cheek, but his response was restrained. His smile, on the other hand, said a great deal. Mostly gloat.

"Who else came with you?" she asked, staring at the empty doorway.

"Seven Dychat, and—"

"Dychat is a Seven now? But he's only . . ."

"He's forty, two years younger than you, Dam. Why don't we sit down?" He gestured her to one seat and took another without waiting for her. His manners had not improved, but yes, he had changed. He was a full-grown man now, with a hard face and the flexibility of a marble statue.

Dychat? She kept thinking of the weedy child who would go to sleep in the Assembly Hall and be carried home in Ledacos's arms. One thing was certain: in all the years since he was chosen, Dychat 702 had never failed to follow his former tutor's lead. He was here as Ledacos's lapdog. Did that mean that the Seventy were split and Podakan had been appointed by the Irona faction? Or was there no Irona faction left?

Podakan took up a pottery flask and sniffed it. The low-temperature ceramic sweated to keep its contents cool, or at least cooler.

"Wine? What I need is a long drink of Source Water."

She shook her head. Kell had none and he must know that.

He studied her face for a moment, nodding slightly to show that he could see how she had aged. If he thought he was being subtle, he still had much to learn.

"You and Dychat and who else? Who's the third?"

"Puchuldiza 711."

Who had been Irona's pupil. Who had turned into both a tramp and a lush. Who was still having prophetic dreams that she never revealed until after they had been fulfilled. If the goddess ever made mistakes in her choosing, Puchuldiza was the worst. Irona felt the waves rocking her coffin, as the Benesh said. A Ledacos crony accompanied by a boy and a fool. And where were the other two? Sending Podakan on ahead for a family greeting would have been a courtesy, but they ought to be here by now, paying their respects.

"So what message do you bring? Have I been acclaimed First, or am I to be dragged home in chains?"

Podakan laughed and filled two goblets with wine. "Not that bad." He offered a toast, "To the Eternal Empire."

"The Empire," she agreed. "Not as bad as being First or not as bad as being dragged home in chains?"

"Well, we have to report and let the Seventy decide, Dam. Dychat for the Seven, Puchie from the Treaty Commission, because the allies are screaming at the cost and want more of the loot. And me to represent Navy."

He watched to see how the old sow would take *that* news.

"*You* are on the Navy Board? Have I slipped a few years? I would have sworn you couldn't have finished your tutelage yet."

He was as transparent as air. He couldn't manage even a faint pretense of modesty. "Tutelage? I grew up in a Chosen's house. I am the only Chosen who's ever rowed a galley to war or fought in a shield line. I killed the Beru, for Caprice's sake! Tutelage? What could fat old Zard ever teach me? After a few months, Ledacos put a military question to me in the Assembly Hall, and I gave him the right answer, all politelike. Then others started doing it, until one day they asked Zard if I was ready and he said yes, so they voted me out of tutelage and onto the Juvenile Court."

"That's a tough assignment, all those poor kids!"

"Snotty little losers." He emptied his beaker and reached for the flagon. "And now I'm on Navy. How old were you when you were first made a Seven?"

"Twenty-seven."

He raised his beaker. "To Podakan at twenty!"

"Do you brag like this to the other Chosen, or just to me?"

His lip curled in a sneer. "Just to you, Dam. I thought you'd be proud to hear how well your little boy is doing."

"I am awed. But you're not my little boy anymore."

Pleased, he flexed his big oarsman shoulders.

Not her little boy, but who? She was haunted by nightmares that her son had died in the hovel at Didicas when the Gren had possessed him. Had he really been taken over that day? Who or what lurked behind those mocking dark eyes?

"What're you staring at?"

"Just seeing how you've changed. So what's the Seventy planning?"

He shrugged. "The king of kings is heading your way with half a million men. He's building a fleet at his end of the Gulf of Berutarube."

"We heard rumors along those lines." Benign was far away, but the Geographical Section had far wider resources than Sazen Hostin did, struggling on his own here in Kell.

"Have you heard that he is going to use Maleficence against you?"

"No. Who says so?"

"Sorry, Dam. Sworn to secrecy on that."

She nodded and sipped wine to hide her fury. Keeping secrets from her? She would see what Dychat had to say. Assuming he knew about the Maleficence. Maybe only Podakan did.

"They call it 'The Woman's War,' you know," he said. "You are 'The Woman.'"

"You're telling me it isn't popular anymore?"

"It never was popular, Dam."

"I heard that people were dancing in the streets of Benign."

"'The people'? The dregs may have danced. We Chosen didn't. The Seventy howled in fury when they heard you'd dragged us into a war with the Three Kingdoms. I was horribly embarrassed, but I was still only a pupil then and couldn't speak up to defend you."

He had his memory trained to remember only what it should.

"'Hitting a lion with a fly whisk,' the First called it," he added.

"Where have your buddies gone?"

"They'll be along in a minute."

"Yes, but where did they go?"

"They wanted a quick word with Chagulak." More unspoken mockery. He took another drink.

She could see now that they wanted their goose cooked before they even started shooting at it. Her long rivalry with Ledacos had ended; he had won, and he was going to have her pelt for a doormat.

A high-pitched voice in the anteroom foretold the arrival of Seven Dychat. A moment later he appeared in the doorway, a tiny man in purple, almost ludicrous against a background of General Chagulak's landscape-sized brawn. Irona lifted her braced leg off the stool and rose so she could bow to the Seven. He greeted her warmly enough, but he could have told her to remain seated.

Puchuldiza's shrill reminiscences echoed out from the anteroom, mingled with Daun's polite responses. She came sweeping in.

"Irona, darling! You are working dear Daun far too hard. I swear he's aged twenty years." *Miaow.*

"It feels like forty," Irona said.

Then came courtesies, and getting seating, and Daun bringing in more wine and another goblet. Chagulak should not be there. Anything he said to the Chosen should be as testimony before the committee, but who could doubt that he had just agreed with hints from Dychat and Puchuldiza that Irona must have made all the major decisions herself, ignoring his objections? He was the subordinate and the fault was all hers, right? In fact she had never overruled Chagulak once and he had always agreed with anything she suggested.

Dychat went swiftly to business. "The king of kings is leading a very large army against you, and building a large fleet . . ."

"We know that, but what's this I hear about Maleficence?"

His annoyed glance at Podakan clearly meant: *Blabbermouth!* "Just guesses. The Kingdoms have often been accused of that evil, and the present king of kings's family came to power two generations ago under very suspicious circumstances. We don't intend to fight on land, and you can't use fixes over water anyway."

"So they say."

"Quite. Now, about our hearings. We shall have to call the general, of course. And he will draw up a list of other witnesses who can provide relevant—"

"May I see your warrant, please?" Irona said.

"Oh. I gave it . . . Podakan? I asked you to bring it."

"I am sorry, Your Honor. I thought you meant me to bring it to the official hearings. Shall I run down to the ship for it? Or they may have brought our baggage up already. . . ."

Great Goddess! They were so transparent that Irona wanted to laugh. It was all meant to look fair: an independent Seven and two other Chosen from major committees. To outsiders, it must even seem to be weighted in her favor, with her son and her former pupil as members. She knew she mustn't trust either of them to take her side. The Seventy wanted Irona's head mounted on the wall for the Empire to see. The Elbrus disaster must be shown to be all her fault.

She almost offered to write the commissioners' report for them.

As soon as they were gone, she hobbled off in search of Veer. She found him in his studio as usual, growling about the heat softening his waxes. After one glance at her, he threw down his spatula and hugged her tight.

"It can't be that bad."

"It couldn't be worse. Dychat's fairly harmless, but Puchuldiza and Podakan? Ugh! I just hope they don't send me to the sea death. If they do, darling, promise me you'll find a way to kill me first."

He squeezed even harder. "Don't be ridiculous. We're going home?"

"Oh yes. Probably not in chains, although I wouldn't rule out anything yet. The army will be withdrawn as fast as possible. So things may get very much worse."

"They told you this?"

"No. They have to hold hearings first. But they have the final report already written, I'm sure."

"Anything I can do?" He squeezed her again, clasping her head against his shoulder. He smelled of wax and hot afternoon and himself.

"Not now," she said, "but if I survive until bedtime, then yes. Definitely."

The Dychat Commission chose that favorite terrace of hers to hold its hearings. They sat behind a table in the shade, with the witness chair in sunlight. There was no recorder present, but all three of them held waxed boards, on which they scratched notes from time to time. They might not have their report already written, but its conclusions were foregone.

She was the first witness, or so she was told.

"Whose idea was it to enter the port of Kell in hot pursuit of the raider?"

"Commodore Chagulak's."

Eyebrows rose to let her know that someone else had told them otherwise. And so it went. But she got her chance eventually, thanks to Puchuldiza, who had the brains of a bat.

"But you admit it was you who got us into this mess?"

"I didn't get anybody into a mess," Irona said crossly. "In less than two years I added three large and prosperous islands and a score of little ones to the Empire."

"And started a war with the Three Kingdoms!"

"They began the killing and looting. I was sent here to stop it—and did so. If the king of kings has a hundred million men standing on the mainland, he still can't march them over the sea. And," she shouted as Puchuldiza tried to interrupt, "if he was a king of kings of kings, he couldn't create a seaworthy fleet and a skilled crew for it in less than ten years. In all its history the Empire has never lost a sea battle to the Kingdoms."

Podakan said, "Hear, hear!"

Dychat glared at him. "If there are no further questions for this witness . . ."

By nightfall it was all over, and Irona was called in to hear their decision. She was even allowed to read their warrant, which recalled Chosen Irona and named Seven Dychat her replacement as admiral, marshal, and acting governor. The other two commissioners were to investigate the situation and advise on future action.

They would decide that tomorrow, Dychat said. Meanwhile, she must haul down her flag and prepare to return to Benign in two days.

"They're pulling out," Podakan said glumly.

He had wandered into Irona's bedroom when she was about to change for the formal dinner. She had shooed her maids away with orders to send in wine and tell Veer to stay out.

For once Podakan was not spoiling for a fight with her. He was glum and perhaps even in need of comforting. She could hardly believe it, but it seemed that she was about to have a confidential tête-à-tête with her hero son for the first time since he gave up sitting on her lap. The evening was relatively cool, with a scented breeze drifting in her windows. It brought sounds of drunken revelry from the streets, where marines were celebrating their recall.

"I thought that was to be decided tomorrow."

"It was decided before we left. There was another motion passed, a secret motion. We were ordered to abandon your conquests unless the three of us voted otherwise unanimously. Which won't happen because Man Mountain Dychat has his orders from 692."

She was impressed that her son had learned Chosen politics so quickly. She had always been inclined to underestimate Podakan. His deliberate rudeness made him seem like a lout, but it hid a ruthless cunning.

"What about the locals who have cooperated with us and accepted our promises not to abandon them?"

"Your promises, not ours."

"So you'll be sending the ships back to their home ports?" When he nodded, she said, "What if the king of kings decides to use this fleet he's building?"

Her son laughed, which had always been rare, even when he was a child. "There's a coastguard flotilla based in Aoba. Dychat's been told to enlarge it, from eight ships to twenty-four, so it will preserve the border through the Gulf of Berutarube. They're idiots, Dam, idiots! They think that wishing makes it so."

"The king of kings will take control of the seas and the Empire will burn."

"Of course." He spoke glumly, but when he looked up at her, she saw fury burning deep in his eyes.

"What would you do, if you were in charge?"

"Sink his fucking fleet before it knows what it's doing."

That would be her own inclination. After a moment, she said, "But Dychat is in charge."

"Ledacos was when his orders were written." Podakan drained his goblet and reached for the flask to refill it. "Stupid, stupid, stupid!

They think they can end a fight by running away from it. You want to sail on the same ship as me?"

"I'd love to. We can have some time together."

"Too much, I'm sure. I rowed straight watches coming here, but Killer Dychat says I mustn't row if I'm in charge. He's going to make me rear admiral to see the fleet home."

"He has to give you some sort of a title, otherwise Puchuldiza and I would both outrank you. Even Dychat can't see her as an admiral, I hope."

He sniggered quietly as the wine began taking hold. "No. He has turds for brains, but he's not that stupid. I wasn't guilty, you know."

"Guilty of what?"

"At Didicas." He looked almost as surprised as she was at the sudden change of topic. "There was a lot of gang raping going on after the battle, but not me. I found her hiding in a cupboard. I said if she'd fuck with me, I'd keep the others away. She agreed, and with every sign of enthusiasm, I might add."

"And did you keep the others away afterward?"

"Of course!"

"You need to practice that response. It was a little too emphatic."

"It wasn't rape!"

"And so was that one. Too forceful."

He glowered at her. "I was not guilty."

"Of course you were," she said, being all motherly. "I was marshal. I was in charge. Dilivost would have done anything in the world to leave you off the list. He'd have given you the benefit of any possible doubt. The evidence against you must have been overwhelming."

Podakan stared into his goblet for a moment, then drained it and wiped his mouth on a brawny arm. "Well, what if I was one of the wolves? Supposing I was even leader of the pack? *You had me flogged!* Your own son, the day after I saved your life, killed the Beru, won the war—you had me flogged like a common criminal."

"Which is what you were. Are you sorry for what you did?"

He banged down the goblet and sprang from his chair. "No. And I'm not sorry for what you did either. I like to know my enemies." He strode out of the room.

Great Goddess! Irona covered her face. Why couldn't he grow up the way other boys did? Why so incredibly mature in some ways and so infantile in others? Whatever would Vly say if he knew?

"Kill him now, Queenie, while you can."

"What?" She stared around. No one.

Veer appeared in the doorway, looking puzzled.

Irona said, "Did you hear someone speak just now?"

He smiled uneasily, eyes still scanning the room. "I thought I heard Podakan. . . . But I'd seen him going down the stairs. You hiding other lovers in here now?" There was nowhere to hide a cat.

"Of course not." She might not have recognized the voice after nineteen years, but the only person who had ever called her Queenie had been Podakan's father.

The heat must be cooking her brains.

Two days later, Rear Admiral Podakan hoisted his flag on *Invincible* and prepared to lead a flotilla of twelve galleys over to Aoba, where six would remain on station while the others carried on to Benign. Irona was already aboard, but Veer had stayed behind to pack up his collection of paintings. Puchuldiza had decided to travel by barque: according to Podakan, she had her eye on a certain bosun. Both Daun Bukit and General Chagulak were remaining in Kell to advise the new governor. Turfan had been promoted to captain and acting commodore. He saluted the surly-faced boy.

"Welcome aboard, Your Honor."

Podakan said, "I chose this galley for my flagship, Captain, because I was told it was the fastest in this squadron."

"Aye, sir."

"Good. I may call you on that boast shortly. Meanwhile I am ready to begin my inspection."

The rear admiral was just barely eighteen, and legally not even that, the youngest man aboard by far, but he knew galleys. He knew where to look and what to look for. He certainly knew the correct nautical language in which to describe *Invincible* as a pile of guano and its crew as a swarm of sexually perverted dung beetles. He rattled off errors that had to be fixed instantly until veins bulged in Turfan's forehead. Yet discipline held, and he continued to snap, "Aye, sir," never mentioning that *Invincible* had been at sea almost continuously for two years and a quarter of its original complement had died in action.

At the end Podakan, amidships, yelled to Irona, up on the afterdeck, "You may as well go home, Dam. This shit bucket isn't fit to go anywhere today."

He then jumped up on the pier and went off to inspect the next vessel under his command. He trashed every one of them.

The next day Podakan did let the squadron leave port. After the men had rowed a fast pace for an hour or so, he ordered a battle drill, involving all ships stripping for action, mounting the bronze ram, both watches donning armor, and then faking a ramming charge. It failed to satisfy him, so he had them repeat it. And again. He made the flotilla spend half the day rowing at top speed in full armor.

Irona became worried about mutiny. "They'll drop you overboard if you don't stop this soon," she said.

He sneered. "Not these jellyfish cripples. They'll do as I say and like it."

He ordered a race back to Kell, with the last two ships fated to spend the night at anchor outside the harbor, in the swell, with no supper. *Invincible* won, and he gave Turfan money to buy the entire crew hangovers. So they cheered him.

Governor Dychat was understandably furious to see them return. He had recalled every imperial ship in the archipelago, and even Kell's great harbor was seriously crowded now. He summoned the rear admiral. Irona was not present, but she heard later how her incorrigible son was overheard lambasting the governor in much the same language he had used on the marines. There was no way, he had said, that he was going to take such a loathsome, slipshod, et cetera, fecal, et cetera, flotilla to sea in the middle of a war zone until he had beaten it into shape.

Dychat ordered him to leave at dawn and threatened to demote him to cabin boy if he came back again.

On its third attempt, the Podakan flotilla did manage to leave port and keep going most of the morning. The rear admiral insisted on a more easterly course than the commodore wanted, but Turfan did not argue. He was going to let the young creep hang himself as soon as possible.

Irona sat under the afterdeck canopy and tried to talk with her son. Podakan was impossibly fidgety, unable to sit still through a whole sentence. He finally ran down to the catwalk, stalked along until he found a smallish rower, and slid in beside him. Then he took the oar and rowed, as if to work off excess energy. His bench mate did not complain at being promoted to passenger.

"What's he up to?" Turfan demanded.

"Wait and see, Captain."

"I know he's your son, ma'am, but . . ."

"Don't let him fool you. He's got something in mind. He's a lot more cunning than he appears."

After a couple of hours Podakan returned to the poop, his tunic soaked with sweat. But then he leaped down to the catwalk again and sprinted to the mast. The whole of the upper deck noticed that. He scrambled up and promptly slid back down at a rate that must have burned his hands. He raced aft again, ablaze with excitement.

"Enemy in sight, Captain."

Turfan stared at the skyline and his jaw dropped. "*Aye, sir!* How many?"

"Too early to tell. You're the fastest. Signal *Intractable* to come alongside. I'm moving my flag. You boil seawater back to Kell and get the rest of the fleet here before dark."

"But—"

"*Do it!*"

Turfan jumped to obey. Podakan sat down beside Irona, shivering with excitement. His eyes shone. The hairs on his arms were standing up.

"How many?" she asked.

"The whole fucking horizon is full of them."

He had known. She couldn't imagine how, but he had wasted two days in Kell and ordered a deviant course today, just so he could intercept the Kingdoms' fleet. Was he in the Kingdoms' pay? Was he using Maleficence? Would he fight them or join them?

"You're going to attack, aren't you?"

"Of course not. You think I'm crazy to take on a fleet that size with just eleven ships? But I'll shadow them until Lapdog Dychat gets here. Whose side do you think I'm on?"

His own, of course, no question there, but she didn't know which team.

"I'll send the fleet, son, but please, *please*, *please*, hold off until it gets here?"

"You think I'm crazy? Death is for losers. We'll show two lanterns on the mast after dark, so they can tell friend from foe. Got that? Attaboy, Dam!" He ran over to the rail and prepared to jump the moment *Intractable* came close enough.

Invincible's crew rowed like madmen, making her dance over the swell. The bosun kept increasing the stroke until Turfan told him to stop or he would have men fainting and fouling the whole watch. They entered the harbor with a war flag flying and trumpeters sounding the muster. The harbor was so packed that there was nowhere left to beach. Men jumped into chest-deep water. Irona was handed down and carried ashore. Then four men ran her toward the town shoulder-high, like a human battering ram.

Dychat had heard the commotion, though, and arrived in a chair before she reached the gate. The moment her feet were set on the ground, she shouted the news to him, bellowing so the fast-gathering crowd would hear it.

"What's that maniac son of yours doing about it?"

"He said he would shadow them, but he was lying. I know him. He'll attack, straight down their throats." She raised her voice to maximum. "If there are any red-blooded Benesh marines here looking for a fight, then now's your chance for glory."

Dychat's angry retort was drowned out in the roar, but he had no choice and he knew it. If the Kingdoms' legions were allowed to land, he would be overrun. He ordered out the fleet.

Dychat also ordered Irona not to go, so she had to stay ashore to chew her fingernails down to the elbow. Fortunately, a full squadron of a dozen galleys under Commodore Garbes had been due to leave Kell the next morning; he led it out within minutes, ready or not. Another dozen or so ships followed as soon as they could, many with pick-up crews.

The sea was very large, but the enemy fleet was too big to miss.

The Empire named naval battles after the opposing leaders and the great clash of 726 was recorded as the Battle of Podakan-Zaozerny. As Irona had predicted, Podakan attacked like a terrier, and no one in his flotilla tried to stop him. The crews might have balked had they known how badly they were outnumbered, but fortunately rowers faced aft and they could not see what they are racing into. The officers could, but they knew that the imperial navy had won against odds of five to one a few times in the past, and they also knew the penalty for mutiny. It was later established that Podakan had been outnumbered about ten to one in ships, and about thirty to one in men, because the Kingdoms' fleet was trying to deliver an army.

More than anything, that fact lost it the battle.

Zaozerny's forces did not know the odds either. When they saw Benesh forces bearing down on them, they naturally assumed it was the vanguard of a much larger fleet. As Irona had argued, the Kingdoms' navy had been hastily enlisted and poorly trained. The sailors were amateurs against pros. Many had never been drilled in what to do when attacked. By rights, the soldiers should have won the contest simply with archery, for their bowmen outnumbered the entire Benesh force many times over, but a great majority of them had never been to sea before, and probably very few could swim. Galleys were cramped for room at the best of times, and the archers could scarcely draw their bows. They panicked, of course.

Even when rammed, a wooden galley would not normally sink. It filled with water and became a floating lumber pile. But the Kingdoms' ships were grossly overloaded with men in armor, all of them struggling to stay above water. Often their combined weight overcame a derelict's buoyancy, causing it to roll or even sink.

The Benesh captains saw that ramming risked being boarded by mobs that greatly outnumbered their own crews. They responded by sideswiping instead. The Kingdoms' training was so poor that their rowers rarely managed to ship oars before the impact, as the Benesh crews did, so half the rowers were mashed by their own oars, and the overloaded ships thrown into chaos.

The first round was a massacre, carrying the Benesh forces right through the larger fleet and leaving dozens of Kingdoms' vessels disabled. Being faster and much more maneuverable, the attackers turned and came at the enemy again from the rear. But numbers must count eventually. According to a couple of survivors, Intractable *sideswiped four galleys and rammed two without taking a bruise. The third ram victim managed to grapple, and hostile troops swarmed aboard. Another Kingdoms' galley then rammed* Intractable *and the Benesh crew were soon cut to pieces. The rest of the flotilla met similar fates.*

The Kingdoms' fleet was starting to celebrate victory—a costly, bloody victory, but better than nothing—when Garbes's flotilla charged out of the sunset and turned triumph into renewed panic. At least a score more ships were sunk or disabled before the survivors fled into the night. Garbes lost two galleys. Two of Podakan's eleven were still afloat, with the others barely distinguishable among the floating wreckage. The rest of the Benesh fleet saw no action, although some ships arrived in time to help rescue both friends and future slaves from the sharks. Admiral Zaozerny was identified and securely bound to a mast for transportation to Kell.

There was no sign of Rear Admiral Podakan.

THE YEAR 727

Veer was still supervising the transport of his paintings, so Irona landed alone in Benign on Midsummer Day, when the city was busy with the festival. The crew commandeered a covered litter for her, and she made her way home to Sebrat House unrecognized until Edziza opened the door. News of the great victory had preceded her, so the first inquiries were about Podakan.

"No news yet," she said. "But I am far from giving up hope. That boy of mine is indestructible."

Drowned? Slain in battle? Eaten by sharks? Or identified by his collar and delivered to the king of kings for his sinister pleasure? Such was that monarch's reputation that the captured Admiral Zaozerny, when offered passage home, threw himself at Dychat's feet and begged for death instead. He was provided with a comfortable cell and a shapely concubine until the Seventy decided what to do with him. Irona was not lying when she said she still had hope. She kept remembering the disembodied voice telling her, *Kill him now, Queenie, while you can.* That did not sound as if Benign had seen the last of the self-chosen Chosen.

It was good to be home, to hobble from one room to another and find everything just as it had been when she left—except for her own reflection, which followed her around, reminding her of graying hair, wrinkled skin, missing teeth, and an overall dullness. Like Redkev and Zajic at Vult, Irona had aged when deprived of Source Water. At least she had served Caprice better than they had.

Next morning Irona reported to the First and that evening limped unheralded into the Scandal Market. Three months ago, the Chosen would have turned their backs on her. Thanks to the Battle of Podakan-Zaozerny, she was greeted with cheers and hugs and bucketfuls of hypocrisy. She was introduced to Eanastick 726, a strikingly pert and pretty girl, and Borawli 727, a solemn lad overwhelmed by his new status but even more impressed by the honor of meeting her.

Irona delivered a brief report on what she knew, although it was a month out of date. When she had left Kell, the threat had already faded. The king of kings had left Elbrus, heading eastward to Acigol-Nevsehir, with the remains of his army trailing behind. Commodore Chagulak had been planning a great raid to burn the remains of the Three Kingdoms' fleet in port. The Empire would hold its new territories for now.

That night the Seventy elected Irona to the Treasury Board. "Just for starters," Ledacos warned her. Rudakov 670 was still First, but lazier and less effective than ever, and the Seventy had shrunk to fifty-eight, the lowest count in memory. Everyone was overworked. If Podakan ever did return, he would be loaded down with offices too.

A month later, Kapalny 664's term as Seven ended. Irona was elected his replacement by acclamation. This was a tribute to her son's success in ending the war, of course, not to hers in starting it. She had agreed in advance to support an obscure procedure whereby a unanimous vote of the Seven declared First Rudakov to be indisposed and in need of rest. The Seventy accepted and elected Mallahle 669 to the post of Acting First—it was part of the procedure that the replacement must be older, so that no rebel band of wild-eyed youngsters could depose one of the old guard. Both men wept. Rudakov took to his bed, refused Source Water, and was dead in a week. Mallahle was mostly admired for his wit and constant good humor, but he was also competent. The wheels of government began to turn again.

If Mallahle lasted ten years, Ledacos would be almost old enough to be seriously considered for First, but Irona would not. Their unspoken rivalry was still in place.

One by one Irona's team followed her home: Sazen Hostin, Daun Bukit, and finally Veer Machin, most welcome of all. An exhibition of his Elbrusian portraits caused a sensation and brought him a fortune.

News dribbled in. Chagulak's raid had destroyed the rest of the enemy fleet, although he had found it beached and neglected. Dychat was organizing the islands as a protectorate. The Seventy voted to name it the Podakan Archipelago, which was effectively an acknowledgment that the conqueror was deemed to be dead.

One night in midwinter, Irona arrived home very late, after a dreary and overlong meeting of the Seventy, and saw that all the lamps in the ballroom were lit.

At that hour she would normally be let in by the night watchman but it was a beaming Edziza who opened the door for her. She guessed right away from his joyful expression.

"*He's back?*"

"Indeed, His Honor has returned, ma'am, but I should . . ."

She did not stay to hear his warning.

The mad thumping of her staff on the tiles announced her approach, of course. The door was open, the fire blazing, and the lamps sparkled. Veer was lounging in his favorite chair, with a good imitation of happiness on his face. Podakan sprang up and came to meet her. He wore a commoner's gray tunic, but he still had his collar and he bore no visible torture scars. He even looked glad to see her and accepted her embrace readily enough.

"Where did you go? How did you get here in this weather? You're looking well. You're a great hero. . . ." Irona realized that she was babbling and stopped.

"I'm well, thank you, Dam. Machin tells me that you are in good health."

"Too old and far too overworked. But tell—" She saw that there was a fourth person present, as Edziza had tried to warn her.

Podakan took her hand and led her over to the stranger, who was standing motionless, eyes downcast. She was tall and very slender, with jet black hair bound high on her head; her face and arms were Elbrusian tan. Her dress was a miracle of some fabric Irona had never seen before, as fine as silk and shimmering in all the tints of oil on water. It covered her from her shoulders to her silver shoes. Her earrings, necklaces, bracelets, and rings all glittered with diamonds, and her diamond-studded belt alone was worth a fortune.

"Dam, may I present my consort, Princess Koriana?"

Irona glanced briefly at Veer, who had his eyebrows raised higher than normal but obviously was not about to comment.

"Princess?"

"That's the closest her title translates," Podakan said, "unless you wish to address her as Precious Gift of the Moon and Stars." If his lifetime ambition was to surprise, he could aim no higher than this. Benign recognized no royalty of its own and paid only grudging respect to the rulers of allied kingdoms. "Won't you say hello?"

"Koriana, you are the most beautiful woman I have ever seen, and the most welcome guest ever to enter my house."

"A bit gushy," Podakan murmured, but he rattled off what must be a translation in a guttural tongue.

The girl responded, but to him, not Irona. They exchanged more words.

"She says you are very gracious. She wishes to kiss your feet, but I told her you would not like it."

Koriana lifted her head a moment, but at the same time covered her eyes with her hands, crossed with palm out, so that Irona caught the briefest possible glimpse of her features before the move was over and the girl was staring at the floor again.

"That's their salute. You'll have to give her time, Dam. She was raised in deep seclusion. At the moment she feels about the way you would feel if you were dragged before strangers stark naked. She had never even seen a man, let alone spoken to one, until she was popped into my bed. Why don't we sit down?"

They did. Veer helped Irona set her useless leg on the footrest and brought her a beaker of wine.

"We thought you had died in the battle," she said. She needed time to think before she asked about the girl.

"So did I, for a while." Podakan raised the hem of his tunic to show a puckered scar in his thigh. "I took an arrow and started bleeding a cataract. Other men were being chopped apart and still fighting, while I was blacking out from one silly little hole. Then *Intractable* rolled and I was in the water, clutching a spar and sending out a blood trail to every shark in the ocean, although there were more bodies than fish there that day. Someone saw my collar and thought it might be valuable. I came with it. So I became a prisoner."

Modesty had never been Podakan's strong point. Lying was. If he wasn't inventing all this tale, he was at least pruning the truth to shape. Koriana sat beside him on the couch with her hands clasped in her lap, fixedly staring at the floor.

"And what happened then?"

"That's a bit fuzzy. They brought me back to life. They soon learned who I was. I was taken before the king of kings in all his splendor. I thought my happy days were over, but he wanted to hear my side of the story—his officers had probably been lying their teeth out to him. He asked how many ships I had led. I said twelve but I had sent one back to bring help in case I needed it. He said there had been over one hundred in his fleet, so why had I attacked. I told him: to sink them."

Podakan smirked. And paused to tell the girl something. She did not react.

"But I did explain that his crews were poorly trained, his ships both badly designed and shoddily built, and they had been so over-loaded with men that they couldn't maneuver. Their archers barely had room to shoot at us and had no experience of shooting from a rolling deck anyway."

"How did he take that news?"

"Very well. His courtiers just stood there with pee running down their legs. He asked me if I could design better ships and train his crews properly. I said I couldn't and wouldn't if I could. And if I could and would, it would take a generation to build a competent navy, even if Benign didn't keep coming around to sink it. He asked how he could get his islands back. I said he couldn't. My mother had started the war and I had finished it, and there was nothing he could do about it."

"What language were you talking?" Irona asked. She was being very careful not to look at Veer, who probably believed much less of this story than she did. Yet she could usually tell when her son was lying and just then she didn't think he was inventing all of this.

"I was speaking Benesh. He was speaking the language of his court, High Cabalian. They have good interpreters."

"That's what you were speaking to Koriana just now?"

He nodded. "See, the king of kings had a loss-of-face problem over the islands. He cannot be seen to lose a war or give up territory. I suggested he marry off a daughter to me and give her the islands as a dowry. And that's what he did. Face saved."

For a moment Irona closed her eyes, trying to imagine the king of kings high on his throne, close to immobilized in all his imperial glory, scowling down at a prostrate Podakan wearing a jade collar, bronze fetters, and probably little more. Any ruler of the Three King-doms had to be a ruthless despot and the present one was reputed to be a fiend in human shape. The boy at his feet had humiliated him before his empire, before history and the world. So he agreed to marry his . . .

She opened her eyes again. "I find that bit a little hard to believe."

Her son grinned. "All right, I admit. . . . It was his idea, not mine. Even I couldn't have thought that one up, Dam. But I'm the clos-est thing to royalty Benign has, see? A Chosen and son of a Cho-sen. I command flotillas and attack fleets ten times their size. They declared me semidivine, because that's the only explanation for my success. Peace treaties are sealed with marriage contracts. That's how their minds work. And the king of kings has problems knowing what to do with daughters. He has twenty sons and I don't know how many . . ." He asked Koriana something; she replied. "She doesn't know either. A whole *lot* of daughters, and nobody royal enough to marry them. So here we are. I came home with a treaty that says the islands now belong to her, but she belongs to me, so Benign owns the islands. Her boobs aren't much to brag about, but she's a pretty good lay in spite of that. She does anything I tell her to. Pass the wine, citizen."

"Yes, Your Honor." Veer rose and took him the wine bottle. Poda-kan held out his goblet to be filled.

"But you know," Irona said hastily, hoping to head off the inevi-table confrontation between those two, "that Chosen cannot marry."

Podakan shrugged. "She's my wife in the Kingdoms. Here she's just my sex toy, like the fat man over there is yours."

"Does she know this?"

"She knows women can own property in Benign. What else mat-ters? When you die, your dauber will get thrown out on his fat ass, and his kids would too, if he'd ever been man enough to put any in you. But Koriana came with two sea chests full of jewels. She's going to buy a palace here and her children can inherit that. I won't trouble the Property Commission." He turned to the girl again and spoke at length, never hesitating over a word.

Irona had asked the Beru how it had learned Benesh so quickly. Dreading that she would hear the same answer again, she said, "How did you become so fluent in Cabalian so quickly?"

Podakan stood up, the girl following his lead instantly. "You'll have to excuse us, Dam. We spent the last two nights in a barque that kept moving in every direction at once. Koriana is very tired and I always need to get my rocks off before I can sleep. See you in the morning." He glanced at Veer. "And you, I suppose."

Irona watched them go, his arm around the girl's incredibly slim waist.

Veer said, "That's twice he dodged that question."

And Irona was fairly sure that Zard 699 had once told her that High Cabalian was the most difficult of all languages to master. "So what do you think the answer is?"

"I think the whole thing is unbelievable: the language, the king of kings's daughter, the jewels, the islands as dowry. It has to be Maleficence at work. The king of kings fixed him."

After a moment she said, "Or Podakan fixed the king of kings?"

This was, after all, the second time her son had performed a miracle. He had apparently killed the Beru, Hayklopevi. And now he had gelded the king of kings, who by rights should have killed him by inches.

"You said that, love, not me."

She sighed. "I'll take him to the First in the morning so he can hand over this draft treaty he claims he has."

"Make sure His Excellency is well guarded," Veer said. "His daughters must be too old to interest your boy, but he may have grandchildren who would."

Podakan's miraculous return sent the city insane. He had won an incredible battle, he had brought peace, he had claimed a daughter of the king of kings as his concubine, he was the hero of the century. When Midsummer came around and Caprice chose a boy called Ayakan, the similarity of his name was at once taken as proof of her approval.

Irona watched her son perform in the Scandal Market and Assembly Hall, and he always impressed. The studied vulgarity he threw at her and Veer was completely absent. In public he was an earnest, respectful, and hardworking young man. She knew it was a mask, but she saw it slip only once.

He was elected to both the Customs Board and Treaty Commission, prestigious offices normally reserved for much older Chosen, but he was kept away from the military committees. A man who is captured by the enemy but released with a king's daughter and a great fortune cannot be free of suspicion. When a vacancy among the Seven came up, young Meluak 723 nominated Podakan 725. That was too much, and not just for the old guard: he was defeated fifty-three to five. He returned to his seat with fists clenched and face scarlet with rage. One thing he had in common with Irona was that they both hated to lose.

INTERLUDE: 728–734

Politically the next few years were uneventful in Benign. Mallahle kept the ship of state on an even keel but explored no new oceans.

True to his word, Podakan did buy a fine palace for his illegal wife, spurning Irona's offers of better homes for token rents. He took on enormous workloads, so that other Chosen hated being on his committees, which might labor far into the night. He was well thought of otherwise, but still excluded from military affairs.

Early in 728, Koriana bore a handsome son with surprising ease for a woman of her gracile build. Podakan refused to name him after his grandfathers, as was customary. Vlyplatin, he said, had been a loser and Koriana's father boasted a dozen names, all unpronounceable. So he named his firstborn Avazan, which he said was High Cabalian for "noisy," and therefore very apt.

In 730 came news that the king of kings had died in spectacular fashion at a banquet. Bloodshed had begun in the palace that very night; civil war would likely follow. The Seventy reacted with cheers and derision, plus many speeches about the drawbacks of hereditary rule, as opposed to Benign's resplendent theocracy. Since Podakan had left the city the previous day on a mission to Genodesa, Irona took it upon herself to break the news to Koriana.

It would also be a chance to meet with her grandchildren. She rarely got to speak with her daughter-in-law at all, and never without Podakan present. Koriana was a recluse. She had used two pregnancies in less than three years as an excuse to decline invitations, but even before or between her confinements, she was rarely seen in public. She still spent more time staring at the floor than looking people in the eye, and she spoke little, although she was now competent in Benesh. So far as Irona knew, she had no friends.

Irona was shown to an upstairs nursery, where she found her daughter-in-law nursing Adwa, her six-month-old daughter. Avazan was sitting in a corner, hammering wooden blocks relentlessly, and ignored his grandmother's arrival. No Benesh woman would have received even a close family member bare breasted, but Koriana seemed quite unconcerned and just asked forgiveness for not rising. She looked lovelier than ever. Veer had begged to paint her, and Podakan had predictably refused. Veer had done so anyway, from memory.

"I am so sorry to disturb you. . . . Goddess, but she's growing fast!"

"Not fast as Avazan. He will have like his father's bigness."

"Yes, he will. Adwa's a lovely name. What does it mean?"

For once, Koriana caught Irona's eye before quickly looking down at her child again. "My husband told you it is most suitable, being Cabalian word for 'messy.'" A rare smile touched her lips.

"I know. But what does it really mean?"

"Dark Jewel."

"She is a jewel, certainly. And what does Avazan mean?"

"He Who Conquers."

"That is good, too." And typical of Podakan. "Koriana, my dear, I am afraid I come with very terrible news."

"You heard that my father is dead?"

For a moment Irona was speechless. Then: "How do you know that?"

"A dream. I told Podakan forty days ago." She spoke with certainty but showed no emotion except happiness as she regarded her nursing child.

"I am sorry. I know how devastating it is to lose a father, although I admit I was not close to mine."

"I never met him." Koriana gently touched Adwa's cheek with one finger.

"Never met your father?"

"And my parents never saw me. Women of our family are very ill-omened. Only our mothers are immune to the bane of our eyes."

Again Irona was at a loss for words. This belief might explain why Koriana had been trained never to look directly at people. It certainly explained why the king of kings had married a daughter to his worst enemy.

"Does Podakan know this?"

"He laughed." Koriana showed a trace of a frown, which was unusual. "He will not even let me keep Avazan away from Adwa."

Not for the first time, Irona wondered if her daughter-in-law was insane. Was it the women or the mad who were regarded as baleful in Acigol-Nevsehir? She changed the subject. "We heard no details of what happened to your father, except that he died at a banquet."

"Oh, no. He died in bed. I saw it."

"*Saw* it?"

"In a seeing." Koriana threw back her head as if staring at the ceiling, except that she covered her eyes with the backs of her hands in that strange gesture. "The hairiest man I have ever seen, in bed with two girls, young ones, new ones. They had been delivered to him naked, of course—no weapons—but they had hidden strangling cords in their bandages."

"Bandages?" Irona asked, at a loss for anything intelligent to say.

"New girls, I told you! The king of kings lies only with blind women and their eyes had not yet healed. He mounted one, the other tried to garrote him, but he wore a powerful *tandikat*. So the cord snapped and it was the girl who choked to death. He laughed as he watched her death throes."

Merciful Goddess! "Just what is a *tandikat*?"

"Word means, 'echo.' You would call it a fix. An assassin slayer. Only works once. He would have had a spare somewhere near, did not reach for it in time. While he was enjoying the first girl's death, the other brought out her cord and killed him."

"You mustn't even talk about fixes in Benign, Koriana. Not even to me. Or about prophetic dreams. However your father died, I expect one of your brothers will succeed?"

"Two already have. More will. It takes a while."

"Are you guessing, or are you certain of that? I mean, do you often have dreams come true?"

Uniquely then, Koriana looked up and stared at Irona for several seconds. Her eyes were enormous and incredibly lustrous. Although Podakan ought to have no complaints about his nursing wife's figure at present, her face was still as spare as carved and polished wood, perfect skin taut over slender bone. Her lips had the brilliance of rubies.

"Special dreams. My husband wishes many children. I have told him I must bear them quickly, while we have time."

"No! You don't mean you will die soon? Or he will?"

"What is soon? Perhaps not dead but not child making. You . . ."

"What about me?"

Koriana changed her mind. "I cannot see so far. My babe has done milking me, go you must now."

"May I just hold her for a moment?" Irona still had wistful hopes of being a better grandmother than she had been mother.

"That would not be proper!" Koriana said. "Or safe for you."

"May I stay and play with Avazan?"

Koriana looked quite shocked. Bewildered, Irona apologized and left.

Koriana was as good as her word and gave birth more often than was decent. Irona, finding herself with so many grandchildren, accused her son of wanting to make her feel old. She was not entirely joking.

In 734, she turned fifty. By the standards of the Chosen, she looked much older, for she had never recovered the years she had lost in Vult and Kell without Source Water. Veer had grown fatter, but he remained undisputed champion among the artists of the Empire. Podakan had thickened, as men do after adolescence, but no one would have mistaken his brawn for fat. He fretted for action and admitted that he longed for another war.

In 734, he got his wish.

The Seventy were called into emergency session. The Treaty Commission presented an appeal from the city of Severny, complaining of raiding by the hill tribes of Muhavura, complete with the usual slaughter, looting, raping, and slaving. Navy reported that it could ship out a thousand men at dawn and muster at least ten thousand from the allies within a month.

Irona happened to be in the chair, but all she could remember about Muhavura was the story Jamarko had told her on her first day as a Chosen, how he had been born there and how lucky he had been to be enslaved. She watched the youngsters fidget in their seats until enough elders had mumbled enough speeches about waiting for more information, considering fiscal implications, and generally doing as little as possible. She recognized Podakan just before he exploded with impatience. He leaped to his feet.

"Your Reverence, what good is our Empire if not for mutual defense? That is what we promise. Here is an ally screaming for help as its men are slaughtered, its children stolen, its women violated—and we sit here talking of taxes? It is our sacred duty. . . ." He was not a great speaker, but he was loud and he could make his point when he felt strongly about something. Again and again, he roared, these barbarians who lived within the boundaries of the Empire had turned their savagery on peaceable people who depended on Benign to defend their homes, their loved ones . . . and so on.

The old guard—and Irona was old guard now—listened stony faced. The firebrand young nodded and applauded. She wondered which way Ledacos would go. He could carry more votes than anyone except herself, and on this problem she had no strong feelings. It was obvious that Benign would have to do something, but what and how much? Send one thousand men or ten thousand? Or, as Podakan roared at the end of his diatribe, fifty thousand and wipe the vermin out?

He won applause, everything from standing ovation to a few polite claps. Irona must call for votes in a moment, but another hand rose, and she recognized Borawli 727. The solemn youngster who had been chosen on the day she returned from Elbrus was still a solemn youngster. He was a loner, belonging to no faction, usually working on judicial matters and the Education Board. He rarely spoke in the Assembly, but always made sense when he did.

"Your Reverence, as the noble Chosen are aware, Muhavura is a peninsula, fertile around its coast, where we count several prosperous cities among our allies. The center is mountainous and good for little but herding. I repeat these well-known truths because none of the previous speakers has mentioned the value of the hill people to our city and Empire."

A few of Podakan's supporters made scoffing noises, which Borawli ignored.

"In peaceful times the hill folk trade wool and hides to the cities, who trade them to us, but they are valuable beyond that. They breed strong people! They breed far too many strong people. About every three generations, as our history shows, one tribe or another finds itself crowded to the point of starvation. Rarely do they try to take over the neighbors' lands, for those are fiercely defended, and the wealthy farmers and merchants of the coast seem more tempting. The young hill men start raiding. Our allies complain to us. We send an army. We kill off dangerous warriors and capture healthy women and children. Honorable Chosen may have noticed how expensive slaves have become in recent years. The supply we obtained from Elbrus is wearing out.

"Your Reverence, the last Muhavura uprising, in 672, was crushed by Chosen Byakal 633, of noble memory. The culprits that time were the Havrani clan, and they paid a high price, in that Byakal exterminated them. Their neighbors inherited their herds and lands, and peace returned. That was sixty-two years ago, so the timing is not unexpected. But I would caution this noble Assembly that the response should be measured. A good gardener will prune his trees to increase their yield. A forester will pollard his forest to grow fresh timber on the same trunks. Both cut; neither tears out by the roots. Clearly it is time to gather another crop in Muhavura, but let us not destroy the orchard." He bowed and sat down.

This time the applause was general and accompanied by laughter. Benign would always support a worthy—meaning profitable—cause.

Discussion must now give way to decision. Irona heaved on her staff to stand up, a move that grew harder every year. There had been no formal agenda or time for prior discussion, so first she had to ask: "Your Honors, I put a question to you: Will you decide this matter now? Those responding 'Aye' will raise their right hands."

The motion carried easily.

"I put another question to you: Should the Empire respond to the appeal by our ally, Severny, by sending a fighting force to Muhavura? Those responding 'Aye' will raise their right hands."

Agreement was unanimous.

"I put another question to you. Who should lead this expedition?"

Several Chosen jumped up, but the senior was Ledacos, and he nominated Podakan 725. She was surprised that he had not nominated someone from within his own faction, but Podakan was an obvious candidate, especially after his rousing speech, and nomination by Ledacos made his election virtually certain.

Podakan came striding forward, eyes bright. He bowed to the First and turned to face the Assembly. Now what? The closest to an opposing view had been stated by Borawli 727, but he was no warrior to run against Podakan. By custom he should now nominate his own preference for leader.

Everyone waited. Irona watched whispers passing, lips pursing, heads nodding as the likely nominee was evaluated. It was a long time since he won the great victory of Podakan-Zaozerny, and the boy had shown no signs of disloyalty . . . this Muhavura nonsense had nothing to do with the Three Kingdoms . . . worked hard . . . respectful to his betters. . . . (*Little did they know!*) And he was the only military hero they had just then.

Borawli rose and was recognized. He moved that nominations be closed.

Podakan made a two-fisted *Yeah!* gesture not allowed under normal rules of procedure, but one that could be ignored in the thunder of applause. Irona sat down.

First Mallahle said, "Noble 725, you are appointed admiral and marshal to lead a force to the aid of our allies in Muhavura. You have the floor."

Podakan did not hesitate an instant. He might have been rehearsing his response for years. "Your Reverence, I would consult with honorable members of the Navy Board right after this meeting, to discuss sending a token force of one thousand men ahead as soon as possible. Tomorrow I will meet with the Treaty Commission and other relevant bodies to finalize more ambitious plans. Noble 700, I ask that this meeting be adjourned until tomorrow evening, when I shall present a detailed proposal for Their Honors' approval."

Irona so ruled, but with a heavy heart. Podakan had just been given a free hand to exterminate the hill folk of Muhavura. The rest of the Chosen had no idea how far he was likely to go.

As usual, her son astonished her. First, Podakan asked for Borawli as his deputy, which surprised everyone, especially Borawli. Next, having gathered a force of twenty thousand and marched them into the territory of the tribe closest to Severny, he shed no blood at all. At a parley, he demanded only release of all captives, return of all stolen goods, and a penalty of one hundred juvenile slaves. Hardly able to believe their good fortune, the tribal leaders complied, turning over some of their loot, many of their prisoners, and one hundred superfluous children seized from their poorest families. They also delivered their previous chief in chains, claiming that he had incited their recent, regrettable, homicidal frenzy.

Podakan released the chief, confident that he was now disgraced and harmless, but took his two sons hostage, just in case. He then spent the summer exploring Muhavura in force, collecting adolescent hostages from all the prominent chiefs. He returned to Benign with forty-nine of them.

Now his choice of deputy made some sense. In a speech to the Seventy, Borawli drew on his experience with the Education Board to explain how these children could be educated in imperial ways at almost no expense to the state. When they were eventually sent home in exchange for others, as had been agreed, they would leaven their people's barbarism with some Benesh civilization.

Any new idea met with opposition among the Chosen. Where were they to be boarded and who would pay for their food? Had he any idea how much fifty adolescents would eat? Podakan replied that there was plenty of unused space in his consort's palace, and he hoped the boys could be put out to work part-time as soon as they understood some simple Benesh. Grumbling on principle, the honorable Seventy gave their approval. Irona suppressed her doubts and voted with the majority.

THE YEAR 737

In early fall, the Seven were informed that First Mallahle had taken to his bed. Ledacos came calling on Irona next morning as she was eating breakfast. She poured him a beaker of wine and Source Water while Veer tactfully withdrew, closing the door.

For a moment 692 sat and smiled conspiratorially. Irona waited, knowing why he had come and content to let him roll the first die.

"He's been a good First, 700."

"Yes, he has." She smiled back. They were the two main power brokers. The last time they had disagreed on something, the Seventy had split narrowly in her favor, but sometimes Ledacos won the majority. Election of a First had uncertainties all its own.

"Just supposing we went head-to-head," he said. "I'd win. You're a woman and too young."

"We're both too young." She was well aware that a stranger judging by looks alone would assume she was older than Ledacos. "Goddess knows who might get picked as a tiebreaker."

He knew that too. "Yes, let's settle it now."

She knew that he was in the stronger position. Not in this election but in the one after this, they would butt heads. If whoever was chosen this time reigned for ten years, as Mallahle had, then Irona would be sixty-three, still too young, and Ledacos seventy-one, about right. The time after that she might be too old to be elected, or even too old to care.

"Can we agree on a candidate?" Ledacos said. "How about Sure-tamatai 683?"

"Your distinguished client and lapdog."

He conceded the point with a shrug. "Makian 682, then?"

"I will fight to the death."

Irona 700 was determined that the first female First must be Irona 700. Even if Makian could be elected, which was doubtful because she had no following of her own, the Seventy would never elect another woman to succeed her.

"Who's your choice, then?" Ledacos said.

Irona had spent half the night thinking about that. The younger the better, from her point of view, to put off the next election as long as possible and give her time to age. Ledacos would prefer someone older for the opposite reason. If they disagreed, his elderly candidate was more likely to carry the day than her younger one, whoever they were.

She said, "Ranau 674."

Understandably, Ledacos was taken aback. "He's only five years younger than Mallahle."

"He's popular and competent. Who says a First must reign for ten years?"

"The goddess, I suppose." Ledacos offered a hand to shake. "Ranau it is, then. You want to tell him, or shall I?"

Later that year, Irona was chatting in the Scandal Market with Haruna 710. The air was cool and the grass wet, but a week ago there had been snow there. Spring was on the way, and that meant sailing weather could not be far behind. The evening's agenda included several seasonal items. Suddenly Podakan 725 was there also, so intent on business that he barely nodded a greeting.

"Item Four," he said. "Election of a governor for Vult. Who gets your vote, Dam?"

"Isn't it Lascar 730's turn?" Irona was not then a Seven, but she still had her clients, and Vult had not come up at their strategy meeting for this agenda because it was routine now. Ever since the governor's term had been reduced from two years to one—on her recommendation—a stint on the edge of the Dread Lands had become a rite of passage for Chosen in their midtwenties.

There had been exceptions, of course. No one had suggested trusting Puchuldiza alone for a year with a hundred men. And Podakan had always escaped, because he had been holding more important offices. Umboi 729 was the present governor, no doubt counting the days until he would be relieved.

"I think it's mine, Dam," he said. "No reason why I should be excluded."

Great Goddess! Needing time to think, Irona looked to Haruna, who had served her term years ago. "He never ceases to amaze me. Have you ever heard of anyone volunteering for Vult?"

What in the world was he was up to this time?

"I expect all those young barbarians boarding in his house have driven him insane." Haruna's humor often exceeded her tact.

"Quite right," Podakan said. "They were a very bad idea and this is probably another, but Lascar is five years my junior, and every Chosen for twenty-five years has taken a turn at Vult latrine duty. Besides, Koriana has just whelped and I can't breed her again for months."

Haruna flushed scarlet. "Then I will certainly vote for you. I just wish it were a five-year term."

"That's the spirit! You should bark more often. Dam, will you nominate me, please?"

"If you wish. Koriana certainly deserves a rest." She had produced three girls and three boys in ten years.

Podakan glanced around the garden. "Good. I'll go and butter up some of the other old relics." He strode away.

Looking quite comically shocked, Haruna said, "There are times, my dear . . ."

"He's always like that with me when we're alone. You got caught in the splash, that's all." But what was he up to?

Irona had still not made up her mind about that when Item Four was called. She raised her hand—she did not stand in the Assembly these days—and nominated Podakan 725. As usual, there was no other nomination.

Within a week he was gone, sailing off to visit his birthplace.

THE YEAR 738

With Podakan away, Irona made more of an effort to befriend Koriana, but with little success. The former princess declined all social invitations and refused to let her children out of the house. Admittedly it was a huge house, whose grounds were spacious by city standards, and she had dozens of servants. She allowed Irona to visit, but made her disapproval obvious. Irona was surprised to learn from a chance remark that the young hostages from Muhavura were no longer billeted in the attic. She had almost forgotten those hostages.

Next day, she requested—which meant commanded—Borawli 727 to drop by her office in the palace, "at his convenience." She might be only a Six at present, but she was still Irona 700, so he came at once. She bade him be seated, offered wine, tried to put him at ease. He didn't look at ease, which was a bad sign when she hadn't yet said why she wanted to see him.

"Hostages?" she said. "I remember the Seventy approving the idea back in 734, but I cannot recall any further discussion. No reports, even."

Borawli squirmed. "That might be because the program was not funded by the Treasury. I left it up to your noble son and . . . he . . . probably . . . forgot?"

In other words, the overpowering Podakan had bullied the low-key scholar into keeping his mouth shut about something. The lowness of his key might explain why the scholar had been chosen as deputy leader for the Muhavura mission in the first place. Irona mentally drew her sword.

"Tell me how it went, then. In your own words."

"Um . . . Quite well to start with. We found some freedmen to teach the kids the language, and . . . various things. Took them to see a public flogging so they would behave themselves." He brightened. "Which they did! You realize that they committed no crimes at all? Not one! Fifty adolescent barbarians loose in Benign and there was not a single complaint about them the whole time they were here."

"I hadn't noticed that. I'm surprised you didn't brag about it to the Seventy."

He hesitated. "Well . . . when we sent them home, we couldn't be sure we had really done any good."

"Just when did you send them home?"

"In 736, as we had promised. And we got another fifty or so in exchange, but they weren't the same."

"Not the same in what way?" She wondered if the sight of a public flogging might loosen his tongue, but of course no Chosen ever got flogged.

His forehead glistened. "They weren't sons or grandsons of elders, like the first lot had been. The chiefs fobbed us off with commoners' spawn. The tribes are very hierarchal in their—"

"Quite. So they were sent back?"

"No. We treated them the same way. But when your honorable son left for Vult, he sent them home and told them not to send any replacements. He didn't want to leave his wife and children at the mercy of young savages."

How thoughtful of him.

"Why were the Seventy told nothing of this?"

Tendons in Borawli's neck were taut as ship's rigging, and his eyes looked anywhere except at Irona's.

"If I may say so, ma'am . . . Your noble son was rather disappointed with the, um, lack of . . . He did promise . . . He told me he was writing . . . It was up to him."

Irona had to be content with that. Certainly Podakan had never been willing to admit mistakes, so he would have kept quiet if his hostage idea had been a failure. And possibly if it had been a success, depending on what it had really been meant to accomplish.

The trouble began as winter was setting in, when the garrison troops who had sailed with Podakan in the spring were relieved and returned to their home bases. One galley had been contributed by Purace and the other by Nedokon Kun, so there was a further delay before mail reached Benign.

Irona received only a very brief note saying that Podakan was well but much too busy to write more. Busy? In Vult? Whatever had he found to do in the rock? Koriana claimed that his letter to her had said no more than that, but she blushed furiously when asked to produce it. It had been destroyed, she said.

The governor's "routine" midterm report was delivered to the Seven. It was anything but routine. The Seven had it read aloud to the Seventy, and it caused a near riot.

There was too little to do at Vult to keep the troops on their toes, Podakan had written. Trogs had been seen again, after an absence of years. He had therefore assembled a flotilla of fishing boats from Fueguino and some of the tiny villages along the coast—small craft that could be manhandled over the weir. He was about to launch an attack on Eldritch. He hoped he could return it to imperial control, but even if he couldn't achieve that much, he could root out some maleficence.

His commission expressly forbade any action more than one bow shot inland from the Eboga Weir, but by this time, it was far too late to send a message north. Even if it arrived, it would almost certainly fail to reach Podakan, unless he had been mad enough to plan his campaign for a Vultian winter. There was nothing to do except wait for the spring sailing season. When the Seventy stopped screaming, they had mostly decided that it must be all Irona's fault. After all, she had nominated him.

Podakan had maneuvered her into that.

Caprice rarely sent troubles alone. On days when the Seventy were due to meet, Irona's major clients would call upon her after breakfast to discuss issues and strategy. That was how the Empire was run. It was a mutual help arrangement, support here traded for opposition there, but the most important votes were always the elections, and one election would be critical. A vacancy had opened among the Seven, the first since Irona had become eligible for another term. If she failed to win, the wind would spread whispers that she was past it, losing her grip, on the way down. Normally she would have been quite confident, but Podakan's insubordination at Vult had thrown the issue into doubt. For the Chosen to vote against her just to spite him would be a meaningless gesture—he could not even hear about it for another half year—but the Seventy's decisions were never based only on logic.

Her clients understood the danger, for if her power waned, their own prospects would dim. They agreed that the day must be spent in campaigning. They were halfway through a triage of the Chosen—the good, the bad, and the buyable—when there came a tap on the door.

Lascar 730, the most junior, rose to answer it, but it could only be Edziza out there, and he would not interrupt lightly. Muttering apologies, Irona reached for her staff. Two men jumped to help her rise. She hated that highlighting of her disability, but lately she had begun to accept it as necessary. Lascar returned to his seat; Edziza waited in the doorway until Irona arrived.

Then he spoke softly. "Princess Koriana here to see you, ma'am. And the boy Avazan."

In almost eleven years, Koriana had never come calling without being invited, rarely even then. Why come on such a vile winter day, with lamps swinging and rain beating against the shutters? Why bring a ten-year-old with her? Irona turned to tell her cohort that she would need a few minutes and would they please carry on with that they were doing. Then she followed Edziza along to the dining hall, where the visitors were waiting.

"Koriana. . . . And wonderful to see you, Avazan. Do please sit, both of you. . . ." Words came automatically as she tried to guess what could have provoked the visit. It was hard to do that when she couldn't see the woman's eyes. The boy was gazing around with a contempt that he must have learned or inherited from his father. His presence was still a mystery to Irona, but a woman of the Three Kingdoms might well believe she must not go out without a male escort.

"I can't spare long just now, dear. In an hour or so . . ."

"It will only take a moment," Koriana told the floor tiles. "I am returning to the Three Kingdoms. And taking my children, of course."

Oh, she was, was she? Irona drew a deep breath and kept her voice soft.

"This is bad news. What provokes this decision?"

"Your son has passed out of my world. He will not be coming back to Benign."

For a moment the words felt like a dagger stab: Maleficence, trogs, Eldritch. . . . Then common sense reared its homely head. The woman was insane. Even if her information were based on reality, why discuss it in front of the boy?

"You believe he is . . . his tide has ebbed?"

"He is gone," Koriana said firmly. "There is nothing more for me to do here."

"You can't sail yet, dear. Not in this season."

"I arrived in such season, I can leave in such season."

Unaccustomed to backtalk, Irona found herself very close to losing her temper. "Until Podakan returns or we are certain that he will never return, I will not let you remove his children from the city. And probably not then. You understand?"

Koriana looked up, eyes flashing fury. "They are my children."

"And my grandchildren."

"No."

Oh, Goddess! "What are you saying, woman?"

"I am saying that your son cannot make children. His seed will not flourish. Oh, he plowed me often, but he had other men sow me so that people would not know his state."

"You are joking." Irona glanced at Avazan, who had blanched, as if his world had just fallen to pieces. It was a small comfort to know that this nonsense was news to him and not something he had been fed for a long while.

"No joke." Koriana was still staring, her face white with rage. "Always I obeyed my lord and submitted. He watched to make sure I did. Men from the docks. Men from visiting ships. Boys from Muhavura."

Irona fought for calm. "You are overwrought. You are alone too much."

"Just look at them!" The princess was close to screaming. "None looks like your son. Or you. Or one another. You've seen Alayta's hair, Chiracha's eyes!"

Yes, but . . . No. This was madness.

Edziza would have stayed close in case he was needed.

"Avazan," Irona said quietly. "Your mother is having a bad dream. Please open the door and ask the man outside to come in again."

Even the election seemed unimportant after that interview. Irona sent an urgent summons to the Palace office for Daun Bukit. She arranged for Koriana to be put under house arrest and doctors to declare her insane. She hired guards and nurses. She pulled more strings than a fishing boat hauling in its nets, but only when both the children and their mother were being supervised day and night was Irona able to relax again. It was going to cost a fortune, but she could afford it.

She did win reelection to the Seven, but she had an opponent for the first time in twenty years, and the vote was too close for comfort.

Koriana refused further discussion of her visions, and Irona would not have believed anything she said anyway. It should have seemed like a long winter, waiting to hear what had happened in Vult, but between the workload of a Seven and getting to know her grandchildren better, she found that the months flashed by. Without Podakan's forbidding presence, she did get to know them at last: Avazan, Adwa, Hanish, Alayta, Chiracha, and baby Olkaria. She and Veer took them on trips around the city and entertained them at Sebrat House. She brought in playmates and tutors, which their father had never done, and she spoiled them with treats of toys and sweetmeats as a grandmother should.

Suddenly it was again time to elect a governor for Vult.

Normally the Seven just put the appointment on the agenda for the next meeting of the Seventy, more or less leaving it to the younger Chosen to decide among themselves whose turn it was in the pillory. But this time the Seven debated it at length, sitting around their octagonal table with First Ranau, seven purple and one red.

They agreed their nominee would have to be Lascar 730. There was some talk of sending Kieyo 731, who made too many speeches for a junior and had a monotonous voice—one honorable Seven suggested extending his term there to five or ten years. But nobody quite knew what the next governor might have to deal with when he arrived, and they trusted Lascar more than Kieyo. Then they discussed sending a senior Chosen along as admiral, to see the junior governor safely installed, but that break with routine might seem like panic. In the end, the Seven agreed to recommend Lascar for the post.

Even that was not the end of it this year. Old Dallol 672, who wasn't frightened of Irona or anyone else, moved that the new governor be provided with a warrant for Podakan 725's arrest on charges of mutiny. All eyes turned to Irona.

This was her moment of truth. He was certainly guilty if he had done what he said he was going to do, and he had lied in his report if he hadn't. Headstrong he had always been, but to attack Eldritch with a mere four hundred men was more like insanity than mutiny. Or it might be treachery, although no one had spoken that word yet. She was not allowed to abstain from a vote. Did she put loyalty to her son ahead of loyalty to the goddess? In truth, that was no choice, because what was going to happen would have already happened despite anything she did or said.

"I agree," she said. "But no summary justice. He is to be brought back here for trial."

They all agreed that this was what they wanted.

"Furthermore," she said, "we tell Navy to send its best two imperial galleys with first-rate captains. No allied trash this time."

That also was agreed, yet that evening the Seventy, in their wisdom, added a third galley. No one quite came out and explained why that might be a good idea, but it was agreed unanimously.

A week before Midsummer Day, when Sevens Irona and Komev were sitting in judgment in Adult Court, they were summoned to attend the First. They had to suspend the sitting, a breach of normal procedure that would set the whole Palace abuzz. As they followed the herald along the corridor, they debated what emergency might have provoked it. The most obvious possibility was news from Vult, but that seemed impossible: bad weather had delayed Lascar 730's departure, and there had simply not been time for him to arrive and send word back.

In the anteroom they found Ledacos 692 and Banahaw 688 already waiting. The herald asked Komev to join them, but he ushered Irona straight into the meeting room, where he helped her position her foot on the low stool kept there for her. As he left by the corridor door, the First entered through the one that led from his own quarters. As usual, Irona made a token effort to rise, and he gestured for her to remain seated.

Ranau 674 had always been a small, spry man. She could remember him as the most junior Seven when she was chosen. Despite his age and snow-white hair, he was still spry, still alert. And now he was very much the ruler of Benign. He ignored his official red chair and took one beside hers, turning it to face her, leaning an elbow on the slate table. He did not smile.

"Bad news," she said. "Not from Vult already?"

He nodded. "A good man, 730."

"What of my son?"

"It looks bad. Irona, I'm sorry. We don't know for certain. We have no eyewitness accounts and no body, but Vult has been sacked."

Too many thoughts stormed into her head all at once. Her son, always wayward, always willful. But always loved, always blood of her blood. Vult, that incredible rock of a fortress. The trogs. Vlyplatin. Those bones at Svinhofdarhrauk. Podakan as a child, screaming with frustration when he wanted to do something and couldn't manage—throwing, jumping, anything. He would keep trying until he collapsed from exhaustion. Podakan the hero, making her heart burst with pride.

"I am sorry to be the bearer of such appalling news," Ranau said. "We gave him up for dead once before, remember, and he came through triumphant."

"No. If Vult has fallen, he is dead." She must cling to that thought, must believe that. The alternative was worse. Trogs . . .

"Which," Ranau said with a steady stare of bright eyes, "is what that Koriana woman has been telling you for months."

Ooof! Irona had hired all the new servants herself. . . . But what did that matter? She managed to hold his gaze. "I did not know the Geographical Section spied on Chosen."

"Geographical spies on everyone, Irona, and its reports come first to me, as you must know or should have guessed. I can forbid any further distribution and often do."

Not just Koriana—he was telling her that there were spies in her house also. Who? Edziza, who had been with her so long? Or even Veer? Oh, not Veer!

Ranau read her thoughts and confirmed them. "It spies on Sevens, also, and I pray to the goddess that it keeps a close watch on the First, in case I'm ever tempted to abuse my powers."

"Koriana is insane."

"Koriana is a witch."

Irona closed her eyes briefly while she took a few deep breaths. When she opened them, Ranau was no longer watching her.

"She could be, I suppose," she said. "Her family has that reputation. But I believe she is mad. You are not going to send the daughter of the king of kings to the sea death, are you?"

Ranau's normally kindly face was frighteningly rigid. "We should, but since she wants to go home, I think we will just put her on a boat without delay. That is what she wants, is it not?"

"But her children? My grandchildren!"

He shook his head.

Oh, no, no!

"Geographical Section won't vouch for all of them, but it is confident that at least four of the six are likely not your grandchildren. Possibly none of them, even the eldest. Your son certainly knew that his wife spread her favors widely. If anyone in that palace was insane, it may have been him, Irona."

"Or he was bewitched," she insisted. "But what happened or did not happen is not their fault. I regard them as my flesh and I love them. May I say farewell to them, later today?"

He nodded. "Tomorrow will do. Geographical has taken over custody already, and we'll have her out of here in a couple of days. I'll see the Property Commission gives her a fair price for the house and contents."

Irona could find nothing else to say. Her world had collapsed around her—her son, her grandchildren, and the Empire itself perhaps. When she did not speak, Ranau rose and strode over to open the private door.

The man waiting behind it came in and knelt to Irona, who recalled him as a fresh-faced youngster on *Invincible* at Kell, so many years ago now. She greeted him by his name, Marapi Kembar, and he beamed at being remembered. Time had weathered him and bulked him up, but mere time would not have brought him his reputation for courage and reliability. He had been sent to Vult as Lascar's commodore, so why was he back here in Benign, reporting to the First? Why he? Why not the admiral, the Chosen?

She told Kembar to rise; he apologized for having brought such terrible news; she absolved him, and by that time the head of state had opened the other door like a common porter. Other Sevens filed in: Komev, Banahaw, Ledacos, Dallol, and Pavouk. Knowing that Irona had been called in ahead of them, they had guessed why. They nodded somberly to her and took their seats in silence. Only two of them knew Kembar, who had returned to his knees.

Ranau closed the door and went to his chair and rapped his seal ring on the table to call the meeting to order.

"Fialovi 694 is reported to be inspecting the new dock. This business seems urgent enough that I propose to start without him. Any objections? Good. I invited Commodore Kembar to report to us. Commodore, please rise and tell us in your own words what happened. I will read out Honorable Lascar's report later, if it seems necessary."

"Y'r Rev'nce, Y'r Honors. . . ." The commodore went to stand behind Fialovi's empty chair and look over his audience. A marine faced enough storms, swords, and missiles in his career that a gaggle of geriatrics around a table did not overawe him. "The goddess sent us fair seas and we made good time to Fueguino, but we found it burned to the ground. We hunted for survivors and found no one, not a dog nor cat, Y'r Honors. We did find three corpses floating in the harbor, and there were some charred bones, that's all."

The listeners sighed. The news changed everything. The war of their ancestors had returned.

"His Honor asked our advice—me and the captains—and we advised proceeding to Vult, as planned, because there we could hope to find news and maybe reinforcements. He said that was his own wish and instructed me to do so.

"I've been to Vult before, Y'r Honors. Found it much changed. The rock's abandoned and the weir breached, so the lake has drained. It's all mud and a few wavy channels now. Stank like . . . like you can't believe. Boats and the entrance stairs had been burned on the shingle, including the galleys *Shark* and *Moray*. We found gnawed bones in the ashes. With His Honor's permission I had a party climb up to the entrance. . . . No easy climb, that! Three men went in, armed. They popped out like coneys chased by ferrets, begging your pardon. They'd almost gotten eaten by a rock worm."

Ledacos said, "If the worms—"

"Questions later," Ranau snapped. "Continue, Commodore."

"Aye, Y'r Rev'nce. A couple of youngsters managed to climb all the way to the summit. One of them fell on the way back down. . . . Th' other reported that the buildings up there had all been burned, and the stairway filled in with rubble. Whoever done it made a good job, Y'r Honors."

Outside the windows of the First's Palace, songbirds were hailing summer. Inside was midwinter. Irona could not recall a report more dire than this one. She sensed an epoch ending and another already begun.

"And what happened then?" the First prompted.

"His Honor had us move down to the river mouth, to camp on the beach overnight. In the morning he sent me home in *Orca* to report to Y'r Rev'nce. He reckoned that whoever had trashed Vult had hit Fueguino too, so he was going to take th' other two ships down the coast and see if he could get ahead of them and warn the villages in their path. If Tokachi was still safe, he would prepare to defend it."

Ranau nodded. "I think you covered everything the admiral wrote in his report." He smiled. "Tell them how many days ago you left the mouth of the Vunuwer River."

"Thirteen, Y'r Rev'nce." Kembar smirked, displaying several gaps in his teeth.

Komev said, "Great Goddess! Did you never sleep?"

"Lads were pretty hungry and thirsty when we got to Brandur, Y'r Honor." He was saying that they had cut across open ocean instead of following the coast. He did not say whether Lascar had ordered such a gamble. From Brandur they could have island-hopped home.

"We'll see they all get a bonus," the First said, "and you, too, Commodore. You have brought us the worst news Benign has heard in centuries, but we do not punish messengers. Admiral Lascar admitted in his report that he had no firm evidence, but he thought the most likely explanation was that Governor Podakan led the garrison, or most of it, inland to attack Eldritch and was defeated in a battle. That left no one to stop whatever dwells in the Dread Lands from sacking Vult. Do you agree with that assessment?"

The marine nodded. "That was what we all thought, Y'r Rev'nce."

"Questions now? You had one, '92."

"It doesn't matter now," Ledacos said. "When did this happen?"

"I'm not certain, Y'r Honor. . . ."

"Of course not. If you'd been there, you'd be dead too. But didn't you even try to estimate?"

Unflustered by such petty efforts to browbeat him, Kembar said, "The corpses at Fueguino were floating. They'd need some days to bloat up in water that cold. The lads thought at least two weeks since Fueguino was hit, which means more'n a month ago now, Y'r Honors." A flotilla of three galleys would usually include at least one man with personal knowledge of anything imaginable, so those estimates were probably reliable. "Vult happened in winter."

"How can you possibly know that?"

"Grass was growing through the bones, Y'r Honor; and they'd been picked clean. Gulls and rats, likely. Rain had washed the ashes well."

The First caught Irona's eye. Winter was when Koriana had started insisting that Podakan was never coming home.

The gloom deepened. Benign would need at least two months more to put an adequate army in the field. Evil had broken out of its ancient cell. How far could Maleficence have advanced in a month? How much farther in two more?

Dallol 672 had a voice like dry leaves blowing across a yard. "I always understood that there was no way along the coast from the Dread Lands to Fueguino and the Empire."

"If there isn't," asked Pavouk 708, "then why do we bother keeping a stronghold at Vult?"

"To keep our own people from trading for fixes, of course. But how did Maleficence get around Cape Imun to Fueguino? Has Maleficence itself taken to the sea now?"

Kembar hesitated, then said, "The boats we saw were all burned or smashed, Y'r Honor. Both places."

"Good reasoning," said Banahaw 688. "When I was sent up there, years ago, we had orders to survey the coast from Vult back to Fueguino, to see if there were any recent settlements we didn't know of. Most of it's sheer cliff dropping into deep water. It's gashed by fiords, so any path along the coast would be much longer than the route a ship takes. I don't say that nimble men, well prepared, couldn't work their way along there in time, but the logistics are impossible. A man can pack only so much food on his back. I'd doubt anyone could carry more than a week's rations over terrain like that, and it would take months to scramble on hands and knees from Vult to Fueguino. They must have come over the mountains."

Surely Maleficence would have crossed the Rampart Ranges long ago if it could? The destruction of both Vult and Fueguino must be more than just coincidence. Kembar said nothing, but Irona thought he would like to.

"What's your opinion, Commodore?" she asked. "You've had longer to think about it than we have."

He avoided her eye. "Dunno the mountains, Your Honors, and the little I've seen of the coast agrees with what Honorable 688 just said."

Irona said, "The problem would be the same either way—carrying enough rations. You can eat birds' eggs in springtime, but a few gannets' eggs won't feed an army." Then she realized what he was thinking, and it was the worst jolt yet. "*Oh, Goddess!* Like the Gren in Achelone? The garrison? The trogs drove their prisoners ahead of them and ate them as needed?" Had Podakan ended as trog dinner?

"That is wild speculation," the First said firmly, "and must not be repeated outside this room. I have a question. If you found so few bodies at Fueguino, isn't it possible that the inhabitants fled inland, or south along the coast, leaving their town to be burned?"

"Could be, Y'r Rev'nce," Kembar said doubtfully.

But there were other possible explanations. The people could have been herded away as livestock. Or they could have been conscripted—*consumed*. Ranau did not mention those possibilities.

"If there are no more questions, Your Honors, I would accept a motion of thanks to Commodore Kembar and his crew for a job well done, with a directive to the Navy Board to issue appropriate bonuses."

There were rumbles of agreement.

"Unanimous. Thank you, Commodore."

Kembar bowed and left by the corridor door.

Now came decision time.

For a compromise candidate, Ranau 674 had turned out to be an excellent First, perhaps the best Irona had served under in all her years as a Seven. He had grown into the job very quickly and now ran meetings like a captain running a ship. Power changed people, a truth too often overlooked.

"This is an extraordinary crisis, Your Honors, and an urgent one. We must summon the Seventy to meet as soon as possible, but only you can decide what to advise them." A hand rose. "708?"

Pavouk said, "I move, as a formality, that we deal with this here and now and do not refer it to committee."

The First glanced around. "I see no objection. Next?"

"Isn't it obvious," said Komev 701, "that we field all the resources of the Empire with all possible haste?"

"I accept that as a motion. Debate?"

Banahaw 688 said, "Probably it should rendezvous at Vyada Kun and then work its way—"

The First slapped the table. "Out of order. We'll deal with the principle now and tactics later."

After a moment, Ledacos murmured, "Question?" and Ranau put the question. The motion carried.

Ledacos raised a hand and received the chair's nod. "And next, I move that we go straight to choosing a leader for this expedition, because in a crisis the Seventy always accept the Sevens' nominee without argument. If we can agree, I would hope to have him found and summoned here immediately."

"We have a motion to nominate a leader," Ranau said. "Objections? I see none. I call for names."

Long silence. A year ago, Irona thought ruefully, the obvious candidate would have been the man who had slain the Beru with a broken sword, shattered the king of kings's armada with a mere eleven ships, and settled the Muhavura rising without a blow struck—the unconquerable Podakan. Now he had gone to Vult and failed most horribly. She *hoped* he had failed. She could not help recalling her old suspicions that he had been conscripted by the Enemy, either in that encounter with the Beru in Didicas, or during his stay in the Three Kingdoms. If that were the case, then he had gone to Vult specifically to loose the hordes of evil trapped in the Dread Lands, and he had succeeded spectacularly. He had betrayed the garrison and sacked the fortress. Now Koriana was eager to return home and tell whichever of her brothers was the present king of kings that the time had come to attack the Empire from the south while her husband wasted it from the north.

Irona didn't really believe all that. She *couldn't* believe that. She *mustn't* believe that. But if his own mother could think it, other people would, too.

She realized that the silence had gone on far too long. Looking around, she saw that were waiting for her to come out of her trance.

The First said, "This is a time of great sorrow for you, 700. It is grossly unfair of us to ask you. We realize this. You have given your life to the Empire and should not be asked for more."

She? They wanted her to lead an army again?

"You are," he continued, "our expert on Maleficence. You defeated it at Vult, at Didicas, and at Elbrus. Can't you turn the tide for us once more?"

Six pairs of eyes watched her. She didn't know what to say, or even what to think. It was impossible, surely. She was old and crippled and bereaved. How could they even ask her?

"I am wondering," Ledacos said softly, "and I suspect we are all wondering, whether you want a chance to avenge your son's death?"

Ledacos knew her better than any of them, and she didn't trust him at all.

But revenge? Yes, perhaps that was the concept her mind had been groping for.

"If you want it, Irona," the First said, "I think it is yours."

"How can you trust me?" she asked, her voice hoarse. "You must see that my son may serve Maleficence. He may have betrayed his men and his homeland. He lived with a woman who may be a spy and is rumored to be a witch. He never did what he was told to do, not at Didicas, not at Kell, not at Muhavura. And certainly not at Vult. Put forward my name to the Seventy and you will have a revolution on your hands."

"We all know you, Irona," Dallol said. "I've watched you in the Assembly Hall for thirty-eight years, and I cannot believe that you are anything but loyal to the goddess and the Empire."

Heads nodded. They might be testing. If she accepted, then she was a traitor too and they would send her to the sea death.

"You may know me," she said, "but I know the Seventy, and they will not appoint me. I could not in good faith accept if they did. I ask leave to stay away from the meeting. They will talk more freely without me."

"Irona," said Pavouk, the youngest one there. "We have no one else! The Empire has been at peace too long. No one who has ever led an army is left alive, except you."

She lifted her foot from the stool and set it down. "No, not if you exile me to Maasok for twenty years. I cannot be leader. You need a young man for that job. And now I ask that I may leave and be alone with my grief."

No one spoke as she limped to the door and left.

She could not bring herself to go home yet. She had her chair carried to the nearest bazaar and sent one of her guards in to buy honey cakes. Then she went to visit Koriana and her children. They might not all be Irona's grandchildren, but some of them might be. She had grown fond of them since she had taken charge of them. Not really loving them, of course, not in the usual sense, because she wasn't a loving sort of person. It had taken her a long time to discover that.

The servants who admitted her were the people she expected, and they did not indicate that anything untoward had happened. If the Geographical Section had taken over, as the First had said, it was being extraordinarily discreet. But when was it not? Irona asked for the children to be sent to her favorite grotto, which was screened from view by a thick laurel hedge and included a noisy fountain. She had no wish for her farewells to be overheard. She also asked for Koriana to be told that she was there.

She had barely settled on the marble bench when Avazan arrived. At ten, he did not look much like Podakan, but he behaved like him. Without a word of greeting he took two cakes and stuffed one in his mouth so he could grab a third before the rest of the children got there. He ruled his siblings with an iron hand. Despotism ran in his mother's family too.

Adwa was eight and had inherited all of her mother's incredible beauty. Her manners were as perfect as her complexion. She greeted her grandmother sweetly and waited to be offered a cake before thanking her and accepting.

Hanish was a year younger and his legs weren't long enough to keep up. He arrived puffing and accepted a cake, without thanks but with a smile than more than made up for that. He had charm, which had not come from either of his official parents.

"Don't gulp it," Irona said. "I have more. I'm not going to be seeing you much in future."

"Dam says we're going to go on a ship," Avazan said through a mouthful of cake. "It's going to have a hole in it."

"*What?*"

"And you won't be meddling any more," Hanish said sadly. "Is giving cakes meddling?"

"I expect so."

"Then I'm sorry you won't be doing it." He accepted another.

"So am I," Irona said, astonished to discover a lump in her throat.

Having an empty hand now, Avazan helped himself to a fourth cake.

And then Koriana arrived, holding Chiracha's hand and accompanied by Alayta. She sat down on the bench as Irona gave the toddlers cakes. As always, Koriana glittered with gems, fit to belle any ball in the Empire. She seemed to be in a conciliatory mood as she addressed Hanish's feet.

"This is very kind of you, ma'am. Olkaria's asleep. Do you want her fetched?"

"No, don't disturb her. I came to tell you that your passage home is being arranged, but Avazan says you've already been told."

"I haven't been told. I just know."

"And what's this about a hole?"

Koriana glanced up and momentarily made eye contact. "Do you really believe that I will be allowed to return to the Three Kingdoms?"

Irona said quickly, "Of course I do!" But did she? Even the Geographical Section might not be ruthless enough to send a ship and all hands to the bottom of the ocean just to score a political point. That would be hard to arrange, anyway, but it would be easy enough to ensure that one particular passenger failed to arrive. A year ago Irona would have said Seven Ranau was incapable of such an atrocity. Today she thought First Ranau might be. "I will make sure that nothing goes wrong."

Koriana just smiled and went back to studying the paving.

"If you wish, I will adopt the children so that they can stay here."

"That doesn't happen."

Irona said, "I can come with you. Do you want me to?"

"Oh no," Koriana said vaguely. "You go the other way, to meet Podakan."

"He is still alive?"

"I see you meeting him, is all."

"Where? Not Vult?" *Please, Goddess, not Vult again!*

The woman shrugged. "I do not know the name, but I saw him when he was there before."

"In Muhavura?" Irona reminded herself that she must not let wishful thinking trap her into believing such ravings. At least Koriana's prophecies were always made before the fact—unlike Puchuldiza's—and some of her visions might have happened to come true by sheer chance. Now she was contradicting herself, saying Podakan was still alive.

"Maybe. I brought this for you, because you have been kind to my children, even knowing they are not of your blood." Koriana opened her hand and let a cord fall dangling, a braid of many colors. "I let each of them choose one of the yarns."

"It will bring you good luck," Avazan said, eyeing the last honey cake.

"I chose the blue one," Adwa said, dark eyes solemn.

"Olkaria chose one too," Hanish said, "the red one, although she didn't know what it meant."

"You tie it around you under your gown," said Alayta, "like this, see?" She lifted her dress to show one like it. While Irona was distracted, Avazan and Hanish both grabbed for the last honey cake. Avazan got it; Hanish landed on his back and his head hit the paving with a crack. Their mother paid no attention.

"I will," Irona promised. "And I am sure it will bring me good luck. And it will remind me of all of you. Hanish, come here, love." She gathered the weeping child to her and tried to comfort him. She was quite shocked to discover that her eyes were misting over. They had never done that before, not ever.

The following morning Irona told her clients to vote any way they liked at the special meeting of the Seventy called for noon, as long as they didn't elect her to anything. She couldn't tell them what the topic would be, because the news had not yet been announced.

Meluak 723 came calling late that evening. He had been a beefy, loud youth when the goddess chose him, sixteen years ago. Now he was a beefier man, almost as loud. He had been the nearest Podakan had to a friend among the Chosen, and Irona had always liked him because he had never taken himself seriously, nor Podakan either. He was the only person Podakan could ever tolerate laughing at him. As soon as Edziza announced him she guessed that he had been appointed to lead the northern expedition. He marched in and waved cheerily to Veer, who was preparing to leave.

"Stay, citizen," he boomed. "This will be all over the city in no time." Then, to Irona's surprise and annoyance, he knelt to her. "I accepted the poison cup, 700."

"Excellent, a splendid choice! Admiral or grand admiral?"

"Grand, the top."

Grand admiral was a supreme office created only in direst emergencies. Meluak could overrule the First, the Seven, or even the Seventy.

"I congratulate—"

"Accepted on two conditions! First, that if we are able to join forces with Lascar, he will outrank me, because he knows an oar from a spear and I don't. Second, that you will be my deputy."

"No!"

He ignored that. "The first thing we must decide is where our rendezvous is to be. Orders must go out at once to all the allies, and we'll need a good harbor to—"

"I said no."

Meluak grew even louder and more abominably cheerful. "I did not and will not hear that word, 700. This is your chance to avenge your son, or rescue him if he's been taken prisoner. If you don't accept, then I will refuse the appointment. I'll do all the work, I promise you, day and night, never sleep. But I need you to tell me *what* to do."

Koriana had predicted that she would meet her son again. The woman was mad. So was Irona, even to think of this. Her only child . . . but if she did not even try, how could she ever bear the pain of wondering what might have happened if she had? A few words of advice on strategy wouldn't commit her to anything more.

Veer read her face and said, "Irona, no!"

"Tombe," she said.

"What?"

"They're past Fueguino, heading south, right? You've got to put the army ahead of them to stop them, just as I had to do at Didicas. If you muster north of their front, you'll be chasing them, and they will outrun you. Tombe has the longest beach I've ever seen. Podakan played on it when he was a toddler. It's capable of holding every ship in the Empire, and I don't know anywhere else that could."

Meluak was aghast. "That far south? You think they'll have reached Muhavura already?"

"You mustn't gamble on stopping them at Lopevi. Karang is hopeless—only one decent harbor, and even that has no access to the interior. Even the Shapeless may not be able to cross Karang. By the time we get to Tombe there should be news of where they are."

Meluak noticed the "we" that had just slipped out. Smiling, he rose and settled into a chair. "So where do *we* begin?"

"*You* begin tonight." She paused to gather her thoughts.

Veer brought wine for the visitor, but Meluak waved it aside without taking his eyes off Irona.

"If we find ourselves fighting on three fronts, we cannot hope to win," she said.

"Three?" Meluak and Veer said simultaneously, with horror.

"Three. Maleficence has broken out at Vult. I have always believed that the Gren were merely Shapeless who had found a back door through or around the Rampart Range into Grensdalur, so we may soon hear that Achelone is being attacked again. If that happens, we shall probably have to withdraw completely from the mainland."

Meluak nodded, aghast. "And the third?"

"The island allies, of course. Will they be with us or against us? If many of them choose to throw off the yoke of empire and turn against us, we cannot possibly win. Even if they merely fail to support us, we cannot survive."

Veer, moving with surprising quietness and without knocking over anything at all, brought some wax tablets and a stylus to the grand admiral, so that he could start taking notes.

Meluak took them. "Your orders, ma'am?"

Irona sighed and accepted that she had been trapped. Like it or not, she was going to war again. "Tonight . . . You said you must notify the allies of the rendezvous, and you are right. But dispatches will not be enough. We must send emissaries of the highest possible rank to convince them of the urgency of this situation and the need to support us."

Stylus poised, Meluak said, "Name them, ma'am."

"Well, Genodesa is the most vital. If it puts its back into this, then the others will likely follow. We need Vyada Kun, of course, and Lenoch, but Genodesa is the key. . . ."

Irona slept badly that night. Never had the Empire faced a worse challenge, and she could not rid herself of the certainty that Podakan was somehow behind it. Guilt ate at her like acid: Didicas, Podakan-Zaozerny, Muhavura, and now Vult—he had carved his initials all around the boundaries of the Empire and she had stayed loyal to a mirage of parenthood. *Kill him now, Queenie, while you can.* Why had she not heeded that warning from the dead?

Unable to bear the frustration any longer, she wakened Veer so he could strap on her brace and let her go to work. When her chair arrived at the Palace, she found it bustling with clerks and officials. Meluak was stirring things up already.

As the sun breached the eastern horizon to brighten the summer sky, she was in her office, seated before a table loaded with memos, notes, and reports. The door flew open and in stormed Ledacos 692. Unshaven, unkempt, and disheveled, he was waving a small tablet.

"What is the meaning of this?" he roared.

Irona looked up with annoyance. "Shut the door."

"Tell me what—"

"Shut the door!"

Grumpily he shut the door and returned to the table to glare down at her.

"What part don't you understand?" she asked mildly. She was torn between fury that he would interrupt her when she was engaged in work so vital, and a despicable satisfaction that the infinitely slippery Ledacos had been cornered at last.

"Genodesa! That's what I don't understand. Send me off as your courier if you must—if that's what your spite requires. Treat me as a slave, but send me to anywhere but Genodesa. You know perfectly well that I was one of the judges who sentenced the present king's father to the sea death!"

"You will, of course, mention that in your representations to His Majesty," she said, and this time she was hard-pressed not to smile at his expression of outrage.

"Bitch! Conniving slut! Genodesa has its own version of the sea death, and if the king is inclined to play traitor, the first thing he will do is send me to it!"

"The grand admiral and I decided that this should maximize your motivation to succeed in your mission. Genodesa is well aware of our politics and your status. By sending you, we display our complete confidence in our ultimate victory and drop an unsubtle hint that he had better not misbehave like his father did."

The normally impassive Ledacos was shaking with fury now. "This disaster is all your fault, cow. You went off to Vult and came back with a monster, an uncontrollable, Maleficence-spawned—"

"Silence!" Had Irona been capable of the move, she would have leaped to her feet at that point. That was much too close to her own fears to pass unchallenged. "On the contrary, it was all your fault, '92."

"Mine? Are you crazy?"

"Not at all. Maleficence preys on our weaknesses, and yours is ruthless ambition. You thought that solving the Vult problem would get you elected to the Seven, but the idea of volunteering to go there in person never entered your head. You needed a puppet, and you chose me. On the day Jamarko was executed, you tried to persuade me. I refused. So then you turned your wiles on Vlyplatin Lavice, right there at Execution Bridge.

"You had done the boy a great kindness when his father died, and you called in the debt. You, a Chosen! A Chosen can bully a mere citizen into anything. But personal favors are not the same as political favors, Ledacos! Political favors can be called in, personal ones can't. They may be returned, but they are not extorted on demand. You never did understand the difference. You warped Vly's gratitude and turned it into guilt. You made him betray his lover by asking me for children. Vly wanted nothing in the world that I did not want, but you twisted him around."

"This is madness, blaming—"

"I expect you told him that Vult was a rural fortress where nothing ever happened, a restful country retreat? So he and I went to Vult, and when he saw how he had been deceived, the truth drove him mad. Your fault, Ledacos. I've never told anyone this before, but in his madness that first night, he forced himself on me. Podakan is a child of rape, and the horror of what he had done sent Vlyplatin reeling out into the darkness, where he fell to his death. My child was a spawn of evil from the moment he was conceived. If now he belongs to Maleficence, the blame is yours."

"Madness, utter madness."

"Sadness, utter sadness. Your failing is ambition; Vly's was gratitude."

Ledacos was portraying extreme disbelief. "This is absurd. Do you also have a weakness, 700?"

"I thought of mine as love, but it was denial. I refused to admit my child's faults; I kept hoping he would change as he grew up. He did, of course—he just got worse. Now go and pack a bag, Ambassador, because if you aren't ready when your ship is, I'll have you marched aboard in chains."

"Trollop! Well, if the Genodesans kill me, my dying breath will cry your name to Bane."

"And I will name you with mine. It is agreed, then—first to die curses the other. Get out of here."

She knew she might be sending him to his death. She was going to send thousands of others to theirs before this was done.

THE YEAR 739

*N*othing mattered in Benign then except the war. People never just walked anywhere. They ran, they shouted, they certainly never questioned. The eye of the storm was Irona's office in the First's Palace, where she spent days quietly dictating to pairs of secretaries. As soon as one pair left, another would enter. Her orders flowed out from there, with a copy to Meluak. Many instructions were verbal, with only the highlights hastily recorded. She arrived before dawn and left after dark, often so tired that she went to sleep in the litter as she was carried home.

The records she consulted might have been written by Byakal 633 himself, or even Eboga 500, but were often her own notes from the Achelone campaign. Meluak saw that her orders were carried out. As he had promised, he seemed never to sleep. His eyes became caves, his face sprouted coppery stubble, but he kept his good humor. The docks, shipyards, and chandlers ran day and night. Even he could not be everywhere, though. At Irona's suggestion he appointed two rear admirals, Kerinci 735 and Caprara 736, without whom everything would have piled up on top of everything else. They got a lot of exercise, but even a twenty-year-old could cow a gang of mutinous dockworkers if he wore a jade collar.

Caprice chose a pregnant girl at the festival and nobody noticed.

~

Soon the first contingents would be arriving at Tombe, and someone must be there to receive them. Since Irona had now organized the organization, and Meluak was still overseeing the performance, she was the logical one to lead the advance party. They agreed on the forces she would take with her. She issued the orders and went home to pack.

That morning she had ordered her travel bags brought up from the cellar, and she found them sitting in the bedroom, already fat. Veer Machin was busily stuffing tunics in a sack. It had never occurred to her that he might be planning to accompany her. She half sat, half leaned on the edge of the bed and watched with mingled fear and affection.

"You can't come this time, love," she said. "I'll be well defended."

He flashed her a mocking look and went back to what he was doing. "That's what I'm afraid of."

"I don't think one in a hundred thousand men could ever get horny enough to menace an old relic like me."

"The other ninety-nine thousand, nine hundred, ninety-nine could. Of course I'm coming. You think I'd trust you around all those brawny young hunks?"

"I'll take a couple of slave girls with me to help with my brace."

"No need, I'll be there. What's this?"

He held up a multicolored cord, about five feet long. Irona's heart twisted in guilt. In the frenzy of war preparations, she had barely spared a thought for Koriana and the children. Had they gone? Were they even still alive?

"Where did you find that?" She needed a moment to think how she would explain that curiosity.

"In your oddments box. I was looking for that little whetting stone I brought back from Kell. Can't find it. But this? It's very curious braiding."

It was typical of his falcon eyesight to notice the braiding.

"It was a keepsake from Koriana." Irona watched his guard go up at mention of the king of kings's daughter. "She let each of the children choose one of the threads."

"Keepsake? Or a fix?"

"She said it would bring me luck."

"I am relieved to hear that you're certain it is not a curse." He carefully wrapped the cord around three fingers until he could tie it in a neat hank. He walked over to Irona and handed it to her. "You'll be taking it with you?"

"I suppose I will."

"Sometimes I think you're crazy."

She sighed. "Most times I know I am." She tried again to talk him out of coming with her, but when Veer made up his mind, nothing would ever change it.

Next morning they shipped out on *Eboga 500*, which Irona suspected had been renamed for the occasion. Her commodore was Marapi Kembar, commanding a fleet of twenty galleys, half a dozen barques, and two of a new class of sailboats called frigates, very fast and designed to carry messages. As the cavalcade passed between the headlands, she saw that they were thick with spectators. Never in a century had Benign sent such a force to war, and more would soon follow.

It was past time for some of the nearer allies to respond to the Empire's call. So, since the sea was calm, she ordered the fleet into line abreast, in the hope of intercepting some messages heading south. Her hunch paid off less than an hour after Benign itself sank over the skyline, when the western end of the line encountered a royal Genodesan galley and sent word to her flagship. Irona could have dallied to read the dispatches it carried, but she was unwilling to waste good sailing weather. She could believe the report that Genodesa was mustering a major force but was inclined to take the claim of fifty galleys with a keg or two of salt, and she could only pray that they would be supporting the right side.

A few days later she reached Yupil, on the coast of Muhavura, and received a welcome both worried and sincere. That prosperous, complacent city was unhappy that nearby Tombe had been chosen as the rallying point. That brought the war uncomfortably close. Yupil itself was arming, as were the nearer hill tribes. So was Vyada Kun, but they had no news from the northern mainland. The fate of Lascar 730's party remained unknown, yet there Irona found a lack of information comforting. If the Shapeless were rampaging through the Empire, a flood of refugees should be heading south by land and sea. In her happiest dreams she imagined young Lascar stopping Maleficence in its tracks and making the great mobilization unnecessary.

From Yupil, Irona sent five ships north to reconnoiter, while the rest carried on to Tombe. She clearly remembered the great beach that could hold many hundred ships, the dunes behind it where a great army could camp, and the Tombe River racing down from the hills to provide ample fresh water; the labor of filling casks would keep the men busy while they waited.

She had hoped to find scores of ships from nearby allies already in place, but there were only half a dozen, all locals. At least this allowed the Benesh to claim the best location, nearest the fresh water supply and the town with its hope of evening entertainment.

She expected that her job for the next couple of weeks would be mostly adjudicating petty disputes between the natives and the visitors. That, and trying to make sense of intelligence reports, would be quite enough to keep her busy. Administrative military matters she could safely leave to General Marapi Kembar. When Grand Marshal Meluak arrived, his army should be ready to move.

By sunset, Irona's camp was set up among the dunes, which sheltered her from the wind but restricted her view. Army had provided her with a splendid pavilion in Chosen green, with fine furniture and silk curtains to separate spacious living quarters from an impressive working area. There she would receive the elders of the city and the leader of each new contingent as it checked in. Veer grumbled that the drapes did not match the carpets, but she knew he was happy not to be sleeping under the stars. Irona herself would not be straying far, because the sand and tough grass of the dunes were impassable for her. From the entrance she had a glimpse of the beach, where the ships lay, and across the inlet to the barren, dusty hills of Karang. The Rampart Range stood somewhere to the northeast, too far off to be visible even from the shore.

The next day news began arriving, a flood of it, beginning badly and growing worse. On his way south from Vult, Kembar had warned the authorities in Brandur and Vyada Kun of the disaster at Vult. Both allies had promptly sent out scouts, but only now did their reports come by various routes to Tombe. Tokachi had suffered the same fate as Fueguino, being found burned and deserted. All the little fishing villages must be assumed to have fallen also. Crews returning to port in Lopevi had found their town ablaze and veered off. Some claimed to have seen a galley burning on the shore, which suggested that Lascar 730 might have tried to make a stand there and been overrun.

Worst of all were eyewitness accounts from the town of Sanbe. Half a dozen men and a couple of women had managed to escape in a fishing boat, and the tales they told repeated the horrors in the historical records almost word for word. Things in the night had attacked without warning: dead things, nightmares, monsters that seemed different to each onlooker and might change form before their eyes. Men had been attacked by half-eaten and obviously dead neighbors, women by their own children. Attackers had swarmed through the town, hundreds of them, which confirmed what the Seventy had feared most—that the victims were being conscripted by their killers. That had happened at Eldritch in the days of Eldborg 300. The horde would grow larger as it proceeded south.

Irona had advised Meluak to muster his army at Tombe in the belief that she was being extremely conservative. She had expected him to carry the war north from there. Now she worried that Malefi-cence might bring it to her before the imperial forces and the allies were properly mustered.

As the days dragged by, it became obvious that the allies were holding back. Two galleys arrived from Genodesa, four from Vyada Kun, one from Biarni. Their commanders insisted that many more would be arriving very soon, offering imaginative excuses for delay: freak storms, outbreaks of belly fever, civic holidays, shortage of funds. Representatives of other towns and cities followed, but in token numbers. No ally was going to be completely absent, for no one had forgotten the vengeance Mother Benign had taken on those who failed her during the Achelone campaign, but most were going to make sure they played on the winning team.

One evening, about a week after her arrival, Irona held a con-ference with Kembar and the senior captains, but they found no reasonable response to the news except to stay where they were. With Lopevi fallen, the Shapeless were already into Karang, and the Empire knew of nothing in there to stop them except the bleak land-scape itself. Even the Tombe locals never went there and knew little about it.

Everyone agreed that the enemy were more likely to cut overland from Lopevi than they were to detour around the coast, so they must be held at the Tombe River. She told Kembar to draw up orders and have them ready by morning, when the chiefs of the Muhavura hill tribes were due to appear.

Irona slept poorly that night. Never before had she seen the Empire in greater danger. Was Podakan behind it all? The sound of Veer's quiet breathing tortured her. She could sense an epochal disaster happening, but why had she brought him into it?

∾

The hill tribes' assistance now looked vital. They knew the terrain and they were close at hand. She and General Kembar would meet their leaders, with no allies present.

Kembar arranged four wicker stools. When lookouts reported that there appeared to be three delegates approaching, Irona called through the drape to Veer to bring out a fifth. The three were ushered in by Hakone Sague, an interpreter from the Treaty Commission's staff—a permanently worried little man, who looked as if he had been dropped into a war by some terrible mistake. The newcomers were deeply tanned, with beards and long braids as dark as jet. They had been required to leave their spears and shields outside and were obviously furious at having to kneel to a woman while Sague recited their names. Irona gave them leave to rise. They sprang up, and two of them then sat, leaving the youngest on his feet.

She decided that Muhavurans must choose their leaders by size. The delegates were both enormous men, clad in leather helmets and sandals, gold strips around their upper arms, numerous tattoos, and kilts of spotted mountain cat skin. The spokesman was Romeral, son of Resago. He had flecks of silver in his beard and was—predictably—the larger. He had brilliant blue eyes, very strange in such dark coloring.

So did the third man, a tall youngster, and apparently an interpreter, for he had not been presented and went to stand behind Romeral just as Sague had walked around to stand behind Irona. He did not qualify for cat skin; his kilt was plain leather and his tattoos few. There was something familiar about him, though. Irona thought she had seen him weeding a garden a couple of years ago, or scything a lawn maybe?

"I know you," she said.

"I am Raung, son of Romeral." He spoke perfect Benesh.

"I am Podakan's mother."

He smiled. "I trust your noble son is well? Also his lovely wife and children?" He added a few words of gibberish, explaining to the others, while keeping a mocking smirk directed at Irona.

Chiracha, Koriana's youngest son, had eyes that color. Koriana had mentioned *boys from Muhavura*. Chiracha, son of Raung son of Romeral son of Resago? It took all Irona's willpower to thrust that abomination from her mind and turn back to the war.

"I am Irona 700, chosen by the goddess, and I speak for the Empire."

Pause for translation, which Raung supplied before Sague could open his mouth. That was good, because the chiefs would trust their own man more.

"The warrior says, 'I am Romeral, son of Resago, taker of eight, and I speak for the twelve nations of the Real People.'"

"Real People, the Empire calls on you to send your brave warriors to its aid, as your oaths bind you."

Conversations through a translator were always slow and cumbersome, but Raung did not hesitate and Sague never corrected him.

"Maleficence has escaped from the Dread Lands. . . . Legions of Shapeless have been sacking towns along the coast. Even as near as Lopevi. . . ."

"The Real People are not frightened by wailing in the night."

"The Shapeless are more than that. General Kembar will show you."

Kembar unwrapped a souvenir he had brought from Vult, a human jawbone, partly charred but also bearing marks of gnawing. First Ranau had forbidden him to show it in Benign, even to the Seven. The four Muhavurans looked queasy, despite their efforts to display bull-hide toughness.

Painstakingly, Irona and Kembar explained the situation. Then they asked about Karang. Could the Shapeless cross Karang? Did anyone at all live there? The people of Tombe believed it was mostly bare rock, with only a few scattered oases inhabited.

Chief Romeral's reply was brief and snappish.

His son said, "My . . . the noble taker of eight says I am to tell you myself, because any stripling of the Real People knows the answer.

Karang, as you call it, is bare rock and gravel, shrubs, spiders, snakes. The only people who live there are the Slug Eaters."

"Tell me about the Slug Eaters."

"They are midgets, dwarfs, and ugly. Not Real People. Not even as human as the soft fat men of Tombe. They go naked in small groups and eat grubs and roots, snakes and vermin. They drink from puddles. They are cowards who poison their arrows."

"Do the Real People ever go there?" Irona asked.

Raung hesitated a moment, then leaned over his father's shoulder to indicate the other man's tattoos. "Licto son of Hornopiren went there on his manhood hunt and brought back two heads. He is a mighty stalker."

Analyzing Raung's body language as well as his words, Irona concluded that the hill folk of Muhavura regarded the tribesmen of Karang as game animals, but dangerous game animals. They would never admit to being scared of midgets, of course, but Licto's medal tattoos were impressively large and elaborate. Clearly no one was willing to cooperate with the nomads. Asked again if the Shapeless could cross Slug Eaters' land, the chiefs insisted they could not. There was no water, no shade. What they seemed to be hinting was that the Slug Eaters would stop the intruders. Irona dared not depend on that.

"We must not let the Shapeless cross the Tombe River," she said. "Benign must defend her Empire by defending Muhavura. We need the great warriors of Muhavura to help us blockade the far bank."

Raung translated, and the chiefs began to argue. Irona took the chance to glance sideways at Kembar and receive his nod of approval. These were the tactics they had hammered out last night.

Hakone Sague leaned over her shoulder to whisper, "They fear these Slug Eaters." Both Irona and Kembar nodded.

"The fierce warriors," Raung announced, "say that it is stupid to defend the far bank of a river. Make your stand on your own side, so the enemy must cross the water to attack you."

That was true, but he might also be hinting that the far bank was dangerous: if the river was the accepted border between Karang and Muhavura, the Slug Eaters might not tolerate trespassers. What might be the correct tactic for the proud warriors of the Real People, and even the Benesh themselves, might not hold for some of the allies, who might panic when the Shapeless appeared. Those would do better with their backs to the river so that they could not run away.

"Remember, warriors," she said, "that the enemy is even now crossing Karang, where there is no water, or very little. Their thirst will be terrible. Better to fight them before they drink than after."

She sensed Romeral's disapproval at once, so he might not be as ignorant of Benesh as he was pretending, and young Raung's contempt as he translated was obvious. There were rules to their form of fighting, and depriving an enemy of needed water would not be sporting. Irona was not worried by their reluctance, because Muhavura would be the first to suffer if the defense failed to block Maleficence's advance. After hard talk and some insults, the Benesh and the Muhavurans agreed in principle that Muhavura must be jointly defended, but on its side of the river. Irona knew of old that a bargaining position should always include some throwaways, and crossing the river had always been a complication.

The hill men also agreed to take the upper reaches of the Tombe River, because they could put an army there much sooner than the Empire could. Mobilization would begin in three days. Kembar and the interpreters led the delegates away to meet other leaders and work out the details.

Irona sagged, feeling the strain. Feeling old!

Veer came through the drapes. "The kid was one of Podakan's pets."

"I think he was."

"I know he was. Irona, do you trust them? The Muhavurans, I mean?"

She looked up at the fear in his eyes and knew what he was thinking. "I have no choice. I must trust them."

"Those savages? That wasn't sweat they were oozing, it was liquid hate. Have the tribes ever fought *for* the Empire before?"

"No."

"Have they ever united before?"

"Not so far as I know."

"But Podakan taught them the advantages of cooperation. Isn't that right? Cooperation against whom, Irona? Cooperation for what purpose, Irona? What did he teach those hundred or so hostages during their stay in Benign, Irona?"

She had no answers.

Later that day, a frigate arrived with reports that Grand Marshal Meluak would be there in a few days if the weather held. The reply Irona sent outlined her plans and would probably condemn Meluak's rowers to double shifts. That evening she addressed all the allied leaders who had arrived so far, reaffirming her intention of holding the Tombe River line. They looked no more enthusiastic than she felt, but no one proposed a better idea.

The river was not navigable far upstream from its mouth, so the army could not travel by boat. It began moving out on foot. Benesh forces went first, because Irona wanted them farthest inland, next to the Muhavurans when—and if—the Shapeless made contact. She did not want the less reliable allied troops panicking and swarming back along the river road, tangling the forces advancing behind them.

Irona had herself carried in the van, right behind the banners and bugles. She wondered if Podakan was leading his army to battle just as she was leading hers. After struggling to deny it for years, she had now pretty much accepted that he had been an agent of Maleficence ever since the Battle of Didicas, and possibly since he was born.

Once again, Veer stubbornly refused to stay away, and Tombe was probably no safer than wherever the army was.

She was dividing the army, which normally was a gross tactical error. Soon the men would be strung out in line of march, glaringly vulnerable to an assault at any point. Even if she ever had her entire force in place and dug in, the line would still be too weak to withstand a determined attack. It would never be able to prevent solitary Shapeless filtering through by night. She was swinging an ax against clouds of gnats.

The last real chance of stopping Maleficence's advance had been at Lopevi. Lascar 730 must have seen that and died trying. But the cause had always been close to hopeless once the Shapeless sacked Vult and passed Cape Imun. A small hole in a dike can let in a great flood.

By noon the countryside had changed. The lush fields and orchards of coastal Muhavura had given way to stony desert, more typical of the far bank, arid Karang, except that it also had a few patches of boggy hollow, which Karang seemed to lack.

At sunset they pitched camp on some hummocky meadowland, too scrubby to make good pasture and too rocky to plow. Irona dismounted from her litter and sat on a boulder while her guards hunted for a place level enough to pitch her tent. She should have been the least weary of anyone, for she alone had not had to walk, but she felt crushed by the weight of responsibility and a dread that she was making a terrible mistake.

Veer came limping up and found a rock to sit on, uncomfortably low for him. He regarded her doubtfully. "Where is everybody? I thought you were leading an army."

"Strung out along the river," she said. "It's not much more than a picket line, and won't be until Meluak arrives. Tomorrow we'll press on until we make contact with the hill tribes. The allies are supposed to follow us and take over the ground we're occupying at the moment. The Muhavurans are supposedly up ahead, and the Shapeless somewhere to the north, crossing Karang." She pointed across the river, which was a placid, humble little stream now.

"That's an awful lot of supposing."

"This is war, dear. War and facts are never found together."

He studied her for longer. He knew her far too well to be deceived, but eventually he just shrugged and said he was thirsty; would it be safe to fill his canteen at the river?

"Better do it now, before the men start washing their feet," she said, and he heaved himself up and limped away.

The missing truth was that both she and her little army were being offered as bait, and she was waiting to see who would bite: Muhavurans, Shapeless, or reprobate allies?

Dark came swiftly: a starless, moonless night. The thorny scrub burned poorly, giving more smoke than heat, but not enough smoke to discourage a plague of biting insects. She retreated with Veer into their tent. The princely silk pavilion had been left behind on the shore, and she must make do with a standard army tent of rough canvas. It was officially large enough for ten marines (plus about eight rocks in that area) but when Veer, two cots, a table, and a document chest were all inside, there was precious little floor space left over for Irona.

They nibbled at a tasteless army-issue supper. The tent was stuffy and hot, the camp outside loud with shouting and clatter. Veer tried to cheer her up and she snapped at him. He did not take offense.

"You're doing your best, love," he said. "Can't do more."

"No," she said. "I can't. But I missed my chance to do better. Years ago, in Kell? You remember that day you thought you heard Podakan speaking after you had seen him going down the stairs? That was his father you heard."

Veer paused with a beaker of wine halfway to his mouth.

"No," she said, "I have not lost my wits, not yet. People taken by the Shapeless are not completely dead. Vlyplatin has communicated with me several times since his son was born. And that time he warned me to kill him while I still could."

"Partially dead?" Veer took a long drink.

"Something survives, sometimes. You heard it, too! Podakan inherited that resonant bass voice of his from his father."

"You couldn't have killed him at Kell. He was a Chosen by then. And if we're going to second-guess ourselves, then I'm to blame, too. Longer ago, when that schoolmaster advised you to give him to the slave traders as incorrigible—that was where I went wrong." He drained the beaker. "I didn't try to talk you into it."

"I wouldn't have listened. I suppose the only real chance I had was when he was born. I could have wrapped the birth cord around his neck and strangled him. But after he was born, he owned my heart."

"No woman would do that. You know, bearing a child at Vult was not a very smart idea, love."

"It certainly wasn't," Irona said, remembering whose idea it had been.

Veer grimaced. "This wine is made from lemons and oak bark. So you think that when the Shapeless attack they'll leave us all half dead?"

He never mocked her like that. The strain was telling on him, too.

"I'm half dead now," she said. "Let's turn in."

The words had barely left her mouth before metal clashed outside her tent, and a guttural male voice said, "Your Honor? Marshal?"

She bade him enter, and the flap rose to reveal Captain Ebulobo, the Vyadian in charge of this camp. She had trouble understanding his thick accent, but his current purpose was obvious, because he stood aside to let another man enter—younger, unarmed, and spattered with mud and leaves, as if he had fallen hard, and more than once. His shins and forearms were bloody. His gear was Benesh.

"Dispatch from Captain Gilolo, Your Honor."

Irona accepted the tablets, two of them, bound with a ribbon. "Did no one warn you against trying to run in the dark?"

He was too weary to smile. "He said it was urgent, ma'am, I mean, Your Honor."

"Well done. Captain, see this man is fed and find him a place to sleep. He must be rewarded."

Apparently the Vyadian could understand her well enough, because he saluted and ushered the messenger out.

Gilolo had gone ahead inland as liaison with the Muhavurans.

"You're sure there won't be a reply?" Veer asked curiously.

"It's too late to do anything tonight. Tomorrow we'll see." She untied the ribbon and held the tablets to the lamp to read the message scratched in the wax. She sighed.

He said, "What?"

"It's coming. Tomorrow or the next day."

Gilolo's report was brief but deadly. Strange little people, mostly women and children, were streaming out of Karang. Nobody could understand their talk, but their sign language was obviously an appeal for sanctuary. Something terrible was close on their heels.

Would the Shapeless follow the same route? Why should they? They could bypass the army, even the hill tribes, for the frontier was simply too long to defend without building a wall along it. The war to keep Maleficence out of the Empire was as good as lost already.

Irona did not sleep long before bugles and drums wakened her. The tent was even hotter and stuffier than before. Men were shouting. And screaming. Sparks flew as Veer blew on tinder to light the lamp. He burned his fingers and cursed loudly.

"My brace!" she said. "Quickly."

"Just a moment." At last a flame grew. Naked, Veer found her brace and helped her strap it on her leg. Then her gown, her shoes, her staff, and finally he hoisted her to her feet. She clung to a tent pole for a moment to catch her balance. Veer turned away to find his tunic.

The clamor grew louder, officers shouting orders, men screaming.

"Untie the flap, please," she said, but Veer had hardly started when they heard Captain Ebulobo outside.

"Your Honor!"

"Enter!" she said. "What's happening?"

A dagger slashed the remaining laces and he hauled the flap aside.

"Fire, Your Honor. The sky is bright to the west! They're burning the ships!"

Nobody could be certain what was burning so far away, but it would take a major blaze to brighten the sky, so either the beached fleet or the city of Tombe was in flames.

The implications were terrifying, and the racket outside told her that the troops had seen that too. She knew what was happening out there without having to decipher Ebulobo's babbling: her troops were panicking, fleeing back to the sea. They knew that without the ships there was no road home, but what could they possibly accomplish when they reached the shore? The burned galleys would be cold ashes, any seaworthy craft would have fled, and the enemy arsoniats would be waiting.

"Let them go!" she said. "Every man for himself."

Veer and Ebulobo both protested, shouting over each other, but she insisted, and obviously it was too late to stop the stampede—the camp was falling quiet already.

"Your litter, ma'am," the captain said, turning to leave. "I'll round up some—"

"No!" she said. "You go. Follow your men and try to form them up in some sort of order. I'm afraid they'll be ambushed on the way and picked off. Go! I'm staying here. I'm waiting for someone."

Still he argued. "Your Honor, I will not—"

"Save your men, Captain! The fleet will arrive tomorrow or the next day, but get your men back to the coast. There may be Shapeless out there, poisoned arrows out of the dark, thousands of vengeful Muhavurans . . ."

He protested again, and it was Veer who shouted him down, bellowing "Go!" and looming over him, unarmed but very big.

Ebulobo spun on his heel and disappeared into the night.

Now there were only two. Veer lit a couple of lamps. Irona stretched out on her cot, and he sat down on his, not even bothering to dress. He stared very hard at her.

"Well?" he said. "What's going on? Who fired the ships? The allies? Malevolence? The Muhavurans?"

"Who knows? I don't know what's happening down at the shore now, nor up at the headwaters." And she might never know.

"But you think you know what's going to happen here? Who're you waiting for?"

"Podakan."

"He's dead, surely?"

"Yes," she said sadly. "My son has been dead for years."

"Don't be chicken stupid, as he used to say. Pardon me while I find my comb."

The flap opened. Raung, son of Romeral, stepped in through the gap, holding a sword and naked, clad only in beads, feathers, and war paint. Lantern light flickered on the deadly blade and caught the eerie blue of his eyes.

"Greetings, mother of Podakan. I was sent to kill you."

She looked up at him in dismay. Just squalid murder by this boy savage? Maleficence, as the Gren, had managed to sniff her out at Didicas, so she had stayed here as bait to draw Podakan, not this barbaric youth. It was too soon for her to die. She wasn't ready to die yet. There was still too much to happen, too many questions unanswered, too many tears unshed.

She pushed herself up and lifted her game leg off the bed in an effort to rise. "Very heroic! How big a tattoo do you get for killing crippled old ladies?"

He scowled. "None. My father promised me he will not tell

anyone who brought him your head, but he says you are dangerous, so you must die and be known to have died."

Veer flung a pillow at the boy's face and snatched up a sword from behind the cot.

Irona screamed, "Stop!" for Veer was no warrior. Had she known of that sword, she would have taken it away from him.

The young tribesman caught the pillow and threw it away. Then he laughed and spread his arms. "Go ahead, fat man—kill me."

Veer tried, thrusting the sword at his opponent's belly. Raung's parry came so fast that it was barely visible, knocking the blow effortlessly aside. *Clank!*

"That's one. You get two more tries."

Veer stepped closer, towering over him, and slashed two-handed, putting all his strength into the move.

Clank! Raung blocked that blow as easily as the first. "Two down. Last chance."

Perched on the edge of her cot, Irona had managed to retrieve her crutch from the floor. She lurched to her feet with its help, a move she had not attempted in years, then raised it to point at the Muhavuran, resting the pad against her shoulder, and keeled forward one step, using the crutch like a lance, remembering how the marines had used lances to defeat the Gren, long years ago.

The result was pathetic. Without even seeming to notice her, the boy just caught the crutch with his free hand and stopped her dead. Meanwhile he parried Veer's sword aside for the third time, before sliding his own blade into the older man's chest. Veer looked astonished. Without a sound he crumpled to his knees and then toppled forward on his face. Raung twisted the crutch out of Irona's grip and tossed it aside. She staggered, clutching at a tent pole for balance.

The killer frowned down at the corpse. "My first score, but I can't claim it. He was too easy. A good kill, though. Did you see? A clean cut; he felt no pain." He retrieved the pillow to wipe his sword, smearing it with Veer's lifeblood.

"Oh, thank you," Irona said bitterly, and somehow she meant it; it was a comfort that he had not suffered—Veer who had never wanted to hurt anyone. Veer gone? No more loving? No more of that divine art? She could not imagine life without Veer Machin. But she did not have to, did she?

"Now you. Ready?"

"Stop," said another, lisping, voice. Hayklopevi climbed into the tent. The Beru seemed even more enormous than Irona remembered it, too tall to straighten up in there, even less human, more reptilian. Its gray hide was bare, flecked with mud and bloodstains, and it carried no weapon. As she well knew, the Gren needed no more than their own claws.

The young Muhavuran screamed in terror, leaped over Veer's corpse, and up on his cot, as far from the monster as he could get. He turned at bay with his sword extended. The point wavered. His eyes were stretched impossibly wide.

Irona was surprised to hear her own voice as if from a long way away. "You haven't met? Raung, son of Romeral, this is Maleficence itself, I think. Also known as the late Hayklopevi, Beru of the Gren. And by other names."

"Certainly we are legion," the lizard man lisped. "And we know the lusty son of Romeral. Long have we wanted to kill that fat one ourselves, Raung, so that he could appreciate the experience. Having denied us the pleasure, you will suffer in his stead. Come to us." It beckoned with a hand of six talons.

The boy croaked, "No!"

Hayklopevi advanced one huge pace—there was no room for more—and reached for Raung. This battle was as one sided as the one before, with Raung now on the losing side. He slashed at the nightmare, but the sword made no impression on the monster's hide. He screamed as it hauled him to it. Blood oozed from its grip on his arm; his sword fell free. The monster lifted him by an arm and a leg as if he weighed no more than a child. "Go away and die!" it said, and hurled him bodily out of the tent. His screams continued.

"There!" the lizard turned to face Irona.

She reeled back, tripped, and fell full length upon her cot. The impact half stunned her, wrenching her hip where the brace was strapped, and knocking all the air out of her. But the fall put her hand near the pillow and the jade-handled dagger hidden under it.

The Beru laughed. It began to melt and bubble. It changed color, shrinking, emitting a rank animal odor, and became Podakan. Yet the tent was still crowded, and he seemed larger than she remembered him in life.

"Greetings, Dam." It . . . he . . . it spoke in the familiar rumbling voice he had inherited from Vlyplatin, not the Beru's lisp. He was naked and lividly dead, but not putrefied, and his only visible wounds were the scars of the long gouges the Beru had cut in him in the hovel at Didicas, long ago. They looked quite recent, though, and he was once again the adolescent who had died there, not the mature man who had sailed off to Vult. "Can you get up?"

"No. Help me!"

"Wouldn't dream of it. You could call Raung back in, but he's in too much agony to be useful. In an hour or so, his remains will be ready to take our orders. Meanwhile you can lie there and despair. Very instructive, despair."

"You and the Muhavurans are allies?" she asked. Her voice sounded quite calm to her, although she knew she was not going to escape from this alive. She probably did not even want to.

"Everyone is our ally, and the bare assed are no more aware of it than most. You have been one of the most helpful."

"When did you recruit Podakan? At Didicas, when you took his shape and pretended he had slain you? Or earlier?" She had a desperate need to keep him talking, to postpone the inevitable.

"It began at Vult. You did it."

"No!" She squirmed to ease the pressure on her spine and let her fingers find the hilt of the dagger.

"Yes, you did. When you were in labor—terrified, writhing in agony, bleeding, all alone—you screamed curses at us. Curses are very potent in Vult!"

"But before that you had perverted Vlyplatin. You drove him mad with guilt. You made him rape me."

Podakan rumbled with laughter. "That was funny, wasn't it? Yes, the rape was when we gained a real entry, as you might say. But why not go even further back and ask why he was suffering so much from guilt? Or think of later, in Benign, when this host was growing up. When you taught me how you had betrayed your principles."

"When I what?"

He . . . it . . . smiled a parody of Podakan's rare smile. "You used to tell us how you hadn't wanted to be a Chosen, how once you had believed the Seventy were evil tyrants. By then you thought that was comical. You thought you had learned better. But we could see how they had bought you, Dam. They twisted you and made you one of themselves. You taught us a good principle there."

She must not let herself be seduced by Maleficence's lies. It wanted to make her feel responsible. It wanted her to suffer. "They taught me how the Empire is a force for good."

"A force for good?" it said with all of Podakan's grating scorn. "Oh, spare me! We wish we had time to discuss this at length just now, but you will understand when you have joined us. We shall consume you, and something of you will dwell in us forever. The Empire is evil, through and through. It kills people for their own good. It takes their money for their own good. It benefits only Benign itself. It follows Craver, and Craver delivers it to us, as he always does."

"If Benign is so evil, why are you against it? It prevents wars between the states. It gives them justice and culture."

"Stupid! It takes their young men to fight its own enemies. It imposes its own justice and its own culture, destroying theirs and demeaning their heritage. The Empire is evil and we are going to absorb it—helped, of course, by all our allies, who were your allies until you drove them away. By next year Benign will barely be a memory. Dust will blow over its ruins, and we shall turn our attention to Genodesa, Vyada Kun, and all the rest, as they turn on one another. Chaos is our ally and our reward."

The corpse advanced a step and leered down at her. Fear drove her to keep it talking, although she had no hope of rescue.

"All your doing, son?"

"Of course. Evil has purpose, but it needs direction."

"What happened in Didicas? You killed the Beru or it killed you?"

It laughed again, with Podakan's deep, scornful laugh, but its breath was Beru carrion. "We combined forces. The rapes were both a reward and a test of our new partner's dedication. Flogging us the next day was a clever idea. The pain almost drove us out of that shape. Was that what you were hoping for?"

She shook her head. "And at Kell? You knew when the Kingdoms' fleet would be coming?"

"Of course. That king of kings was one of ours. We recognized each other the moment we met. I far outranked him by then, of course. He was still human enough to breed sons. Look where that got him!"

"So he gave you Koriana. And who fathered her children?"

The monster chuckled. "Not this body, Dam, not Podakan! After we consumed it at Didicas, the Podakan part of us could not create life and we didn't want people wondering why. It amused us to pimp the king of kings's daughter like a free harlot. She was the nightly prize for good behavior, and the Muhavuran lads were very well behaved. If she complained, we just sent for a few more. But it doesn't matter now. She and all her litter are dead, killed by your benevolent Empire—on the orders of your Reverenced First."

She said, "You are enjoying tormenting me, but I see through your lies, as I have always seen through them. One more question. When you had Podakan put the spider in Fagatele Fiucha's bed, that night in Achelone City, did he know it might bite?"

The monster scowled. "You should ask rather why it didn't bite him."

"That answers my question. It didn't bite him, or he would have known it was dangerous. He might have died, and Maleficence didn't want that, did it? But Podakan thought it would be a good prank to make his tutor wake up screaming with a hairy, many-legged thing in under his sheet with him. It turned out otherwise. He was a very humble, repentant little boy for months after that. For a while I almost believed he was going to grow up to be a decent, honest man."

"You didn't try hard enough, so we didn't, I'm glad to say. Now, you will join us." He reached down and gripped her shoulder.

"No!"

"Yes. We are ready to consume you, Irona 700." He opened his mouth and bent to her throat.

She stabbed her son's image, ramming the dagger into its ribs. It straightened up, laughing and making no effort to remove the gruesome trophy protruding from its chest. The wound did not bleed. "You think that will stop us, woman?"

"It is the blade that cut your birth cord."

"Why should that matter? But we shall keep it as a souvenir," it said, looking down admiringly at the hilt. Then the Podakan thing shimmered one hand back into a Gren's taloned paw and slashed her breasts.

She heard her dress rip, but all she felt was a jolt of power from the cord around her waist. The monster's features displayed both surprise and rage.

"What are you doing, woman? How—*You are wearing a tandikat!*"

Tandikat: assassin killer, the gift Koriana and her children had given Irona for just this purpose. She did not speak, just watched, amazed, as the Beru unraveled. A torrent of identities came pouring out of it and faded away into space. She caught glimpses of her juve-nile bodyguards at Didicas: Silay, Biam, Dofen; there was Lascar 730, dead at Lopevi; Koriana was there and all her children seek-ing revenge for their shameful heritage; and others, a multitude slain by Maleficence rushing by her: the four hundred betrayed at Vult; Raung, son of Romeral, laughing at his killer's fate; the countless dead betrayed at the Battle of Podakan-Zaozerny . . . Veer Machin, still astonished. At the end she thought she heard a cry of, "Well done, Queenie!" or could it have been, "Well done, Dam"? Their voices had been so alike.

Maleficence was gone, dissolved. Even Raung's screams outside had ended. Irona was alone in the tent with Veer's body.

It wasn't fair! Why should she be still alive, when so many thousands must have died in the night? They would all have wanted to live, and she only yearned to die. But there was sunshine and birdsong outside the tent, and inside two corpses and one crippled old woman lying on the floor, wishing she could die.

Eventually it was thirst that forced her to move. The ground was impossible for her to walk on, a tangle of rocks and tree roots, but she dragged herself on two hands and one knee down to the river. Raung's was not the only corpse around, so the rats and ravens did not molest her. It was late on the following day before Meluak's men arrived.

She was, unfortunately, still alive, so they dosed her with Source Water and rushed her down to the town for some loving care. She was beyond caring, beyond speech, beyond eating, but they would not let her die.

The next day, or perhaps the day after, she was slumped in a chair in the same dingy little room, which stank of onions and had roaches. She was watching an industrious spider in the dormer window alcove, spinning a web—climbing, rappeling, going to the center to test its architecture, then spinning more. Grand Admiral Meluak himself came to see her, big and loud and odiously cheerful.

She ignored him; her world was closed, and he wasn't part of it, less important than the spider.

"Irona? I'm truly sorry about your consort."

Go away.

He sent everyone else away and pulled up a chair.

"You did it again, Irona."

Who cared?

"You weren't very popular, keeping us at sea, all those ships. We were running out of water, out of food; lot of seasickness. The allies were threatening to head for home, some of my own captains were ready to throw me overboard."

Why didn't he just go away? Veer was dead, Podakan was dead, and she couldn't weep for them.

"It was lucky the savages attacked at night. We saw the light when they fired the ships, and there was still enough evening breeze that we could come in under sail.

"What we found . . . It was heartbreaking. We were far too late to help. Our lads must have put up a good fight, but the odds had been hopeless. By the time we arrived, the ships were ashes and the tribes were heading for Tombe itself to do a little recreational looting and raping. I was so mad I ordered, 'No quarter,' but I don't think what I said made any difference. The numbers were on our side then; we slew without mercy. Tombe River ran red under the moon. Of course, the next day, when we started up the river, we found more of the same—Benesh corpses everywhere.

"But now we're ready to clean up the interior, the villages: the women and children. Benign can have a slave girl in every kitchen. We're going to depopulate Muhavura and sell it off as garden plots."

Lots of suffering. Podakan would have been pleased. He would have been pleased whichever side lost.

"Irona!" The big man pulled his chair closer and bent so far forward that he could peer up at her face. "Where are the Shapeless? Did they join in? Haven't they arrived yet?"

When she didn't speak, he grew louder. "Irona! I must know! There were reports of Shapeless seen in Tombe, but then they disappeared. *Irona 700, tell me!*"

"Gone," she whispered, wishing more than anything that he would just go away.

"Gone where?"

Shrug—*don't know.*

"Will they be coming back?"

Shake.

"You're sure of that?"

Nod.

He regarded her doubtfully, perhaps wondering if she were a Shapeless herself.

"Is it the casualties that are worrying you? Don't worry about that! Yes, you brought an army here and then staked it out as a lure and ordered me to keep the main army away until the prey took the bait, but don't worry about it! Such things have to be done in war sometimes. You won! You saved the Empire yet again. We saw a few Shapeless, but they sort of melted and disappeared and that was that. Saw the game was up, I expect. So it won't be held against you. They'll fete you back in Benesh when you get there. You're a shoo-in to be the next First, Irona!"

She closed her eyes. Let Ledacos or anyone have it. Veer was dead, Podakan was dead. Ambition was dead. She would refuse all Source Water and just die.

"If we can stop worrying about Shapeless now," Meluak said, "there's another little war waiting. All the allies rallied to our call this time—some more than others, o' course—all except Genodesa. So it's next! The loot will be incredible, gold and art and slaves galore. The allies are all salivating at the thought of their shares. I think I'll just let them loose and turn up for the sharing-out."

To the victors the spoils.

The big man rose and put the chair back where he'd found it. "One other thing you won't have heard yet. The Genodesans didn't just sit back with their arms folded. They put Ledacos 692 to the sea death. That's why they're marked for destruction."

Ledacos? It took a moment to sink in. Podakan, Veer Machin, *and Ledacos*—those three had defined her life, and now they were all gone. All of them.

The dam broke at last and she began to weep.

"That's good," Meluak said, rising. "Tears are human." He went away, shutting the door and leaving Irona to sob.

ABOUT THE AUTHOR

Dave Duncan was born in Scotland. After graduating from the University of Saint Andrews, he moved to Canada, where he worked as a petroleum geologist for thirty years. He is the author of many science fiction and fantasy novels, among them *A Rose-Red City*, *Magic Casement*, and *The Reaver Road*, as well as the historical novel *Daughter of Troy*, which he published under the pseudonym Sarah B. Franklin. Under the name Ken Hood, he wrote the Longdirk series, which includes *Demon Sword*, *Demon Knight*, and *Demon Rider*. *Children of Chaos* (2006) was nominated for both the Prix Aurora Award and the Endeavour Award. Duncan is a founding and honorary life member of SF Canada. He continues to live in Canada with his wife, children, and grandchildren. Visit the author at daveduncan.com and openroadmedia.com/dave-duncan.

EBOOKS BY DAVE DUNCAN

FROM OPEN ROAD MEDIA

These and more available wherever ebooks are sold

OPEN ROAD
INTEGRATED MEDIA

OPEN ROAD
INTEGRATED MEDIA

Open Road Integrated Media is a digital publisher and multimedia content company. Open Road creates connections between authors and their audiences by marketing its ebooks through a new proprietary online platform, which uses premium video content and social media.

Videos, Archival Documents, and New Releases

Sign up for the Open Road Media newsletter and get news delivered straight to your inbox.

Sign up now at
www.openroadmedia.com/newsletters

FIND OUT MORE AT
WWW.OPENROADMEDIA.COM

FOLLOW US:
@openroadmedia and
Facebook.com/OpenRoadMedia

31901056416268

CPSIA information can be obtained at www.ICGtesting.com
Printed in the USA
BVOW08s2136260715

409830BV00001B/1/P

9 781504 002189